Jas Singh is a globetrotting Environment, Health and Safety scientist. He grew up in Punjab but has spent the last five decades of his life in the USA. He was a witness to many of the events described in this book. While living in the USA, Dr. Singh has been a regular visitor to his native India to visit friends and relatives and to document many of the changes in the country. Jas is the author of the popular book *Jas – Chronicles of Intrigue, Folly and Laughter in the Global Workplace.*

Dedication

To my family

Jas Singh

ONLY IN INDIA
STORIES UNTOLD

AUSTIN MACAULEY PUBLISHERS™

London ★ Cambridge ★ New York ★ Sharjah

A CIP catalogue record for this title is available from the British Library.

ISBN 9781786930903 (Paperback)
ISBN 9781786930910 (Hardback)
ISBN 9781786930927 (E-Book)

www.austinmacauley.com

First Published (2017)
Austin Macauley Publishers Ltd.
25 Canada Square
Canary Wharf
London
E14 5LQ

Acknowledgments

I could not have completed this project without the daily assistance of Mary Singh, my wife and partner of fifty years. Mary put aside countless chores to help get these stories written. She also helped me recall many details of the stories in which she has participated. At times, she remembered more names and places than my own memory allowed. Mary also tried to keep the book rating within G to PG (meaning suitable for readers of all ages) ratings. There are, perhaps three or four stories where parental guidance

(PG) is advised. The material may be too mature for children although the content is only suggestive and not overt.

I am indebted to my friend and business partner, Greg Beckstrom, who toiled as my chief editor, researcher, wordsmith, and fact checker. Greg and I worked together for several years at the same company and collaborated on my first book, *JAS – Chronicles of intrigue, folly, and laughter in the global workplace.*

Greg is a writer, geologist, business manager, and world traveler who has worked in energy exploration, environmental services, and engineering/consulting. He has held a wide variety of positions including consultant, exploration geologist, technical writer, marketing manager, business development manager, and operations manager. Greg and I used to work together at Golder Associates and developed a common bond based on our mutual appreciation for exotic foods, dusty villages, hotel club lounges, global travel, and paths seldom travelled. Greg holds a B.Sc. degree in Geology from the University of Wisconsin and a MBA from the University of St. Thomas. He lives in Minneapolis, is the proud father of two young adults, and can be reached at gab4254@gmail.com or via LinkedIn.

Another key contributor is Carol Nagan, a talented artist, and a wonderful human being. Carol illustrated my first book and illustrated several of the stories in this book. Although Carol had no prior experience with India, she brought many of these characters and settings to life, which you will see in "Paradise Found and Lost" and "Bureaucracy Par Excellence."

My cousin, Danny Uppal, an enormously talented artist and a versatile individual, illustrated most of the stories in this book.

Danny had an amazing upbringing. He was born in Kyaukse, a small village about twenty-five miles south of Mandalay in Burma. His colorful heritage includes a Punjabi father; an engineer like himself, and a Burmese mother. With few kids to play with in his small Burmese village, his father encouraged him to paint plants, animals, and construction sites.

In 1962, a military coup overthrew Burma's president and implemented a dictatorship. In 1964, his father decided to take his family back to India to his village, Bassian, where Danny grew up. For the next twenty years, he attended the nearby educational institutions and continued painting. His paintings have been displayed in national art galleries throughout India. Danny also illustrated a children's health book for United Nations Children's Fund. The range of his artistic imaginary is evident from the diversity of the scenarios he has created.

Danny later moved to USA. He is employed as an engineer with CALTRANS, the California Department of Transportation. Working as an engineer, he has never abandoned his passion for art. Some of his portraits, including that of Mother Teresa, have won praise from art critics. His depiction of Indian scenes is entirely authentic as he lived in those places when growing up. Danny now lives in Sacramento, California with his wife and two sons, both of whom are engineers.

I could not have written a few of the stories without help from David Paul Singh, a graduate of the University of Michigan business school and a research analyst at a global high tech company. David is an international traveler and, therefore, could relate to the environments I have described in a few of these stories. He is a subject of one of my stories. I will let you decide which one.

When writing these stories, I also relied upon three brilliant, dynamic, and highly-educated Indian women to interview them to assure that I did not stray too far from the real Indian values after being absent from India for fifty-five years.

Ms. Navjot Sidhu, my niece, whom I fondly call Dr. Peggy (she is a medical graduate from Patiala Medical College), was my advisor and censor on several of the stories. Peggy is an avid literature reader and a tough critic. She would grade my stories on a one to ten scale. Sad to say, I did not always score ten on  Peggy's scale, but most of the time I followed her recommendations.

Ms. Shamini Samuel reviewed several of the stories, including the one in which she is a one of the stars ("Merchants of Disease"). Shamini is a Canadian with an Indian and Malaysian heritage.

She is a leading professional in the Industrial Hygiene field and is manager of health and safety at an international energy company. Shamini is a delightful conversationalist and dinner companion. She can light up any party anywhere. Shamini lives with her engineer husband, Abe (a delightful beer companion), and their three children in Calgary, Canada.

Chitra Murali, a graduate of the elite Indian Institute of Technology (IIT) in Mumbai, is one of the smartest people I have come across anywhere. When I want to be sure of my facts, I call on Chitra. She works for Golder Associates, a multinational environmental engineering company, and lives with her husband and son in Chennai, India.

My thanks are also due to Rajesh Jackson, from Kuala Lumpur, Malaysia, who let me use his real name and his hot pepper episode in, "Addicted to Heat"; to Mr. Amarjit Khare, for arranging meetings with Mohinder Brar (the revolutionary's daughter); to Mr. J. Singh, manager of the Mastuana Sahib complex, for a tour of the "The Best Fortified Primary School in India"; to Narinder Bai, for giving me a copy of his brother Tej's autopsy report; to Adarsh Sidhu for researching opium use in Punjab villages today; and my brother Jagjit, who is an author and historian himself, for research and fact checking.

This book is also possible due to the encouragement and participation of my family. My daughter, Monica, my son, David (already acknowledge above), and their progeny (my grandchildren), who are my incentive for telling these stories.

Last but not least, I am thankful to my nephew Sher Singh and his wife Adarsh (Navjot's parents) who in my opinion are the most gracious hosts in the world. Their house in Patiala is our Indian headquarters whenever Mary and I visit India.

Table Of Contents

INTRODUCTION

Fifty-two years ago, I left India and have lived in the USA for most of my adult life ever since. I have achieved the American dream by most measures. Much of who I am today was molded in my early youth in India. A part of my soul still resides in India, even though I encounter more challenges entering the country of my birth than any of the other fifty countries I have visited for work or pleasure. Never mind, I am still drawn to my birth village.

In every man's life there comes a time when he wonders if life could have gone in a different direction. It is with this perspective that I wrote this book.

The stories herein span the seven decades of Indian history of which I have been a part of and some older events explained to me by my mother and other elders. These events have impacted my adult life. The stories reflect Indian historical events viewed through the lens of a child and young adult living in India and later as an American émigré with intense interest in India.

Most of my life I have been troubled by India's institutionalized caste system. The well-entrenched social classification system is so degrading and divisive that as a child I was left wondering how a civilized society could deem some members so inferior and unloved by virtue of their birth status. One day I asked my father, a Sikh scholar and admirer of ancient Hindu philosophy, about the caste system. He did not have a satisfactory explanation. He did tell me that the caste system is to be condemned and that many Hindu reformists such as Swami Dayanand, founder of the reformist organization Arya Samaj, had come out against untouchability.

When my brothers and sisters reached college age, we rebelled against the practice. That is the basis for the story *"Bring Your Own Bowl."* More than fifty years later and despite legal pronouncements, class discrimination continues to be widely practiced at all levels in Indian society.

"Preeti Gill Got Married – Almost" is a story about dowry demands

15

placed on a bride's parents. I do not know if it is the same all over India, but in Punjab, this extortionist practice has not diminished, but has actually evolved. Currently the practice has adopted innovative dowry math with higher and higher sums being demanded of the bride's family when the groom is an employed professional.

"Bridesmaids Gone Wild" describes a Punjabi wedding ritual where women from the bride's side of the wedding party subject the groom to extreme verbal hazing, all in good fun. I cannot recall the name for this ritual, but it provides a remarkable insight into a rite that grants unfettered freedom of expression to women in a very conservative environment.

The mass killings of innocent civilians following India's partition with Pakistan in 1947 left a deep impression upon me. The scope of atrocities, and the sheer abandonment of human virtues on a mass scale after the partition, may be second only to the Jewish Holocaust a few years earlier. Unlike the Holocaust, however, little has been written about the 1947 massacres and much of it one-sided. Two stories, *"The Best Fortified Primary School in India"* and *"Paradise Found and Lost"*, look at the partition as viewed through the eyes of a ten-year-old boy from the Indian side of the border. Both stories describe events when Muslim residents in nearby villages were forced to flee across the newly created India-Pakistan border (the Radcliff Line) to seek refuge in Muslim-dominated Pakistan. Many did not make it. *"Paradise Found and Lost"* is about a bachelor farmer who claimed to have rescued a young Muslim woman from harm by bands of fanatic Hindu and Sikh residents after her parents fled to Pakistan or were killed on their way to the border. After a long wait, the two were married, only to later be separated again by force.

My saddest memory concerning India happened on October 31, 1984, the day I read the news of the assassination of the popular Indian leader Indira Gandhi, followed immediately by the massacre of thousands of Sikh men, women, and children by fanatic mobs. When I returned to my hotel in London, where I was working at the time, I shared my grief and horror with the Sikh guard at the five-star hotel in Piccadilly Circus. When I asked him if he was in danger because of his Sikh appearance, his exact words were "Oh no, sir, a Sikh is never at risk in the UK just because of our looks. This is the safest place for a Sikh. British people remember our service to the Crown."

In my room, I kept thinking about what he had said and his words made me sad and agitated. How ironic, I thought? A Sikh in a foreign country, thousands of miles away from home, feels perfectly safe but not in his own country where his faith originated and where his soul resides.

The tragedy triggered by Mrs. Gandhi's assassination continued for a decade in the aftermath of the ill-named and ill-advised "Operation Blue Star", which killed many innocent pilgrims and demolished part of the holiest Sikh shrine, the "Sikh Vatican." In the ensuing revengeful era, my cousin Tej was beaten to death by Punjab police in full view of a handful of people. Tej's violent death inspired me to write the story *"Last Stand of the Blue Warrior"*.

British rule in India forms the background for four stories. Much of the colonial history of India has been sugarcoated by the victors. This is not unique. History is usually written by the conquerors. Expecting neutrality is being naïve. British rule in India is no exception. Evidence of this is the account of the first organized military uprising at the Meerut Military Cantonment in 1857. English historians have described the event as a common mutiny, yet the Indian name for the same event is the First War of Independence. The 1928 Ahmedgarh attempted robbery of a train carrying British treasure was a major anti-British act of Indian freedom fighters to finance their violent anti-British campaign, but to the outside world it was presented as a bunch of village dacoits. To sort out the truth, I did some research and located the only known book about the incident, which is called, *Sangrami Pind*, meaning 'Revolutionary Village'. That is the story behind *"The Failed Train Robbery that Shook the British Raj"*.

The last thirty years of British rule, starting with the Ghadar party uprisings in 1917, followed by the Jalianwalla massacre of 1919, and through the Indian National Army (The Azad Hind Fauj) activities, brought increasingly violent times. Thousands of Punjabi farmers were killed fighting either for the British on World War II fronts or against the British as INA soldiers in support of the Japanese in hopes of hastening the British exit from India. I can count relatives among the fighters. These events are captured in *"Revolutionary's Daughter"*.

I hold the British responsible for much of the tobacco and opium addiction in India despite the fact that India was no stranger to hallucinogens before the arrival of the British and the Portuguese, as well as the fact that Indian tobacco merchants have been outdoing each other in promoting tobacco in more recent years. The stories *"Merchants of Disease I – The Opium Trail"* and *"Merchants of Disease II, The Smoking Gun"* are about innovative schemes by Western companies and their local partners to get millions of Indians addicted to opium and tobacco. Some readers will judge me as being too harsh on tobacco. I offer no apologies. Being a health scientist (Industrial Hygienist), I know the facts. I have studied toxicology. Preventing exposure to harmful chemicals is my job.

Some of my friends might also find me too critical of British rule. Perhaps I am, but the fact is that no colonial ruler has left a happy legacy. It is not possible considering that the whole idea of colonization is to divert scarce, precious, or valuable resources of the occupied land to the colonists' mother country. On a relative scale, however, the English treated their subjects better that the Portuguese in India, the Dutch in South Africa, the Spaniards in Latin America, and the Belgians in Congo.

The story "*Datura Eaters*" describes the easy availability of naturally occurring hallucinogens in India. Their acceptance in Indian society on spiritual and religious grounds has justified their widespread use.

My best memories of India are from my years at the university campus in the beautiful city of Chandigarh, and my travels into the Himalayan foothills. Indian hill resorts are some of the most enchanted places. The stories "*The Slow Train to Her Majesty's Summer Capital*" and "*Annapoorna Entrepreneur*" attest to that. The ride to Shimla, the summer capital of British India on a narrow-gauge train, was recently featured in Anthony Bourdain's popular *Parts Unknown* television show. "*Kite Runners of Bathinda*" is a story of my happy childhood and so is "*Bibi Mehraan, May She Live in Peace*", a bittersweet memory from my early childhood. The sophisticated woman practicing her ancient trade while living in my neighborhood, and her violent and unsolved murder, were remarkable and traumatic events in my preteen life.

"*Addicted to Heat*" is a tale of hot and hotter peppers. I cannot imagine Indian food without chili peppers. Many countries have spicy cuisine. None can match the imaginative uses of capsicum as Indians can.

I am amused when Westerners fail to discover humor in Asian countries relative to the USA where commercialized humor (TV shows, nightclubs, and comedy clubs) is a staple of daily existence. I can understand why Westerners miss it altogether. Much of it cannot be translated, only felt. The fact is that almost every village in Punjab had a comedy club when I was growing up. The humor was derived from everyday insignificant occurrences of life in the manner of the popular *Seinfeld* TV show. The story "*Seinfeld in Every Village*" is my attempt to highlight Indian humor.

The story "*Bureaucracy Par Excellence*" results from my years of frustration with the Indian bureaucratic system. Even today, when I visit India, I dread clearing Indian customs even though I carry valid entry papers and carry nothing to import. Bureaucracy notwithstanding, I am drawn to India. Part of my family is there, and part of my soul is there. For this, I am willing to bear such bureaucratic indignities.

I am happy about the progress India has made and I want people to write about the positive changes when they are deserved. However, glorifying things is not my style. I want to write about it all – the good, the bad, and the ugly. I am mindful of the significant progress that has been made, but I am also disappointed that some vexing ills still hamper change. Despite legislative efforts, India remains mired in communal violence, caste discrimination, institutional corruption, environmental degradation, gender inequality, and a growing disparity between the haves and the have-nots. The electronic revolution has not benefited the Indian masses, especially rural workers and farmers.

I have one wish. When I am ninety-nine years old, in good health but toothless, I will go to India with all my documents in order. The immigration officer will look at my toothless grin, observe my jet black hair ("better living through chemistry"), verify my birthdate, smile back at me and say, "Welcome back, Dr. Singh."

FOREWORD

I met Dr. Jaswant (Jas) Singh in 2008 at a conference in Minneapolis, Minnesota. We both worked at the same company, and he was coming to my turf. As the local manager in Minneapolis, I wanted to know who this guy was. Once I learned more about him, and of his reputation as a "must meet" personality in the health and safety consulting world, we considered taking a full length photograph of Jas and placing it in our booth with a sign saying "Have your picture taken with the famous Jas Singh." When clearer thinking prevailed, the idea lost its appeal.

What did not go away was my appreciation for him as a remarkable professional. After Minneapolis, Jas and I managed to reconnect once or twice a year at various industry events, company meetings, or client initiatives in places like Shanghai, Portland, and Delhi. We learned that we had similar approaches to business – have fun, work hard, treat clients fairly, and respect our profession.

As the years passed, our connection evolved from being professional acquaintances to collaborating on some writing projects. When Jas conceived of his first book – *Jas – Chronicles of intrigue, folly, and laughter in the global workplace* – he asked me to work with him. As many of Jas's friends and acquaintances know, he is a fantastic storyteller. With my background as a science writer, editor, photographer, researcher, and producer, it was a natural fit for Jas and me to work together on that project.

For this project – *Only in India* – the challenge was very different. How do we tell stories about a country as vast and complex as India in a way that is fair, accurate, and honest? What Jas has done with *Only in India* is to share a series of stories about his birth country through his eyes, his memory, and his imagination. This is the best he can do given that so much of India's history, at least as it relates to everyday life in rural areas and small Punjabi villages, is undocumented.

Only in India is not a series of love letters about the country that was. Nor does it describe the country as it is today. India is a complex country

20

with thousands of years of human history, complex social relationships, maddening traffic (lookout for the buffalo!), and political and religious divisions that seem to threaten to tear the country apart. Yet the people are remarkably friendly, resilient, patient, and tolerant. Somehow it all works.

Growing up in India, at least until he was a young adult, helped motivate Jas to do his very best in his career, yet he is humble and deeply appreciative. He has achieved professional success, is highly respected by his peers, is a sought after speaker and mentor, and is a seasoned world traveler. Professional accolades don't define Jas. What makes him special are the relationships that he forges with clients, young professionals, university professors, students, and others who learn from him. He has a wealth of knowledge that he shares widely. This is his gift.

I have been fortunate to work with Jas for a few years. In doing some research for this book, I travelled with him and his wife Mary throughout Northern India. I have dined with his extended family, visited his birth village, travelled by a narrow-gauge train to Shimla, met some of his university contacts in Chandigarh, and visited the schools he attended prior to his move to the USA for his advanced studies at the University of Southern California. What he writes about in this book, with a few exceptions to protect the identity of some characters who may prefer to remain anonymous, is based on real people and actual events. Jas, in his quest to document the country through the eyes of a keen observer, spares no one, yet is gracious about his criticisms. He also writes about some of the customs and rituals of India, such as India's social caste system that still influences where people live, what they eat, how they dress, whom they marry, etc. Therefore, this collaboration, which we hope you find interesting and entertaining, and sometimes maddening, should help you gain a better appreciation, dare I say respect, for a country that I know Jas loves.

I hope you enjoy learning more about the amazing history of India and have a better understanding of the good, the bad, and the ugly events that shaped the country. If you haven't visited India, please do. I can assure you that all of your senses will be stimulated – vibrant colors, the noise of cars honking to announce that they are passing and the smell of curry from roadside food stalls will come back to you long after you leave. Moreover, if you have Indian roots, come home again someday. Your family misses you.

Greg Beckstrom, Minneapolis, Minnesota, USA

CHAPTER 1

REVOLUTIONARY'S DAUGHTER

We were late. She was waiting. She stepped forward and greeted us with folded hands. A middle-aged man named Amarjit introduced her as Mohinder. I gestured for a hug, and she engulfed me in a tight embrace and started crying. I made no effort to break her grip. Knowing some of the history that she likely possessed, and the difficulties she experienced, certainly brought forth feelings of sadness in me. Here I was in the arms of a woman only five or six years younger than myself and whom I had not known existed until three weeks earlier. I had discovered her after many attempts to locate anyone alive who knew her late father Kehar Brar, a revolutionary warrior in the Indian independence struggle. As I searched, I could not remember if Kehar had had any children. After much exploring, I learned that a cousin from my mother's side lived near Kehar's daughter (Mohinder) and is, coincidently, a distant relative of hers. The cousin himself was too young to know much about Kehar, the revolutionary.

We sat down next to each other in Amarjit's family room. Amarjit, a college educated man, articulate, friendly, and handsome with a regal bearing, had arranged this meeting.

"You don't remember me, do you?" She fired the first question. I had not, and I struggled for an appropriate response. "I am trying to think where we had met and when? After six decades, my memory is not as good as it once was," I confessed.

"We played together for few days when you and your mother came to visit my mother and me in Bahadurpur. That was my mom's village, and, as a matter of fact, your mother's village too," she said as she smiled. "Bapuji (father) was not in Bahadurpur at the time because the police were looking for him. He was on the run."

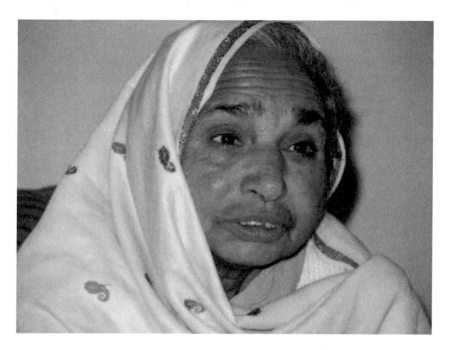

"Yes, I remember now." (I was lying). "Those are good memories." Before I finished the sentence, I realized my blunder. Those were not good memories. Those were bad memories and hard times, very hard. It was coming to me now. My mother and I were visiting Dhiyan Brar, Mohinder's mom, when they were refugees several years after an explosion had destroyed their house and Mohinder's father went missing. She had no clear memory of her father at that early time, where he was, or what he did.

Mohinder's father was dedicated to the rebellious Indian National Army (INA), also called the "Azad Hind Fauj" meaning the "Free India Army" (*note: The term INA should not be confused with the modern Indian National Army. The term is reserved by most Indians for the anti-British guerrilla army during the Indian independence movement.*) According to information passed down from my mother and other personal items in Kehar's possession, it is apparent that he took orders from the INA commanders to carry out activities that would help accelerate the British departure from India. I wondered where he had acquired such anti-British feelings. Could it be from the infamous Jallianwala Massacre (1) where an estimated one thousand peaceful protestors were gunned down by Brigadier Reginald Dyer in Amritsar in 1919? Alternatively, perhaps he was influenced by the earlier Ghadar (2) movement for Indian independence. The Ghadar independence movement originated in America and Canada

23

and was imported to India by expatriates living on the West Coast of North America in 1913, long before the INA.

Kehar Brar had plenty of company in his antagonism towards the British. Much of Punjab was in the grip of anti-British fervor. At the peak of this activity, the INA had over 43,000 soldiers fighting against the British in several countries including an estimated 3,000 soldiers fighting in Europe under German command (the Legion Indienne) (3) and over 40,000 Indian soldiers forced to fight for the Japanese in territories occupied by Japan during World War II.

Mahatma Gandhi's nonviolent "quit India" movement had won the hearts of many Indians, but in Kehar's neighborhood, there was little interest in Mahatma's slow movement to persuade the British to grant independence to India. Kehar may have associated with some of the most active members of the INA, including the likes of Sher Jung, one of the smartest and most charismatic members of the organization. Kehar, already under the watchful eyes of the British police, eluded capture and paid fleeting visits to his family when it appeared safe.

Right: Kehar Singh Brar (no photographs of Kehar as an adult could be found. This illustration by Danny Uppal is based on descriptions of Kehar)

All that changed on one Sunday afternoon. Kehar quietly slipped into his house after dusk. As told to Mohinder by her mother years later, he gathered his chemistry set, which included a few wires, and started experimenting with small quantities of explosives he had procured. Something went wrong and there was an explosion. One of the walls and most of the roof of his home were blown away. The rubble blocked half of the street behind their home. Although Kehar sustained minor injuries, he picked himself up, rushed through the streets, leaving a trail of blood, and disappeared before people could gather. He knew that the police would be there soon and the outcome was predictable. He would face a very brief trial and would be hanged according to British law.

With the roof of their home blown away, his wife and daughter had no cover over their heads. Dhiyan picked up Mohinder, who was nine months old at the time, gathered whatever she could and went to the neighbor's house with the intention of spending the night. After considering her options, she decided not to stay at the neighbor's house because it would expose the neighbor to police harassment. Because she was married to a subversive, she knew that it was just a matter of hours before British police would come to investigate the explosion. She left some of their belongings at the friend's house, grabbed a few essentials, and decided to set out on foot to her parents' house several hours away. With darkness approaching, the neighbor realized that it was a dangerous and impossible task for Dhiyan to walk several miles while clutching her nine-month-old baby. According to stories passed down from family members, he quickly arranged a camel ride with an escort to take them to their destination.

Early the next day, the police came looking for them at Dhiyan's parents' house. They questioned Dhiyan and her parents for a long time and left with a warning to call police if Kehar came to see them. Failing that, they would be charged as accomplices. The police were certain that Kehar would be drawn to his in-laws' home to see his wife and baby daughter. They were right. Sometime later, Kehar started visiting Dhiyan and Mohinder at night. Someone notified the police about Kehar's visits, who then increased their visits to Bahadurpur. The frequency of the police visits soon made Kehar's midnight rendezvous too dangerous. There were too many prying eyes. Someone could tip the police when Kehar was visiting to gain favor with the government, or to claim a reward (if one existed) for his capture. The interrogations by the police became increasingly threatening and abusive. Kehar knew it was only a matter of time until physical force would be used by the police to get the truth about the fugitive's whereabouts and his activities.

Kehar soon realized that he was putting his family at risk. One night, he said good-bye to them and told them not to expect him back until times were better. He also told Dhiyan not to search for him and not to talk about him with the neighbors. If someone asked, she was to say that he vanished and most likely had been killed by the police or, worse, sent to Kaale Pani ("black water"), the dreaded "prison of no return" in the Andaman Sea.

Months passed and Mohinder and her mother had no news of Kehar. Dhiyan was beginning to think of all those possibilities that Kehar had mentioned about his fate if he was captured and, although Dhiyan had no reliable information, preferred to believe the black water prison scenario. This meant that he was still alive although, for practical purposes, he would have been dead in the sense that she would never hear from him again. No prisoner charged with treason had ever returned from the prison of no return.

Relatives wondered what was so special about Kehar that merited such an intense search. Everybody knew about the explosion at his house and the fact that he was an active member of the Azad Hind Fauj (Free India Army) which had been founded by General Mohan Singh (4), the right hand man of Subhas Chandra Bose (5), the charismatic leader of the INA independence movement. Beyond that, they did not know any specifics.

Kehar was a brilliant student in his school days. He was interested in chemistry and engineering. His command of the English language was enviable. He stood out as someone who had been educated outside of India; such was his intellectual aptitude and international style, though there was no evidence of him having lived abroad when he was young. He had been experimenting with explosives for some time and may have received training at an INA bomb-making factory in Lohat Baddi village, which was only a few miles from his house. Punjab was a hotbed of anti-British activity at this time, so there were probably several illegal weapons-making operations in the region. The Azad Hind Fauj goal was "independence by any means" which included targeted assassinations, bombings, and train robberies.

The explosion that demolished his modest home placed Kehar on India's "most wanted list". There is no evidence that Kehar had any part in the most violent incidents of the time such as Shaheed Bhagat Singh's (6) bombing of the Legislative Assembly or Udham Singh's revenge killing in London for the April 13, 1919 Jallianwala Garden attack. He elevated his activist credentials, however, by associating with another high profile revolutionary named Sher Jung, the unsung hero of the Indian independence struggle according to Indians sympathetic to the cause of independence by any means. Sher Jung was a scholar and a wildlife conservationist best known for his book, *Tryst with Tigers*. (See the related story, "*Failed Train Robbery that Shook the British Raj*").

After the explosion, Kehar disappeared with no clue to his location or communications with his family. He was not heard from for the next few years (Dhiyan and Mohinder lived with Dhiyan's parents during this time). Kehar's precise whereabouts during that time are shrouded in mystery, but based on my conversations with Mohinder, it was evident that he had slipped out of the country and very likely joined the INA and the Japanese in Malaya.

THE PRISON OF NO RETURN

As time passed, the frequency of the police visits to Bahadurpur declined. No one saw anyone who fit his description in the area. People assumed that either he was caught, tried, and hanged by the British, or he had fled to a distant land that was not under British control. Other exotic stories emerged about his whereabouts, among them imprisonment in the remote Kaale Pani prison in the Andaman Sea (7).

"Did you ever think your father was alive in Kaale Pani when you had no news of him for years?" I asked Mohinder.

"I never believed he was sent to Kaale Pani," she replied. "As far as I knew, only high-profile political prisoners were sent there because from there they could not cause trouble, but the public knew they were still alive. For less important activists, it was more expedient and far less expensive to just hang them and tell their families that the criminal was executed under British sedition laws instead of keeping them alive at the costly Andaman facility. An even better way for the police was to inform the family that their relative was killed in an armed encounter," she continued.

"I was sure all this time Bapuji must be alive because the police never came knocking on our door informing us of his death. I wanted to believe he was alive in some other country serving the cause of independence, maybe in Germany, but more likely in Japanese occupied Malaya (now Malaysia) or Singapore," she added.

INDISCHE LEGION

I was particularly intrigued about her mention of Germany as a possible refuge for Kehar because most people today do not know about the Punjabi farmers, who as prisoners of war, were pressed into service under Nazi command in Germany. Why Germany, I thought? Then I remembered reading about the Indian Legion (Indische Legion), officially Legion Freies Indien.

Mohinder reached for a brown envelope with some newspaper clippings and old photos she had brought with her for me to review. She pulled out a reprint of a large legal-size article in Punjabi celebrating a speech in Berlin by the INA head Subhas Chandra Bose asking Germany to help India expel the British. It was common knowledge that Bose went to Germany to meet with Hitler. While in Germany, there seems to be documentation that he met with several German leaders, but it is doubtful that he met Hitler. The most popular photograph showing him shaking hands with Hitler appears to be a fake.

Mohinder agreed that Kehar Singh being in Hitler's army was a remote possibility. It is possible, however, that he would have known some of the estimated 3,000 Indians who served in the Indische Legion because almost all of them were prisoners of war captured by the Japanese after the disastrous allied defeat in Singapore. Many of the captured men were villagers from Punjab.

"Did Bapuji know any soldiers from around here who served in Hitler's army, or what happened to them when Germany lost the war?" I asked her.

"I don't know, but it is quite possible. As to what happened to them after the Nazi defeat, one can only guess. Probably they slipped into neutral Switzerland and made their way from there back to India only to face a court martial, or charges of desertion and treason," she said with a bit of authority.

Mohinder's understanding of the history of Indian independence stunned me. Why did she possess such a detailed and intimate knowledge of this phase of India's history, and how did she know about the events from World War II? I wondered and concluded that when your entire life, your loved one's life, and your very existence depended on the outcome of the war, and India's struggle for independence, she probably made it her mission to learn everything about those events. I do not know if I am right, but this is my opinion and one that seems to make the most sense.

Her in-depth knowledge of the events made me wonder about her level of schooling. I decided not to ask because I suspected that she never went beyond high school, considering her family's circumstances. She just decided to know everything about why she was deprived of her father's love for most of her young life.

THE JAPANESE CONNECTION

Taking a different tact, I asked Mohinder if her father served in the Japanese army as thousands of Indian soldiers did after the fall of Singapore. "I do not think he served under the Japanese. He was not a soldier. He was a planner or a technician, you might say. One thing seems certain. When he was missing in Malaya, he must have met with General Mohan Singh, the INA founder and the man he admired and with whom he had a great deal in common. He never talked about his war years with his family, friends, or neighbors, maybe only with his comrades in the INA. One thing I remember is he mentioned Major Fujiwara a few times.

"I heard a few INA members went to Japan. Did your father go to Japan to get training?" I asked.

"Thank God he did not because rumors were that when Japan lost the war and signed a treaty with America, such people became a liability for the Japanese and they would execute them instead of repatriating them back to India where they would have been executed anyway as traitors under British laws." (This was pure speculation on her part I realized).

We had been talking for two and a half hours nonstop. The conversation was an emotional roller coaster ride for her. She wiped away tears many times during our conversation. We decided to have a break for tea and snacks while looking at the photos and mementos she had brought with her for our meeting.

HOME COMING, A FLEETING FAMILY LIFE

"Let us talk about happier times," I said. "Bapuji did return home from wherever he was after years of absence. Tell me about it. How did you feel upon his return?"

Mohinder did not perk up as I expected. She was still in a pensive mood. "You know the British won the war. They promised Gandhi, Nehru, and other Indian leaders that India would be granted independence soon and that everyone should be patient. The first thing the British had to decide was what to do with the 40,000 INA commandos like Bapuji. Therefore, although the war was over, we did not hear any word about him. We were sure he was alive. Still, we were not celebrating. The rumor was that thousands of INA soldiers would be charged as traitors and some would be hanged. There were to be trials at the Red Fort," she said. "We waited."

The British were faced with a dilemma. Should they imprison thousands of Indians just before they left India? Did the British rulers want to leave this legacy? After much contemplation, they decided not to charge most of the thousands for treason. Only the high-profile cases would be tried. Lord Mountbatten, the Governor General of India, and Jawaharlal Nehru, the lead lawyer defending the INA, agreed that ordinary INA soldiers would be set free after cashiering (a military term for dismissal of an individual for breach of discipline and forfeiture of their pay and allowance). In addition, they would not be permitted to be inducted into the free India National Army. Later on, it was decided to pardon even the INA leaders, including General Mohan Singh. *Note: Despite the bloodshed and violence during the long independence struggle, the British leaders had maintained relatively good relationships with the Indian political leaders, and when compared to the other European colonial powers, British rule in India ended rather quietly without any incidents or reprisals against the British still remaining in India.*

Kehar stayed away while all the legal wrangling was going on and finally returned home after making sure that he would not face any reprisals.

I asked Mohinder about her life at home after Kehar returned. "When Bapuji finally came home, was there a big celebration?" I asked.

"Yes there was, but it was so short. I barely got to know him." She sighed. "And then it was the same all over again."

"What happened?"

"He was not happy at home. He was bored. He missed the action. After years of being on the run, he could not adjust to a normal life. He had no friends here. He had some relatives, but he never knew any of them. They had all shunned him during his years as a fugitive because they would be at risk if the police knew they were harboring him or associating with him in any way. They just excluded him from their lives. He was a foreigner in his own village. He wanted action and excitement," she said.

Kehar did not have to wait long for action. The slow process of the independence movement in Portuguese-occupied India picked up steam after the British exited the country. Many people thought that the Portuguese would follow suit and would immediately leave India, but they did not. They liked Goa and its beaches. Many had made Goa their home. Unlike the British, who never mixed with the Indians except for some intermarriages in the East resulting in a small Angelo-Indian community, the Portuguese intermarried on a much larger scale. They built many

Catholic churches, promoted the Portuguese language, and became more integrated into Indian society. There were reluctant to just pack up and go.

The independence movement in Goa intensified and used multiple tactics, including violent protests. Kehar joined the protests. He was arrested but released beyond the Goa border into the Indian side with a warning to never return to Goa. The Portuguese dealt with the local protesters harshly, but they reserved their fury for outsiders entering Goa. They believed Goa still belonged to Portugal.

According to Mohinder, Kehar could not stay away from Goa. He visited there off and on for seven years until one day he and about a dozen other revolutionaries tried to bring down the Portuguese flag on the Governor's house and replace it with the tri-color Indian flag. They were arrested, beaten, and jailed. Apparently, repeat offenders like Kehar received particularly harsh treatment including beatings with rifle butts. Mohinder did not know how long he stayed in prison after the flag incident, but she seemed positive that the Portuguese poisoned him while he was in their captivity.

She continued, "To end the struggle, India finally invaded Goa in 1961. Goa was incorporated into the Indian Union although Portugal did not acknowledge the annexation until 1975. Kehar ended up in a hospital in Bombay (Mumbai) from where he was transferred to a hospital in Nabha (closer to Kehar's home and family) with the help of the Maharaja of Nabha, who admired Kehar."

Mohinder wiped tears again and continued, "He was discharged from the Nabha hospital and came home. Back at home, he was not the same man. He was always in pain, so he started taking opium to dull the pain. The opium also made him sleepy. He seemed depressed and restless. He became paranoid and started reacting as though someone was chasing him. Whenever we went out to the fields for a walk, he would look around and behind his back even if no one was around. One time I asked him to go out with me into the mustard fields. It was Basant, the springtime. The normally dry and sometimes parched fields were a beautiful bright yellow carpet as far as the eye could see. It was as if nature had laid a yellow carpet to celebrate some important occasion. I told him, 'Bapuji, look, this is a yellow carpet to welcome you back home.' He looked at me and did not smile. I cried. This was not the father I remembered. Someone had poisoned him, damaging his nervous system. Who did this to him? We left the fields and came home. He went straight to bed. On the way home, he did not say a word." Mohinder paused, drank some tea, wiped her tears, and continued. "Apart from opium, Bapuji started drinking which he had rarely done before. He would stay in bed very late, contrary to his earlier life style."

ONE SPRING MORNING HE DID NOT WAKE UP

"This is a sad story. I feel your pain," I assured her. "Times have changed, but what do you say to the people who claim that it was wrong for the INA to rush into the arms of Hitler and the Japanese to expedite the British exit? Gandhi's pacifist approach was working, according to them, and why did Subhas Bose and General Mohan Singh think that the Germans or the Japanese, who have their own dark history when it comes to racial relations, would be any kinder to India than the British if the war had gone the other way?"

Mohinder stared at the ceiling searching for answer. She did not want to comment. I realized that I should not have asked such a question because it implied a diminished role of the INA and the futility of the hardships and sacrifices made by many like her father. She managed an answer.

"I don't know what to say to them. They (INA) gave their lives for this country. They wanted to live in a free India. Maybe they did not have time to think about life under the Japanese or Germans."

That was an exquisite answer, I thought. "You are so right. Backtracking is easy. Living through such times is not," I said.

Kehar's death, unlike his life, was quiet and uneventful. One morning he was found dead in his home. After decades of fighting the British and Portuguese, surviving at least one bomb accident and numerous beatings, and enduring countless difficult journeys, his passing somehow seemed anti-climactic. As to the cause of his death, no one knows. At that time in India, autopsies were rare.

It was time for us to depart. We prepared to leave, but Amarjit's wife motioned for us to stay seated and have another cup of tea before taking the long drive back to Patiala. After tea, we said good-bye and walked to the car and the driver who was waiting to take us home. Mohinder followed us outside and gave my wife and me a warm hug.

"Thank you so much. It has been many years since anyone has wanted to know about my father. It is as if he never existed. Thank you for letting me share my grief and remembrance of him. Promise to come back and bring me a copy of the book you are writing when I see you next."

"I will," I promised. We got in the car. She waved until the car turned into the side street.

1) **Jallianwala Massacre**: On 13 April 1919 a crowd of nonviolent protesters, along with Golden Temple pilgrims, had gathered in the Jallianwala Garden in support of Indian independence. Brigadier Reginald Dyer told the crowd to leave. When they failed to disperse, he ordered his troops to fire on the crowd. They kept firing for ten minutes until they ran out of ammunition. Official count by the British government was 370 dead and 1200 wounded. Other sources placed the number of dead at well over 1000. After the massacre, Brigadier Dyer made Indians crawl along a street where apparently two English women had been harassed. Dyer became a celebrated hero in Britain along with many other people connected with the British Empire's long rule of India.

In 1997, Queen Elizabeth visited the site of the massacre to pay homage to those killed. The New York Times reported her visit in October 15, 1997 under the headline: **In India, Queen Bows Her Head Over a Massacre in 1919:** *AMRITSAR, India, Oct. 14 (1997)—In an act of contrition for Britain's colonial past, Queen Elizabeth came to this Punjab city today and paid 30 seconds of silent homage at the site of the Amritsar massacre of April 13, 1919, one of the British Empire's darkest days. The Queen removed her shoes and laid a wreath of white and gold marigolds at a pink granite memorial at Jallianwala Bagh, the walled garden where Brig. Reginald Dyer, a British officer administering martial law in Amritsar, ordered 50 soldiers to open fire on a crowd of about 10,000 unarmed Indians...*

2) **The Ghadar Party** was founded in 1913 by Punjabi Indians in the United States (California) and Canada (Vancouver) with the aim of securing India's independence from British rule. Key members included Lala Har Dayal, Sohan Singh Bhakna, Kartar Singh Sarabha, and Rashbehari Bose. Though predominantly Sikh, the Ghadar Party included members and leaders of many religions. After the outbreak of World War I, Ghadar party members returned to Punjab to agitate for freedom from Britain. As early as in 1915, they conducted revolutionary activities in central Punjab and organized uprisings. Their presence alarmed the British Empire, and police surveillance of Punjabi villages increased to crush the rebellion. The Ghadar Party set the foundation for future Indian revolutionary movements and served as a stepping-stone for independence. (Source: Wikipedia)

3) **Indische Legion,** officially the Free India Legion (Legion Freies Indien) and later the Indian Volunteer Legion of the Waffen, was a military unit raised during World War II in Nazi Germany. Intended to serve as a liberation force for British-ruled India, it was comprised of Indian prisoners

of war and Indian expatriates in Europe. Because of its origins in the Indian independence movement, it was also known as the "Tiger Legion", and the "Azad Hind Fauj", the Free India Army. Initially raised as part of the German Army, it was later part of the Waffen SS. Subhas Chandra Bose, the INA leader, initiated the legion's formation when he visited Berlin in 1941, seeking German aid as part of his efforts to win India's independence from Britain. (Wikipedia)

4) **General Mohan Singh** was an Indian army officer who later served as a member of the Indian Parliament. He was born to a farming family in Ugoke village in the Sialkot district in Punjab (now part of Pakistan). He was the founding father of the INA, which he formed in Malaya with the help of the Japanese. Major Fujiwara Iwaichi, Chief of Intelligence of the Japanese 15th Army, handed over 40,000 captured Indian soldiers in the fall of Singapore to Mohan Singh to form the INA in exile. Mohan Singh later became disenchanted and suspicious of the Japanese motives and dissolved the INA in December 1942. INA was later re-organized by Subhas Chandra Bose. In the Indian partition of 1947, Mohan Singh's village fell on the Pakistan side of the border. He had to flee to the Indian side where, with the Government's help, he settled in a village in Ludhiana District. Mohan Singh Died in 1989. (Source: Wikipedia)

5) **Subhas Chandra Bose**, popularly known as Netaji ("respected leader") was educated at the University of Cambridge. He secretly married Emilie Shenket, an Austrian, in 1937. She bore him a daughter named Anita Bose Pfaff. Bose kept his marriage secret while he was President of the Indian National Congress. In 1938, he was ousted from the Congress Party because of differences with Gandhi and the Congress Party's leadership. Bose went to Germany in 1942 to seek German help for Indian independence. Historians have questioned the wisdom of his efforts to seek an alliance with Hitler. Hitler hated many ethnicities and racial groups including Asians and Africans. His alliance with the Japanese was of pure necessity. There is no clear evidence that Hitler ever met Bose, although some photos have recently appeared on the internet without authentication. It is plausible that Bose met with several members of the Nazi high command, including Himmler. Bose was familiar with Germany. He studied there. He spoke fluent German at home because his wife's native language was German. In time, Bose also became disillusioned with Germany. One reason may have been Hitler's decision to invade Russia. Bose had Marxist leanings. In 1943, he left Germany. Hitler felt that Bose would be more useful to the war effort if he was in India, so he provided Bose passage on German submarine U-180 around the Cape of Good Hope

to Madagascar where he was transferred to a Japanese submarine for the rest of the journey. Bose never made it back to India. The details of his death are shrouded in mystery. Common belief is that he died in a plane crash somewhere in Manchuria, but no definite proof of that exists.

6) **Bombing of the Central Legislative Assembly:** On April 8, 1929, Bhagat Singh, also referred to as Shaheed Bhagat Singh, and his accomplice Batukeshwar Dutta from the Hindustan Socialist Republican Association (HSRA), threw two bombs and many leaflets inside the Central Legislative Assembly from the Visitor's Gallery. Both Singh and Dutta were sentenced to life in prison under Section 307 of the Indian Penal Code & Section 4 of the Explosive Substances Act (Times of India). Dutta was exiled to the Kaale Pani prison in the Andaman and Nicobar.

During the trials, sufficient evidence emerged against Bhagat Singh for the murder of assistant police superintendent John Saunders. Bhagat Singh and his accomplice Sukhdev Thapar had plotted to kill James Scott, superintendent of police in Lahore to revenge the killing of Lala Lajpat Rai, a noted writer and politician. In a case of mistaken identity, however, John Saunders, the assistant superintendent of police was killed. Bhagat Singh was convicted and subsequently hanged for his participation in the murder. He was to be hanged on March 23, 1931. Instead, his execution was brought forward and he was hanged eleven hours earlier. He remained defiant until his death. His last words before he died were, "Down with British Imperialism." He was twenty-three at the time of his death. Bhagat Singh continues to be an idol to many Indians. His memorials dot the land, including a bronze statue in the Parliament of India.

7) **Kaale Pani (Black Waters)** prison in the remote Andaman and Nicobar Islands was constructed between 1896 and 1906, although the British had been using the Andaman islands as a prison since the days in the immediate aftermath of the "Sepoy Mutiny of 1857" (called the "First War of Independence" by Indian historians). Many activists were imprisoned there during the independence struggle. Famous inmates of the Kaale Pani Jail included; Diwan Singh Kalepani, Yogendra Shukla, Batukeshwar Dutt, Maulana Ahmadullah, Movli Abdul Rahim Sadiqpuri, Maulvi Liaquat Ali, Babarao Savarkar, and Vinayak and Damodar Savarkar.

The remote islands were an ideal place for solitary confinement, political isolation, and social exclusion. The convicts were treated harshly and were used in chain gangs to construct other buildings and harbor facilities. Many died serving their sentences.

Many prisoners attempted to escape. In 1868, 238 prisoners tried to escape. All were caught and punished. Eighty-seven of the escapees were hanged. Japan captured the Andaman Islands in 1942. In 1945, the British resumed control at the end of World War II. (From Wikipedia and several other sources)

CHAPTER 2
FAILED TRAIN ROBBERY THAT SHOOK
THE BRITISH RAJ

The normally uneventful night train came to a screeching halt before it reached the Ahmedgarh station. While passengers peered out of the windows in the moonless night, the train conductor came out of the engine room to see what the emergency was and to find out who had pulled the emergency chain. As soon as the engineer stepped foot on the ground, he was greeted with gunshots. He presumed the passenger who had pulled the emergency chain fired the shots.

The wounded conductor fell to the ground. The attacker felt no urgency to finish off the wounded man but rather rushed towards the compartment where the rest of his group, five in all, were already busy whacking away at an industrial safe with sledgehammers. The compartment under attack was a fortified railroad car on its way to Delhi, the Capital of British India.

Regaining his composure, the bleeding conductor dragged himself to safety and disappeared in the bushes. The train robbers continued to pound furiously at the impenetrable steel locks on the safe. The robbers were driven to get their hands on the cash collected from the Indian hinterlands that was destined for the British treasury.

The robbers were well armed. They had at least two shotguns, a revolver, and hand-to-hand combat weapons. They also had hammers and crowbars. Minutes passed and the frustration of the robbers, unable to make any dent in the safe, increased. Their tools would not let them get any closer to the treasure located behind the multi-layered steel locks. Minutes were ticking away. Someone in the group noticed lights from several fast moving vehicles approaching from a distance. They knew that a motor vehicle at night in that area was a rarity and believed the approaching vehicles must be police. The leader gave everyone the signal to leave. The robbers picked up their tools and disappeared into the dark.

In the following days, there were no reports of the failed train robbery in the Indian papers. The British police, however, knew right away that it was not a simple attempted robbery by a bunch of Punjabi farmers. It was an attack on the British treasury by activists determined to harm British rule by any means possible, including inflicting financial pain on the Raj (1).

British India had mastered the techniques to censure news of such anti-British activities from the Indian public and, more importantly, from fellow Britons back home. Many British leaders were already beginning to question the wisdom of holding onto India much longer. Emotions were running high in the aftermath of violent incidents which included the assassination of assistant police superintendent John Saunders by Shaheed Bhagat Singh and the assassination of Brigadier Reginald Dyer in London by a Punjabi villager named Udham Singh.

On the scale of attempted train robberies in general, the Ahmedgarh robbery was a small, and unproductive, event. Nevertheless, coming on the heels of the assassinations of Saunders and Dyer, the Ahmedgarh train robbery was a major anti-British event. It shook up the governments in Delhi and in England. All available resources of the Empire were allocated to finding and punishing the perpetrators of this attack. While there were few clues, the robbers were suspected of being from Punjab.

An immediate causality of the robbery investigation was the closing of the local college. The Akal College in Mastuana was the only institution of higher education in the area at that time.

IN THE SHADOWS OF THE DEFUNCT COLLEGE

Seventeen years after the Ahmedgarh attempted train robbery, I enrolled as a student at the Akal high school in Mastuana. Students from the surrounding farming villages constituted the majority of the school's enrollment. A few hundred feet from my high-school classroom stood the empty, haunted, multi-story building of the former Akal College. At that time, the structure was only serving as a refuge for thousands of pigeons, owls, and other critters and crawlers, although the building was still structurally sound and suitable for other purposes. I never received a satisfactory answer to my questions about why the Akal College was abandoned.

There were a variety of stories about what led to the college's demise, but none made sense. The most prevalent explanation given was that the college was closed after several students were implicated in the 1928-attempted train robbery. The theory was that the college was short on funds and some devoted students and alumni could not bear the thought of their beloved institution being closed for lack of money. Consequently, they decided to rob the train, which passed within a few miles of the college. This train was rumored to carry British treasure to Delhi, the capitol of British India. When the attempt to break into the safe failed, the robbers fled in a hurry, leaving behind a hammer bearing the inscription: "Property of Akal College." This led police to immediately seize college property and close the institution. This explanation had elements of truth but never completely made sense to me. College students robbing a train to keep their institution financially solvent? I had never heard of such a thing.

RISING FROM THE ASHES

Mastuana today is a rejuvenated and bustling educational center where one of my nieces attended the Mastuana Pharmacy College a couple of years ago. I decided to revisit Mastuana, my high-school alma mater, and to visit with my niece at the pharmacy school where I could dig deeper into the college's history and especially into the attempted train robbery mystery. I soon hit a brick wall during my search. Beyond some anecdotal information, I was unable to find any details on the attempted robbery. Internet information was scant and unreliable. Most people in Mastuana with whom I spoke, either did not know any details or gave me the impression that the topic should be avoided. Current Mastuana alumni and faculty did not seem to want to know their history and the management was not interested. None of the available Mastuana literature mentions the train robbery and the closing of the college. The reason for this lack of information may be deliberate. Some people believe that history need not be recorded unless it is glorious. What is important to the residents of the area is that Mastuana is now back with institutes of learning and a growing student population.

I decided to try to learn more because the Ahmedgarh train robbery was a defining moment in British occupation of India. To the surprise of many in England, this and several other sensational acts of violence revealed the extent of anti-British sentiment in India.

Further investigation disclosed that the closure of the Akal College had nothing to do with funding the educational institution. The need for additional funds was to finance the underground activities related to the Indian independence movement. Mastuana had become a hotbed of anti-British activity. All anti-British activities were considered legitimate as long as they advanced the goal of accelerating the exit of the British from India. Inflicting financial damage upon Britain, by looting the treasury, fell within those objectives.

Five of the six perpetrators of the Ahmedgarh robbery were associated with the Mastuana College. Not all were students (2). They belonged to several revolutionary groups of like-minded individuals who hung around campus in a relatively secure and secluded environment. Among those groups was the Praja Mandal. Mastuana College had become a distribution center for Praja Mandal literature.

The incident sent shock waves throughout the British Empire. To the outside world, the British Government in India presented the incident as a common attempted robbery by a group of village dacoits (the word dacoit is an anglicized version of the Punjabi word "dakoo" meaning a robber or a bandit. It was a favorite British term to apply to the mischief-makers. Another term frequently used was bandit). The following news item in the British-friendly *Sydney Morning Herald* illustrated the extent to which the Government would go to conceal the true nature of the incident.

AHMEDGARH TRAIN ROBBERY

An article in the British-friendly *Sydney Morning Herald* described the train robbery as a common theft by a bunch of area farmers, not as an anti-British act. However, the report had little bearing on the facts. The bandits were political activists and included several well-known freedom fighters.

Among them was Sher Jung, one of the most celebrated anti-British activists of the time.

Soon the British police sprang into action. The potential perpetrators were quickly identified. Photos of the robbery suspects were posted on railway stations and bus stands all over Punjab. A reward of 2,000 rupees was offered to anyone who provided information that would lead to the arrest of the culprits. It took a while, but the offer of a reward eventually bore results. A tip from a relative led to the arrest of Sahib Singh Salana on January 20, 1930. Others were apprehended soon after, including Harnam Singh Chamak, another well-known revolutionary, and Sher Jung, the leader. Mr. Chamak, Salana, and Sher Jung were quickly tried and then given life sentences to be served at the Kaale Pani prison in the Andaman Sea. Others were given five- to ten-year terms depending on the roles they played. Other reports indicated that Sher Jung was tried and found guilty of sedition, of waging a war against the King-Emperor, and sentenced to death. The sentence, however, was commuted following the Independence of India.

Another famous name among the six was Harnam Singh Chamak, who had impressive credentials among the early revolutionaries (3). Chamak was a famous alumnus of the Mastuana College. He was an active participant in the Ghadar Party movement against the British. The Ghadar Party, formed by the Indian expatriates in the USA and Canada, imported armed resistance to India around 1913. Chamak's credentials also included establishing the only clandestine bomb-making factory in a house in Lohat Baddi, Punjab.

LEADER OF THE PACK – SHER JUNG

There has been an ongoing debate in India about the role of anti-British revolutionaries during the Indian independence struggle. Many Indians cite the relatively peaceful freedom marches of Mahatma Gandhi as a hallmark of the Indian low-key approach. Perhaps an equal number of Indians consider the more violent tactics adopted by the INA (Indian National Army) and the various splinter groups and individual revolutionaries as the real heroes of the Indian independence movement. Statues of these revolutionaries stand all over India, including in small villages where they were born. Missing conspicuously among those is Sher Jung. To date, no memorials have been built commemorating Sher Jung. There is, however, a renewed interest in India to accord Sher Jung his due place in the Indian independence struggle.

Sher Jung was perhaps the most charismatic figure among anti-British revolutionaries. Unlike most of his accomplices in the Ahmedgarh train robbery, who were farmers, Sher Jung had an aristocratic upbringing and had mastered multiple languages including French, German, Persian, Hindi, and Bengali. His literary acumen won admirers among many in Indian society. The French Revolution, which occurred early in the previous century, greatly impacted his thinking and inspired his actions. After the British left India in 1947, the Indian Prime Minister Jawaharlal Nehru appointed Sher Jung as a colonel in the Indian Army because of his role in fighting along the Kashmir border.

Nehru was not the only Indian Prime Minister who admired Sher Jung. Another Indian Prime Minister, I K Gujral, wrote in a preface to a book on Sher Jung, "When I joined college in Lahore, the youth would sing songs of Sher Jung's bravery."

Col. Sher Jung authored several books including *Tryst with Tigers* (1967) and *Ramblings in Tigerland* (1970).

In his later years, Sher Jung settled down in Delhi and founded a shooting club. He passed away in Delhi on December 15, 1996. His home state, Himachal Pradesh, recently renamed the Simbalwara National Park in Sirmaur as the Sher Jung National Park to recognize his contributions.

Sher Jung passed on his legacy of a sharpshooter to his grandson, Samaresh Jung who was called, "Goldfinger of India", after he won five gold medals in the air pistol shooting events in the 2006 Commonwealth Games at Melbourne.

1) **British Raj,** or just "Raj," sometimes refers to the rule of the British Crown from 1858 to 1947 over the Indian subcontinent. British occupation of India from 1757 to 1858 was under the rule of East India Company. Although a trading company, the East India Company soon became an occupying force with its own military and governing structure. It is only after the 1857 mutiny, according to British historians, or the "First War of Independence" by Indian writers, that the British Crown took over the governance of India.

2) *Sangrami Pind* (Revolutionary Village) by Jarnail Singh Acharwal. Tarak Bharta Prakashka (Publisher), Barnala, Punjab, 2004.

3)   Oral history obtained by Jas Singh through private communications with Mr. Jagit Singh, M.A, a retired school principal, a local historian, and author of "Bhai Bahlo, an area celebrity".

CHAPTER 3

KITE RUNNERS OF BATHINDA

Declared the ultimate contest, "Thrilla in Manila" *, was seemingly like the Super Bowl and the Formula One all combined into one. The time had come to settle forever who the king of kite fighting was in Bathinda. The championship was to be held on the first day of spring. Astrologers were consulted and religious events were screened to assure that nothing could distract from the fight. The only unexpected event that could derail the super contest would have been if Lord Mountbatten, the Viceroy of India, suddenly decided to be in Bathinda. That was unlikely. The viceroy's visits were not announced in advance because of security concerns.

Bathinda had other competitive sports besides kite fighting. There were soccer and field hockey matches at several of the schools and the Rajendra College. These sports attracted limited crowds, mostly students and their parents. Kabaddi** was another sport and it attracted larger crowds. Competitive "Guli Danda" (Punjabi baseball) was also popular, but there were no Guli Danda championships. Kite fighting and pigeon flying contests were the events that drew the Bathinda masses. The best kite fighters and their handlers were Muslims but such details were unimportant. Kite fighting was a community affair that celebrated the arrival of spring and spring was non-denominational and neutral.

LIFE IN BATHINDA – ONE YEAR BEFORE (1947) PARTITION

Bathinda had three religious communities when I was growing up there: Muslims, Sikhs, and Hindus in that census order. The three communities lived in harmony. Bathinda's neighborhoods were well integrated with only a few enclaves of exclusivity. Religious groups interacted within their own circles when celebrating weddings and attending funerals or religious

44

events. The communities were fully integrated in sports whether soccer, kabaddi, or kite contests. This harmony was also manifested during poetry and musical contests that were held in Urdu. Urdu poetry recitals always erased ethnic and religious divides. I spent six years of my childhood in Bathinda. The most imposing structure in town was the massive two thousand years old historical fort called "Qila Mubarak" (Urdu: قلعہ مبارک) which was only five blocks from my home.

QILA MUBARAK

The historical fort has been largely ignored by visitors and authorities alike, although its history and mystique rivals that of the Red Fort of Delhi. This fort, established by Hindu rulers of the "Bhatti" clan (probably origin of the name Bathinda), was occupied and reoccupied by the Hindu, Muslim, and Sikh rulers during its 2,000-year tumultuous history. Perhaps the most notable of all the events in the long-recorded history of the fort was the imprisonment of Razia Sultan, the first female Empress of India. Razia was not typical of the Delhi rulers of the time. She believed in equality of men and women and she was more secular than the other Mogul rulers were. Razia's reign did not last long. She was imprisoned in the Bathinda Fort in April 1240, and released in August of the same year. From here, the story gets fuzzy. According to some accounts, she married a man named Altunia and tried to reclaim her Delhi Sultanate, but she was killed in a town called Kaithal before reaching Delhi. At the Bathinda Fort, the story told by the guards is different. According to them, Razia escaped the prison cell by jumping off the fort parapet outside her royal prison. She survived the fall, married Altunia, and tried unsuccessfully to reclaim her Sultanate. There is general agreement, however, on her date of death as October 13, 1240. Visitors liked to see the site of Empress Razia's prison cell and the exact location of the escape. Rumors said that a half-human and half-bull creature akin to the Minotaur of Crete, who was slain by the Athenian hero Theseus, patrolled the halls surrounding her royal prison cell. Later there were accounts of visitors being chased out of empress Razia's prison cell by the angry bull.

Author in the Bathinda Fort

To a casual eye, Bathinda of sixty years ago had nothing except the fort to offer to a ten-year-old for fun and entertainment. The fact is that there were other attractions. Fort exploring itself could consume many weekends and when you became tired of unravelling the mysteries of the fort, you could head for the gigantic railway station, popularly known as "Bathinda Junction". Bathinda railway station was one of the largest in India at the time and rivaled those of Delhi, Calcutta, Bombay, and Madras (now Chennai). Seven railroad lines emanated from the Bathinda Junction in all geographic directions, including a one-meter gauge line that snaked through the sandy Rajasthan Desert.

The railway station (outskirts) had the only cinema in town. All of it was open air except for the screen and projection equipment that were covered. Patrons sat on the ground under the stars to watch the show. Later renovations provided canvas tarpaulin cover for the patrons and rudimentary toilet facilities. Prior to that, such functions were performed Viking style in the nearby open field. The majority of the cinema patrons were passengers waiting for their train departures. Sometimes when the passengers were in the thick of the story plot, a man would appear on the stage with a bullhorn and announce, "Brothers and sisters, the express train to Delhi will leave in exactly one hour. Make sure to assemble all your belongings before leaving and do not forget to take your "Khase" (the usually dark brown thick cotton blanket) with you. Do not delay. God willing, the next train may be available twenty four hours from now." After a pause, he would adlib, "And if the God is not willing, the train may never show up." He would then burst out in laughter at his own joke.

The railway station itself was popular for just aimless loitering (reminds me of modern teenagers at the malls). Ruffians found plentiful opportunities at the crowded platforms to brush against unaccompanied young females and then quickly disappear in the crowd while ignoring a hail of insults and yells from the young victims and the nearby passengers. Rarely were they caught but when they were, they were thoroughly thrashed.

THE MOST DANGEROUS SPORT IN THE WORLD

Kite flying requires skill as in any sport. When the kite is flown with the flying line (string) taut, it bends from the wind pressure and stabilizes the kite, but when you let out more line to gain height, the kite becomes unstable and begins to rock from side to side and sometimes starts spinning. A skilled flyer can re-stabilize the kite by applying the right amount of tension on thin line. Success in kite fighting is a combination of the flying skills as well as the equipment available to the fighter. This generally means the lethality of the line (string), quality of the spools holding the line, and the dexterity of the assistants ("pit crew") to make sure the right amount of the unwounded line is instantaneously made available to the player for maneuvering of the kite from the ground.

The most important of these is the line (the string) itself. In Afghanistan, where the sport originated, it is called "taar", but in Punjab, it is called "manjha" or "dore". The shape of the kite itself matters but was a lessor factor because all fighters used similar kites called "patang". Effective "kite kills" depended upon "weaponzing" the cotton line. The technology of weaponzing the string was a carefully guarded secret of champions of the sport. The commonly known formula was coating the line with a mixture of adhesive and finely grounded glass applied to the cotton line in several layers. Some fighters, however, appeared to have superior and deadlier lines, and thus an advantage.

Kite flying and kite running were dangerous sports. Of the two, kite flying itself was relatively safe. The only injuries were cuts and bruises from touching the razor sharp line, except occasionally the drifting player would run into traffic or an animal while keeping his eyes fixed on the sky. This could result in a serious injury.

Kite running, on the other hand, was extremely hazardous. Kite running involved chasing the dead (cut) kite while running through traffic and other obstacles, and sometimes crossing adjoining, unguarded rooftops. Injuries included cuts to the hands, wrists, necks, and throats. Fatalities resulted due to falls from rooftops, being run over by vehicles, or slashes on the throat or neck when the runner became tangled in the razor sharp line.

Note: The forgotten sport has staged a comeback in India and Pakistan. The traditional reinforced coated cotton line has been replaced by synthetic line imported from China. The imported synthetic line is deadlier. ***

At the time of my youth, there were no safety regulations to curb injuries. There were even reports of overzealous entrepreneurs attaching metal blades to the line to cut the opponent's line.

MEET THE CHAMPIONS

Finalists Nasser and Bashir had many victories before reaching the finals. Of the two, Bashir had a few more victories to his credit. People were uncertain of the reason for this superior record. Bashir, an imposing thirty-year-old young man lived in my neighborhood and was my hero. (*See related Story: "Bibi Mehraan, may she rest in peace."*)

Bashir Khan, the Kite fighting Champion

The opponent, Nasser, was shorter, heavier, very fair-colored, and wore a long curled moustache. He did not look Indian. He looked like an Afghan, or a Turk. Both men flew almost identical kites, the standard fighting patang, which was favored in Punjab. Each of the two fighters had their own entourage of young boys who prepared the abrasives and wound up hundreds of feet of manjha string on the spools.

The winning edge of the competition seemed to be in the coated line.

Bashir's line, everyone believed, must have been coated with an additional secret chemical besides the crushed glass and adhesive. It was. His opponents often conducted spying missions to learn his secret formula. They always failed. Bashir's "pit crew," which included Salim, my close friend, and Jamaal, another boy from my neighborhood, only knew the secret. The two were confidants of Bashir. I was not in the inner circle, but I hovered at the edge because of my friendship with Salim. He trusted me. One day he let me in on the chemical secret and allowed me to watch him while he and Jamaal applied the secret mixture to the cotton line. The secret ingredient was a very hard white porous material. I had never seen anything like that before. Salim swore me to secrecy and told me that the strange material was "Samunder Jhugg" (ocean froth). A friend of Bashir's had brought the material from the ocean floor in Bombay. It was believed that when mixed with ground glass, it made the cutting line even more abrasive. Years later, I realized that the hardened ocean froth was sea coral.

CHAMPIONSHIP VENUE

The contest would take place in front of the ancient fort, a popular venue for many sports. One reason for the popularity of the site was that besides the main event, there were many ancillary attractions to keep one entertained before the match started or during any delay with the featured event.

The sideshow entertainers were both animals and humans. Small-time kite flyers, showed their talents while the main contestants were preparing. Snake charmers, monkey shows, and black bear dances filled the void when there was a lull in the activity. The most popular of the shows were the aphrodisiac peddlers with money-back guarantees for the pharmaceutical they were selling.

Competitive kite fighting was a team sport. Assistants ("the pit crews") were crucial to wins. They assured the consistency of the coated manjha, held the loose line between the flier and the spool holder, and sometimes acted as kite runners to retrieve the fallen kite if it was a special trophy.

The big events were well advertised and promoted with the help of loud speakers mounted on bicycle rickshaws adorned with posters. The rickshaw driver would peddle slowly to the war like beat of the cattle drums accompanying them.

CLASH OF THE TITANS

On Championship Day, spring flowers were in full bloom. The nightingale birds and pigeons nested comfortably in the perforated walls of the two thousand-year-old fort. There was not a cloud on the horizon. The historical fort provided a perfect backdrop for a clash of the titans. Bashir arrived first with Salim and Jamaal by his side. Both boys were in festive wedding-like clothing. Nasser arrived with his equally impressive entourage. The names of his assistants, not from my neighborhood, were not known to me. By all accounts, this was an even match. The statistics of their wins were close with Bashir holding a razor-thin edge. Both teams quickly began preparing their staging areas. Crowds streamed in to claim prime spots close to the starting line.

Salim had a plan. He knew that the "killing" would take place somewhere high up in the sky where the atmosphere was more stable and maneuverability better. The best observation point would be on the nearby rooftops, which joined, in a long row. He had become somewhat of an expert in meteorology. He could predict wind patterns and the speeds of a falling kite to a pinpoint accuracy. His estimate of where the mortally wounded kite would hit the ground was usually accurate. As a result, he had more fallen kite trophies to his credit than anyone else. Catching a kite fallen in a battle was exciting enough, but retrieving the fallen one belonging to the enemy was special. That was a "head hunting" trophy worthy of displaying in your living room. As kites became airborne, one of the young assistants would assume the role of manning the spool or the "slack line". Although the flyer would maneuver the kite by holding the line itself, the assistant helped manage the slack line between the flyer and the spool, a critical task. The "spool man" had to be quick to unwind the needed string in a hurry and rewind it if it started accumulating on the ground.

Bashir's two assistants, both from my neighborhood, knew how to make the secret chemical coating which made his line so deadly. Thinking back, the secret was not just the coral they added to the crushed glass, but Salim and Jamaal were grinding the glass much finer. In doing so, they were creating submicron-size particles reaching "nanometers" (one billionth of a meter) diameters. When you grind a material to very small size, the same chemical assumes different and amazing properties. The same amount of glass crushed ultrafine would have a much larger surface area and more contact sites. When these particles contacted the opponent's line, millions of these tiny soldiers started nibbling at the enemy line instead of just few larger particles in a coarsly ground coating.

The contest started the way it always had. The two fighters stationed themselves near each other and at a slight elevation above the ground level. Bashir gave permission to Salim to watch the contest from a rooftop vantage point. He had other competent help. Jamaal manned the slack line. The game had no rules other than the time when the two flying kites will be released by a neutral third party. Kites were released on a count of three. Everyone stepped back to watch the drama unfold. Salim went up on the nearby rooftops to claim his vantage point.

Bashir held the manjha line in his hands wearing leather gloves for protection from cuts. Jamaal supplied the slack line to Bashir when prompted. Jamaal wore no protection. A second assistant held the spool at a few feet away and ready to unleash tens of feet of the line to the intermediary, Jamaal, who fed it to Bashir. This maneuver required dexterity because any delay in feeding the unwound line to the player could cost the fighter the match. The fighter needed to react quickly and pull his kite away from the predator in time.

TO GREATER HEIGHTS

Both kites ascended at a steady rate. They drifted apart as they rose but started to converge until within inches of each other. From the ground they looked like they were touching, but the fighters knew better. The crowd grew excited as contact was made. People started yelling, "Now! Now! Kill! Kill!" Bashir gave a gentle tug to the line. The kite responded as intended. With one more tug, Bashir put his Green Giant on top of the Red Devil (Nasser's kite). Nasser tried to get from underneath, and in the process, the two kites tangled. Both flyers furiously tried to slash each other's line. It didn't happen. The kites gobbled up more and more of the razor-sharp line while the kites kept ascending.

Suddenly the crowd roared. The kites were drifting apart. Cries of "boo kata" **** filled the sky! It was difficult to tell who the victor was. Salim let out a loud cry from the rooftop. He could tell that Bashir's line was still taut which meant that it was Nasser's line that had been severed. Dozens of young men started running towards the anticipated trajectory of landing of the fallen kite. Salim started galloping across the endless adjoining roofs to intercept the trophy before anyone else would.

The drama was not over. Bashir encircled the trailing line of the severed kite before it drifted away from him. Once secured, he could pull both kites together and bring in the prize (the enemy kite) to give to Salim. The crowd noticed this and went wild. Salim started galloping across the joined roofs with both arms stretched to claim the trophy.

The entangled kites descended together. Bashir guided the pair to deliver the trophy to Salim who was poised to leap in the air to embrace the trophy at any moment. He leapt forward and jumped in the air. When he was about to land, he noticed that there was no roof underneath him. He had run out of surface to land. The rows of rooftops were separated by a large gully.

Salim hurtled to the ground below. In falling, he hit an abandoned metal manifold on the ground. The impact opened a big gash on his forehead. He was bleeding profusely. The crowd rushed towards him. Bashir and Jamaal were running towards him yelling, "No, No! Oh God!" They looked toward the sky as if to say, why?

Bashir put Salim's' head in his lap and started crying like a baby. No ambulance was nearby and there were no other emergency vehicles. At the site, there was a man there with a small truck. He offered to take Salim to the hospital half an hour away. Bashir put the bleeding Salim in his lap and they sped away. Salim was pronounced dead on arrival when the hospital was reached.

THE DAY AFTER

I stepped out to answer the knock on our door from the mailman. Across the street, Bashir was talking with Bibi Mehraan, the middle-aged single woman living alone in the small house directly across from our house. Bibi was trying to console him. Bashir was telling Bibi that he was quitting the sport. He was feeling guilty about Salim's death. He kept repeating, "I caused Salim's death. I got greedy. By pulling both kites, I altered the predicted descent, making Salim misjudge the landing. I cannot do it anymore. Salim will always be on my mind. There will be no more kite fights for me."

"You must not quit. Do at least one more fight and dedicate it to Salim. It will be the biggest event in Bathinda. Do it for Salim," said Bibi.

"I will think about it, Bibi," he said, putting his head on Bibi's shoulder. Then he departed.

LAST CONTEST

The Bashir-Nasser match was heavily advertised. It was to be held at the Fort again. On the appointed day, an even larger crowd gathered. Jamaal was there to oversee the preparations. He had help from two other kids to act as the "spool man" and the middle "string man".

The contest started as usual. The kites started skywards, separated by at least fifty feet, and began converging after reaching an aerodynamically stable altitude. Bashir maneuvered his kite above Nasser's and started tugging at the Red Devil. The crowd roared.

Only a few seconds later, a hush fell over the crowd. Bashir's Green Giant was limping down to the ground, dragging with it the long lifeless manjha line. The humiliation was not over. Nasser encircled the limp line, entangled it with his own line and started pulling it towards him. The crowed started booing.

"Leave him alone. Do not rub his nose. He is doing it for Salim," many in the crowd were shouting. Nasser kept pulling both kites towards him until he grabbed both. He reached for a knife, cut the extra line from the kites, walked up to Bashir and said, "These are for Salim. Please keep them." He then locked Bashir into an embrace. Many clapped. Some cried.

*Thrilla in Manila was the famous boxing match in 1975 in Quezon City near Manila between Muhammad Ali and Joe Frazier for the Heavyweight Championship. The contest's name is derived from the frequently cited promotional phrase by the Mohammad Ali

Kabaddi A popular game in Tamil Nadu, Punjab, and Andhra Pradesh in India. Two teams of seven members each occupy opposite halves of a field of approximately thirty by forty feet. To win points, the team sends a "raider" who tries to tag a member of the other team and retreats successfully to his side. The opposing team tries to tackle the raider and restrain him from crossing the line to his side. The member tagged successfully is "out" and temporarily sent off the field.

The 2013 World Kabaddi Cup was held in December 2013 with the Opening Ceremonies in Bathinda, Punjab. *** "Vague order banning Chinese strings makes kite flying risky."

CHANDIGARH: Menacing Chinese strings used for flying kites have already claimed the life of one child and injured many in Punjab during the ongoing kite-flying season despite the ban orders. With no specifications of the strings identified in the vague order, a variety of industrial threads being used for kite flying continue to be used. The dangerous strings, that were initially imported but now are being locally made, have flooded the markets despite a ban imposed by Punjab government.... A day before this, a 13-year-old Jaskaran Kaur, daughter of a police officer from Batala suffered multiple injuries to her neck when a stray piece of Chinese kite string slit her throat. After a complicated operation, the damaged muscles of her voice box were repaired and joined together. It will take around a month for her to regain her voice.

Vibhor Mohan, TNN | Dec 18, 2014.

****BOO KATA:** An expression heard when an opponent's kite is cut and go down. Origin of the word is not clear, but may relate to "Boos" who are fictional ghosts from Japan. As every young person knows, Boo ghosts attack by sneaking up from behind.

CHAPTER 4

BIBI MEHRAN MAY SHE REST IN PEACE

She was the most beautiful woman on my street. Correction. She was the most beautiful woman in my town. Her name was Bibi Mehran. Translated into English, it meant, Miss Merciful, but it could also be Miss Congeniality. I like Miss Congeniality better.

To a nine-year-old boy, she looked very grown up. I do not want to say "old", but I knew she was close to my mother's age, perhaps five or six years younger. Other than age, my mother and Bibi Mehran had nothing in common. In fact, they were polar opposites. My mother was composed, modest, conservative, and well educated. Bibi was outgoing, flashy, talkative, and friendly, very friendly indeed. She had no schooling except rudimentary reading and writing skills in Urdu.

Bibi had many friends. While we would be lucky to have a visitor or two in a week (not counting routine street vendors who delivered fresh milk, vegetables, and other daily necessities), on a busy day, Bibi had several visitors in addition to the many street hawkers, food vendors, and hijras (transsexual or transgender singers).

Her personal visitors were colorful just like Bibi. They wore gaudy clothes and made fashion statements but not the kind of statement that well-to-do folks in business or academia did. Their fashion was akin to the dandy extras in Bombay's "Bollywood" movies who depicted villains, gangsters, and gangster's sidekicks. I kept track of most of her regular visitors because Bibi lived directly across the street from our house. I spent a lot of time outside on the street playing with other kids of my age, and I was curious.

OUR NEIGHBORHOOD

Bathinda was a unique town in the middle of the Punjab desert. The town had grown in the shadow of the massive Bathinda Fort, a living monument to two thousand years of Indian history. Bathinda was not a beautiful town. There were no public parks, entertainment districts, lush waterways, or other natural wonders except miles and miles of sand dunes all around the city. This is not to say that Bathinda was devoid of fun and entertainment. Not at all. In fact, the seven years that my family lived in Bathinda are the most memorable of my life. If we consider kite fighting and pigeon races as sports, Bathinda was the sports capital of Punjab *(see the related story: Kite Runners of Bathinda).*

Bathinda was also a cultural oasis. It was the center of Urdu poetry. People came from afar to enjoy poetry recitals called mushairas.

Of the many unique features of Bathinda at the time, the most outstanding was its multi-faith, multiethnic neighborhoods that were amazingly integrated. The largest ethnic group was Muslim, which were in majority until the 1947 Indian partition, after which most of them fled to newly created Pakistan because of safety concerns. That was a difficult time in India's history.

The street on which I lived was a prime example of this ethnic and cultural mosaic. It was a narrow, dead-end street. There were only ten families who lived in closely spaced homes, spacious in overall square footage, but stingy on covered space. Of the neighbors I remember, there were two well-to-do families. The house to our left belonged to a family with a father who was a senior railway engineer at the Bathinda railway station.

My family socialized most with the railway family. They had two sons named Jugi and Sunni. Jugi was the older boy. Both boys wore long, braided hair, which was knotted on the top into a neat six-inch arc above the head. Wearing long, braided hair was not unusual for very young Sikh boys. I wore a similar hairdo until I was older. When the boys grew up, they would support colorful turbans. Jugi and Sunni were always well dressed and stood out as cultured and affluent in the mostly lower middle-class neighborhood. My mother and their mother were friends and went to the temple together.

The man two houses down was a minor government bureaucrat. His name was Ram Chand. I think Ram was an accountant. He was in his fifties and ready to retire at Punjab's mandatory retirement age of fifty-five. He lived with his wife who had a very difficult Sanskrit name. I think it was Arundhati (अरुंधती) which means "unrestrained." The title was a misnomer. Arundhati was very restrained. She never spoke more than few words. Apparently, she had mastered the phrase my mother emphasized all her life.

"Pehle tolo, phir bolo."

"WEIGH IT BEFORE YOU SAY IT."

Ram and Arundhati had children, but they were grown up, employed, and settled outside Punjab. The couple kept mostly to themselves and never said much to anybody else. On Diwali, the Hindu festival celebrated by all Indians, they brought sweets to everybody.

Next to Ram and Arundhati lived a tall and lanky middle-aged man. His name was Sharif Nawaz. He looked older than he was because of his light and bony frame. He was single and he dressed very well. I wondered if he had a secret girlfriend but, thinking out loud, I don't think he would have dared. One thing was clear, he did not like Bibi. He never said anything hurtful, but he gave Bibi disapproving looks when the two crossed paths. He would never look into her eyes. He always wore black. Sharif Nawaz did not approve of Bibi's social activities, neither did he like the way she dressed, nor did he like any of her friends. Consequently, he never talked to Bibi.

Toward the end of the street lived two middle-aged men. Both worked as security guards on the other side of the town. They worked nights and slept during the days. I only saw them a couple of times, usually at our neighborhood block parties. They were pleasant and they set off fireworks during the Diwali festival. To my knowledge, no woman ever graced their abode. There just weren't many dating prospects. There was a severe shortage of women in Bathinda. Only the lucky ones had spouses, not to mention, girlfriends.

HOUSE AT THE END OF THE STREET

An interesting feature of our little street was the house at the end of the street. There were no homes beyond it, only wheat fields. It was strange. It was like in a movie where in one frame you see a busy street and in the other instant, mountains or lush farmland. When you exited the house through the backdoor, after traversing the spacious courtyard, you landed at the periphery of a vast wheat field. The farmer who owned the big farmhouse was a substantial property owner. His name was Kirpaal Sidhu. It is not that Kirpaal suddenly decided to build a farmhouse replete with animals in the middle of urban Bathinda. He was living in his ancestral home built by his forefathers several generations earlier when it was all farmland or desert. My family bonded with the Kirpaal family for a variety of reasons. We were both Jat Sikh farmers, culturally, and ethnically alike. My mother and Kirpaal's wife were like sisters, although Mrs. Kirpaal was twenty years older than my mother was. The Kirpaal house was very spacious. They kept cows and water buffaloes and were a source of fresh milk for neighbors. I sometimes went there to get milk in the morning soon after they finished milking the cows and buffaloes. When there was a choice, I preferred buffalo milk. It was very creamy compared to milk from cows. Cream from buffalo was prized more than any other food item. It was consumed as pure butter or as clarified butter called "ghee", and added to savory curry foods as well as sweet desserts. Chubby cheeks were much admired. The Kirpaal family was popular. In addition to being wealthy, Kirpaal was also liberal, secular, and jolly. With his flowing platinum beard, he looked like Santa Claus. He threw great parties at his house where home-brewed alcohol flowed freely. Kids were allowed to watch from a distance, but they could not touch any alcohol. Women were also forbidden to drink alcohol. Bibi Mehran was always invited. She might have been tempted to down a "peg" or two, but did not in deference to other ladies present.

Bibi's presence seemed to make the parties more fun. I chatted with Bibi during these parties. Kirpaal's parties were the longest that I can remember. Only on one occasion did my mother take me home early. On that night, the lovable Santa Claus got drunk after he had too many beverages.

One day I noticed a visitor to Bibi's home whom I recognized as Bashir Khan, the champion kite fighter. To kids in my neighborhood, Bashir was a celebrity.

From my perspective, Bathinda was the sports capital of Punjab. There were sports for all kinds of people, which appealed to various pocket books and social classes. Like every aspect of Indian life, sports were associated with class and status. Kite fighting and pigeon racing were the most popular in my neighborhood but were not considered classy. School dropouts and shadowy characters dominated these sports. There was a hierarchy of social acceptance of these sports. Pigeon racing was considered less honorable than kite fighting. Cock fighting was next lower in status. Heavy betting and violence were illegal. Common wisdom was that betting led to gambling and thus pimping was only a step away.

The pigeon racers were a different breed from the kite fighters. They were called "Kabooter Baaz" and were involved in serious betting and gambling. Pigeon racing required greater training skills and financial resources than kite fighting. The irony was that while significant sums of money changed hands in this sport, most skilled Kabooter Baaz were poor. Only the top two or three players had money. Although a betting game, pigeon racing was popular along all social strata. It was called pigeon racing, but in reality it was a pigeon flying endurance contest. The contest would start with all competitors simultaneously releasing the birds in the air. The pigeon that stayed airborne the longest won the contest. Pigeons would stay afloat for many hours testing the endurance of spectators and the owners, as well as the birds.

DANGEROUS LIAISONS

On one occasion, I noticed the well-known pigeon racer named Imran Khan visiting Bibi. Imran was a celebrity. Everybody called him "Ustaad" (master) Imran. He would open Bibi's front door and without hesitation walk inside. The rumor was that he was Bibi's favorite. Imran always wore gold chains, a necklace, and a heavy gold bracelet. I believe he even had a couple of gold-clad teeth. He was different from most pigeon racers who were poor. Imran may have been the wealthiest Kabooter Baaz in Bathinda.

I had the urge to ask Bibi to introduce me to Imran, but I hesitated. I anticipated opposition from my mother because of the social stigma attached to his sport. My mother considered this game more harmful for a kid than kite fighting even though many more kids were killed or maimed chasing fallen kites than watching live pigeons flying in the sky. The sport was a time waster, for sure. Despite my desire to be introduced to Imran, I decided to focus on getting to know Bashir, the kite champion through courtesy of Bibi Mehran. If Bibi could put in a good word for me, perhaps I could get a seat (standing space actually) close to the champion in the upcoming kite fighting championship match being advertised all over town.

Besides an introduction to sports celebrities, there were other reasons to befriend Bibi. She had the charm, openness, and magnetism that I found absent in other women in the neighborhood. She was approachable. She made a point of talking to me whenever I bumped into her on the street. She also talked to my younger sister and my baby brother.

Bibi was very fond of my sister Kulwant, who was five years old. People had commented that Kulwant was the prettiest one in my family and someday would rival the Mumbai film stars if we gave her the chance. We called her "Guddi" (doll), a popular nickname for little girls. Bibi nicknamed her Anarkali (pomegranate blossom). Reflecting back, I think Bibi longed for her own little Anarkali. One time she told my mother, "Guddi looks like an Iranian girl. My forefathers came to India from a part of Iran called Isfahan; the Garden of Eden, my grandmother used to tell me about." As she said this, Bibi became very sentimental. My mother wanted to know about her childhood and what brought her to Bathinda. Bibi refused to talk more about her childhood or her family. She changed the subject.

Our little Anarkali (Kulwant) never got the chance to blossom. She died of typhoid. All attempts to save her life failed. Bibi came to our house to console my mother. She cried as if she had lost her own little girl. My mother never fully recovered from the loss of her only birth daughter. Every year she would go in the back windowless room on Guddi's death anniversary, close the door, and cry. No one was allowed to go in to share her grief. She wanted to do it alone. Later, she tried to get over this by bonding with my two cousin sisters; daughters of her deceased and beloved younger sister.

Bibi was always dressed up as if she was going to a party, a concert, or a wedding. She wore her favorite crimson-red lipstick called "Surkhi." *(Many Bathinda women, whether poor or well to do, wore generous amounts of surkhi. I do not know what company made the crimson-red lipstick. L'Oréal was still six decades away from building a plant in Poona, India.)*

Besides physical appearance, Bibi had other interests that fueled my resolve to befriend her. She loved Urdu poetry, which was the rage in our area. Urdu poetry was laced with romance, sarcasm, acidic wit, and dangerous liaisons (Romeo and Juliette style). Despite such adult themes, Urdu poetry was enjoyed by all ages and genders. The reason for this was that there was no overt sexual content; only suggestion.

Poetry recitals were the biggest cultural events and were held in open air to accommodate large number of patrons. The open-air forum provided cool fresh air in the usually hot desert environment interrupted only occasionally by rain. The recitals lasted into the wee hours to the thunderous applause of "Wah! Wah!" (Wow) similar to rock concerts of the 1970s. Even at nine years of age, I was enthralled with Urdu poetry and could recite verses for hours. I could read and write Urdu. Accompanied by Persian script, Urdu was the medium of instruction at my school. At home, we spoke Punjabi and wrote in Gurmukhi (Devanagari script). Bibi had a reasonable mastery of Urdu, although her conversational language was Punjabi. She often sang Urdu poetry when walking in the street. When she noticed someone observing this, she would smile, wink, and make a very seductive face, just as occured in the films.

I wanted Bibi to take me to one of the open-air poetry recitals, but I knew that such an activity would be impossible. The recitals were held at night and continued into the wee hours of the morning, so I never asked her. The opportunity to attend such a program presented itself during one summer when the schools were on recess. One of my uncles, a teacher at a junior college, came to visit my family. He was somewhat of a poet himself but in the minor league.

One morning this uncle and I bumped into Bibi. I introduced her and told her of his poetical prowess. The two immediately delved into comparing poets and their newest compositions. Bibi came up with a proposition for my uncle. "Tomorrow night there is a Mushaira (recital) at the high school. Some of the big names will be there. My cousin Bashir and I will be going. Do you want to go? And you can bring Jesse with you," she said to my uncle.

"Yes, of course, I would not want to miss the chance. As for Jesse, I will have to ask his mother," my uncle replied.

"Yes, yes," I exclaimed as I jumped into the air, even knowing of the potential curfew. To my delight, the ban was lifted as long as I was accompanied by my dear uncle. Uncle and I went to the recital. We made it a dinner-recital evening and my uncle allowed me to violate every dietary restriction.

The Mushaira recital was as exciting as anticipated. We did not notice Bibi and her cousin (who in hindsight, was not her cousin) Bashir until after one particular verse when I heard a shrill, "Wah! Wah!" The voice was unmistakably Bibi's. I traced the sound, spotted Bibi, and started waving like a mad man. Bibi smiled and threw an aerial kiss at us. I did not reciprocate. I was not sure what is appropriate in such situations. Uncle was mesmerized. He did not know what to do either, except he whispered, "Beautiful lady!" We made no effort to join Bibi and her friend despite my observation that Uncle would have liked it. The place was too crowded. Uncle had to leave the next day. It was better that way.

One day I asked my mother, "Mom, Bibi is so nice. She is good to us and talks to you often. She has so many friends. Can I be friends with Bibi?"

"Yes, Bibi has many friends and she is very talented. You can talk to her, but you cannot be her friend because you are too young. You are better off making friends with kids your own age," she said. Her explanation did not make complete sense to me, but I reluctantly accepted her wishes. The full implication of her advice did not become apparent to me until years later. My mother liked Bibi, but she was also leery of her. She liked Bibi's friendly nature and kind disposition but wondered about Bibi's profession. She suspected Bibi was a lady of pleasure, a high-class one. It was evident that Bibi was not a streetwalker or a call girl, but she was definitely not like other ladies in the neighborhood.

My mother would not approve any more contact with Bibi than just a hello and a neighborly chat. She was not worried about any intimacy developing between Bibi and me because of the age difference. She was more concerned with my secondary contacts with Bibi's friends. My mother acknowledged that Bibi was a good person at heart. At one time, I overheard my mother and Bibi having a sincere talk. The topic was marriage and children. Bibi desperately wanted her own children. My mother told her that being an attractive and good-natured lady she would make a nice wife for some lucky man if she could extract herself from her current situation. My mother was facing a dilemma. She worried about my fascination with Bibi but could not outright prohibit my association with Bibi because that would be against her own preaching regarding meeting neighbors and learning to socialize. As she was unable to make a case for me to avoid Bibi, she tolerated my "fascination". The uneasy neighborhood relationship and accommodation between the two ladies was unusual. I think the whole situation was unique with a woman like Bibi living peacefully in a middle-class neighborhood. As far as I know, no one ever made a fuss. No bricks were thrown at Bibi's door or obscenities plastered on her walls. I am so glad. That would have been utterly uncivilized. This co-existence surprises me even today. Thinking back on my mother's acceptance of Bibi's presence in the neighborhood, her occasional chats with Bibi, and lack of malice, make me proud of my mother. She was ahead of the times. I had always wondered about what kind of relationship Bibi had with several of her secret admirers who zealously protected their identities. One of them was a police captain.

BATHINDA FORT

I wanted to visit the legendry Bathinda Fort, which was only five blocks from my house. Daily on my way to and from school, I passed by the fort, looked up, and wondered about the exact spot on the parapet the legendary Indian Empress Razia had chosen for her fatal plunge. I wanted to go all the way up and see the location, but it was off limits. A story circulated that once a daredevil tried to duplicate the suicidal jump with a homemade parachute, which failed so he plummeted to his death. The daredevil's experience discouraged people from breaching the upper levels of the two thousand-year-old structure which was unsafe and crumbling in places.

As a child, I was allowed to go to the massive fort if my parents or another dependable adult accompanied me. Such freedom applied only to the first two levels of the fort, one of which supported a relatively new Sikh temple, a favorite of my mother's. The historic temple was a significant

64

attraction, but I wanted to see the upper levels and the Minotaur. I was not allowed to venture higher.

THE BREAKTHROUGH

One day while playing in the street, I overheard Bibi talking to her friend Bashir outside her house. They were planning to go to the fort on the following Sunday. My ears perked up. I gathered courage, moved closer, rudely interrupted their conversation, and said, "Bibi, may I go with you and Bashir to the fort?"

"Oh sure, Jesse (Bibi was the only one to call me Jesse. I loved that and wished more people would call me Jesse), but you better get permission from your mom," she replied.

I knew full well that there was no way my mom would allow me to go sightseeing with this woman, especially if she was accompanied by a big beefy man who looked like a gangster. I tried to think positive. "Sure Bibi. I will ask mom. I don't think she will mind."

"Okay, then you meet Bashir and me at the fort at noon just outside the main gate," she said.

My planning started for the Sunday adventure. Being absent from home for a couple of hours on Sundays was not a problem for me. Every Sunday I went to play kabaddi* or soccer with the kids in the neighborhood at a nearby field. The thought of not telling my mother, however, was gnawing at me. I had not done that before. Nevertheless, I started fantasizing. Wouldn't it even be nicer if Bashir could not make it and Bibi and I alone could explore the fort? Wouldn't people be envious of me with the prettiest woman in whole of Bathinda? What would Bibi be wearing to visit Razia Sultana's 1200-year-old prison palace in the fort**. I started comparing Bibi to Empress Razia, convinced that next to the Empress of India (Razia), Bibi might be the best dressed and the prettiest, although Bibi lived in a two-room house that was modest even by Bathinda standards. I thought of telling some of my buddies who lived in the neighborhood to be at the fort gate as a proof that I had a date. I decided against it because of unanticipated complications.

65

Razia sultan's prison quarters

Half hour earlier than agreed upon, I arrived at the fort gate and started pacing. A few minutes later Bibi arrived without Bashir. My heart started pumping faster. I was secretly reciting a prayer to the Guru. I must have done something good to merit my first ever date with not just any girl on the block, but the shiniest and best-dressed woman in town. I forgot that I was only nine and Bibi was almost as old as my mother was. I wanted to hold Bibi's hand, but I hesitated. In India, you did not hold hands in public with a lady unless she was your mom, an aunt, or a younger sister.

Bibi started apologizing. "Too bad Jesse, Bashir could not come. He was going to protect us when we trespassed the monster bull's territory. Now my dear, you have to protect Bibi." Then she took one-step forward, and grabbed my left hand, and we started walking.

A high-voltage current ran through my tiny frame. The current seem to exit my body as soon as it had entered (in the engineering jargon that is called grounding). I realized it was not a real current but it felt like one. My chest filled with pride and I declared, "No problem, Bibi. Jesse will protect you." Arm-in-arm, Bibi and I explored the fort. We could not go all the way up, nor did we visit the Minotaur. Suddenly those two items had dropped in priority. Walking with Bibi was more adventurous than anything else. I still wanted to confront the Minotaur mainly to show Bibi I was not a chicken. I also suspected that perhaps the talk about the half-man and half-animal was all bull! I was conscious walking with Bibi although we could have been mother and son on a Sunday stroll. Still, we were an odd pair. Bibi was over-dressed even after she had toned down her appearance. She wore little or no surkhi to ward off stares. You can minimize stares by trying to blend into the background, but preventing stares is impossible in India. Staring at people is a national pastime. We did not attract as many stares as I feared. Maybe most onlookers assumed this was an aristocratic mother taking her son on a Sunday stroll.

What worried me most were the potential taunts that onlookers could hurl in Urdu poetry. One I particularly despised went like:

"Pehlue hoor mein langoor, Khuda Ki Kudrit"
"A beauty under a chimpanzee armpit – wonders of God!"
"Kavve ki chonch me angoor khuda ki Kudrit"
"A grape in a crow's beak – wonders of God!"

No such taunts followed our tour. For one thing, I was not an ugly crow or a chimpanzee, I rationalized. My mother had assured me that I was a good-looking boy. My aunt had seconded her opinion.

Halfway through our tour, Bibi and I found a patch of grassy lawn and sat down. Bibi took out some kalakand (milk cake) from her purse. She asked me to close my eyes and open my mouth wide. She then dropped a large piece of the heavenly treat straight into my throat. I swallowed the piece and thanked her with my eyes. Bibi started humming, at first, she was barely audible and then she sang in full force. There were no people around.

She had a beautiful voice and knew many Urdu songs. She stopped singing and asked me if I had ever heard the story of the slave girl called Anarkali (the pomegranate blossom). I had not. I asked her to tell me. Bibi was eager to tell the story. She started, "Anarkali (Urdu: انارکلی) was born as Nadira Begum in Iran and migrated to Lahore, Punjab (in present day Pakistan) with a trader's caravan. She later moved to Delhi and became a court dancer in Emperor Akbar's court. One day when she was tiptoeing through the royal gardens for a secret rendezvous with Prince Salim, she caught the eye of the emperor. The Emperor of India was so enamored with her that he offered to give her an award. Nadira politely refused but said that she would be honored if His Highness gave her an anarkali (pomegranate blossom) from his garden. The emperor obliged and gave her

67

the name "Anarkali"

***

Bibi related the haunting sad story as if she was reciting a poem. I think she identified with Anarkali, who was also of Iranian origin. Like Anarkali, Bibi was looking for her Prince Salim who would never come. Instead, she ended up entertaining others. She would not find her own love. I sat motionless. I had never before heard the story, which six years later became a Bollywood blockbuster movie.

Sitting on the fort lawn, I saw an opportunity to ask Bibi about another one of my dreams, visiting a cinema. Indian cinema was in its infancy and Bathinda had its own rudimentary theater (if you could call it that) by the railway station. I was forbidden to go to the movies, no matter the theme. My friends, who faced no such banes, raved about the entertainment. Bibi was an avid moviegoer. I gathered enough courage and asked, "Bibi, would you do me one more favor?"

"What is it, Jesse? Spit it out," she responded.

"Would you take me to a movie on a Sunday matinee? I know I cannot go at night. I have very few restrictions on my activities during the day when the school is off," I said.

"Are you crazy, Jesse? Take you to a movie? You think I am crazy?" Bibi seem annoyed at the suggestion. "Your mom would kill you if she found out and I would not want to make your mother mad. She is nice to me and I cannot even imagine what would happen to you, kid. All I know is we both would be in deep trouble."

I dropped the movie idea as fast as I could. Five years would pass before I saw a film. The one I saw was a religious, mythical story about a saint who emerged out of an inferno unscathed because of his intense prayers.

Bibi and I lingered longer than planned. On our way back, we stopped by a street vendor and Bibi bought me a scoop of ice cream. This was another violation of mom's protocol – no visits to the fort and no food from strangers. I was rationalizing the fort excursion in my mind. I reasoned; how could I refuse this offer from the pretty woman with a heart of gold? Bibi was not a stranger, I reasoned. She was a neighbor and one who often talked with my mom about things. My mother never discouraged me from talking to Bibi, although neither did she endorse my socializing with her. Upon returning home, I went straight to bed, which also served as my study desk, and pretended to do homework.

The next day, before lunchtime, I noticed my mother and Bibi talking to each other outside our house. I knew it was about something serious. They were not laughing but they were not yelling at each other (my mom never yelled) either but it did not look pretty. It was different from their previous chitchats. I went inside my bedroom and pretended to be studying.

My mother entered the room. She asked me to follow her, without saying a word; she led me to the windowless inner room and motioned for me to sit down on the bed. "You betrayed me. I never expected this from you. Why didn't you ask me first? I have taken you to the fort several times, on the Guru's birthday, and Baisakhi, the harvest festival, among other times. Why did you decide to go with Bibi, a woman you know nothing about? Do you even know if she is a person of good moral character? You know I worry about your safety in this neighborhood?"

My jaw dropped. This was the first time ever my mother had implied anything negative to Bibi's character. I interrupted my mother, "I am sorry, mom. I should have asked you first. I thought you would not object to my going with Bibi. Bibi likes us and I thought that her friend was going to be with us. He is very strong and not afraid of anything. I would have been safe," I said.

"Bibi's fearless friend is not a good company for you. He is thirty years older than you," my mother reminded me.

"Okay, I will not go with Bibi again..." but before completing the sentence, I said, "...without your permission."

I still could not accept her implication that Bibi was a stranger and her fleeting comment about Bibi's character. I blurted out, "Mom, Bibi is really a nice person. She is kind and polite and that is why she has so many visitors."

"Yes, she is nice and kind. As to why she has so many friends, I cannot tell you. You would know when you are a grown up. Now it is time for you to finish your school work."

My mom's last statement kept me thinking late in the night. What did she mean when she said I would find out when I was grown up? I vowed to find it out now. I knew some older kids but was not sure if I should approach any of them. In India, any age difference at that stage is a major barrier in taking such liberties. Indian schools offered no sex education; you learned it all on the street. I figured I would learn about this sooner rather than later. It was sooner than later.

THE CRIMSON SUNRISE

On a Sunday morning, I was returning from soccer practice at the nearby middle school. There was a commotion outside my house. People were yelling, screaming, and trying to get into Bibi's house through the narrow open door. I followed the crowd, wiggled around the adults, and reached Bibi's bedroom and froze. Bibi was lying in a pool of blood. Her throat had been slit and her blood had traversed to her mouth where it became mixed with the surkhi, her favorite crimson-red lipstick. I grabbed my stomach to prevent myself from throwing up. I was crying. Then I noticed my mother walk in with a cry of, "Oh God, Oh God," several times while covering half her face with the headscarf (chunni) she always wore. She noticed me and immediately grabbed my left arm to lead me back inside the house. She was shaking. So was I. "I am sorry you saw this. I can't reverse it but try to pretend it did not happen. I know Bibi was your friend. She was very fond of you. Wish her peace wherever she is." She tried to console me. We hugged each other.

THE KILLER HUNT THAT NEVER WAS

Police soon arrived and pushed the crowd back to secure the crime scene. They knew it would not be easy to track down the killer or killers. Police in Punjab did not have the tools or the desire to spend department resources on unimportant cases. Bibi was not a prominent citizen. She did not merit the effort.

Theories surfaced on the motive for Bibi's killing. Most people theorized that the cause for this murder was a dispute over money or jealousy between two lovers. People speculated that someone who was in her company all night refused to pay his bill. Bibi may have demanded her fee. When the argument grew loud, the visitor, who may have been a respectable member of society, could have panicked. He may not have had cash, but he carried a dagger. He may have ended the confrontation by slashing Bibi's throat and then exited before the fast rising sun appeared from behind the sand dunes. This seemed to be a plausible theory, but it soon faded in competition with a more forceful motive. Attention focused on Bibi's most frequent visitors.

Bibi had two known suitors. Her first love was Bashir, the kite-fighting champion, but she also liked Imran, the pigeon racer. Because pigeon betting involved more money than kite fights, everyone assumed that Imran was rich and that Bibi was attracted to him because of his wealth. Imran was handsome and a few years younger than Bashir. Unlike Bashir, Imran was not friendly. He looked down on people, rarely smiled, and often behaved as if he were special. I know Bibi preferred Bashir. She had indicated her preference on several occasions without my asking her. She wanted Bashir to marry her. I wanted that to happen because it would make Bibi happy and if Bibi decided to marry Bashir, I assumed I would be an invited guest at her wedding. Imran had started showing increased signs of jealousy because of Bibi's affection for Bashir. He was intensely competitive. He hated to lose. One theory was that on the fateful morning, an argument erupted. When Bibi told Imran that Bashir was her man, he could not take it and ended her life.

Focus later shifted to Nawaz Sharif, the shy religious man who lived next door to Bibi. Maybe he had had it with Bibi. This theory was fueled further when someone claimed that a man wearing black and of Sharif's description was seen loitering on the street in the early morning hours on the day that Bibi was murdered. This theory never went further. Ultimately, people decided that Sharif was not the killer type. He may have despised Bibi but not to the point of killing her. There was nothing violent in his past. The story about a man wearing black and wandering near Bibi's house in the early morning that day persisted nevertheless and was corroborated by others.

Rumors of a more plausible theory soon emerged. It was suggested that a secret lover, a prominent and respected police captain in Bathinda at the time, might have murdered Bibi. He was fair-complexioned, mustached, fun-loving, and was considered the most handsome man around. He was seen around Urdu poem recitals and at one "invitation only" social club. On a couple of occasions, he may have taken Bibi, in disguise, with him to such parties and told people she was his new love after he had separated from his first wife. It was said that he saw Bibi secretively often under some kind of a disguise, because if someone saw him entering Bibi's house, and his identity was revealed, he would be disgraced and surely lose his job. He had no obligation to go home at any set time because he was single. He could have visited Bibi late at night when there were no prying eyes. Nevertheless, some people claimed they saw someone meeting the captain's physical description visiting Bibi on several occasions. The man who claimed to have noticed the captain entering Bibi's house went silent. No way was he going to name a police chief as a suspect. He knew better.

A motive for the captain to murder Bibi soon surfaced. Apparently, the captain and Bibi had fallen in love. The captain emerged as her Prince

Salim. Bibi started pressing him to marry her now that he was a single man. She was aware of the social barriers between them. Not only was her social status an impediment, but the religious divide was like that of climbing Mount Everest. The speculation was that Bibi suggested that if he really loved her, he should quit his job, they could elope, and go to some far corner of India where they could start a new life together. This was unacceptable to the captain. He did not want to risk his job and his family name. He did not have the guts.

Things probably got ugly. Bibi was tired of being jilted by men who used her and then abandoned her. She may have given him an ultimatum. The socially conscious police captain could have panicked. Rather than using his pistol, he may have pulled out the dagger he always carried.

Two years later the police captain married a pretty Bathinda socialite.

Bibi's killer was never found.

ANARKALI REVISITED

Six years after Bibi's murder (in 1953), the movie *Anarkali* was released. It was a Bollywood blockbuster. Fights erupted at theaters as patrons claimed priority in line. I thought of the fort lawn where Bibi had told me the story of the pomegranate blossom in such dramatic fashion. I wanted to see the movie. I waited until the crowds thinned out and went to a theater in a city away from my home where I was continuing my education. After months of showing the film, the theater was still packed. On the screen, everyone's favorite scene was when Anarkali was auctioned to the highest bidder. She was handcuffed and whipped by two burly men in black with faces covered except for little cut outs for their eyes. The men in black took turns whipping Anarkali, who was sobbing but was also able to continue singing while being whipped. There was absolute silence in the usually boisterous theater.

Anarkali was singing:

"Aja, Ab to Aja. Meri kismet ke Kharidar, ab to Aja"
"Come now my savior, custodian of my destiny"
"Take me away from these barbarians"

Anarkali kept sobbing and singing with occasional hick-ups blended into the accompanying music.

"Sabh ne lagai Boli, Lalchai hur nazar"
"Every one is tempted. Everyone wants to bid for me"
"Mein teri ho Chuki hoon, Dunya hai bekhabar"
"I am yours. Little does the world know"
"Come now, oh custodian of my destiny…"

The song transported me to the Bathinda fort lawn six years before when Bibi had told me the Anarkali story in a poetic style. I could not get back into the movie and missed many crucial conversations, which my friends later said were the highlights. I decided to return the next week and the week after. I watched Anarkali six times in different theaters.

PS: Five years ago, I went back to Bathinda with my wife and daughter. The vicinity around the Bathinda Fort had changed. Bathinda has become much more crowded. By spotting a few landmarks, that are still there, we found my street. Most of the old houses were gone, replaced with more modern and bigger houses. There now stands a two-story house where Bibi once lived. I had a hard time recognizing the lot where my house had stood. All the residents of the street were either Hindus or Sikhs. The Muslims fled to Pakistan in 1947.

* **Kabaddi** is a contact sport based on wrestling and originated in India. It is the national game of Nepal and Bangladesh. The 2013 World Kabaddi Cup was held in December 2013 with the opening ceremonies in Bathinda, Punjab.

** **Razia Sultan** was the first woman emperor of India. She was deposed by her enemies and imprisoned in the Bathinda Fort from which she escaped and tried to reclaim her throne, but was killed on her way to Delhi on October 13, 1240. Her name was Razia Sultana, but she renamed herself Razia Sultan because the word Sultana implied a woman and, therefore, not equal to the male rulers.

*** **Emperor Akbar** ran into Anarkali a second time when she was tending to his son Prince Salim after he had returned home from a battle in Kabul where he had sustained a serious wound. What Akbar had not realized was that Anarkali was in his garden in the first place for a secret rendezvous with his son, Prince Salim. The Prince never showed up. The third time Akbar saw Anarkali was at a royal performance where Anarkali sang and danced while intoxicated and unleashing all her spent up emotions for not uniting with her prince. Akbar was furious. It was also the first time Akbar realized that she was in love with the prince who would be the next emperor of India someday. He ordered Anarkali shackled and imprisoned.

73

She was later offered to the highest bidder in a public auction.

Note: *The ultimate fate of Anarkali is fuzzy. Some accounts note that she was entombed alive. This has never been proven, but the story has captivated generations of Indians. Price Salim later assumed the Indian throne under the name of Emperor Jahangir and built the fabled Taj Mahal in memory of his beloved wife Noor Jehan. His son Aurangzeb, the tyrant Moghul emperor who developed animosity towards his own father, had Jahangir imprisoned in the historical Agra Fort until Jahangir's death. Aurangzeb did make one concession. He imprisoned his father in picturesque quarters overlooking the Yamuna River where he had an unobstructed view of the Taj Mahal, which he had built in memory of his wife.*

CHAPTER 5

THE BEST-FORTIFIED SCHOOL IN

INDIA

On August 15, 1947, the United Kingdom Parliament passed the Indian Independence Act declaring the end of British rule of the Indian subcontinent. Following this, India was divided into two separate nations: the Indian Union and the Pakistan Dominion, which later became the Republic of Pakistan. Two days later, a border, called the Radcliff Line, between these two counties was unveiled replete with its contours, jogs, uncertainties, and imperfections.

Despite widespread dissatisfaction, the border was absolute. It was non-negotiable. The next morning, millions of Indians woke up wondering which country was theirs. The consequences were mind-boggling. If you were a Hindu or a Sikh and woke up in mostly Muslim Pakistan, you better pack up your belongings and head for the border while praying along the way for safety. The same was true if you were a Muslim and woke up in the heartland of India where the dominant religion was Hindu. There was no time to waste. Some people were too late packing. They never made it to their new home (wherever it happened to be) assigned to them by Sir Radcliff, architect of the border.

Radcliff had little familiarity with the Indian subcontinent. He was given five weeks to complete the task of dividing the Indian subcontinent. This was a tall order, but the Englishman decided to meet the challenge, no matter if his thin red line ran through the middle of villages, close-knit communities, and, in at least one high-profile case, through the middle of a single mud house in a multiethnic neighborhood.

Radcliff was in a hurry to go back home to England for several reasons. The most pressing driver was to get away from the stifling August heat in Northern India. By working quickly, he was able to leave for the UK just

75

ahead of the public unveiling of the border. Chaos and riots erupted even before his plane touched UK soil.

AN OASIS OF LEARNING

On August 17 1947, my family was living in an enclave in Punjab, India known as Mastuana Sahib, which was situated four miles west of Sangrur City. Sant (Saint) Attar Singh, a revered pious man from a nearby village, founded Mastuana. He was an educational missionary who wanted to put his power and intellect into developing an education center that would be ahead of its time. It was.

Attar Singh scouted real estate in the area and settled on a piece of wooded property strategically located between several large towns, a nearby railway station, and the important regional business center called Sangrur. People in the area were delighted the Sant had selected their neighborhood as the nucleus of his spiritual and educational endeavors. As early as in 1920, he established a high school and a degree college in Mastuana.

Mastuana was an idyllic place well suited to serve as an academic and spiritual center. In the 1920s and 1930s, it flourished and became a magnet for people seeking knowledge and spirituality. Coincidentally, these were also some of the most violent times in the developing Indian independence movement. Mastuana College started attracting activists who advocated immediate British exit from India. In time, the college became a hotbed of activity against the British Raj. The culminating protests lead to the Ahmedgarh train robbery in 1928, one of the most brazen anti-British acts. After the attempted train robbery, the college, known as the Akal (divine) College, was immediately and permanently closed.

Nineteen years after the train robbery, my family moved to Mastuana. Only the shell of the big building, which housed the degree college, still dominated the landscape. The empty Akal College building towered three stories high and contained impressive cathedral ceilings. When we moved to Mastuana, the abandoned degree college was serving as a refuge for pigeons, not a center of learning for knowledge-hungry students.

The nearby primary school and the high school in Mastuana had remained in good standing and were supported by an active academic pre-university program. In the year of the Indian partition, the resident population of Mastuana numbered fewer than fifty people. During weekdays, the daytime population would swell by a few hundred visitors.

This number included day scholars and those who came to pay homage to the holy saint, to gawk at the gleaming marble temples, and to visit the holy pools.

In one corner of the walled complex, there were lush gardens with pomegranate trees and guava orchards. Religious hymns were sung throughout the day with the accompaniment of harmonium wind instruments

My family was among the approximately fifty residents of this more than a thousand-acre complex. My father was employed there as a religious scholar and a teacher. Although the school served as a Sikh educational center, the high school in Mastuana had a significant number of students from other religions. This was uncommon for denominational schools in India at the time.

By most measures, the Mastuana school and temple complexes were heaven on earth, a great place for learning, and an ideal location to raise a family by anyone fortunate enough to have employment there. The complex included two large swimming pools in the tradition of the great Sarovar (pool) in Amritsar, the ultimate Sikh shrine, the Sikh Vatican. Mastuana's pools were open at all hours. The pools were not for just swimming, but also to obtain the gratuitous blessing from the Guru, given when your head was dunked into the holy water.

Guards with navy-blue uniforms hovered around and remained mostly out of sight but were close enough to come to the rescue if there was trouble, which happened only occasionally. An important duty of the guards was to chase away any unscrupulous visitors who happened to step on the marble "Parkarma" (circular pathway around an altar) wearing leather shoes. Guards would ambush the unsuspecting wanderer, yelling and screaming insults and giving him or her a tongue lashing to ensure that the ignorant intruder would never again step on the holy space with shoes made from animal hides. Such an act was considered the ultimate desecration, which showed a lack of culture and dignity.

Most of the violators were men. Women were more thoughtful and reverent. If occasionally someone violated the space, the blue guards ("Nihangs") would come running and yell rebukes, but they were relatively civil towards the ladies. Occasionally the infuriated blue guard would reinforce the protocol with a whack of a spear butt on the covered toe of the violator (1).

Akali Temple in 1947

Administratively, Mastuana was divided into two functional units. The North side was called the "Bihangam" and the south side the "Akali Abode." The high school, the defunct college, the medical dispensary, and the post office came under Akali governance, which had a larger budget. White-robed Bihangams were content with managing the south temple and the large amounts of money donated by the rich donors whose need for divine help and blessings from the holy men was greater than the Akalis or just ordinary folks. The Bihangham side was more spacious, better landscaped, and had fruit orchards.

Bihangham Temple in 1947

The pool on the Akali side had a small built-in private bathing facility for women only. It was called "The Pona" (towel). Pona was an attached masonry thirty feet by twenty feet enclosure, on west side of the pool. A fully dressed woman could enter the big towel (Pona), change clothes, bathe, dry, and emerge fully dressed ready to attend the religious services. A fleeting "peek-a-boo" by any male into Pona's interior would earn him, at a minimum, a good old-fashioned thrashing from a blue guard or the potential loss of an important part of anatomy in the extreme case.

Men had no private changing room and no dress code. They could walk up to any side of the pool, other than the Pona, shed their clothes (except the underwear), and just jump in.

IDYLLIC HAVEN LOST

Mastuana of 1947 was not quite the idyllic haven the great Sant Attar Singh had envisioned. The tranquility and calm was replaced by heavy vehicle traffic on the new roads that crisscrossed the area. Increasing sectarian violence and political divisions had shattered the peace and communal harmony that was the hallmark of Mastuana when it was conceived. The degree college and the train robbery were now just memories. Whatever calm and harmony still existed was shattered in one big blow on the morning of August 1947 when Radcliff's red line first appeared in the morning papers.

RUN FOR THE BORDER

Viceroy Mountbatten and Sir Radcliff anticipated dissatisfaction and demonstrations subsequent to the unveiling of the partition line. The ferocity of the riots and the massacres that followed was not in their calculations. Even after governing India for 200 years, the British had not fully fathomed the degree of religious distrust and hatred in India. They were aware of such feelings and had actually exploited them to execute their "Divide and Rule" doctrine.

Killings started before sunrise. Refugee stations and transfer points to hasten the movement of people were arranged in a hurry to repatriate an estimated 15 million people to their new destinations wherever they happened to be. This did not guarantee safe transfers. Fleeing victims were chased and sometimes hacked to death inside the supposedly safe havens of the transfer points.

Owing to its location in extreme northwestern India along the border of newly created Pakistan, chaos engulfed the entire state of Punjab as soon as the partition was unveiled. Fleeing families traveled by foot, bullock carts, and camels, or traveled perched on rooftops of overloaded railway trains clutching children and any valuables they had. Religion-fueled killings were widespread on both sides of the border. Claims were heard that the onslaught was fiercer for refugees fleeing from the newly created Pakistan to the east of the dividing line into India. Many people never made it. An estimated 200,000 to 500,000 people were slaughtered in a matter of days.

As pandemonium broke out, rumors spread that the suddenly trapped Muslims in the nearby village of Badbar were fleeing to Pakistan, but en route they would unload their frustrations and anger by attacking Mastuana as the symbol of evil and hatred. *(See the related story, "Paradise found and lost".)*

It was a school holiday, which meant that the population of Mastuana was at its lowest. The occupants included the Sikh priests from the two temples, resident schoolteachers and their families, cooks, the cleaning staff, the part-time resident post-master, a paramedic, the two pool guards, and the security guards who operated the gates on both ends of the property.

There was an overall security chief for the complex. He was a retired military man who possessed the only gun in the enclave. Everybody called him Soobedar (pronounced soo-bay-daar). It was not his real name but a military title and, therefore, more impressive. Soobedar also served on the high-school faculty as a sports teacher and a drillmaster. His gun was a double barrel shotgun (do-nali) and the envy of many who would have killed to own such a prestigious weapon. Private gun ownership was impossible under India's ironclad gun control laws.

With the attack imminent, all eyes turned to Soobedar to organize the defense of Mastuana. Instantly, he became the de facto commander and did not hesitate to assume his duties. His first job was to compile an inventory of all available weaponry. Besides his double barrel shotgun, the only other firepower was a World War II vintage pistol belonging to one of the resident priests. The priest had acquired the weapon when he served in the British Sikh regiment years prior to the 1947 partition. In addition to the shotgun and the pistol, there were spears and swords carried by some Sikhs. These weapons belonged to the blue warriors (Nihang Singh's – a specialized militarized Sikh sect) who believed in staying alert in the belief that the enemy, who has not been spotted in 300 years, was still bent on wiping out Sikhs. Why take chances?

Soobedar was confident and methodical. His British military training came in handy. He raised his left hand high and shouted, "If necessary, each man, woman, and child will go down fighting. There will be no captives. We will see to that."

His last statement, "We will see to that", sent chills down my spine. What did he mean when he said, "We will see to that"? Did he mean that everyone would fight to the finish or be sacrificed? I was not clear of the implications of his last pronouncement, but when I think of it now, I can visualize Masada in Israel (2).

After inventorying available weaponry, Soobedar turned his attention to the defenders available. He focused first on the adult males. There were fewer than twenty-five available. Each of them was assigned a spear and a sword. Many Sikhs also carried Kirpans (mini-swords) (3) which were plentiful in Mastuana. Children below the age of eight were given no combat assignments. They were to stick around close to their mothers or an adult male. Nine to fourteen years olds (my unit) were considered battle worthy.

Among the male adults was one Nihang Singh (blue warrior). He was always dressed in the old Sikh warrior tradition, wearing navy-blue from head to toe, save for a saffron scarf around his massive turban. His name was Fauja Singh, which literally translated as "Army Singh." He claimed he served in the British military for a short time but was discharged after he sustained an injury unrelated to combat. His imposing frame, handlebar mustache, and fierce gaze instilled fear or confidence depending on your side. Fauja Singh could let out the loudest blood-curdling war cry. Psychologically, his war cry could prove more demoralizing to the enemy than Soobedar's shotgun.

His presence gave a morale boost to all of us. A unique weapon that Fauja possessed could have been as lethal as the Soobedar's gun. It was the chakra, twelve-inch diameter circular ring that was razor sharp. In the hands of an expert, the ancient weapon could sever an enemy's head in one strike from one hundred yards away. No one knew what expertise Fauja had in hurling the death circle. Unfortunately, if he missed, there would be no second opportunity because he had no spares. The absence of spare chakras did not seem to bother him. To all gathered, he explained, "Ladies and gentlemen, the chakra is as much of a psychological weapon in warfare as it is lethal. You aim it at the head of the enemy chief. The spectacle of an officer's head rolling in the dirt like a cantaloupe is so dramatic and horrifying that it will send the enemy fleeing in terror." He cited ancient battles in support of his hypothesis.

Armed to the teeth: Resident Blue Warrior Fauja Singh (Army Singh) with Sword, Chakra, Dhala (vest), and hand-to-hand combat weapons tucked in turban folds.

Soobedar re-stated the battle assignments to each age group and announced weapon allocations. I did not qualify for a spear or sword because I was under age. I did however; qualify for a knife, a kirpan, and an inventory of bricks with instructions on when and how to toss the bricks at the approaching enemy. Soobedar was trained in every aspect of warfare, including psychological weaponry. He called my age group close to him and said, "The residents of Badbar will be passing through here this evening on their way to Pakistan. Rumor is that they plan to kill every man, woman, and child in Mastuana before going further. We must defend ourselves. You are young. I do not believe in sending youngsters to war but today's encounter could be a do-or-die situation. Let me remind you that when the tenth Guru was surrounded in the Chamkaur fortress with only forty faithful followers, the same number we have today, and he needed everyone, including his children, his wife, and his mother, to be involved in the cause. So don't be afraid."

"I am not afraid sir," I announced. "I am ready to die." I shouted this while steadying my shaking body and hiding my fear.

"You make me proud son." Soobedar vigorously patted my right shoulder and moved on to assure each of the youngsters individually.

Among the weapons assigned to my group (nine- to fourteen-year-olds) were bricks and knives. Bricks were pre-positioned on the rooftop of the abandoned college building which provided an unrestricted view of the surrounding flat terrain. Soobedar also had a pair of binoculars from his military days. He was stationed on the rooftop among most of the others. Three of the adults were assigned to the three outer entrances to the enclave. One of them had the vintage pistol.

February 2015: Author checks bricks, reported to be leftover from the 1947 "siege."

83

Mr. Singh, the current resident manager, pointing out the likely location of the fortifications on the day of attack (that never happened).

Darkness approached. Our instructions were that when the attackers came close, Soobedar would fire a few shots and hopefully would hit someone. If that did not happen and the enemy kept advancing, more shots would be fired. If they kept coming and were within range, Soobedar would shout "chalo" (go!) and we would shower the enemy with the bricks stacked nearby. It was hoped that Soobedar's precise aim would bring down the attacker's advance man who would be carrying the enemy flag, and that the enemy might just give up and retreat after the first casualty.

Part of the strategy was also to make as much noise as we could by beating the six-foot diameter war drum called "Negara" which normally was used only at special prayers and celebrations. For the impending do-or-die battle, the Negara was hauled to the rooftop from inside the main temple.

Just before the sun went down, a male guard came running and directed Soobedar to look westward. There was movement and a drifting cloud of dust accompanied by a faint noise emanating from the direction of the Badbar village. In the twilight, nothing was clear. The commotion could

84

have been a herd of water buffaloes or a frightened wild deer in the distance.

Soobedar gave the order to start beating the Negara. The brick squad moved into position. Small kids started crying. Mothers tightly hugged their babies. No one panicked, but fear was evident.

For the next tense minutes, whatever was heard in the distance was getting closer and louder. Suddenly the noise faded and disappeared. Soobedar reminded everybody that the danger was not over. He shouted, "It is never over until you are sure it is over."

The sun was going down fast. The impending darkness added to fear. We tightened our grips on swords, spears, and bricks. Minutes passed. Nothing happened. Soobedar's orders were to keep the drum going. The arms of the muscular adults assigned to drum beating were getting tired. The danger seemed to have passed, but Soobedar kept the drum going until early dawn when it was certain that we had scared the enemy away.

When the drum halted, there was an eerie quiet. At daybreak, Soobedar gathered everyone and declared victory saying, "We have scared the enemy without firing a shot or tossing a brick." He shook hands and warmly hugged everyone he was allowed to hug.

Before we dispersed, the fully weaponized blue warrior stepped up, declared victory, and motioned everyone to sing along with him the Sikh victory hymn, "**Raj Karega Khalsa, Aaki Rahe na Koy**" which meant that the purest (meaning Sikhs) will rule and there will be no holdovers. Everyone applauded and dispersed to reassemble soon for "Langar," the communal lunch.

PS: Writing the story while sitting in my back porch in Hawaii, I kept thinking. "How in the world we could have believed that we could be attacked by a handful of Muslim villagers who were fleeing for their own safety to get to the border of their new country (Pakistan)?" Many of the fleeing Muslims from Badbar did not make it. Bodies were found floating in a nearby canal. It was easy to tell who they were. They were all circumcised.

1) I received this treatment once when I stepped on the temple Parkarma at the great Damdamma Sahib, one of the holiest Sikh shrines. The blue guard came running, yelling insults on the top of his lungs, "Don't you have any sense you moron, stepping on the space with your filthy leather hides where the Guru used to walk in the evenings while reciting Lord's prayers?" To scare me further, he gestured as if he was going to jam the sharp end of the eight-foot long spear on my toe. Luckily, he only scraped the front half of my tennis shoe with the spear handle. I apologized

and promised never to do such a stupid thing again as long as I lived.

2) Masada is the biblical fortress on top of a mesa-like rock in the Judean Desert in Israel. Herod the Great built palaces on the mountain and fortified Masada a few years before Christ's birth. Roman troops encircled Masada to force out Jewish rebels. The long siege finally ended with 960 Jews committing mass suicide rather than surrendering to the Romans.

3) Punjabi- ਕਿਰਪਾਨ), a mini-sword. Most baptized ("Amritdharis") Sikhs carried a kirpan. Although mostly ceremonial, a kirpan could easily kill someone if used in hand-to-hand combat. Several adult females in Mastuana, including my mother, carried Kirpans.

CHAPTER 6

JEETO – THE UNCUT DIAMOND

As a teenager in India, I was addicted to "Bollywood" movies. These movies were designed to fulfill all your fantasies: palatial homes, beautiful women, exotic food, dancing and music, and more music even when the moment did not call for music.

The formula for success was standardized. You could not hope to make a commercially viable Indian film unless you had all the standard ingredients. The recipe had been perfected from hundreds of trials: boy meets a girl and immediately sets out on a complex but predictable romantic journey that starts with the boy teasing the girl, generally by singing amorous songs. Such impromptu displays of intimacy would first irritate and offend any respectable potential heroine. At first, she would strongly resent such crude attention and tell the pursuer to get lost. She would have nothing to do with the likes of him. But wait. This tongue lashing would be temporary. Soon the stone would start softening as the suitor persisted. Softening of the stone would be evident when the same tongue lashing is delivered in the form of a song replete with the full orchestra in the background even if the encounter is at a lonely public park. The musical rebuff would be like the song from my favorite Bollywood movie called *Mr. and Mrs. 55* (1955).

और कोई घर देखिये
(Go look for some other venue)
दिल को यहाँ मत फेंकिये
(Don't throw away/waste your heart here)

The heroine singing the song would be the most gorgeous girl around and would be dressed to the hilt even if the venue is a dilapidated city park. If the park happens to have a few decent trees, the boy and girl must run around the trees several times and that would often blossom into a game of hide and seek *(Bollywood movies have come a long way from my time. Although the basic theme remains the same, the boy and girl are now flown to places like Switzerland to run around more lush trees on the Swiss mountains or roll over in piles of fresh, white snow)*. The boy then will erupt into his own song and will plead for permission to peek inside the girl's "aanchal" which is the long wrap around headwear. Sometimes he will be more daring and ask the girl if he can hide under her aanchal ("mujhe aanchal mein chhupa lo") knowing full well that there is not enough space there to hide, and moreover, it is of a transparent fabric and the prying eyes can still see inside. If the hide and seek goes as expected, then the path from there on is pretty smooth, punctuated only by temporary setbacks which the viewer knows will be overcome without a serious glitch.

As a kid, I used to wonder where in the world such women were found. They looked Indian, but they were nothing like the babes (I had not discovered the term at that time) in my village. I know this because if there were women like those in my village, I would have noticed them.

Not finding the kind of women, the palatial homes, the nightclubs, and the glitter in my village propelled me to the movies every weekend to experience such luxury. I had become a movie addict despite my mother's objections. She wanted me to practice algebra.

As a teenager, I did not live in the village of my birth. I lived in the big city (if you could call it that) where there was a middle school because my village did not offer education beyond the fourth grade. I returned to my village only during summer holidays, except for the Diwali (the festival of lights), and for an occasional wedding or a funeral.

My village had no facilities or opportunities for amusement, but I still liked it there. I liked to go to the fields with my cousin who never went to a school and died recently, still an uneducated farmer. He had, however, a fantastic sense of humor. For some strange reason, I also liked the unpolished and unsophisticated girls in the village despite the fact that most of them seemed perpetually covered with a fine tropical dust and a top thinner layer that looked like organic microfibers composed mostly of cow dung.

THE COW DUNG PYRAMIDS

Cow dung reigned supreme in my village. There were heaps of the fresh, green aromatic commodity waiting to be transported to the open yards either to dry out for later use as fuel or to be composted. This was truly the green revolution; all natural, organic, and biodegradable. Larger quantities, destined for composting, were transported by machines and loaded by burly mustachioed men with muscles hardened and dried under the hot North Indian sun. Smaller quantities of the green gold were converted into perfectly shaped discs (cow patties), dried in the sun, and stacked into smaller and smaller circles from the base up, forming perfect pyramids rivaling the Egyptian masterpieces but on a mini scale. The architecturally symmetrical structures were later coated with layers of mud and clay to insulate them so tightly that even a molecule of water could not penetrate. After the relentless monsoons, when everything was soaking wet, you could open these gigantic hives and find bone-dry organic fuel that contained no trace of manmade additives and toxins. Breaching the pyramids to recover dry fuel in the cold and wet season was like finding Tutankhamen's treasure. I am sure that the first time I witnessed the breaching of one of the monstrous pyramids, I must have felt like Howard Carter, discoverer of King Tut's tomb.

Much of the hauling of the green gold was carried out by village girls between the ages of twelve and eighteen. They would haul the semisolid material that had the consistency of creamed spinach for long distances to a common work area. There, they would turn the precious commodity into discs by forming round patties with their bare hands and would then arrange the discs into neat rows to dry out under the hot sun. They would then neatly arrange the dried discs of dung inside the symmetrical pyramids. I was certain that their labor sustained the daily life in the village by providing light, heat, and fuel for the cooking pits. You might say they were responsible for fueling the economy of my village. The men just sat around all day yelling insults at the young boys who were either hired cow herders but more often than not buffalo herders. Bull sh!t flowed unchecked during such gossip gatherings but, unlike the cow dung, there was no one designated to clean it up.

THE VIA CANDIOTTI OF GURNE

Paris has the Champs Elysees. Rome has the Via Veneto. And Milan boasts of its fashionable Via Candiotti where you can shop or simply ogle at the beautiful people. The Via Candiotti of Gurne (my birth village) was the street on which my house was located. All the beautiful people went by it. So did the ugly ones. The street had no name. None of the streets in the village had a name or a street sign. To find an address, you had to find someone who would know the person(s) you were seeking. It may sound complicated, but it always worked. It was more reliable than MapQuest or a GPS system. Usually, someone who knew the house would escort you and sometimes not before you accepted a cup of tea at the escort's own house.

On summer days, I would sit on my front porch, on a jute cot with a big fat pillow to support my back and where I was just wasting away time. That was all I did during my summers except for ogling the girls hauling the green gold to the field to be shaped into symmetrical discs.

On the way to the cow dung disc-forming sites, the girls would walk right in front of my house. My porch afforded me a front row seat and an unobstructed view of the workers transporting this raw material. No one could wrongly accuse me of staring at the girls carrying the smelly stuff. Staring is generally not frowned upon in India. To the contrary, staring at women is a national pastime. I mean, why object to it? God's wonderful creatures are meant to be admired. It should be known that while staring was permissible, any verbal and/or physical contact was strictly verboten.

After my first couple of days in the village, I started noticing certain patterns. Every day, at almost the same time, a pretty girl, maybe fourteen or fifteen years old, would emerge from the right side of my field of vision and soon appear in full glory.

I took a good look at the young lady and my heart sank. Even under the sagging weight of probably seventy pounds of dung packed in a leaky cane basket, she radiated beauty, charm, and raw sexuality. I was smitten. I described my feelings to my brother's wife who was my ardent supporter and confidant. Mentioning such feelings to my mother would have meant immediate assignment to other more productive activities including studies, sports, or some sort of community service, the kind of activities that were way down on my list of priorities. My mother would have done anything to steer me away from the staring game in which I was engaged.

My sister-in-law Deepa was an angel. She did not approve of my sudden new crush, but she was willing to share with me information about this newly discovered treasure. She told me that the girl's name was Jeeto and that she was fifteen years old. Jeeto lived on the east side of the village where many people of her clan lived, which was not too far from our house. My sister-in-law, however, warned me not to get too ambitious for several reasons.

Jeeto was underage (*so was I at the time*). Jeeto was from a different ethnic group, a major obstacle to advancing the scope of my project. Moreover, if my mother found out, I would be banished back to my dormitory in the drab city or advised to visit relatives in another village. Worst of all, if Jeeto's father found out, Jeeto's path would be diverted away from the Via Candiotti of Gurne. None of these alternatives sounded attractive. I assured Deepa that she did not need to worry. I would do nothing stupid (*a false promise*) to bring shame to our or Jeeto's family.

91

I was hooked. The next day, I made sure I was well positioned on my woven jute cot when Jeeto came by. As if controlled by an atomic clock, Jeeto appeared from the right at precisely the same time as the day before. She noticed my behavior and seemed willing to play along with my game. Jeeto wore the same long Panjabi salwar that she had worn the day before. Sporting an erect posture, even under the seventy-pound weight on her head, she walked as if she was a seasoned model for a Milano fashion house (which of course I did not know about at that time). Bracing seventy pounds of cow manure, she still exuded the grace, pride, and confidence of an Italian model. When she approached the same latitude I was, she ever so slightly tilted her head (probably no more than an ergonomically safe fifteen degrees) towards me but only for a second or so it seemed. During that flash of a moment, she gave me a beautiful but subdued smile. Then as quickly as she had tilted her head towards me, she withdrew it in one quick action as if she was saying:

'*Ok, this is all you get. This is all you deserve you slacker. Show me why you deserve more? Earn it if you can.*' She resumed her walk as if nothing had happened.

I slumped in my jute bed. I was mush. I was putty, silly putty at that. I could not resist telling Deepa of my plight, which resulted in another friendly warning.

"Watch out kid, you are getting into muddy water."

I assured Deepa of no potential harm but continued the cat and mouse game. Every day Jeeto would appear at the same precise moment and look at me. The duration of her glances were getting longer and the smiles broader. Her eyes were now clearly saying '*Hello handsome. How are you today? Why aren't you studying hard so you can become a doctor and then ask my parents for my hand?*' I have no proof that Jeeto thought of such things. It might have been just my imagination.

I often dreamed of going to America and taking Jeeto with me. It did not matter if she had no college education or could not speak English. I would give her a crash course in English. She would go to a school. She would learn American etiquette and when we got to Los Angeles, I would take her to a fashion house in Beverly Hills to get the diamond polished. Los Angeles was the only city in America I knew anything about. I had heard wonderful things about Hollywood, Beverly Hills, and the Sunset Boulevard from a distant relative who had lived in California. In my daydreams, when the Beverly Hills fashion house was finished working on Jeeto, she would rival any model in the land of fruits and nuts. I would walk with Jeeto hand-in-hand on Sunset Boulevard and heads would turn. The rich California boys would have their fancy cars and their platinum-blonde girlfriends, but only I would have Jeeto. They would stare at me and be filled with jealousy and wonder *'where did this farmer guy pick up this diamond?'*

No longer could I contain my feelings. I wanted to share my dreams. The next day at breakfast (my favorite meal of the day in my village), I casually blurted: "Mom, don't you think that Jeeto girl is gorgeous? The way she walks and smiles. What strong muscles she must have carrying a ton of that disgusting stuff on her pretty head, and yet her beauty and grace shines through from under all that grit."

DISASTER CONTROL

My mother's jaw dropped. She smelled big trouble, both literally and figuratively. Her baby was growing up. The hormone harvest had arrived prematurely. She reacted as if I had just announced that I had a terminal disease. She immediately went into disaster-recovery mode, pulled me close to her chest like when I was five years old. She lowered her voice so no one could hear it even though there was not a soul in sight. She cupped both hands around my chubby cheeks and said: "Listen son, you have a beautiful future ahead of you. You are so young. One day soon you will be a doctor. People will greet you with folded hands. They will think of you as a life savior. Parents of well-educated girls from prominent families in Patiala or Delhi will be knocking on our creaky door to engage their daughters to my Jas." She gave me a big squeeze, her eyes filled with moisture. She composed herself and continued: "Just be patient. You will have plenty of girlfriends when it is time. You are such a handsome boy. I know you are destined for America. You could even be the heartthrob of some American lady" (she knew the exact Panjabi equivalent of heartthrob). The word is escaping me now. Then she got to the point.

"So why are you wasting your precious time dreaming about this uneducated, unsophisticated village girl with spindly legs and an unstable frame like a prematurely born 'Shutermurg' (ostrich) baby?" Jeeto was tall for her age. "She is always covered with dirt and cow dung and she walks like she just recovered from a polio seizure."

"Okay mom, please stop. First of all, Jeeto does not have spindly legs or walk like she has just recovered from a polio seizure. She has beautiful legs and her walk is deliberate and graceful like those Bollywood actresses in the movies. In fact, she walks like a fashion model even under all that weight on her head. Yes, she is always covered with grit and sh!t." I hesitated, reversed a bit and said, "Cow dung." And continued, "Mom, please look at it rationally. Jeeto is like an uncut diamond. She just needs to be polished. Just imagine if someone gave her a thorough scrubbing with an industrial strength detergent and then a coating of perfumed oil, she would shine like a jewel and you would be proud to imagine her as your daughter-in-law."

"And I guess you would be the one to give her that industrial strength scrub?" She looked at me and could not hide her smirk despite her best effort to look serious and concerned. Mom was not about to give up. She again tried to convince me to wait and resist all such distractions. I would be rewarded later.

I had heard such promises before. Our village priest had been drilling into my head that if I was a good boy, and refrained from bad things, sex being on the top of that list, good things would happen to me in the afterlife. I could never take that advice seriously. Maybe I could hold off for the time-frame my mother had proscribed for me, but not the life-long commitment the preacher wanted. No way. I knew I did not have that kind of patience and actually neither did the preacher. A year later I found out that the preacher was accused of child molestation and he was sanctioned by the authorities.

I did not want to ignore my mother's wishes. She had a lot invested in me. She wanted to be proud of me and my two brothers. She wanted to show the villagers that she was a successful mother.

THE LAST GLANCE

I did not to want to disappoint my mother. She did not have to worry. My vacation was almost over. The next day, I was scheduled to leave Gurne to go back to the city to resume my studies. Somehow the whole village knew it. Rumor spread that I was going somewhere far away like America, perhaps never to return. The rumor was false. I was only going to Calcutta to explore educational opportunities. My last day to see Jeeto was at hand. She came at the usual time. Normally she would turn her head only slightly to look at me for a few fleeting seconds, leaving me craving for more. This was different. Today she tilted her head a full ninety degrees, a painful gesture no doubt under the enormous weight on her head. And instead of a few fleeting seconds, she stared at me for what seemed like forever. Luckily (or perhaps unluckily) there were no passersby to interrupt the painful gaze which was full of sadness, despair, and anger. Gone was the heavenly smile, the mischievous teasing eyes, and her gentle grace. No words were exchanged, but the text was there for me to read in black ink and large font. None of it was pleasant. Jeeto's big beautiful black eyes were telling me in no uncertain terms:

'Why did you do this? Why did you play with my emotions? Why did you lead me on if it was to end this way? You may have lot of things in your brain, but your heart is an empty shell with nothing in it. Absolutely nothing! Go back to your world where this is just a game and it is all about winning.'

Jeeto was still staring at me. I always craved for more attention from her, but today I could take it no more. I wanted it to end. I wished she did not look at me. I felt bad. I felt like the green goo Jeeto was carrying on her head. Finally, she turned her head with one swift jerk and continued her march to the cow dung yard. She didn't look back.

Obviously she had heard from the neighbors that I was going away the next day, possibly never to return. What is the point of smiling if there is no continuity in this play? This was just a dream, a dream with no theme. Who said life is fair?

I never saw Jeeto again. A year later, when I came back to my village, Deepa (my confidant and sister-in-law) told me that Jeeto had grown into a woman. Ruffians on the street had taunted her. One of them even tried to molest her. Her parents decided she should stay home. Deepa went on "…Jeeto no longer comes out this way. I have not seen her in months and if you are thinking of seeing her, forget it. It will do you no good. You will only cause grief to your mother and to us all."

I heeded Deepa's advice and did not attempt to see Jeeto or even walk by her house.

Another year went by. I came home again for a couple of weeks. Still I could not resist asking Deepa if she would help me to find Jeeto, only to see what she looks like now. I suggested that Deepa and I go to Jeeto's house, knock on the door pretending we are collecting donations for an orphanage.

"Forget it Jas. Give up. I cannot be party to any such stunt. Moreover, you will not see Jeeto anyway even if you show up at her house everyday dressed up as a miserable beggar." Deepa continued… "Let me tell you something you may not want to hear. Jeeto is married now. Her parents found a suitable match for her in a neighboring village. It was a big wedding. I saw her husband. The man is lot older than Jeeto, maybe fifty-ish and not much to look at, but apparently he has money. They say he has 150 acres of land and a hefty bank account which he amassed when he lived in Kenya. I don't know what he did, but apparently he brought a lot of dough with him when he returned to the village."

"Okay, I know it is over. I have known it for two years. I just wanted to see what she looks like. I wanted to say I'm sorry to her, but I know it is just a dream like everything else."

"I wish I had better news for you, brother." Deepa tapped my shoulder.

'*I doubt if Jeeto is happy, but I know she will no longer have to haul that cow dung,*' I consoled myself.

A LIFETIME LATER

In 2010, I visited my birth village accompanied by my wife Mary and my daughter Monica. At my request, my relatives set up woven jute cots on the porch where I used to sit and watch Jeeto walk by. So it seemed like absolutely nothing had changed in the village until my niece brought to me her brand new laptop computer equipped with Wi-Fi. She said I should test it. Without thinking too deeply, I opened up Google, typed "Jeeto – the Uncut Diamond", and pressed enter. Hundreds of records and documents showed up, many related to illegal and immoral diamond trade in Sierra Leone. It also brought up several Jeetos, one of whom seemed to be a well-educated professional woman in India.

The Jeeto I was looking for was nowhere in the database. Even Google could not find her. The diamond was to remain unpolished and undiscovered.

Monica came from behind and tapped me on my shoulder and said: "Snap out of it, Dad! It's time to leave. The driver is getting anxious. We need to get to Delhi on time to catch our flight to L.A."

CHAPTER 7

PARADISE FOUND AND LOST

Seva wanted to know if his friend Rahim was safe. Rumors of rioting and violence had spread only a day after the Indian partition was announced. He reached the outskirts of Badbar, a town he had known as well as he knew his own village. He did not see anyone on the streets at the edge of town. An eerie feeling came over him. Where were the people? The streets seemed to be empty. He knocked on one wide opened door, called to the residents, and walked in. No one was in the house. He tried a few other houses with the same result. Everyone had fled. Even the animals were gone except for some stray dogs and a sickly old cow. Something terrible had happened, he thought, to lead to such hurried flight. Apparently, looters had moved through the area and taken household possessions as well. Once a thriving village, Badbar (1) was now a ghost town. It all must have happened within the last few hours.

Seva expected some turmoil and panic after the news of the partition, but he never imagined anything like this. He wondered, are there any people in the village? Besides Rahim's family, he had known several residents in this neighboring Muslim village. He went to Rahim's house. The door was open, but no one was inside. He wandered throughout the house, a mansion by Badbar standards. Gone was the poster of the Taj Mahal and of Delhi's red fort and a portrait of Rahim's two sons that had hung there for years. The green sofa he sat on many occasions was also gone, an indication that looters had already scoured the place.

Seva had an uncomfortable feeling. With fear and trepidation, he went to a neighbor's house. A stray dog followed him. "Go away," he yelled at the dog. The dog took off immediately. Inside the house, everything was gone – stools, chairs, cots, clothes, toys, and even the kerosene lamps. Only the penetrating smell of the fuel remained. He wondered if someone tried to set the place on fire.

"What happened to all the people?"

Badbar was a Muslim village. They must have been in a hurry to reach the transit center to make their way to Pakistan, he thought, hoping no one was harmed on the way by zealous religious mobs. He was overwhelmed by the eerie surroundings. He sat down on a cot in the front yard and started imagining the horror that must have happened here only a few hours earlier. He had heard rumors of communal clashes in some distant villages when he had woken up that morning but never imagined a scene like this in his own area. He started wondering.

Not all the inhabitants were Muslims. There were a few Hindu and Sikh families in the predominantly Muslim village. So why did they flee? Where did they go? He wondered. Badbar must have become a dangerous place to hang around. Anything could happen. Better leave, he thought.

As he was about to leave the neighbor's house, Seva heard a faint sound. He looked around. I must be hearing things. There is no one in the house. Maybe I am too spooked, he thought, and started to get up to go back to his own house in the nearby village of Bahadurpur before darkness set in.

He heard another sound, this time unmistakably human. It was coming from the corner room, which was dark and windowless. Seva started looking inside the dark room and, when his eyes adjusted to the lack of light, he finally saw the silhouette of a person. Then he heard the sobbing sound of a teenage girl.

Seva was soon looking into the eyes of a young woman who was wrapped in a brick red sheet adorned with flowers, a typical Punjabi fabric called "fulkari."

"Please do not hurt me, please! I will do whatever you want. I will clean your house, sweep your floors, haul water from the well, but please do not kill me."

"I will not harm you. You must believe me. I want to help you. I will take you to my village and give you food and water. My mother will take care of you. Hurry, let us leave before it gets dark. It is dangerous here. On the way, if someone asks, I will tell him you are my daughter. By the way, what is your name?"

"My name is Reshma but please tell anyone who asks that my name is Reva (a Hindu name). That way I will be safe. They are killing all Muslims," Reshma said while still sobbing and shaking.

"Don't worry Reshma, you are safe with me. No one will bother us when they see this," he pointed at his kirpan, the eighteen-inch curved dagger he always wore on his belt.

"Hurry up. We must go quickly!"

Reshma and Seva started walking towards his village, a good thirty minute walk away from Badbar. No one saw them. No one was around.

Seva was a tall and well-built farmer of thirty-five years of age. He had never received schooling beyond a couple years at a nearby primary school. He lived with his sixty-year-old mother in a small but comfortable house. He had several head of cattle, two oxen, a camel, a milk-bearing water buffalo, essential farm tools, and a new bullock cart. He owned several acres of irrigated land, which he cultivated, with the help of a young Chamaar (a lower caste farm hand) boy. All this made him self-sufficient and qualified him as middle-class by local standards.

Essentially he had been successful enough to support a wife and raise a family. His prospects of finding a wife, however, were low. Although tall and healthy, Seva was not much to look at. He had lost one eye as a child because of a small pox infection. He had no education beyond primary school and had to depend on the village clerk to help him manage his finances. The village clerk, although sweet tongued, was not known for his honesty. Seva never knew whether what sold at the auction was a fair price for his wheat crop and whether the broker's commission he paid was fair and legitimate. In any case, he had few options for financial expertise. Once or twice, he did get some help from a cousin who had a high-school education until the cousin joined the military and moved away.

Seva was not alone in his unsuccessful pursuit of a bride. Many men in the village were in the same situation. Punjab villages had a chronic shortage of women. The male-female ratio was ten males to seven females. This lopsided math meant that three out of ten men had no prospect of finding love. To be sure of finding a bride, you had to be rich, educated, or good looking. If, however, you had all three attributes, you had plenty of prospects. Parents of girls would come knocking on your door.

Seva and Reshma entered his house. Seva firmly bolted the door behind them and proceeded to introduce Reshma to his mother Daani. Before Seva could utter a word, Daani shouted, "You idiot! What have you done? You abducted this Muslim girl from her village. This is not the way to find a wife, stupid! I am trying my best to set you up. I have already identified two good prospects for you. Take this girl back where you found her before they come looking for you, beat you up, and lock you up forever. Worse yet, they will probably kill you before they ask any questions."

"Mother. Calm down. I did not abduct her. Her family had to flee, the whole village of Badbar had to flee, and everyone is gone. I mean everyone including Rahim's family. I assume that they are on their way to the transit center in Talwandi village hoping to go on to Pakistan. I do not even know if they made it safely. They might have been killed enroute," Seva said. "Any attempt to take Reshma to the shelter would be a disaster for both of us. She can't leave," he continued. "I did not touch Reshma. I saved her from real harm. You can ask Reshma herself," he said emphatically.

Reshma nodded in support of Seva's claim. She seemed relieved at the sight of the grandmotherly woman. She started telling Daani the events of the past few hours and pleaded for help to find her parents. Daani gave Reshma some warm milk and other food. Reshma had not eaten for many hours.

Seva went to a friend's house and told him about Reshma. From the friend, he heard rumors of wholesale attacks on Muslim villages and those fleeing to the transit center in Talwandi. The canal only a few miles away was rumored to have many bodies floating in it. The bodies were all Muslims. You could tell from how they dressed.

Word spread in the village that Reshma was at Seva's house. Curious neighbors suspected that Seva had abducted the girl. At his mother's urging, Seva went to the police station, told the constable on duty about Reshma, and asked if they would be of assistance in locating Reshma's parents or news of them? He did not know if they were alive.

"Do you realize you are asking for the impossible? Don't you know what is happening out there? Bodies are being dumped in the canal. No one knows who they are. You are foolish to bring this up. Just keep quiet. Maybe things will settle down someday," the police constable advised Seva.

"Fat chance," the policeman sitting at the next desk said. "I think this is the end of the world as the holy men have predicted for decades," he declared. Then he moved a little closer to Seva, smiled, and asked, "Are you a married man, brother?"

"No, I am not," Seva replied with some shame in his voice.

"Then consider yourself lucky that you found a potential wife and don't even whisper to anyone. By the way, is she pretty? I know some of those Badbar girls are knock outs."

"I will consider your suggestion, sir," Seva replied curtly and returned home. Seva told his mother about the visit to the police station. She agreed it was best to stay put.

Months passed. No news of Reshma's parents surfaced and no one came looking for her. This was not a surprise. Everyday more and more tales of massacres surfaced with trains packed with dead bodies arriving from Pakistan into Indian railway stations. Stories spread of anxious friends and relatives waiting at railway stations to greet returning loved ones only to find dead bodies inside the trains. The ghastly phenomenon may have been repeated in the other direction (India to Pakistan), but I did not hear those reports. With such genocide occurring all over the country, no one had any interest in locating the parents of a young Muslim woman.

With each passing day, Reshma adjusted to the reality that perhaps she would never see her parents again, and that they may not even be alive. If they were, they would have made an effort to locate the daughter they left behind.

Daani was good to Reshma. She let her do the cooking and serve the food. The regimen of this household was not strange for Reshma. She had eaten exactly the same food and spoken the same language in her home as at Seva's house. They shared identical culture, civic manners, and just about everything except religion. She bonded with Seva's mother who was acting now as a surrogate mother.

DREAMING OF A BRIDE

Years passed. No news of her parents emerged. Reshma had now accepted the inevitable. Danni's health was deteriorating and had suddenly taken a turn for the worse. One afternoon after returning from the fields where she and Reshma had gone to deliver fresh food to Seva and his helper, Daani collapsed on her bed and died.

Seva and Reshma were alone now. Thoughts of taking Reshma as his bride soon filled his head as he remembered the police constable's advice. Seva wanted to bring up the issue of marriage to Reshma, but he did not know how to approach her. He was a shy man and he never acquired the vocabulary to express such intimate thoughts. He sought advice from a married friend, and one day shortly afterwards, he approached Reshma on the subject. To his surprise and delight, Reshma, now twenty-two years old, did not get upset or angry. She responded in a measured and thoughtful way.

"It is not crazy to think about our future, our lives together," she said, "but there are obstacles, as you know. We are of different religions. The community will never accept a marriage. Some people will be outright hostile".

Seva had no answer to this. Reshma thought for a while and said, "But we can go to Patiala (2) and ask for a marriage certificate from a clerk of the court. The court clerk can pronounce us man and wife. Then people will accept us once we can show them that we are legally married under the Angrez (British) laws."

"You are not only pretty but also smart," Seva exulted. This was the first time Seva had said that she was pretty. Reshma smiled then wiped her tears with the corner of her chunni (headscarf).

The next week, accompanied by a high-school student who presumably knew English, Seva went to the court in Patiala and asked the clerk to marry him and Reshma.

"Not a chance, Mister," the clerk replied. "Under the British Law, which is still the law of the land despite the fact that British are gone, a wedding between people of different religious faiths is not valid," he said. In addition, as a proof, he shoved the English document into Seva's face knowing fully well that Seva could not read. Seva was disappointed, but he was not about to challenge the British Crown. He thanked the clerk and went home dejected.

He had another idea. He would ask the Sikh priest in nearby Sangrur City to marry them in a Sikh ceremony. The priest was sympathetic to his cause but told him the same thing. A marriage between a Sikh man and a Muslim woman would not receive the Guru's blessing, he said, although he did not know. This was his own interpretation, he admitted. As Seva turned to leave, the priest had an idea.

"Reshma can change her first name to a Sikh name, renounce her religion, and become a Sikh in the presence of two others and the Adi Granth (Holy Book). Then we can perform the marriage," he declared.

Seva returned home, full of hope, but he had to convince Reshma to accept this. He was not going to force her. After a long discussion and with reluctance, Reshma agreed.

Preparations were begun for Reshma to adopt a new name and religion so she could marry Seva. He decided that it had to be a low-key affair, simple, and fast. When the Sangrur City priest seemed reluctant to perform the ceremony, Seva decided to go to Patiala, which is a city larger than Sangrur and the capital of the famous princely state of Patiala. More importantly, Patiala had a large and historic Sikh temple, many resources, and a head priest who could decide things.

Seva planned the event in an efficient way. Reshma would receive the Amrit (the baptism nectar) and then change her name. Then on the same day, they would be married in a simple ceremony in the presence of the Granthi (the Sikh Priest) at the historic temple.

All went as planned. Reshma took the name of Sharan Kaur, which means Guru's shelter. Sharan is perhaps the most famous and prestigious historic name for a Sikh woman (3). The priest pronounced them man and wife and congratulated them. He gave them a handwritten wedding certificate with his signature and the time and date of the ceremony. The certificate listed Sikh as the religion for both of them. He then told Seva that with that paper, he could go back to the court in Sangrur if he wanted and the British law will not stand in his way. Seva considered it unnecessary. The court clerk did not outrank the priest in his estimation. Why bother, he thought.

Seva was ecstatic. He decided to remain in Patiala for a few more days. That would be their honeymoon. While in Patiala, he took his bride to dinner and a movie at the new theater in town. The movie turned out to be a tearjerker as many Bollywood movies are. She cried all the time because it was quite an experience for her. She had never been to a movie before and neither had Seva.

Seva was on top of the world. His life changed for the better. They started going to movies every month in the nearby city of Sangrur. He started wearing nicer clothes. Sharan convinced him to cut down on his alcohol consumption. He adored Sharan and why not? While three out of ten men in the village could never find a bride, not only did he have one, but she was a trophy wife. Heads turned when Sharan walked with him, although she was always three or four feet behind him as the custom dictated. No catcalls followed – perhaps because Seva always had a Kirpan on his belt.

Seva worshipped Sharan. He thought that the gods must have smiled on him, although he could not think of a reason why. He discussed having children with her and promised that if they had a son, he would send him to a school and not involve him in farming as his father and grandfather had done before him. He promised Sharan that one day he would take her to the Golden Temple in the fabulous city of Amritsar (the pool of nectar).

Seva kept that promise. The next year's wheat crop was the best in five years and the price it fetched on the open market was high. Seva was flush with rupees. Not only did he take Sharan to Amritsar, but he also took her on an extended trip to see more of India, which he himself had never had the opportunity to do. He took Sharan to Hyderabad Deccan in Southern India where one of the five holiest Sikh shrines is located. They both enjoyed the long trip.

TROUBLE IN PARADISE

One day in April, when Seva was examining his wheat crop which would soon be harvested and bring him another good year of income, a man came running and told him, "Seva, you better come home. The police are looking for you. There are five or six of them including a police lady and a man in white clothes. They have two jeeps. They want you there in a hurry."

Seva ran as fast he could and froze at what he saw when he reached home. The uniformed men including one in white civilian clothes had surrounded his house and were questioning Sharan who was crying. Seva tried to console her but was stopped by two policemen. The man in white said, "You are living in sin with this woman. Your marriage in null and void. For one thing, she is of a different religion and secondly it looks like you abducted her. You are lucky. We will not press abduction charges against you, but we must return this lady to her relatives in Pakistan." The man who said this was apparently a Pakistani representative belonging to the Repatriation Commission, (4) according to a villager.

"You cannot do that, sir. I did not abduct her. I rescued her, gave her shelter, and married her in accordance with the religious edicts and in accordance with British laws. She does not have any relatives in Pakistan. Her parents must have been killed while fleeing; otherwise, they would have made the effort to reunite with their daughter. They knew exactly where to look for her." Seva challenged the man in white clothes.

"Well, she does have an uncle in Pakistan. His name is Sher Khan. You should know that it has taken five years to implement a procedure to locate people left abandoned. We are now reuniting families on both sides of the border," said the man in white.

Sharan interrupted him, "Sir, I do not have an uncle named Sher Khan. I knew all my relatives in Badbar. I was almost an adult when the horrible things happened. I do not know who this Sher Khan is who wants me in Pakistan, but he is not a relative and even if he is, I am settled here. I love my husband and we are happy. Moreover, I will not be accepted in Pakistan by any relatives once they know I am married to a man of a different faith. I will be a pariah," she said emphatically while wiping away her tears.

"Madam, this is our mandate. We must send you to Pakistan where the rest of your people are and where you belong. This is the understanding reached between the two countries to unite uprooted families."

The lady police officer seemed sympathetic to Sharan's pleas. She asked the man in white if Sharan could be an exception under the circumstances.

The man in white shook his head in a negative way and motioned to the officers to transport Sharan in one of the police jeeps. Sharan started screaming as more villagers gathered. Seva grabbed Sharan to break her away from the police officers and the white clothed man who was helping Sharan to get in the vehicle.

"Get this idiot off her," the man in white shouted. The policemen started to drag Seva away from Sharan. The man in white then yelled that Seva was reaching for his Kirpan. All the policemen, except the lady, jumped on Seva, wrestled him to ground, and started pummeling him with their fists. Seva was moaning in pain while yelling, "Please do not take Sharan away. Do not take my wife away." Then he started yelling obscenities at the police. The police lady covered her ears with her hands. The beating continued until Seva stopped resisting. He was barely moving.

With help of the lady officer, Sharon was put into the jeep between the man in white and the police lady. The jeep sped off, leaving a cloud of thick brown dust behind. Seva was lying in the dirt, moaning and pleading, "Please do not take Sharan away!"

PARADISE LOST

Seva was a desperate and lonely man again. For days, he would not come out of his house. He became a recluse. He started drinking every day and began to lose weight. His crops failed. The farm hand who worked for him was not able to manage all the work, so he leased his land to a neighbor who farmed it for him and gave him a share of the profit.

Seva lived for seven more years. He never heard anything from Sharan. One day he was found dead at his house from natural causes. He was only forty-seven years old.

Author's note: There are no historical references to this story. Nonetheless, this happened in my mother's village near Mastuana where I spent much of my childhood during and after the partition of 1947. This story is like one of thousands and would have barely merited mention in a newspaper.

End Notes:

1) Badbar today is a thriving village resettled mostly by displaced refugees from Pakistan in 1947. Displaced individuals were allocated land by the Indian Government as compensation for the land they left behind when they fled to the Indian side. Badbar now has a population of approximately 7,000 Sikhs and Hindus and is seventy-two percent literate according to the 2011 Indian census (www.census2011.co.in)

2) Patiala (Punjabi: ਪਟਿਆਲਾ) is a city in southeastern Punjab. It is the administrative capital of Patiala District. Formerly a princely state, Patiala was ruled by the Jat Sikh Maharaja Narendra Singh from 1845 to 1862. He fortified the city by constructing ramparts and ten gates. The Patiala Royal house is now headed by His Highness Captain Amarinder Singh, who served as the Chief Minister of Punjab from 2002 to 2007. The Patiala Royals command great respect and loyalty among the public.

3) Sharan Kaur Pabla was a Sikh martyr who, according to several Sikh historians, was slain in 1705 by Mughal soldiers while cremating the bodies of two older sons of Guru Gobind Singh, the 10th Sikh Guru.

4) In the aftermath of the genocide, both India and Pakistan agreed to restore women abducted or abandoned on both sides of the border. The Indian government claimed that 33,000 Hindu and Sikh women were abducted, and the Pakistani government claimed that 50,000 Muslim women were abducted during the 1947 riots. By 1954, according to one estimate, there were 20,728 recovered Muslim women and 9,032 Hindu and Sikh women recovered from Pakistan *(Borders & boundaries: women in India's partition – Ritu Menon, Kamla Bhasi. Google Books (24 April 1993).* Many refused to be repatriated for fear of rejection by their families for cohabitation with members of other religions.

CHAPTER 8

BRING YOUR OWN BOWL

No one knew his real name. Not his first name, middle name, or his last name. Not having a middle name was no big deal. Very few Indians had middle names, but not having a last name is unusual, even in India.

He must have had a last name. The last name defines who you are in India's social hierarchy – your status; your education, career, and marriage prospects; your business and professional associations; where you lived; what you ate; how you dressed, etc.

My family and the other villagers called him Boda ("Toothless") as he had lost most of his teeth when he was a child. No one knew how. It could have been tooth decay from a bacterial infection. On the other hand, perhaps he had his teeth knocked out in a fight or a fall.

The reason no longer mattered. Boda had accepted his lot in life. Not once did he complain or ask people to use his real name, whatever it was. He saw no point to it. He never went to school, where someone would need to know his real name for record keeping or issuing him a certificate. He had no police or medical records. He just accepted this as inevitable and ordained by the Lord, although he was not positive which deity was responsible for his welfare and upkeep.

I asked him on more than one occasion what was his religion. This was not an impolite inquiry as everyone in India had a religion. Religion, along with your last name, also helped determine one's social status, one's existence. Without religion, you were nobody. Even the lowest caste "Shudra" people, known as "untouchables" in the Indian social order, had a religion.

Ultimately, I discovered the reason for his ambivalence. He simultaneously belonged to not one, but two religions. He was a combination of Sikh and Hindu, which in India's present, more hardened social order, may seem odd. This was common in Punjab State seventy years ago. Hindus and Sikhs did not go out of their way to differentiate themselves from each other. This "not sure of religion" classification was successful in maintaining community harmony. Unless there was an issue of caste. A caste difference always trumped religious differences.

Boda was a young boy when I first met him. My mother, upon the recommendation of my uncle, had just hired Boda. His job was to be a farm hand and an errand boy.

He was thought to be about twelve years old at that time. No one could ascertain his real age, as happened with many kids in the village. We did have an old man whose job was to keep track of births and deaths in the town and to apprise people of their age and their birth dates. Unfortunately, the old man suffered from poor vision, a fading memory, and inadequate writing skills. When you asked him someone's age, he would make a calculated guess. He was usually correct.

Before hiring him, my mother wanted to subject Boda to this local procedure but she soon found a better solution. Quite by chance, at that time, some government people happened to be in town to update the ten-year census. Questioning the census taker would be a good way to ascertain Boda's age, she thought. The census taker had superior techniques to determine people's ages so he agreed to estimate Boda's age.

He examined Boda's less-than-perfect teeth, thought for a while, and declared that the boy was twelve. The census taker regularly used this technique (teeth inspection) to estimate the ages of people without birth certificates. He knew that farmers used the same technique when purchasing cows and water buffalo at cattle fairs.

The census taker's verdict satisfied my mother, as it was good enough for her purpose. She needed a reasonable estimate of Boda's age so she could determine his compensation. A worker's age was a more important factor than his skills in this computation. Other than for payment purposes, Boda's age or his birthdate were of little significance. Indians of that day were not concerned about child labor. In Boda's situation, working for my mother, his duties would be considered light labor.

Although the distinction between being a Sikh or a Hindu in a Punjab village was unimportant, I still wanted to know which religious sect he followed. Boda's answer to this quandary thrilled and charmed me.

"Sardarji (Chief), I am the same as you are," he replied with a grin. I felt silly but delighted and wished we were the same.

He was implying that he was also a Sikh, but we both knew that there was a wide gulf between us. He came from the Chamaar caste, which meant he was an untouchable (a Dalit in today's polished Indian jargon). Boda occupied a very low spot in the caste hierarchy prescribed by Manu, the caste architect.

Manusmriti (मनुस्मृति), the Indian Caste Primer

Manusmriti, the Holy Scripture dictated by the great Manu about two thousand years ago, has **been described as the Law of Society and the Standard Point of Reference for all future Hindu behavior.** The manuscript is impressive in its size, the range of social issues addressed, and scholarship. The text was translated into English by Sir William Jones in 1794. Manu's document has drawn praise from some scholars, including Wilhelm Nietzsche, the noted German philosopher and cultural critic. Nietzsche, however, disagreed with Manu's class division.

The "Manu totem pole" places Brahmins on the apex and the others below in the following descending order.

Brahmins (priests, scholars)

Kshatriyas (warriors)

Vaishyas (merchants, workers)

Shudras (servants and subordinates to the upper classes)

Manu did not put women in a separate category, but he did not spare them. Derogatory comments about women are plentiful in Manu's text.

On the Manu social scale, Boda would have been placed in the Shudra class. Some Manu followers were so enamored with the utility of the caste system that they decided to split the untouchable class even further. In North India, the untouchable Chamaars* were placed higher in social order than an even more untouchable group called Choohras (Punjabi: ਚੁੜ੍ਹਾ) or Bhanghis who were assigned to clean human waste and handle animal carcasses, the absolute bottom level of the caste pyramid. On this expanded scale, Boda, by being a Chamaar, would have been a little more touchable than had he been a Choohra.

Apart from being a notch higher than a Choohra on the social scale, Boda's physical appearance also made him more acceptable to the three classes above him. He was a handsome boy with a lighter complexion when compared to most of the other villagers, and shy but witty in his own way. He was proficient in carrying out his responsibilities and well mannered.

BRITISH ROLE IN CASTE SEGREGATION

The British have earned both praise and criticism for their handling of the caste issue. They made no effort to change the caste system, but they provided opportunities to the lower castes in the British army in India and even promoted some of them to the Officer ranks. On balance, however, the British, to whom social classification was not alien, promoted caste divisions. They were comfortable with a divided population based on economic, religious, social class, and family status. They needed the caste system to help them maintain their hold in India, which was for many years the British Empire's most valuable and populous possession.

The arrival of the British, nevertheless, created opportunities in the military for the lower castes. Grabbing this opportunity, the untouchables, especially the Choohras who were on the bottom, developed a reputation as good soldiers. British recruiters actively sought "Mazhabi" (Choohra) Sikhs and a special elite regiment composed of Choohra Sikhs was created. The division was named the "Mazhabhi Sikh Regiment" and later renamed the Sikh Light Infantry of the Indian Army. Chamaars like Boda were also attracted to the military where they usually found instant elevation in their status and life style.

Under the influence of the Christian missionaries and with the support of the British army, a majority of Choohra Sikhs converted to Christianity. Low caste Hindus also adopted Christianity, although in lesser numbers.

THE CONTRACT

Boda's contract with my family was simple and informal. He would receive no cash, but would earn a share of the crop yield (almost all in wheat). The crop sharing process was transparent as wheat was sold on the open market where everyone could see the amount auctioned and the price. His contract included two additional provisions. My family would cover the cost of his clothing and provide him with food. The clothing and food bonus did not extend to his family though. Nevertheless, Boda was happy with his contract and especially with his clothing allowance which allowed him to dress better than his peers. He wore the same style of clothing as the other higher caste kids. His food was the same as ours, which meant that it was much better than what his own family could afford to feed him.

Boda ate his meals at our house at the same time as we did. Rather than take his food to his home, he chose to eat at our house when the food was still hot (highly recommended when eating Indian food). This allowed him to have second helpings, which he enjoyed. By eating before going home, he was also available to perform a variety of after-dinner chores for my mother.

There was one complication. Boda, being a Chamaar, was not allowed to use our kitchen utensils, as was the custom in our village. Once used by a Chamaar, the utensil would become unfit for use by persons of higher castes. This was not our rule, but was dictated by our society. A utensil used by an untouchable could not be "reclaimed" by washing with soap and hot water according to the Laws of Society. Only another untouchable would be permitted to use such a utensil. A valuable metal object touched by a low caste Shudra, however, could be purified by annealing it in flame and then cleaning it with sand and soap.

Boda offered an easy solution to this problem. He would maintain his own brass bowl in the tool shed in our house. He would clean the bowl after every meal, sometimes with silica sand that was always on hand, dry it, and carefully tuck it in the corner where he also kept a change of clothing and some other valuables. One reason he would take such meticulous care of his brass bowl was that it was an expensive article, hand carved, and very ornate. My mother had given him the bowl on the day of signing of his employment contract in an effort to demonstrate that he would be treated as part of our family. There was a mutual understanding that because he was a Chamaar, he was expected to use his own utensils (on one occasion my mother confided to my brothers and sisters that she felt bad about this custom, but she did not have the stamina or the resources to challenge the system.)

Apart from dealing with such issues and supporting his family, Boda worried about the safety of his sister Bholi ("Novice"). Bholi was a beautiful girl as were many Chamaar girls. She was maybe thirteen years old when Boda first started working for us, but she looked much older. This was proving worrisome to Boda and his ailing father (Boda's mother had passed away a few years earlier). The fair-complexioned Chamaar girls were the target of well-to-do Jat property owners who lusted after them and did not hesitate to molest them if they spotted them working in the sugar cane fields. They considered the Chamaar girls fair game because of their lower social status. While the untouchability stigma did not apply in molestation cases, this brutal behavior sometimes led to violence. There may have been laws against raping a Chamaar girl, but I do not recall an occasion where there was a conviction or other serious punishment for committing such a crime.

Boda need not have worried. There were no reports or rumors of any attempts of molesting Bholi. One reason could be that besides being pretty, Bholi was also intelligent and wise.

RAYS OF HOPE

Boda started working for my family just as my elder brother entered junior college. I was still in high school and my sister, Nikki, was pursuing a Public Health Nursing degree at the nearby Miss Brown Christian Medical College in Ludhiana, Punjab.

In our classes, we were reading books on history and social behavior in other parts of the world. As a result, we started challenging age-old practices in our community that seemed illogical and discriminatory. Simultaneously, several Hindu reformist movements, among them the powerful "Arya Samaj," started speaking out against the caste system. These ideas raised our awareness of Boda's brass bowl custom.

In the summer when Nikki was home, we engaged in a debate about the untouchability system and decided to rebel. That evening after dinner, we confronted our father, a religious scholar, and asked him to explain Manu's caste system. He was delighted to enlighten us. Knowing much about ancient Indian history, religions, and Hindu philosophy, he confessed that he did not think much of the Manu's caste system. To support his opinions, he read dreadful Manusmriti passages thought to be particularly offensive.

We were horrified! Almost in unison, we questioned him about Boda's plight and proposed that the practice be ended.

My father had no ready answer. He went into his usual pensive mood when confronted with such controversial issues. After a while, he said, "It should not be like this. I am glad that you have raised the issue. Talk to your mother about this." He then proceeded to take his usual seat under the shady Neem tree in our backyard to read his thick leather bound, "Mahan-Kosh," the Punjabi language encyclopedia.

"Talk to your mother" was his standard answer whenever he was confronted with a complex and sensitive issue. He respected my mother and referred all such complexities to her, knowing that she could tackle hard problems. She always came through.

At his suggestion, we talked with my mother who belonged to a very conservative, but reformist, Sikh movement. This faction emphasized the Sikh Guru's stand against the caste system. We asked her, "If we do not believe in the caste system, why then are we paranoid about Boda using our utensils and demanding that he carry his own bowl? Maybe he does not have to sit down with us to eat, but why couldn't he just grab one of the dishes in the pile at meal time?"

My mother was caught off-guard. She did not have an answer, although I knew she agreed with us. Finally, she managed to answer.

"You know, I agree with you, but the rest of the village does not. We can work slowly to change the practice, but if we push too fast, we could alienate the neighbors and become ostracized ourselves. This could also be dangerous for Boda. Let us work out the solution carefully and slowly."

The issue came to a conclusion sooner than anticipated. One week later was the birthday of Guru Nanak, founder of the Sikh religion. For a Sikh, this is the most auspicious day and must be celebrated with great joy and enthusiasm. There had to be festive clothing and fancier food than at other times. On such occasions, my mother made everyone's favorite dessert, kheer (a rice-milk pudding).

Kheer was on the top of Boda's list of culinary preferences. When my mother made this dessert, she made sure there was plenty for Boda. She topped it with extra pistachios and slivered almonds.

That evening, Boda came to dinner dressed for the occasion. He wore his shiny blue Sanforized cotton shirt (*Sanforization is* a treatment used for cotton textiles). Everyone sat down for the meal. Before he took his usual seat on the floor, Boda went to the tool shed to fetch his prized brass bowl. To his horror, it was not there. He looked all around but found no bowl. It had vanished. Someone had stolen it. His bowl was gone. This was a disaster! How was he going to eat his meal on this holy day?

By the time of his return, we had started eating, using my mother's ornate dishes. These dishes had been a part of her dowry and were reserved for such occasions.

Boda told my mother that he had no bowl. This presented a quandary to my mother. What could she give to him on the most auspicious day of the year? She scanned the remaining utensils. Nothing matched the quality and the luster of the utensils in front of us. There were no spare bowls in her cabinet to suit the occasion. After some thought, she rose and headed for the back room. We looked at each other with surprise and alarm. What was she up to? As we wondered, we sat motionless until she reappeared. She was clutching a beautiful bowl – a seven-inch diameter bronze utensil carved on the outside with anarkali (pomegranate) leaves. The ornate bowl was more magnificent than the ones she had offered to us. She headed straight for Boda, handed him the ornate bowl and said,

"Now young man, take good care of this bowl. My mother gave me three of these jewels as part of my wedding dowry. This one is yours. Don't you let anyone steal it from you! Next week I will take you to the shop so you can get a lock for the storeroom. You must promise to keep your bowl locked and remember this bowl is for special occasions like today. This is not for your daily meals." Boda looked at her with apprehension, wondering what he was going to use for the everyday meal.

My mother continued, "From now on, when you want to eat, you grab any utensil from the pile and after eating, rinse it and put it in the dirty dishes pile like everybody else. Remember, you are not any more or less special than anyone else here." She winked as she said this.

The three of us shrieked in unison and started clapping. Boda was speechless. He grabbed the bowl, stared at it, and started to bow down to touch her feet, as was the way respect was shown. My mother took a half step back, lifted him off the ground, and embraced him in a hug of the kind reserved only for her own children.

Boda hesitated but made no effort to break away. He had not felt such a touch since his own mother had passed away. He did not say a word. He just cried. He had no words because he had not been schooled in the verbal or written etiquette of expressing thanks.

Even if he had been schooled in ways of giving thanks, there are not many words for thanks in the Punjabi vocabulary. (In the Indian culture, gratitude is to be felt and expressed through emotion and body language, not verbalized.) He did not need to say thanks. His eyes spoke for him. He just looked in my mother's eyes and sobbed. We clapped. A taboo had been broken!

YEARS LATER

Time passed and Boda faded from my memory. Then, in 2010, while visiting my birth village, I recalled his connection with my family. I wondered aloud if anyone in the village knew what happened to him. Where did he end up? How was he doing? No one seemed to know.

Sitting in the old creaky porch of my parent's home, I kept wondering: did he just disappear among the vast Indian population, relocate somewhere far off, find a job as a busboy in a restaurant in Delhi or Bombay, or did he adopt a respectable Brahmin name and declared himself upper class? This probably never occurred to him. He must have believed that it was not possible. At least not in Boda's India.

As luck would have it, the day before I was to leave the village a neighbor arrived and told me that many years back Boda had found an opportunity with the military. Somehow, he learned about the fabled Sikh Light Infantry composed entirely of Untouchables. The Sikh Light Infantry had earned many decorations for their heroic deeds when fighting in WWII under British command.

Apparently, Boda had joined the 10th Regiment of the Sikh Light Infantry. Soon afterwards, following the marriage of his sister Bholi, his father moved away leaving no clues to the family's whereabouts. I asked the neighbor if he had Boda's picture. He smiled and said, "You should know we don't have such fancy things around here, but you can imagine what he would look like. He would have looked very impressive as a military man. He was a good-looking boy."

I thanked the neighbor for the update, but kept wondering how he would really look today.

I hope Boda had a good life in the military. There, I know, he would not have to worry about supplying his own bowl.

PS: I am still trying to locate Boda and hope he is alive. He would have

117

retired from the army a long time ago. I would like to see his picture in the Infantry uniform. I am sure he looked magnificent!

I have not given up my search. I could try searching internet or military records, but I do not know his last name or his true first name.

*In today's India, Chamaars have made much progress, but a Chooras's lot has not improved to the same extent despite some legal protections and job opportunities with large corporations. While some may have been successful in throwing off the yoke of caste classifications, many Chooras are still engulfed in the age-old struggle as evident from the periodic Dalit riots in today's India.

CHAPTER 9

SEINFELD IN EVERY VILLAGE

When I first arrived in America, people would ask me, "Do Indians enjoy humor as much as Americans do? Are there comedy clubs in India and can you tell us a few Indian jokes?" I always hesitated. My English was not good enough to translate Indian humor and, humor does not translate unless you know the two cultures equally well. I would try to convince people, often unsuccessfully, that Indians enjoyed humor as much as anyone else and perhaps more, although I could only speak for my home state of Punjab. There, almost every village had what you could call a comedy club, a gathering place to share impromptu puns, mild insults, and "did you hear" anecdotes. My village had such a place, but the best one was in my mother's village, Bahadurpur, where I spent many of my summers. Much of the village humor was derived from everyday insignificant occurrences in life in the manner of the *Seinfeld* show, so named for Jerry Seinfeld, a popular US comedian. Often the humor was based on an individual's shortcomings or the absurdities of daily life. Sometimes it was crude and bordered on cruel. Occasionally the humor was delivered as poetry, a more cherished form of joke telling. (1)

THE BBSC CLUB

I had heard about the Bahadurpur village gossip society for years. It was the unorganized comedy club. There was no name for this organization. After my first visit to this "no name" fraternity, I decided to call it BCC, the Bahadurpur Comedy Club. After gaining English language proficiency in America I decided to rename it as the BBS; Bahadurpur Bull Shit Club. At the BBS club, members discussed politics, scandals, and rumors; but making fun of insignificant daily occurrences, *Seinfeld* style, was their forte.

Bahadurpur had no village square, plaza, or meeting hall to accommodate community gatherings. There was a religious temple, but the BBS club was not welcome there. Club members, however, found a home for their gatherings. It was the village entry gate called Darwaza-meaning gateway. The village Darwaza was a replica of the grand arched Mughal gateways, modest in size but ornate.

A village gate in Punjab

Every visitor to Bahadurpur had to pass through the Darwaza to enter the village interior. All modes of traffic, including pedestrians, bullock carts, camels, and an occasional motor vehicle flowed through the gate. On each side of the covered passage was a brick platform where villagers sat. Some brought their own cushions. The more comfort-minded people brought a stool or a chair. Darwaza served as the community hall for game contests, village council meetings, and impromptu gatherings. It was well suited for the evening or Sunday afternoon meetings of the BBS club.

As a youth, I was not allowed to attend the BBS sessions because the material was often R-rated (but never X-rated). Children passed through the Darwaza all the time but did not stop. Women also went by and the mature ones partially covered their faces in deference to stares from the elderly men. The term "dirty old men" was occasionally whispered. Young women and old ladies felt no reason to cover their faces, but the married women felt the necessity to partially cover their faces, and let the men guess who they were. To facilitate identification, the women walked slowly and unobtrusively through the gate. Neither party ever admitted the existence of this silent hide and seek sport, so obvious to any casual observer. Club members usually lowered the volume and cleaned up their vocabulary when youngsters and ladies were passing through.

WHEN NATURE CALLS

My first visit to the BBS club happened by chance. I was on my way to my relatives' home when I passed through the Darwaza. About twenty-five men were huddled under brown blankets around a coal-fired stove positioned on the larger of the two brick platforms. With my brown blanket, I blended in and squatted on the platform like everyone else.

A tall funny man was telling a story. He looked a bit odd and wore an oversized turban. Someone called him Nihala (the happy one). Nihala cleared his throat and started, "Gentlemen, last month I attended an unusual wedding in the neighboring village; the one where folks are only half as intelligent as we are in our village." Everyone looked around to guess which town he was referring. He continued, "The two priests belonging to different religious congregations competed against each other to perform the wedding ceremony. The older and more experienced priest proposed an elaborate ancient ceremony. The younger one favored a simpler and less sumptuous affair. He considered himself modern. The father of the groom awarded the event to the younger priest because it would be less costly. The older priest did not take rejection kindly. He was furious. He felt humiliated, but he did not show it. This was a small, close-knit community. He had to preserve his reputation. He swallowed his pride, congratulated the father of the groom, and promised to fully cooperate and participate in the joyous occasion. Internally, however, the old man was seething and vowed to avenge his humiliation.

"On the day of the wedding, the humiliated old priest showed up before the start of the ceremony. He greeted guests and congratulated the mother and father of the groom. He then asked that he be allowed to serve ceremonial tea as a gesture of goodwill from the bride's side because he was the bride's family priest.

"Spiced tea was served to guests before the ceremony started. The older priest insisted that he personally serve the tea to the groom and his father in

121

ornate ceremonial cups. His gesture was appreciated. The old priest went inside the kitchen and without anyone noticing, slipped a calculated amount of an herbal extract into the two cups reserved for the groom and his father.

"The music started as the colorfully dressed musicians started plucking the harmonium key board. The drummer tightened the goat hide on his dholak to get the desired sound. The groom, his father, the bride, and their guests assumed their assigned positions on the heavily cushioned and carpeted floor.

"A few people sitting in the front noticed that the groom seemed fidgety. Every new couple goes through 'buyer's remorse', they thought. They disregarded their initial apprehensions, but then noticed that the groom was growing more uncomfortable by the minute. They saw him whisper to his father who was sitting behind him.

"The father came on to the stage and announced, 'Ladies and gentlemen, there will be a slight delay in the ceremony. The groom has a minor medical emergency. Nothing to worry about, he will be back in a few minutes. Please have another cup of tea, munch on the snacks, and listen to the beautiful music. The ceremony will resume soon.' The guests followed his instructions and began to enjoy a little chitchat.

"The groom rose and exited the large tent that housed the ceremony. His older brother, who understood the nature of the urgency, followed. As soon as the groom cleared the property line, he started galloping across the field in search of a bush as the herbal extract churned inside his stomach."

Nihala, the storyteller, took a breather at this point and commented, "Can you imagine the dressed up groom wearing a shiny Sehra Crown and a flowered pink tunic galloping towards a bush to answer the call of nature?" The club members shook their heads in disgust. He continued.

"The groom reappeared from behind a bush after a couple of minutes. Uniting with his brother, the two headed back to the ceremony with a quick stop at an animal pond on their way to freshen up. The guests were patiently waiting. Everyone breathed a sigh of relief. None of them witnessed the race in the field.

"The music began with a big thump of the drum. The ceremony began and proceeded without a hitch until the groom's father felt a pang. The herbal extract in his tea began to affect him. Without saying a word, he motioned to the head musician to slow down the progress a little until further notice. He then quietly slipped out of the tent and made the same dash to the fields as his son. He moved more quickly than his son did. As soon as he could, he returned to the ceremony and motioned to the head musician to speed up the process. He suggested that the musicians should skip a few of the hymns and begin the marriage vows. The father was an experienced man and knew that an herbal aftershock could hit at any time. The strategy worked. The couple exchanged vows. The old priest, with a heavenly glow on his face, congratulated the couple."

GAS TRAPPER

On my second visit to the BBS club, members were engaged in a heated discussion when I entered. I sat down on the carpeted floor. Our neighbor, "Lakkha" (meaning a deci-millionaire), introduced me to the group. "Gentlemen, this is the young man I told you about. Next month he is going to Bihar province to assume his duties as an engineer at the big chemical factory that has just been constructed. Never before has any of our alumni gone anywhere farther than two hundred miles, not even to Delhi to see a moving picture, let alone to take up an engineering position. This is some achievement. We need more young men like Jas to make us proud!"

Everyone clapped and a barrage of questions followed. Foremost among the inquiries were such questions as: How much money I would earn? What benefits would I receive? Would I be given a house with electricity? Who would cook for me because I did not have a wife? Shouldn't I get married first?

I warded off the pay issue saying I would not know exactly what was my pay scale and the benefits until I arrived there, but yes, I would have company accommodations with electricity. As to how I would manage the food, I was not worried. It would work out.

The focus next turned to work attire. To my dismay, everyone seemed to be staring at my long khaki pants. "What will you wear at work?" someone asked. Before I could answer, a young man named Sohna answered the question, "When you are an engineer, you always wear the 'Fart Trapper', either white or brown, depending on your rank."

Before the laughter died, a serious looking middle-aged man said, "That is a shame because the gas trapper is not comfortable clothing. It must be hot inside, but most of all, it is not airy and ventilated. How do you even stay in it for hours?"

I realized now that this was a "Roast" (an event where a guest of honor, is subjected to good-natured jokes to amuse the audience) and not an ordinary sendoff. I should have suspected this.

"Yes, it is not as comfortable as the village dhoti" (2), I admitted, "but it looks sharp and there are opportunities for ventilation. For example, when you answer nature's calls, and when you come home, the first thing you do is to toss off the Trapper.

"I say the dhoti is still preferable, comfortable, cheap, and easy to take on and off," the middle-aged man said. Then he proceeded to show how to tie and untie the Punjabi dhoti called Bhotha. He untied the Bhotha he was wearing, exposing his underwear, a G-string like undergarment called Janghia. Then as quickly as he had untied the Botha, he tied it again with a simple double knot to demonstrate the efficiency of the village wear. Everyone agreed that dhoti was a smarter choice. Nevertheless, they agreed that for me, an engineer, the less comfortable fart trapper was appropriate.

The discussion of the appropriate dress was not over. Another man, Gunja (bald), raised hand and declared, "Gentlemen if you are going to wear a dhoti make sure you have proper under garments. Let me tell you my experience two weeks ago while travelling on the night train from Ludhiana." He went on with his story, which I decided not to include in this book.

I decided to leave the session after that tale. When I was leaving, I was invited to report to the club on my experiences at my first professional job. I promised I would.

FERTILIZER EXPERT

Things did not go well for me at the Sindri (3) fertilizer factory. The first few weeks were interesting. I learned new things. My first paycheck was good enough for me to live a lifestyle well above the average citizen in the area. I was meeting foreigners for the first time in my life. The fertilizer factory was built by an Italian engineering firm called Montecatini. At the time of my arrival, it was undergoing full-scale trial runs and was soon to be handed over to the Indian management team. I enjoyed getting to know several Italians who were looking forward to going home soon after the factory was handed over to the Indians.

One time several of the Italians invited me to go to Calcutta with them on the weekend to enjoy the Ice Follies show, which was all the rage in Calcutta at the time. On another occasion, they invited me to go with them to the "girly" joints in the big city. Calcutta was full of such places. Visiting girly joints in the company of foreigners was a privilege for a young Indian man like me. The Italians spent freely on entertainment, including my part of the expenses. The foreigners also benefited from my company as I assumed the role of translator and fun-loving escort. Despite such privileges, I was not happy in Bihar. I was homesick for Punjab. I missed the food, my friends, and the gossip. The factory work also had become monotonous and was dangerous to my health. Sometimes I would sit all day on top of the coke ovens that were spewing noxious chemicals into the air. There were no masks or respirators to ward off the toxins.

I started sending resumes in search of better career opportunities. After many rejections, I received a letter from the Khalsa College in Ludhiana promising me a junior lecturer's job to teach chemistry classes. I promptly resigned my fertilizer plant job and headed home to Punjab.

Rumor had spread that I would be coming to Bahadurpur after eight months at the most advanced foreign factory in India. An invitation from the BBS club was already waiting for me. On Sunday after my arrival, I went to the BBS club. I was greeted with enthusiasm. The barrage started immediately. What is a foreign factory like? What do Italians look like? Are they like the English or different? Are they friendly? The club members salivated when I told them I had gone to half a dozen girly joints in Calcutta in the company of the Italians.

"Lucky man," I heard several of them say. Questions about my title, my pay, and what product I was making at the all-important new factory resumed.

"I made ammonium sulfate, a popular fertilizer. It helps grow crops, and thus helps to alleviate food shortages," I said.

A hush fell over the crowd as if I had delivered bad news. One older man wondered aloud, "Did you say you made khaad (fertilizer)? Is that what you do? Frankly, we are surprised. You have a lot potential, son! We have plenty of idiots in the village who can make fertilizer. All they have to do is follow the buffaloes and scoop up the shit as soon as it hits the ground. It does not require a college education," he declared to the concurrence of many.

I was dumbfounded and felt insulted. I wanted to leave but felt obligated to respond. "It is not about gathering buffalo dung," I responded. "Ammonium Sulfate is a chemical, white as a snow (this was not a good simile as none of them had seen snow), and much more effective than buffalo manure. At the factory we can manufacture immense quantities that even one lakh (one hundred thousand) of buffaloes could not produce." My last sentence brought some positive response but not enough.

"Yes, but khaad is still khaad. You have greater potential son," the old man, whose name was Bakshi, reiterated.

To regain respect, I started to say that I had resigned from my fertilizer job to accept a teaching job at the Khalsa College but I thought better.

Becoming a teacher, even as a college lecturer would impress no one in that crowd. Teaching jobs were not prized because they paid a pittance in comparison to Government jobs, which promised under the table payments. I pondered for a few seconds and said, "I am thinking about how I can tap my potential as Uncle Bakshi mentioned. For the next few months I will teach college classes in Ludhiana and then I will go to America where I already have some other prospects" (which was true). A raucous applause erupted. Bakshi Uncle pointed at me and exhorted others to give me another round of applause. As soon as the applause died, I left after making a promise to give a full report to the club about life in America upon my first visit back to the village.

THE WORLD MAY NOT BE ROUND

Nine years lapsed before my return to India. In the meantime, I had acquired my US citizenship and passport. I went back to India in triumph. I had a job, an American wife, citizenship papers, and money to spend. I had achieved the American Dream! The BBS club delivered a verbal invitation to my folks in Bahadurpur for me to attend their special session. I was glad to oblige. They were waiting. It was a different scene than before. The meeting was in a recently constructed schoolroom. There were benches. In front of the benches, a rattan chair was positioned. The chair was for me, the honored guest. Uncle Bakshi was not there (I found out later that he had died from a heart ailment). Another man who was a village councilor introduced me to the new members, said many words of praise using phrases like "favorite son", and then opened the floor for questions.

There were many questions. Among the questions were, is America farther than England? Was money more plentiful in America than in England? Then came the more challenging question from a man who had the face of a comedian. His name was Banta.

"So Bai (brother) is the world really round or is that just BS like the kind we dish out here? If so, how do you know it is round?"

I struggled for the proper answer and said, "The best proof we have is that we have someone from the neighboring village who took the western route to Vancouver, Canada through England. I took the Eastern route through Japan and reached the American West, right next to Vancouver, Canada, proof that the world must be round."

Banta was not convinced and said, "But Bai, that is not a concrete proof. The fact is that on these long trips, they put you in that long metal tube (airplane), close the door, and they never tell you if you are going East or West and what is happening until they release you at the destination," he said with a smile on his face.

"You have a point, but there are instruments you can check," I said. I decided not to challenge him further.

EDIBLE PLATE (MUKKI DI ROTI)

Several other of the group's questions related to western food, women, and the standard of living in America. It all went well and then Banta, the man who had challenged the earth's shape, asked another zinger. "Bai, are Americans and English a lot smarter than we are? I mean can you match their intellect?"

"Yes, but they have had more opportunities to advance over the past few hundred years. The rest of the people have the same intelligence, but have not had the same opportunities. Now they are catching up. I have had opportunities and yes, I am as smart as any average American."

He accepted my explanation but apparently, he had his own story to show that the American and the English are not smarter than the Indians are. He cited the following story in support of his hypothesis.

"Several years ago an English man, piloting a small, single-engine airplane which he rented at the Delhi flying club, crashed in the middle of the desert in southwestern Punjab. He was lucky. He landed in sand and was not hurt except that he was stranded with no food, water, or humans in sight. Hungry and thirsty, he walked until he reached a small hamlet. Upon his arrival, the villagers gathered around him and offered assistance. They gave him water to drink and a cot and a pillow so he could lie down. Through sign language, they figured out that, he had crashed his airplane and had had nothing to eat for many hours. They believed they should feed this hungry man and proceeded to offer him their best food. They chose slow cooked mustard greens (saag) topped with butter that was placed upon a flat piece of fried corn bread (mukki di roti). The hungry Englishman ate the delicious buttery stew with his fingers and asked for second helpings. When finished, he tossed the corn bread into the trash thinking it was a homemade disposable plate." The surprised and delighted onlookers clapped.

"As soon as the nearby police rescue team arrived, he said good bye. He had already profusely thanked the villagers for their hospitality."

Banta delightedly pointed out, "The Englishman was not as brilliant as expected because he could not tell the difference between corn bread and a plate. Most Indians could do that!"

(1) "When Nature Calls" story is memorialized in a hilarious poem by Mr. Dhanna Singh, the "Poet Laureate" in the area of my village. I have recited the poem dozens of times to groups of Indians in the US on special gatherings.

(2) Dhoti is a traditional men's garment worn in many parts of India with some variations. It is a long piece of unstitched cloth, wrapped around the waist and the legs and knotted at the waist. The Punjabi version called Bhotha is not wrapped around legs but is more like a long skirt stretching down to the feet.

(3) Sindri Fertilizer Company was built by Montecatini, an Italian chemicals company. It was inaugurated in March 1952 with great hoopla as a symbol of developing an independent India. In his factory inauguration speech, the Prime Minister of India, at the time, Jawaharlal Nehru, called it a temple of modern India.

Update: Banta, the fellow who had questioned whether the earth is round or flat, took his first long trip in an airplane. He flew to Singapore on a wide body jet. He was part of an organized tour group that went to Singapore for shopping and sightseeing. Banta had money. He benefited when land values skyrocketed. His father had left him with a sizeable tract of land.

The tall guy who told the "When Nature Calls" story, found a job as a driver with one of the biggest bus companies transporting passengers between Chandigarh and Delhi. I am sure his passengers enjoyed his sense of humor.

CHAPTER 10

MERCHANTS OF DISEASE

THE OPIUM TRAIL RAN THROUGH MY NEIGHBOR'S YARD

We had relatives who lived in more interesting places than my dusty village. I longed for the villages where my father's sisters lived. The youngest of the three lived in a town that had shops, playgrounds, and a railway station where you could roam and watch monkeys play in the terminal buildings as well as the two daily trains coming and going. My aunt was a sweet woman who was very fond of me. She would invite me to spend part of my summers at her house and I always did. However, in the summer of 1949 she did not extend the hoped-for invitation because her husband had passed away from some unknown ailment and she decided to move back home where she could live with her parents.

My summers were now limited to two options. I could go to my father's middle sister's house to spend part of my summer in a village called Baghuwala at the edge of the Hissar desert in Punjab. This was a good prospect. Her three sons, all-older than me, were athletic and fun loving. They had many acres of land and owned horses, which we sometimes rode for fun.

My other option was to go to the eldest of the three aunts who lived in a village in the Fazilka district not far from the border of today's Pakistan. She had only one son whose name was Mukhtar, which means "chosen one" or the head of a village or a neighborhood. Mukhtar sounded like an Arabic name, but my cousin was born and raised in Punjab as a typical Sikh boy. He had an imposing figure and with his black beard, a handlebar mustache, and in his neatly tied turban, he commanded attention and respect.

Cousin Mukhtar Sidhu was much older than I was. He had a college degree, was well dressed, and was a very affluent man. His wife Gurmeet

129

was also college educated and was employed as a teacher in a girl's primary school. Mukhtar's father had died a few years earlier in a shooting accident.

The Sidhus lived in a magnificent house, had servants, and went to restaurants whenever they wished. Despite being twenty years older than I was, Mukhtar treated me like an equal. He was a funny man. For obvious reasons, I longed to spend as much of my summer at their place as possible.

The reason the Sidhu family lived well was that Mukhtar owned a legal and licensed opium outlet. Opium sales in India were promoted under the British rule (and even after the British left) because the trade was owned and controlled by the British merchants and their Indian partners. People coveted the greyish black gold (opium) even though it was not available on the open market at the time I visited cousin Mukhtar. It had to be controlled and licensed for a variety of reasons; high profits being one.

Profits from the sale of opium were enormous and the demand was high. After a century of promoting its use, millions of Indians were addicted and desperate to get their fix at any price. Obtaining a legal license to sell opium was like winning the lottery. You had to be a respectable citizen, a loyal subject of the Crown or the regional Maharaja, and a man of wealth. This was necessary because many negotiations were needed, forms had to be filled out, and "facilitation payments" had to be made in order to secure a coveted license.

Cousin Mukhtar had everything required to win the opium contract, the – THEKA. This he did, and the license he held covered not only his village but also the whole region, which included several smaller outlets he regularly visited.

THE SUMMER OF 1949

Mukhtar invited me to spend the summer with his family. One of the incentives he offered was that during the day, I could go to his shop and watch a stream of hard-core addicts, as well as new initiates, come to his shop to beg for or buy opium. Of special interest would be derelicts on their last gasp until they got their fix. Mukhtar told me that watching a stoned addict pleading for mercy could be hilarious and tragic at the same time. The neurotoxic drug could affect user behavior in weird and unanticipated ways.

Harvesting opium from a poppy plant.

LOST IN HIS OWN HOME TOWN

Mukhtar told me a story of one of his regular customers.

Sucha was a farmer in a nearby village. He was about fity years old and owned 100 acres of irrigated land, which was sufficient to support a family of four in a comfortable house in the middle of the village. Sucha registered his oldest son in the village school, which meant he would not be available to work on the farm except doing minor chores, but decided that his youngest son should ply the father's trade and stay as a full-time farmer. Sucha was very fond of his wife, a personable and educated lady who had attended school up to the eighth grade. Although he felt that things were going well for him, he still felt something was amiss.

Sucha went to the local doctor and confided to him that he could not make his wife "happy." He always disappointed her when it came to intimacy. He felt ashamed and inadequate. To remedy it, he consumed generous amounts of milk, ghee (clarified butter), and yogurt as well as following a regular exercise regime. Compared to other men, he was muscular, but he believed he always failed where it mattered most. The village herbal doctor did not have anything specific for him but advised him to drink more milk, do more exercise, and say more prayers. Sucha tried all to no avail.

One day, while talking with a neighbor, he was advised to try opium. This he did and the results were a success. He felt like he was reliving his honeymoon of thirty years earlier. Sucha had reclaimed his lost paradise with just a few grains of the musty greyish black plant extract.

Sucha became regular at Mukhtar's opium clinic. His dose and frequency increased with time. Addiction was beginning to take hold. His weight began to fall and his eyes started to sink into his sunken cheeks. He became perpetually tired and disoriented. The regained paradise was slipping away. Something seemed about to happen for the worst.

A relative he rarely visited on the other side of town asked him to help celebrate his son's wedding. The day before the wedding, Sucha's wife instructed him to deliver the wedding presents to the relative because they would not be able to attend the ceremony the next morning.

Sucha picked up the beautifully wrapped package, took his daily energy (opium) ball-a little larger than usual-for the one-mile long walk, and proceeded on his journey. Near his destination, as darkness fell, he got confused and disoriented. Just before reaching the house, he became turned around and started traversing the opposite route in the direction of his own house. The distance to the relative's house seemed longer to him than he remembered from previous trips. Perhaps he was walking too slowly, he thought. As he got closer to his intended destination, he was astonished by the similarity of the surroundings and landmarks. There was the same kind of temple around the corner as in his town. Next, he saw the freshly whitewashed post office, a street intersection similar to his own, and a Mithai (sweets) shop similar to the one he liked to frequent.

Sucha was transfixed. "What a marvel of nature?" he thought. The exact same features in this part of town paralled the landmarks near his own house! Who but the good Lord could have arranged it this way?

He started to think, "If this is all God's doing, then there must be a pinkish grey house just like my own at the next turn. And maybe the man's wife might look like my own wife!"

He turned the corner and there it was, just as he anticipated; a pinkish grey house with a worn out wooden door and brass handles. His racing heart speeded up even further as he opened the door. A woman with the likeness of his wife greeted him at the door. Surprisingly she asked him, "What happened? Why do you still have all the gifts?"

"These are for your son, the groom, my dear lady. My wife and I apologize to you for missing the wonderful ceremony tomorrow but please accept our regrets. By the way, I am amazed how similar everything here is to my own neighborhood and if I may say madam, you look as lovely as my wife. Could you two be sisters? In any case, you have similar looks and good tastes no doubt."

Sucha's wife was not amused. She knew he had gone beyond the threshold. She cupped her hands around her mouth and yelled at him, "You idiot! You are talking to your own wife. This is your own damn house and you are the same old miserable man you always were. Listen to me. If you don't quit this habit of taking opium, I will be gone and you will rot in your bed."

Sucha snapped out of the trance and tried to apologize but he was too far gone. He slumped in the nearby jute cot and fell sleep.

The next day Sucha went to the shop to get his fix. He told Mukhtar about the incident the previous night and of the ultimatum from his wife. She had said she would leave him if he did not overcome his addiction.

Mukhtar was in a quandary. He did not want him to lose his wife yet he knew Sucha could not just quit. He suggested to Sucha a gradual withdrawal regimen. Every week he would sell him a smaller amount until he would not need the drug anymore. Sucha agreed to the plan. In the beginning it worked.

"It has been three weeks now since Sucha has had any of the drug," Mukhtar said to me with pride and he knocked on wood for good luck. Mukhtar, the drug merchant, had acted as a therapist as he had done on many previous occasions. Unlike other merchants, he did not need more customers. He was already running short on supplies. His license restricted him to a certain quota and he had reached his limit. The only way he could get an increased supply was to bribe a few higher ups. He decided he did not want to do that. He was making a great living as it was.

Mukhtar's stories fascinated me. He had many tales. I urged him to tell me more. He referred me to his wife Gurmeet for another good story at dinnertime.

FROZEN TO THE WALL

Gurmeet told me the story of one of their neighbors named Billa ("cat eyes") who was also addicted to opium. Mukhtar and Gurmeet Sidhu had a big house with a large front parlor where they kept spare furniture; a few chairs, a folding table, and several cots made of jute, which were leaned carefully against the wall. Neighbors knew of this resource and because of

Gurmeet's good nature and friendly attitude, people did not hesitate to borrow a piece of furniture stacked in the foyer.

One day, a man from the next village came to their house after dark. He told Gurmeet that he expected a few guests later that night and asked if he could borrow one of the cots that was leaning against the wall.

"Well of course, Billa. Take what you need and you can return it tomorrow when your guests are gone," she said.

"Thanks Bhabiji (sister). You are very generous," he said haltingly as he proceeded to untangle the cots on the wall.

Gurmeet left and returned to her regular chores. The next morning she rose early as usual and went to the front parlor. She was startled to see a man frozen against the cots on the wall as if trying to break one loose from the pack.

"Oh Billa, you did not have to return the cot this early in the morning. It could have waited," she said.

The man was startled. He shook himself violently like a drenched animal, rubbed his eyes, reassembled himself and said, "Sorry Bhabiji, I am not here to return the bed. I must have fallen sleep. Actually, I have not yet left." Then in embarrassment, he rushed out with a cot on his head while muttering, "Oh God, I am so late. I wonder what my guests must have been doing all this time."

OPIUM TRADER FOR A DAY

One day, Mukhtar had several errands to attend to in the afternoon, but he did not want to close his shop. Several regulars would be coming for the precious commodity and there was no way to inform them in advance of the temporary closure. He asked me to tend the shop for a few hours when he was away.

This was a generous offer. I readily accepted the challenge and assured Mukhtar that I could handle the task. My math skills were developed enough to calculate the price, I could follow the limits on the quantity sold, and I could accurately guess the age of a customer so as not to sell the drug to a minor.

Mukhtar was satisfied. He had faith in my mathematical skills and my decision-making abilities, but as I was a novice in the trade, additional instructions were necessary. "Do not sell to anyone, no matter how deserving or respectable looking, any opium until you have collected the cash, in legal and crisp rupees. Some will plead, beg, sob like a child, promise to pay later, and try to barter, but show no mercy. Remember, cash is King!" he repeated the old adage.

"Got it. Not a problem. You go and tend to your business," I assured him.

Mukhtar hopped on his motorbike and sped away.

As soon as he left, the challenges began. A respectable looking woman of the same age as my mother walked into the shop and asked for two "Tolas" of opium. This posed no problem. I was well versed in Tola math. A Tola unit was created in 1833 by the East India Company to trade precious commodities like gold, silver, tobacco, and opium. One Tola equaled three eighths of a troy ounce (about 23 grams). The shop was equipped with a sensitive Tola scale to precisely weigh the precious commodity.

Looking at the customer, I realized that something was worrying me despite the fact that the motherly woman looked respectable and composed, and not like an addict in need of fix. I started thinking. Why does she need the drug? Could she be buying the drug for someone else? How do I know it will not be for a minor? Do I dare challenge a lady who looks like my mother?

135

"Okay young man, hurry up. I do not have a whole day to waste and my baby is screaming bloody murder. I must give him his daily dose to keep him pacified for a while so I can tend to a million other chores."

I understood immediately. She had a legitimate need for the hallucinogen even though cousin Mukhtar had failed to warn me that not all customers would be desperate and dependent old men. A good number will be household wives and mothers who regularly used a controlled amount of the drug to keep babies happy and pacified. The poppy salesmen were telling childbearing women that a dash of the black herbal extract is the safest way to pacify an overactive toddler and free up the mother to perform daily chores without interruption. [1]

I dispensed the drug to the eager mom. Before leaving, she gave me an approving look. "Smart young man," She said. "You must be attending an English school. You are the lucky one. My older son also started school but unfortunately, it is a terrible school. The good ones are too far away from here."

Business was brisk. The customer parade continued. I was feeling increasingly confident with my role as a drug dealer. I would not mind if cousin Mukhtar did not return when he said he would.

The next customer was a man in his fifties. He was tall, fair complexioned, and slender. In fact, the ratio of his height to his weight was so disproportional that he looked like a scarecrow standing in a cornfield.

He came right to me and said, "Sunny, I need the usual. Please hurry!"

"Okay uncle," I started to say, but hesitated. The etiquette in our society was that every adult man in the neighborhood was an uncle and every adult woman was an aunt. That was the culturally appropriate and polite thing to say, but looking at the man, I could not bring myself to call someone an uncle who looked like a derelict. I stood strait and demanded cash up front.

"Oh Sunny, give me the stuff quick! I am not feeling well. I forgot to grab the cash when I left home in a hurry. Just give me one Tola and I will be back in five minutes with cash."

"No sir, I cannot give you the opium until you show me the cash. Cousin Mukhtar told me not to give the drug to anyone without money, no matter what. Please come back with cash and make sure the rupees are new and crisp and not some greasy and tattered notes ready to expire," I said with confidence.

The man became very agitated. He started pleading and begging. He claimed that if he did not get his fix, he would die right on the steps of the shop and Cousin Mukhtar would never forgive me. Moreover, I would have his death on my conscious as long as I lived.

This was too much for me to withstand. I relented a little. "Okay sir, I can give you a Tola for now but only if you leave a deposit which you can reclaim when you bring cash." This seemed like a reasonable offer.

Mr. Scarecrow readily accepted the offer. He went to the corner of the shop and laid his slippers near the door. I dispensed the promised Tola and he left saying, "You are a smart lad. Someday, you will make a good businessman, even better than your cousin!" He then darted out the door on bare feet, hopping on the pavement stones that were baking under the tropical sun. I felt bad not knowing how far he had to walk on bare feet over the scorched earth.

Mukhtar returned sooner than expected. He had a smile on his face. Apparently, the errands had gone well. "Did everything go alright? I see you are still in one piece and you are smiling," he said to me while sporting a grin on his face.

"Yes Bai (brother), I encountered no crises in your absence. The whole thing was a breeze but there is one thing I should tell you. A tall lanky man who was in dire need wanted the fix had come with no money. I had never seen a grown up man in such pathetic straights. So I gave him the drug and demanded that he leave a suitable deposit. This he did," I said that with confidence.

"You did what? Gave the drug without cash to a junky? And what precious deposit did he leave behind?"

I pointed to the slippers in the corner.

Mukhtar erupted into laughter and started yelling while still laughing uncontrollably. "You gave him the merchandise in exchange for his tattered slippers? I was wondering why the shop is smelling like shit! Now we must inform the Bhangi (the janitor) to haul this crap away when he comes to clean the latrines," he was still laughing out loud.

Before I could say sorry, Mukhtar stopped laughing and said, "My dear cousin, you are very smart. So what would you like to be when you grow up?" He sounded serious.

"I want to be a scientist, an engineer, or a doctor when I get out of college which unfortunately is still very far away," I told him.

"Excellent!" he exclaimed. I think you are cut out for any of those. I am glad you did not choose business because, my dear brother, you are not cut out for business," he firmly declared. Before I could fully comprehend the insult, Mukhtar resumed his hyena laughter. I joined him.

AN OPIUM PRIMER

My day at the opium shop raised many questions in my mind. I was intrigued and troubled. I wanted to know all about opium; the history of trade, its uses, effects, impact on neighbors, and the benefits, if any? Most of all, how could tens of millions of Indians pay fortunes for a tiny ball of greyish gummy stuff?

At dinner, I peppered Mukhtar with questions. Apparently, he was ready. He was very informed on the subject and knew all about the merchandise that made him a very wealthy man.

I questioned him first on the health effects of the material he was selling. He hesitated a bit but replied, "Bai, I am not sure, because as you know, I did not study chemistry, biology, or medicine in college. I was a business major with history as a minor. I do know, however, that the effects are not good, especially for habitual users. You witnessed this at the shop. Most of the effects I see are hallucinogenic and psychological, and often there are tragic outcomes. I am sure there are other diseases associated with the continued use, although I must tell you that it does help some people in distress," he continued. "One thing I can say for sure is that an opium smoker is often suspended between sleeping and being awake. Many of them describe having frequent erotic daydreams, short-term euphoria, and a persistent lucky feeling. The euphoric effects lead to increasing psychological dependence. I have also heard of cases of organ failure and people suffering from damaging effects on the liver, kidneys, and brain."

I saw an opportunity to ask him if he ever uses the stuff, he sells?

"No Bai, I would not touch the stuff, although I tried it when I first started the business. It does not interest me a bit. My preference is English whisky, single malt Solan No.1, brewed in Kasauli in the Himalayan hills. I also like Black Knight."

He paused and asked the Mundu (the thirteen-year-old errand boy they employed) to bring him a drink. The boy knew what to do. He brought a bottle of Solan No.1, two glasses, crushed ice, some spicy mango pickles, and some salty noodles. Mundu offered me a drink, but I declined. Instead of a drink, I munched on the spicy noodles and pickled green mango.

Mukhtar was now ready to enlighten me on more opium issues, especially opium marketing and promotion. He went into his study and brought several books and old newspaper articles for me to look over and read later when I had time.

MERCHANTS OF DISEASE

I learned that the opium trade was a triangular business arrangement between India, China, and Britain. The trade was complex but efficient. China had a positive trade balance with the British. To enhance their balance with China, the British promoted opium use in China and they delivered the opium from India's Eastern Provinces that were under British control. Opium cultivation and supply in India was controlled by the East India Company (EIC) as a monopoly of the British government. Calcutta was the ideal port to supply China with Indian opium. Calcutta was closer to China and the Bengali opium was the best of the best. Many Chinese people quickly became addicted. Attempts by the Chinese government to destroy the opium stock and to stop opium imports led to the First Opium War (1839–1842), in which Britain defeated China. Opium supplies to China continued and flourished.

A number of American and British companies were involved in the lucrative trade. Jardine Matheson [2] and their agents Augustine Heard and Company had the biggest share, but American and British companies were not the only ones benefiting from the opium trade. In Mumbai, much of the trade was in Parsee [3] hands. A Parsee businessman named Pastinjee Bomanjee Wada was known to have devoted thirty-nine ships to opium trade through the busy ports of Bombay, Goa (Daman), and Calcutta. One of the ships he later sold to the Sultan of Muscat (Oman) was refurbished by the Sultan and named the Prince of Wales. David Sasson, a Persian Jew living in Bombay, ultimately cornered the opium trade driving the Angelo American giant, Jardine Matheson, out of the opium business.

Mukhtar took another sip of the Solan No. 1 and said, "But Bai, the British and Americans were not directly involved in popularizing the drug to the masses. There were many Indian entrepreneurs to take the message door-to-door in a truly grass-roots effort. A salesman would go door-to-door, especially ones with screaming babies, and tell the anguished mothers how to pacify their child with just a pinch of the god-given herbal product. Free samples were handed out with instructions for use and information about where to buy the medicine if they liked it.

Similar sales demonstrations were held in village squares to large gatherings of men to convince them how their miserable sex lives would be miraculously transformed with a mere pinch of the natural plant extract. Their sales pitches centered on opium's ability to enhance their romantic encounters from ridiculously short sojourns to never-ending romantic interludes. These street demonstrations were vulgar but entertaining. The resulting sales statistics, however, would be the envy of any modern pharmaceutical industry-marketing person. This sex-appeal aspect of the poppy gave rise to several very popular soft-core pornographic publications that were sold strictly in the underground market.

Another door-to-door demonstration was to show the pain-killing potency of opium. Opium's well-documented pain-killing properties were perhaps the most convincing demonstration. You could always find someone in the audience who suffered from severe pain who would provide rave reviews about the drug's effectiveness.

The Indian film industry pitched in to help popularize the drug just as it made cigarette smoking fashionable. Poppy addicts were featured in Bollywood movies as carefree and lovable characters. In Punjab, a movie about a lovable poppy addict called Posti (Punjabi: ਪੋਸਤੀ) was released in 1950. It did very well at the box office and launched the singing career of Asha Bhosle, who became one of the most beloved singers on the Indian big screen. One particular duet that became popular went something like:

"Tu Peengh te mein parchhavaan, tere naal hulare khawaan, la lei dosti

"You are the swing and I am the shadow, let us swing together. Let us fall in love."

Mukhtar was on a roll, but it was dinnertime. Gurmeet joined us for dinner. I had more questions, but realized I had two more weeks to learn. Dinner over, we said good night to each other. Gurmeet brought me a glass of warm milk and I went to bed.

For the rest of my stay, I went to the shop at every opportunity. There was something different every day. One day I heard a commotion on the street. There were two men each carrying a red flag with a hammer and sickle and a bagful of pamphlets in Punjabi, which they readily gave to the onlookers. The men belonged to the Communist Party of India (CPI) and were a part of the grassroots effort to bring Marxism to India. I had witnessed similar displays near my school back home. One of the men was a Sikh gentleman with a neatly combed beard and mustache who wore a pink turban. He held a large placard written in English. It read:

"RELIGION IS OPIUM OF THE MASSES" – KARL MARX

FAST FORWARD TO 2015

I never had the opportunity to spend another summer with Mukhtar although I saw him on a couple of occasions when he came to visit my parents. I concentrated on studying during my later summer breaks. I desperately wanted to go to America to pursue chemistry.

On a recent trip to India, I wanted to follow up on my opium obsession. The Central Bureau of Narcotics now controls opium cultivation and distribution in India. Opium shops still dot the landscape. According to 2008-2009 numbers, there were over 44,000 opium licenses in effect, the amount of illegal harvesting and outlets notwithstanding.

I inquired about the use of opium in today's India from one of my old classmates. He said opium use in India is at epidemic proportions and it is still the pharmaceutical of choice among villagers for many reasons. Medical facilities are not always on hand and if they do exist, the cost is too high for most people. A pinch of opium can come in handy when someone has a cut, a severe headache, an injury, or convulsions. To demonstrate how common the use of opium in Punjab households is, he motioned to his fourteen-year-old son, whispered something in his ear, and dispatched him to bring some opium to show his American uncle.

The boy took off like a rocket. Within fifteen minutes, he returned with a black ball about one centimeter in diameter and wrapped tightly in three layers of cellophane paper. He spread it on the dinner table.

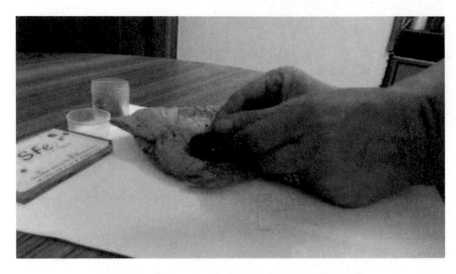

Photo: Emergency medicine in a Punjab village

Endnotes:

1) The opium pacifier procedure has been blamed for a number of toddler deaths from overdosing. No convictions have ever occurred because the British law apparently had no provisions for prosecuting deaths from opium ingestion. Moreover, there was probably not a toxicology lab in India that could prove opiate residue in a child's body.

2) Jardine Matheson Holdings was a multinational company incorporated in Bermuda, and listed on the London Stock Exchange. Much of its business was in Asia with Hong Kong as its hub.

3) **The India-China Opium Trade in the Nineteenth Century** by Hunt Janin, Library of Congress: ISBN 0-7864-0175-8

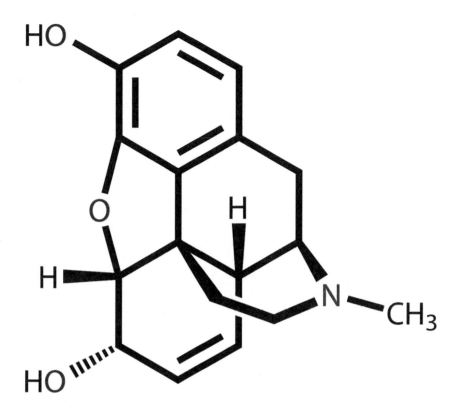

Chemical Formula of Morphine, the primary biological active chemical in opium. Source: Shutterstock

CHAPTER 11

MERCHANTS OF DISEASE II

The Smoking Gun

She opened the door, walked in, and headed straight to our table in the crowded restaurant in Bangsar, a thriving suburb of Kuala Lumpur, Malaysia. The attendant at the door tried to say hello to her, but she paid no attention to him and kept walking toward us.

LUCKY STRIKE IN MALAYSIA

My friends Abe and Shamini recommended that I meet them at a recently opened restaurant called "Spice." We had known each other for several years. I had previously lived in Malaysia and managed a small US-based health and safety company. Shamini had worked with me there while Abe was a plant manager at a plastic manufacturing plant owned by another US multinational company. This was my first visit back to Malaysia since I had returned to the US after finishing my assignment in Malaysia. We looked forward to exchanging personal stories and catching up on gossip.

The brazen intruder walked up to me, tapped on my shoulder, and said, "Hello stranger, my name is Candy. What is yours? And what brings you to my country?" She had guessed from my floral Hawaiian shirt that I was not a local.

Without waiting for an answer, she turned to Abe and said, "Haven't I seen you before but where? Right here, I think." She answered her own inquiry, smiled, and looked at Shamini after addressing her husband. She must have figured out that Shamini was Abe's spouse or his Friday night date. With this knowledge, Candy adjusted her attitude towards Shamini and made no physical contact with Abe.

Candy was not a typical Malaysian woman. She wore heavy lipstick (although that is not atypical in Malaysia), a very short dress, had an aggressive and sporty demeanor, and wore a perfume not commonly worn in Malaysia. It was Elizabeth Arden's® Red Door Eau de Toilette, a fragrance that one of my administrative assistants in California used to wear. My assistant's generous use of Red Door conflicted with another administrative assistant's favorite "Evening in Paris Eau de Parfum." Years ago, the dispute between these two women erupted into a full-scale "perfume war" (1) which took time and resources to quell. Candy's perfume was not that overwhelming.

Candy quickly came to the point of her visit to our table. She reached into her oversized golden purse, took out a pack of American cigarettes, and deposited two samples each in front of Abe and me. Then turning to Shamini, she reached into a smaller pink purse and pulled out two other cigarettes of a different variety, longer, and thinner. She handed those to Shamini. These were Lucky Strikes produced by the British American Tobacco Company. Candy knew that sophisticated Bangsar women preferred Lucky Strikes. She picked one of the Luckies, held it close to Shamini's lips, and offered to light it for her. Shamini refused her offer. She then offered the same cigarette to Abe and asked him to hold the cigarette between his lips so she could light it for him. Abe did as instructed but then removed the cigarette from his mouth and said, "No thanks." Later he told me that he was tempted to smoke it but decided not to do so because of me and my views on smoking. Moreover, he did not want to be seen smoking a woman's cigarette.

Undaunted, Candy had one more trick. She took out her chrome cigarette case adorned with the Victorian era floral designs, grabbed one of the cigarettes, and asked me to part my lips so she could insert one in my mouth and light it for me.

I addressed her directly saying, "I do not touch these things, Candy, and you should know that you are pushing a drug, a cancer-causing substance. How would you feel if one of your regular customers developed lung cancer as a result of your free gifts?"

Candy did not know what to say, but before she could muster an answer, I was ready to dump more guilt on the young woman who was just trying to make a few ringgits (Malaysian dollars). I continued my moralistic sermon, "I know you are an educated woman. You speak excellent English. You could be a public relations employee for a multinational company, a sales supervisor at a fashionable clothing store, or a flight attendant for Malaysian Airlines or Singapore Airline."

Candy was listening. I continued, "If you would like a higher-paying job, you could work as a hostess in one of the many night clubs in town because you have the looks and the demeanor. You might even consider working at a private karaoke club where singing is never a pre-requisite."

I heard a "swish-h h" sound and looked towards Abe. Apparently, he had choked on my last career suggestion and released a fine spray of Tiger Beer© (brewed locally by Heineken). Shamini passed a napkin to him to tidy up the table.

"I will consider your suggestions, sir," Candy said, "but right now I am happy with what I am doing." She briskly walked away from our table to others in waiting.

Abe turned to me and said, "Jas, what you said to Candy was kind of harsh. Many of the private karaoke joints around here are fronts for other activities that exploit young women. I did not expect that from you, my friend!" he said emphatically.

"Yes, I shouldn't have said that. I will apologize to Candy if I see her again, but I was irritated at the whole charade. Normally, as you know, I am gracious towards pretty women, but Candy angered me with her aggressiveness, interruption of our conversation, and dared to imply that she could turn me, a supposed health and safety expert, into a tobacco junky," I said.

"Okay man. I still say, you overreacted, but let us resume our story where we left before Candy interrupted us." Abe then motioned to the nearby waiter to bring three more "Tigers."

Candy moved to other tables. She distributed the free goodies and left the restaurant without looking at us. The restaurant filled up and became warm and stuffy. About three couples were waiting for a seat. Friday was the busiest night at Spice.

Every table Candy visited became a smoke generator. Our eyes started burning from the aldehydes and other lachrymators in the smoke. Shamini called one of the waiters to our table. "The air was nice when we first came in," she said, "but now it is like Los Angeles smog on a really bad day. Why do you permit cigarette sellers in the restaurant while your paying customers, many of them non-smokers, are enjoying their dinners and not expecting to be disturbed by hawkers or subjected to other people's smoke?"

"I apologize, madam, but it is legal, and the presence of such cigarette ladies in restaurants is common in Bangsar and enjoyed by many customers," the waiter replied and added, "Miss Candy is good for business. Some customers come on Fridays probably just to get free samples and to say hello to her. The boss is particularly fond of Miss Candy," he said with a knowing smile.

"Can't blame the boss!" both Abe and I said almost simultaneously. We left the restaurant laughing although Shamini and I were also crying from inhaling the smog, courtesy of Candy and her new friends.

From Spice restaurant, we moved on to a new swanky bar called Journey's End, in the next block. Sticking our heads inside the bar, we realized that more cigarette smoke awaited us. The air density of the smoke was thicker than at the place we just left.

We found a seat outdoors and ordered drinks. There was cigarette smoke outside, too, but the air density felt closer to the average on planet Earth. A gentle breeze was blowing. The air was warm and humid but still a welcome reprieve from the smoke filled interiors of the Spice restaurant and Journey's End bar.

The acrid cigarette smoke from the Spice restaurant was still on our minds and in our clothing (tobacco combustion products carrying cancer-causing soot particles fall out of the air onto clothes, hair, eyes, and into the nostrils). With the soot and smell of smoke still with us, I told Abe and Shamini a story about tobacco promotion in India when I was growing up there as a teenage boy.

MIND READER IN CONNAUGHT PLACE

My first ever visit to Delhi was approaching. As a teenage boy in India, this would be a big deal. I had dreamed of visiting India's capital but never before had the opportunity to do so. A relative of ours, a medical practitioner, recommended that my mother see a specialist in Delhi because of a health problem. My mother and my sister Nikki, who was studying to be a Public Health Nurse at the Christian Medical College in Ludhiana, were going to Delhi and they took me along. We stayed with a relative who happened to live near the fabled Connaught Place. This was a dream come true!

The British built Connaught Place in 1929 to create a small piece of England thousands of miles away from home. It was named after H.R.H. Field Marshal, the 1st Duke of Connaught and Strathearn. When an Englishman entered Connaught Place, he must have felt both at home and homesick at the same time. *(Author's Digression. To create a feeling of home away from home, the British also built another enclave hundreds of miles away from the crowds, dust, heat, and humidity of Delhi in the cool foothills of the Himalayan Mountains. They called it Shimla and made it the summer capital of India. See the story "Slow Train to Her Majesty's Summer Capital").*

Before the British left India in 1947, Connaught Circle was a special place. You did not see much riff raff at that location according to my aunt, our host in Delhi. She had lived all her life in the Connaught Place neighborhood. Three years after the British had left, it was a place on a downward spiral, she said. It was crowded and had become a haven for street shows, merchandise hawkers, and salesmen promoting cheap, Indian-made "Bidi" cigarettes (Note: Connaught Place has recovered its luster in recent years and is now one of the busiest business centers in Delhi).

Once the visit to the doctor was over, my mother, my sister Nikki, and I went to Connaught Place. The two ladies shopped while I gawked at the demonstrations occurring there.

A crowd of people gathered around some musicians who were performing Hindi songs with a dancing girl accompanied by a harmonium and a drum. The catchy and familiar tune caught my attention. Nikki noticed and said to me, "Massiji (auntie) and I will check a few shops and you can see the show, whatever it is. Just stay there until we come back."

"I will be here, right here," I said, pounding the pavement with my right heel as if it was critical to identify the rendezvous spot within a few centimeters.

Once on my own, I slipped between the adults to occupy a front seat close to the dancing girl. She was sixteen or seventeen years old, had curly black hair, and wore a red ruffled skirt, as well as heavy brass jewelry and a nose ring. The leading man introduced her as Miss Choomi. This told everyone that she was a gypsy. Choomi, which in Punjabi and Hindi means, "kiss," is a popular gypsy name in India and abroad.

Although she wore a Rajasthani dress, Choomi looked very cosmopolitan. As an adult, I have seen Choomi lookalikes (tanned complexion, curly hair, and an affinity for red clothing) in many countries. They always looked familiar to me as if they were kin. It is possible that they had gypsy heritage and were descendants of the Rajasthani and Punjabi nomads who migrated to Europe long ago. In Europe, they are called Romas. In Hindi, the equivalent word is Romani (रोमानी). (2)

The man in charge, Choomi's boss, was a non-descript Delhi urbanite, short, thin, and dark with a pleasant disposition. A harmonium hung around his neck but was positioned at his waist. The third member of the cast, a young boy of about fifteen, had a large drum that perched on his stomach. He was introduced as Bittoo. The harmonium man, the leader, did not introduce himself.

Bittoo hit the drum. The harmonium player sounded a crescendo on the keyboard. Choomi began to dance. She raised her head towards the sky, tilted her waist at an uncomfortable forty-five degree angle, and began dancing inside the semi-circle formed by a wall of spectators. She completed the circle, mimicking a classical Bharathanatyam star.

She began a second lap around the circle. When she came to me, she stopped singing but still gyrated to the drumbeat, directed a jet of warm breath into the middle of her cupped palm and pointed towards me. Her "paan" (3) scented breath ricocheted off her palm and hit me in the middle of my face. It smelled delicious and inviting, a sensation I had never felt before! Choomi seemed to have kissed me in front of one hundred spectators. I was elated. I entered dreamland and hoped that Nikki and my mom had more shopping to do. I did not realize that they were just around the corner. Choomi resumed dancing and completed another round. When she came close to me, she stopped, rolled her eyes, pointed at my heart and sang:

"Tere Mun Ki Baat Bataa Doongi"
(I know what is on your mind)

My heart sank. It cannot be. How would she know what is on my mind? My thoughts are my own. No one has access to those. I kept my innermost thoughts in a deep dark secret locker.

Choomi made another full circle, stopped when she came to me, rolled her eyes again, and repeated:

"Tere Mun Kl Baat Bataa Doongi"
(I know what is on your mind)

I was now in complete panic mode. Obviously, she knew what was on my mind. Otherwise, why would she pick on me out of a hundred gawkers? I was elated by her attention, but the problem was that everything on my mind was filthy and X-rated.

What if she told my mother when she showed up that her teenage son with a G-rated brain was harboring X-rated thoughts about Choomi?

Suddenly she stopped dancing, picked up a box, and started dispensing Bidi cigarette samples while encouraging everyone to try the free samples. She offered to light up a Bidi if someone did not have a match. She brought a Bidi close to my lips and said, "Want to try it pretty boy! You will like it. You will feel like a man!"

I declined by turning my head 180 degrees from left to right at least twice. Choomi moved on to other more suitable onlookers.

Two blocks away another crowd gathered. It was a competitive cigarette promotion demonstration. A person next to me started to leave saying,

"You should watch that one. I have seen it twice. The man has a monkey who smokes. He gives the monkey a lighted cigarette to smoke. The monkey puffs on it, makes a face, and tosses the cigarette to the ground. The man then gives him another cigarette, his favorite brand. The monkey happily accepts it and starts puffing. Once in awhile the monkey grabs the cigarette too fast and mistakenly inserts the lighted end in his mouth. Then he screams like a baby. It is funny when he does that," the man said.

I was tempted to see the smoking monkey but did not dare to leave the rendezvous spot that I had clearly marked with my right foot. (4)

My mother and Nikki returned. They spotted me in the crowd. My mother put her hand on my shoulder and said, "Tell me you did not try one."

"I did not, mom, I swear," I answered. Choomi heard and came to my defense.

"No Bibi, (mom) he did not try any. I did not even offer one to him (that was a lie) but I sang to him. He is a cute boy, Bibi. If he were little older, I would marry him."

My mother laughed and said, "Thank God he is not older. He has to go to college and then to America for more studies."

We started walking towards my aunt's house. My mother had not yet completed her anti-smoking lecture. She warned me again, this time stating more dire consequences if I ever smoked.

"For a Sikh, smoking is a sin according to the 10th Guru Gobind," she said. "It is not just the intoxication or adverse health effects. It is a sin, period."

151

"What if a Sikh breaks the rule and commits the sin?" I wanted to know.

"He would be banished from his family or disowned forever if he does not reform," she said confidently.

The word banishment sent chills down my spine. The only time I had heard the word "banish" was in reference to Ramayana, my all-time favorite classic story. In the story, Prince Rama, his wife Sita, and brother Laxman were banished for fourteen years to roam around in the dangerous jungles of Sri Lanka a long time ago. I grabbed my mother's hand and promised, "I will never smoke, mom, not as long as I live." She gave me a warm and motherly choomi.

Bidi's promotion was merchandising at its best. If you can hook twelve- or thirteen-year-old kids, you have fifty years or longer to sell the drug. What a bonanza for tobacco merchants. Some estimates show that sixty-five percent of males in India smoke tobacco and over 120 million are regular users. Unlike in the US, there is no reduction in the number of smokers because essentially there are no smoking cessation campaigns in India. If such exist, they are ignored.

MERCHANTS OF DISEASE

Portuguese merchants introduced tobacco to India in 1600 and it was most commonly consumed in the form of a hookah pipe. By 1610, smoking had extended to all socioeconomic levels. In the East, some new initiates smoked "Chutta" which involved placing a large clump of tobacco with the lighted end inside the mouth.

The Portuguese were not the only ones to introduce tobacco to its colonies. Most European colonial powers recognized tobacco as an ideal resource for consolidating their grip on occupied territories. It was a profitable commodity and, being addictive, it turned natives into smoking addicts, thus weakening their resolve to resist their masters.

English tobacco merchants arrived later in India but they had intimate knowledge of the country. With the might of the British Empire behind them, they soon established a vast tobacco empire. Indian masses were ready for the tobacco invasion. After all, cannabis smoking had been a tradition in India since 2000 BC as mentioned in some Indian medical classics such as *Atharvaveda*. Introduced as a product to be smoked, tobacco quickly found other uses. The inclusion of tobacco as one of the ingredients of paan enhanced its social acceptability. Currently, India is the second-largest producer of tobacco in the world with the highest consumption among the least educated and the poor. Before the merchandising of fancier foreign products, the traditional Indian cigarette was the hand-rolled and inexpensive Bidi, which most poor and uneducated Indians smoked. More educated and affluent Indians smoked western cigarettes.

Indian smoking habits increased markedly when R.J. Reynolds launched its campaign for the lovable Camel brand and the sexy Lucky Strike women's brand.

NO PLACE TO HIDE FROM NICOTINE

Tobacco contains a chemical called nicotine. Nicotine is an addictive substance.

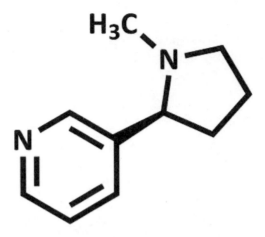

Chemical Formula of Nicotine

Tobacco smoke contains more than 4,000 chemicals, at least forty of which are cancer causing. Nicotine combustion produces carcinogenic polycyclic aromatic compounds with formulas that look like Lego® structural blocks. One of the polycyclic chemicals in tobacco is Benzo (a) Pyrene, a highly potent cancer-causing substance believed to be the smoking gun in the intense debate about the main culprit as the causative agent in inducing lung cancer and mesothelioma, a cancer of the lining of lung and chest cavities.

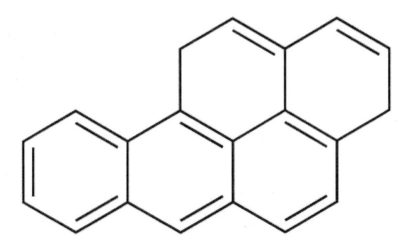

Benzo (a) Pyrene molecule

SAFE SMOKE

Drug merchants now have a new product, smokeless/electronic cigarettes, or vapor smoke. Venders claim that there is no danger from tobacco consumption if one ingests tobacco or inhales pure tobacco extract (which contains the addictive Nicotine). With this misunderstanding, more people are being lured to the addictive substance as I recently witnessed during a sales demonstration of electronic cigarettes at a retail mall near Palm Desert, California.

India passed a law that prohibited smoking in public places in October 2008. The rule is widely ignored. According to the World Health Organization (WHO), India has twelve percent of the world's smokers. In 2009, the annual death rate in India associated with smoking was approximately 900,000 people. Statistics may vary from one source to another, but no matter which source you choose to believe, the statistics are grim.

Despite such grim statistics, Indian Tobacco Company (ITC), successor to the giant British Tobacco Company, is flourishing and admired. Unlike the US tobacco companies, which are demonized for promoting their products to minors on TV and through other means, tobacco merchants in India have felt no pressure or shame from the public or the government. In 2013, the Indian Tobacco Company received the Rajiv Gandhi National Quality Award. It remains the third most admired company in India, the 900,000 deaths caused by tobacco consumption every year, notwithstanding.

1) Linda, who was my assistant when I worked in California, complained bitterly about Joanna's "Paris by Night perfume" and the quantities she was using, forgetting that she herself could be accused of the same with her "Red Door." One morning Linda came to my office and said:

"Can you smell it? I cannot stand her perfume. It is making me sick. You can ask others in the office. I love my job, but if this continues, I will have to update my resume," she said. It dawned on me that a full-scale perfume war had erupted in my office. It was the kind of crisis for which I had received no prior training.

Battle of the Perfumes: "Red Door" vs. "Evening in Paris Eau de Parfum." No winners.

2) Gypsies are of North Indian origin, mostly from Rajasthan and Punjab provinces. They arrived in West Asia sometime between the sixth and seventh centuries A.D. and then in Europe shortly thereafter. European gypsies have since spread all over the world, including the USA and Brazil. An estimated one million Americans are believed to have gypsy origins.

3) Paan is a preparation combining betel leaf, areca nut, and sometimes tobacco. It is chewed for its psychoactive effects. After chewing, it is either spat out or swallowed. Paan comes in different varieties. It is addictive and carcinogenic to habitual users (it can cause cancer of the mouth).

4) I told the smoking monkey story to my granddaughter, Asha Haley, in Los Angeles during a family get together in 2013. She found it funny but troubling.

"What kind of person would do that to an animal?" she asked me.

"One animal to another animal," I replied.

Asha laughed, but she had many more questions.

"Why do people smoke? Does it taste good?"

Eight-year-old Asha drew a picture of a smoking monkey and showed it to her teacher.

The teacher was amused but was also worried.

This child is fascinated by smoking, the teacher must have thought. Could it be that her parents smoke? She called Asha's parents. Asha's mom and dad met with the teacher and assured her that Asha hates cigarettes but she loves monkeys.

The hilarious monkey was smoking cigarette that was as filthy as an ol pellet.

CHAPTER 12

DATURA EATERS

Young Jeev lay in bed in a coma. His parents were in a panic. No one in the village had seen anything like this. There were no injuries to the child's body. The six-year-old Jeev (Jeevan) was usually one of the healthiest kids in the neighborhood. The first thing that came to everyone's mind was to take little Jeev to the local holy man, a hermit-like and trusted soul who was an expert in psychoactive natural plants. With that knowledge, the holy man had become the de facto medicine man when modern medicine was not easily accessible or preferred.

He examined the child and looked into Jeev's severely dilated eyes. He immediately identified the child's symptoms as muscle paralysis and postulated that the child must have been exposed to one of the toxic weeds in the neighborhood. The toxic wild plant could be either milkweed, known as aak, or the more potent, datura. The holy man should have known, he himself was a heavy datura user. He used datura in seeking union with the almighty above. Nevertheless, he was furious about the child's condition and declared, "This child has been given datura. This is not right. Datura should not be given to children. It is for adults and only for those adults who are in need of meditation and communion with the heavens. The use of sacred datura requires practice and such knowledge as I have acquired after years of meditation," he said with authority.

The villagers had seen the holy man in an altered state many times before. A few concerned souls had tried to provide medical assistance, thinking that the pious man was dying, only to incur the wrath of the holy man when he accused them of ruining his meditation at a time when he was very close to reaching the almighty. After once experiencing his wrath, no one would dare to disturb him again, regardless of his physical state.

Jeev was the youngest of four siblings and was the favorite child of his uncle, a teacher at the primary school in a nearby village. After the holy man's visit, the uncle advised the parents to take Jeev to the hospital in Patiala City. At the hospital, the physicians concurred with the holy man's diagnosis, but then the question arose regarding where and how the child had consumed the toxin? With proper medical care, Jeev made a recovery, but concerns about his long-term neurological health lingered. To avoid a reoccurrence, the physician recommended that an effort be made to determine how and where the child was exposed to such a high dose of the neurotoxin.

The mystery was soon solved. Jeev had swallowed the poison on a recent weed-hunting outing with his older siblings. On previous outings, he had touched milkweed latex and complained about his skin itching. Apparently, he had never ingested the weed or the flower. On the last go round, however, according to one of the brothers, Jeev wandered away to an area where the toxic datura plant grew and he likely ingested some purple flowers before he was corralled and brought back by his brothers. The siblings never reported the incident, thinking it was no big deal.

MILK WEED HUNT

Harvesting wild milkweed was a significant part of my early childhood adventures. We called the plant aak, which sounded like yuck, the English slang for something that tastes bad or gross. The filaments from milkweed pods have many desirable properties. Its soft silky touch, lumpiness, shiny appearance, and thermal insulation properties made it a material of choice for pillow stuffing, cushions, and rugs. Due to these desirable characteristics, milkweed carpets were highly prized textiles in the area. Making a carpet from milkweed requires hours of labor and tremendous skill. My aunt was one of the most skilled milkweed carpet-makers in our village. Her handmade masterpieces were coveted and some are still on display in lacquered wooden cases in my old village. Farmers in the area did not need to cultivate milkweed because acres and acres of the wild plants grew on their own throughout the region. My cousins and I would regularly go milkweed picking. After several outings, we would amass enough cocoons to make a modest-sized rug. It was a wonderful outdoor activity, and for each outing, we earned enough money to buy an ice cream cone when the kulfi hawker came around.

My friends and I had encountered the white, sticky milkweed latex many times. It was an unavoidable occupational hazard and caused mild dermatitis. If the latex entered a skin wound, the dermatitis was severe and

159

took weeks to heal. We were smart enough to avoid eating the plant.

Asclepius L, the milkweed I grew up with, was a genus of perennial plants that include many species. Its white, milky sap was once tried as a commercial rubber substitute. The plant contains Belladonna (1) alkaloids and several other toxic compounds.

Datura: Embedded deep inside the seeds of this beautiful shoulder-high plant are some of the most toxic and hallucinogenic chemicals with names like scopolamine, hyoscyamine, and atropine.

HALLUCINOGENS GALORE – THE BELLA DONNA KINGDOM

India is awash in psychotropic chemicals. In addition to opium poppies, with ingredients such as morphine and codeine, a wide variety of mind-altering herbs and plants are only steps away. You had choices whether you wanted to deliver the hallucinogen via inhalation, ingestion, a body rub, or some other innovative route to achieve a spiritual high or for some nefarious purpose. Users had varied objectives such as:

- Holy men in search of heavenly unions
- Younger men in search of earthly unions
- Desperate individuals wanting to commit suicide
- Recreational users – looking for kicks
- Dispatching (killing) an adversary through a friendly drink served with Belladonna – laced pakoras (Indian fries)
- Thugs wanting to incapacitate a person to rob, rape, or kidnap

DATURA EATERS

Perhaps because of its sacramental use in India and the Americas, datura has been the choice of many yearning for a higher state of consciousness. Of the varieties available, Datura Stramonium seems to be the preferred weed.

Datura Stramonium

Datura is a revered intoxicant. In the ancient Sanskrit language, it was called धत्तूरह ("dhattūrāh") and was used in Ayurveda medicine as an aphrodisiac. The Native Americans ("American Indians") used this plant in sacred ceremonies.

TO NEW HIGHS IN NEPAL

Holy men of India use datura as a spiritual tool and often smoke it with cannabis in a traditional pipe (chillums). Datura provides a visionary journey that facilitates a shape-shifting process. Transformations into birds are a frequent experience described by people under the influence of datura.

In the United States, datura is called jimson weed, hell's bells (based on the flower's shape), or Jamestown weed (2). The effects have been described as a "living dream." When under the influence of datura, consciousness comes and goes. Conversations are conducted with people who do not exist or are far away. The effects can last for days.

Datura is a psychotropic substance that crosses the blood–brain barrier where it acts primarily upon the central nervous system and affects brain function. The results can be alterations in perception, mood, consciousness, cognition impairment, or behavior change. Hallucinogenic effects of datura are due to the presence of chemical substances known as amines with names such as scopolamine and atropine.

Scopolamine easily crosses the blood-brain barrier and is the chemical of choice for criminal gangs who wish to incapacitate their victims. When administered in powder or liquid form, scopolamine can render a victim unconscious for twenty-four hours or more. In large doses, it can cause respiratory failure and death. In controlled doses, it has been used to treat central nervous system depression. Cases of modern misuse of scopolamine abound. The majority of these incidents occur in nightclubs and bars. Men who are perceived to be wealthy are frequent victims.

ZOMBIE CHEMISTRY

Another psychoactive chemical used for mind control is tetrodotoxin (3), commonly called TTX. It is approximately 100 times more poisonous than potassium cyanide, the chemical that was used in the mass suicide/murder at the Jonestown Temple in Guyana in 1978. Recorded cases of TTX poisoning can be found in the ship's log of Captain James Cook (4).

At very high doses, TTX can leave a person in a state of paralysis and near-death for several days. For this reason, TTX has been alleged to be an ingredient in Haitian Voodoo rituals. Some victims have approached a zombie state, the status popularized by Harvard-trained ethno-botanist, Davis Wade. (5)

The word datura remained hidden in my memory for many years after I left India until one day a friend told me about a 1985 movie called *The Serpent and the Rainbow*. The movie was based on the work by the Harvard researcher Davis Wade, who investigated alleged cases of man-made zombie slaves on the Caribbean Island of Haiti.

Wade's investigation presented the case of Clairvius Narcisse, a man who had been a zombie working as a slave laborer at a remote farm in Haiti for many years. Dr. Wade postulated that the zombification was likely the result of forced-feeding psychoactive chemicals to the man by mischievous individuals. The complex interaction of the chemical tetrodotoxin (the puffer fish toxin) and the datura, coupled with the cultural voodoo beliefs, produced the zombie-like effects which included severe muscle paralysis.

From local sources, Wade concluded that the victim was fed a potent psychotropic mixture called zombie powder. Ingredients of the powder included: puffer fish, human remains, freshly killed blue lizards, dried toad wrapped in a sea worm, and the datura plant.

I had heard of a similar incident in India where a holy man appeared to be clinically dead. He would hold his breath for many hours at a time and then would come alive again. This was explained as control of body and mind, which he had perfected after years of practice. I suspect, although I have no proof, that his mind and body control were augmented by a healthy dose of psychotropic chemicals.

On a recent trip to India, I saw a saffron-clad sadhu in a deep trance in Ahmedabad, not far from my hotel. The man was motionless. I ventured close with reverence. I was certain he was experiencing complete muscle paralysis. I know he was alive, but I kept wondering, what was the chemical that allowed him to achieve such a state? Was he just using mind control and concentration or was his state assisted by a toxic chemical? I wondered if he could have been using datura.

Where has all the Datura Gone?

When I returned to my Punjab village in 2015, I went out looking for the purple flowered weed in the fields outside of town to see if the prolific the weed was still as widespread as it was when I was a kid. Datura plants had vanished. Without datura, I wondered, how do you achieve contact with the heavens? I did not have to wonder long. Technology and chemical knowledge have come to our aid. We can achieve even higher levels of consciousness (or unconsciousness) with synthetic chemicals such as cocaine, angel dust, ecstasy, and many fabricated mind-altering substitutes.

(1) Belladonna Alkaloid plants have long history of use as a medicine, cosmetics and as psychotropic hallucinogens. Romans used such plants as a poison. The Belladonna alkaloid plants acquired their name because of their use by Italian women to dilate their pupils to look more seductive. The pupil dilation properties of the belladonna alkaloids are responsible for the zombie-like gaze of the severely affected users (the walking dead).

(2) Jamestown, Virginia, where British soldiers were secretly, or accidentally drugged with datura, while attempting to suppress Bacon's Rebellion. They spent several days generally appearing to have gone insane, and failed at their mission.

(3) Tetrodotoxin also referred to as TTX, is a neurotoxin. Its name derives from tetraodontiformes, a species that includes puffer fish, porcupine fish, ocean sunfish, and even some octopus species that carry the toxin.

(4) Clairvius Narcisse, born in 1922 in Haiti, is the man reported to have been a zombie. Narcisse returned home to his village eighteen years after being confirmed dead and buried. After the funeral, his body was dug up by the man who had cursed him — a Haitian voodoo sorcerer and he was given a paste made from datura. This all happened late that night. The sorcerer dug up Narcisse and transported him to a sugar plantation where other zombie slaves worked. There, regular doses of datura produced amnesia, delirium, and vulnerability; significant factors in his long and obedient enslavement. (*From various articles published by Davis Wade, a Canadian ethno-botanist, author, and photographer, whose work has focused on worldwide indigenous cultures especially involving the traditional uses and beliefs associated with psychoactive plants. Davis came to prominence with his 1985 best-selling book* The Serpent and the Rainbow *about the zombies of Haiti).*

(5) James Cook's records show his crew ate puffer fish, and then fed the remains to the pigs kept on board their ship. While the crew experienced numbness and shortness of breath, the pigs who received a much higher dose, were all found dead the next morning (Wikipedia).

CHAPTER 13

ANNAPOORNA ENTREPRENEUR FROM THE HILLS

To pursue graduate studies, I chose Punjab University in Chandigarh, a modern city designed by the famous French architect Le Corbusier. Punjab University campus had several canteens throughout the sprawling campus to keep the young scholars from straying towards unhealthy and unclean street food. The main fare offered at these canteens were tea and snacks. On my very first day at the university, I was introduced to a tall and slender man named Karma, who ran the canteen that served tea and snacks to the students at the chemistry department and the neighboring schools of botany and zoology. Karma's canteen was to become my dining base for the next two years. It was also the feeding local of many day scholars, the BSc. honors students, and the elite research scholars who were pursuing Masters and PhD degrees at the University.

Karma, the proprietor, soon became my friend. He was born in a small village in the Kangra district in the Chamba Hills. He and his younger sister Aarti were the only siblings in a poor family where both the father and the mother worked as cooks for upper-income families. Both parents suffered from poor health. His father had chronic bronchitis and was later diagnosed with tuberculosis. After many years of poor health, he succumbed to this disease. Karma was only nine years old at the time of his father's death. His mother continued her employment working for a property owner who traced his pedigree from the famous Raja Gopal Singh in the Himalayan Mountains. There had been many rajas (royals) at one time in the hills. Rajas owned vast tracts of land, employed many servants, and were entitled to collect tariffs from their subjects, who were mostly tenant farmers. As generations passed, their properties were subdivided and handed down among the siblings of each generation. By the time of Karma's mother's employment, the descendants of the raja she worked for had a considerably diminished fortune. In such circumstances, the not-so-rich raja did not see himself as a commoner and still wished to live in an affluent style. Sadly, his assets were not adequate for his requirements. He paid a mere pittance to Karma's mother.

Karma's mother eventually found a better position with the local police chief. In this home, Karma began his employment as an errand boy. Young Karma helped when there were parties at the chief's house and procured the local moonshine whisky, called Rudi Brand (1). The first distillate of this moonshine (the "premium cut") would produce a speedy intoxication from the volatile and toxic compounds, as the aldehydes were relatively abundant in the premium fraction. The more affluent customers favored this expensive cut.

The police chief and his elite friends loved this potent brew as the good feeling arrived immediately after ingesting the beverage. Karma's mother prepared the meals for these wild, drunken men. Several of them were important and influential citizens and one was a district judge in the area. Karma, now ten years old, knew that these men could get rowdy, vulgar, and would occasionally pass out. Therefore, he never allowed Aarti, his baby sister, to help his mother during such parties. Instead, he would always arrange to be there. That way, he figured, his presence assured that his mother, an attractive woman, was safe from the wild, raucous behavior of the police chief's guests. In any case, the police chief, a widower, admired Karma's mother and would not have tolerated any mistreatment of her by his guests.

Because there were no jobs in the hills suitable to his skills and needs, Karma soon decided to move into a city in the plains. Once there, he found employment as a child cook with a middle-income family. This allowed him to be a more successful provider for his family. To market himself, he decided not to use his birth name, Karam Singh, but adopted the name Karma instead. In this way, he could simplify matters, he thought. His general demeanor was one of a curious youth with a subdued toothy smile. This, he believed, would convey respect but not necessarily warmth and familiarity. Overall, he displayed a sad disposition.

There were many young boys in India who performed adult chores. Terms such as "child labor" or "exploitation" were unknown. No one used terms like "stolen childhood" or "missed opportunities." Generally the younger the child worker, the more admiration he received from his employer and neighbors for his role in the support of his family. Middle-class Indian families eagerly sought child workers from the hills because they had a reputation as excellent errand runners or cooks. Even families who had not yet achieved the middle-class status aspired to possess a child cook from the hills. Such cooks would work for low wages, were obedient, and were trainable. Housewives with child cooks were seen as privileged.

Measured against such desirable traits as obedience, and eagerness to please, Karma could have been considered spoiled. This was a term used by the employers when a child cook started displaying independent behavior and tried to assert minor decision-making authority. When I met, Karma he was already spoiled compared to the fresh imports from the hills.

CANTEEN MANAGER

After carefully surveying his opportunities, Karma found employment in the tea canteen at the university. He began to know his customers by name. He always greeted me warmly and called me "Doctor Sahib." I was not a doctor, but rather a student hoping to earn my Ph.D. that would enable me to use the word 'doctor' before my name someday. To Karma, all graduate students at the campus were doctors.

As a canteen cook, Karma was able to make his own decisions and enjoyed not being told what to do. When he began the canteen work, he was fifteen years old. His last job, prior to the canteen, had lasted for five years.

The employer for that job was a low-level government official and his wife, who was a primary school teacher. The pay they gave him, they said, was market wages, but in truth, it was below average. Karma hated the job but endured it for all those many years because he was the only wage earner in the family at the time. By that time, his mother had died of a liver complication and his sister was at a boarding school.

Karma's sister, Aarti, started attending school and he would not permit her to take any housemaid jobs. He would not allow her to do the work of their mother. To succeed at this promise, he contracted with a distant uncle to have him raise Aarti. He promised that he would send part of his own wages to pay his sister's costs and to help support the schooling of the uncle's young son. A deal was struck and Karma headed for the plains and his future.

Once securely settled in his canteen job, Karma had some status. He called himself the Canteen Manager, although he could not read or write. The real manager/owner was another person who was employed as an accountant with the State Irrigation Department. This owner only surfaced when the time came to renegotiate the canteen contract with the university. At all other times, Karma was the boss, but not a part of any profit-sharing scheme. He was paid a salary that was less than fifteen percent of the pay of a junior professor. Each year he received a raise that permitted him to keep up with the increasing school fee for his baby sister Aarti. She walked the four miles each way to attend the decent school her brother and the distant uncle had selected for her.

Before much time passed, Karma and I became friends. I began sharing my personal stories after listening to stories of his life growing up in the hills. We generally saw each other during the breaks between my classes when I was drinking tea at his canteen. During one of these tea sessions, Karma had me promise that I would visit his village in the Kangra District. The area was known to be beautiful and cleaner than towns in Punjab. Generally, Indian hill towns presented a stark contrast to the hot, humid, noisy, and dusty environment of the plains towns, even though there was more poverty in the hills.

Karma talked about his baby sister at length and wanted me to meet her. She was now thirteen and beginning to show signs of maturing into a woman. This worried Karma. He told me she could benefit from my sage advice. He wanted me to advise her on her studies, the value of a college education, and to try to motivate her to achieve success as I had done. He was greatly impressed that I was going to America.

THE ANNAPOORNA CONTRACT

In the ancient language Sanskrit, अन्नपूर्णा, means *provider of food and nourishment.* Annapoorna, also spelled as Annapurna, is the goddess of nourishment, an important deity in India. The goddess's home is Kashi in the modern city of Varanasi or Benares. Goddess Annapoorna, however, also likes the cool Himalayan Mountains because that is the home of some of the best cooks. Karma was the perfect devotee of the Goddess. He spent all his working hours providing meals to others from tasty food that he prepared with his own two hands with little help from others. He held this position essentially all his life.

After awhile, he began to feel that the university canteen did not meet his needs. The canteen owner did not pay him adequately, he thought, for his culinary skills and his superior performance. His salary was low by Indian pay scales at the time. Additionally, he did not feel he could adequately display his culinary skills with such a limited menu. Running a daytime college canteen limited him to making gallons of sweet white tea, spicy fritters (pakoras), and a daily menu of daal (lentils) with whole-wheat chapattis. This routine was punctuated occasionally with a fresh garden vegetable and cucumber salad (raita). The Annapoorna entrepreneur knew he had more to offer.

While Karma was immersed in this dilemma, some of his loyal customers devised a plan. Three of us graduate students (all of whom were research scholars) found a chemistry faculty member who would join us in our plan. We decided to pool our resources, rent a four-bedroom condominium (flat) in the new section named Model Town, which was near the campus, and hire Karma as our cook. We found a town house that came equipped with a kitchen, running water (cold water only – but still a good thing!), and a western-style bathroom with a shower. This place was an absolute luxury even for the modern city of Chandigarh (2), which was designed by Le Corbusier. The Annapoorna entrepreneur was excited by the idea and came to the apartment to explore the opportunity. Oh how his eyes grew in size when he first saw the brand-new kitchen. His inspection was sealed with a tremendous shriek of approval!

"This is the kind of kitchen I deserve for my cooking!" he said.

"Then why don't you join us?" one of my flatmates replied.

"Is this for real?" Karma blurted in his Kangri dialect.

"You have the job, Mr. Annapoorna," I assured him.

We celebrated Karma's hiring with a noisy party the following week.

Potent Mohan Meakin Dyer whisky was consumed in generous amounts. Karma prepared his spicy deep-fried concoctions and considered it an honor to inaugurate the newly painted and modern kitchen. Two weeks later, Karma resigned from his university canteen job and became our full-time cook. He had found a replacement, a mundu (small kid) from his village, to work at the canteen. The mundu was already in town but fed up with his current employer due to the house madam's unending demands. Some of the tasks the house madam demanded were beyond the mundu's ability at the time. The university job was a promotion for him. Mundu had a name that his mother had given him, but most employers ignored that in favor of the generic term mundu, meaning child servant.

The four-bedroom flat we rented had no provision for a servant or a cook to live in. Later, such amenities became a standard feature in upscale townhouses designed for emerging upper-middle-class families. When provided, the servant quarters usually contained a closet-size apartment with enough room for a cot, a small desk, and some hooks and hangers for clothing. Fortunately, this lack of accommodation for the cook was not a deal breaker. Karma agreed to stay in the little shack where he was already living with two mundu cooks from the valley. He contentedly walked the short distance from there to his new place of employment.

The four of us believed we had found heaven on earth. We dreamt that the cook would arrive at 6 AM punctually every morning to serve us bed tea when we were still in bed and half asleep. The bed tea concept was developed by the British colonists as a way to start the tropical mornings without haste. They were in no hurry to report to work. They had no fear of anyone yelling at them for being late to work. We felt we should live like the colonial masters. With our stipends from the university and the help of our supporting parents, we believed we should mimic the colonial lifestyle. The first step towards this goal was to be served tea in bed.

After we had settled into our routines in the flat, I approached Karma with the bed tea proposition. He was shocked. He had not encountered such a decadent bourgeois request from any of his previous masters. He considered the matter and looked at the ceiling for a time. "That would be all right, Doctor Sahib, but it would be great if someone could first give me a hot cup of tea because I am usually groggy very early in the morning."

While I was still analyzing the implications of what he had just said, Karma realized the absurdity of his own statement and said, "Oh that was stupid of me. I told you it takes me awhile in the morning to get going!"

172

MICHELIN THREE-STARS IN OUR OWN KITCHEN

The colonial routine was on. Karma would serve the steamy perfumed tea to each of us while we were still in bed. Immediately afterward, he would start preparing the daily special (breakfast), the details of which he never revealed before the meal was served. Soon we understood the reason for this secrecy. Why ruin the anticipation? Every meal was akin to dining in a three-star Michelin restaurant, only Indian style. First came another cup of tea but spiced less heavily (than the bed tea) with cinnamon, cloves, cardamom, and a touch of ginger. Corn flakes (a novelty in Chandigarh in those days) soaked in warm unpasteurized milk followed this. A savory omelet stuffed with onion, green pepper, and a generous dose of chili pepper came next. The omelet was always accompanied by a thin parantha (pancake) smothered with fresh butter. Some days, the omelet was replaced by a pair of paranthas stuffed with cooked mashed potatoes or finely grated cauliflower. The parantha was occasionally replaced with a poori, the fried and fluffy wafers, which were delicious and greasy.

Karma's cooking was strictly timed to when the patrons were ready to sit down for the meal. Lunches were not part of this regimen. We ate lunches at the college canteen now run by Karma's mundu friend from the hills. On weekends, we ate at the cinema because that was where everybody else went to eat and watch the PG-13 Hollywood matinee offerings. To watch R-rated and X-rated foreign films, you needed connections and money. Those were not available to us.

Karma was a movie addict. He had seen some of his favorite movies multiple times. Maybe he was wasting money he needed to educate his sister, but this was the only entertainment he could afford. Movies were cheap if you did not care where you sat. We cleared his Sundays to allow him to pursue his passion. Karma appreciated this. We were a different sort of employer than he had before. He even invited his two cook friends to see that he was living well. They were impressed and jealous.

The four of us flatmates were a diverse lot. Although we were all Panjabis; the fact that we came from different parts of Punjab and spoke slightly different dialects gave us a feeling of diversity. We made fun of each other's pronunciations and we corrected each other's joke endings. Sometimes Karma tried to mediate, but such an action was pointless. We never understood his reasoning nor his humor.

One of our flatmates was a full-faculty member in the chemistry department. He had just returned from the USA where he had earned his

173

PhD at Tulane University in New Orleans. He was four or five years older than the rest of us but looked older. The reason for this was his long flowing dark beard that made him look like a religious preacher. His real name was M. K. Singh, but we called him Maulvi. He did not object to his given name because it implied the learned one.

Having recently returned from America, Maulvi's conversation was tinged with western idioms and mannerisms. He would constantly correct us by saying, "That is not how Americans do this." One time Raji and I had a fight over something. Maulvi brokered the peace and gave us a mild tongue-lashing. I asked him, "How do Americans mediate fights among friends?"

He gave me a disdainful look and said, "Americans don't fight. Only Indians do. Americans express their displeasure in more civilized ways." *(Living in America now for the last five decades, I wish Maulvi's pronouncements were true.)*

Maulvi became the de facto head of the house; a position he filled well.

Fondly called Uncle, our eldest roommate Surjeet, deserved the position because of his regal appearance and his sage manners, but the fact that Maulvi was educated in America trumped every other qualification or skill that Surjeet possessed. We gladly accepted Maulvi's leadership realizing that he was, America-returned, when none of us had even been to Calcutta at that time.

Being, America-returned also gave Maulvi a leg up over the several dozen, England-returned in town. The England-returned crowd included dentists, teachers, auto mechanics, and a couple of tailors who had adorned their billboards outside their shops with the, "England Returned", testimonials. There was no evidence that any of them had gone to UK to get an education at Oxford or Cambridge. Two of our faculty indeed had been to those bastions of scholarship, but they were too sophisticated to hang a banner on their doors and so was Maulvi. He ridiculed all our suggestions of hanging a placard on our front door stating that an "America-returned Ph.D. resided in this humble abode."

THE KARMA MATH INITIATIVE

The traditional Indian class barriers separating cooks from masters were crumbling in our household due to some extent to Maulvi's regular sermons of equality. We started thinking of Karma as a member of our family and every now and then, we asked him to sit down with us to eat. He always

174

rejected this request with the argument that he could not serve fresh-off-the-grill chapattis to us if he was sitting with us at the dinner table cracking jokes. "Who will be serving the food if we were all sitting at the table waiting to be served?" He looked at us waiting for an answer. He was certain that such action would be a disgrace to his profession and he would be breaking his Annapoorna oath. (An oath, which he never took in the first place.) He never shared a table with us except one night before I was to leave for the USA. His two "hill-mates" served the meal.

One day during breakfast, we concurred that his culinary skills, hard work, and his desire to please, would make him a great restaurant owner and he could be earning more money than serving tea to the graduate students at a university canteen or as a private cook. Maulvi even suggested a name for his future restaurant, "Karma's Cajun Dhaba" (roadside diner). The rest of us had no idea at the time what the word Cajun meant or how Cajun food tasted. Maulvi told us that Cajun food was spicy like Karma's creations. He also argued that the foreign-sounding restaurant name would attract the curious university crowd.

Karma's biggest problem was that he lacked basic mathematical skills. For simple calculations, he was entirely dependent on his fingers and his two thumbs, one of which he had accidently chopped in half as a child when slicing a head of cauliflower. I thought we could teach him basic math that would allow him to run a restaurant. When he had a profit, he could hire a bookkeeper. We dubbed the math project as the "Karma Math Initiative" and I volunteered to be Karma's math teacher. I sat Karma down one day and said, "We will start slowly and then pick up speed. Let us start with math that will help you right away with your current job."

"Yes, Doctor, let us go," Karma agreed.

The lessons began.

"Okay, Karma, when you go to the farmer's market this Saturday, buy two dozen eggs (we consumed large amounts of eggs). Tell me, if one egg was half a rupee, how much should the bill be for twenty-four eggs?"

Karma could not believe his ears. He gave me a disbelieving look as if he was questioning my fitness to pursue a Ph.D. He blurted out, "Excuse me, but what kind of an idiot would pay that much for eggs? I pay less than half for the best ones on the market!"

I felt like saying, "Karma, actually you are looking at such an idiot." but I refrained. That would have been over the limit and breach of a protocol between an employer and his cook even for us as perceived liberals.

I asked Maulvi to take over the "Annapoorna Math Project" for a while. After all, he was the American-trained scholar. Maulvi gladly took over the project with good results probably using techniques he leaned at Tulane.

MATCH MAKER

Despite my failure as a teacher of math, Karma and I were bonding. He started talking more and more about his family. He told me about his childhood, the beautiful Himalayan sunrises, haunting music of the Kangra valley, and the beautiful and shy "pahari" maidens. He talked about his baby sister Aarti and repeated his resolve to send her to college. In his mind, she would not be a housemaid for some rich person as his mother was or someone's cook for the rest of her life. I interrupted him, "Maybe she could be the proprietor of the wildly popular "Karma's Cajun Dhaba." This produced a subdued smile, but he continued, "Doctor, I really want you to visit my village. As you know, I am going home for one month in June to visit my family. June is the best month in the hills. Soon you might be headed for America. Who knows, you may never have another opportunity. You must visit the Chamba Hills before leaving India. You will enjoy the break," he emphasized.

"You have convinced me, Karma. I would love to go to your village. You will be my tour guide. We will have good time. Let us take something nice for Aarti," I said. In an instant, he started to pull out his right hand for a shake but settled for a weak high-five instead.

SWITZERLAND OF INDIA

Karma peppered me with elaborate descriptions of his enchanted Kangra Valley, one of the most picturesque and luxuriant valleys of the lower Himalayas. I already knew the facts. The town called Kangra is only at an elevation of about 2,500 feet above sea level but the valley quickly rises to eye-popping heights above 16,000 feet.

Karma's home was near a town called Chamba at an estimated 4500 feet elevation. From his home, Karma assured me, you could see the high Himalayan peaks as if they were a short walking distance. Despite its small size, Chamba has a rich history going back thousands of years, but Karma did not elaborate upon that. He never read any books. He never learned to read.

I needed no more prompting. I was sold. Moreover, I had another important reason to visit Karma's world. My sister Nikki had just been transferred to a hill town called Baijnath in the Kangra Valley to manage a

Health Clinic. Nikki was a public health nurse and had graduated from the Miss Brown's Memorial Christian Medical College in Ludhiana, Punjab. In a short time at her new assignment, she had attained celebrity status in Baijnath and the surrounding villages due to her kindness and passion for helping the sick and the poor who were plentiful in the area. How great! I thought. I would visit Karma's home and spend a few days in Baijnath. I was very excited.

A week after Karma went to his village; I followed on the same route for the long bus ride to Chamba. Karma had arranged for me to stay at the nearby rest house operated by the forest ranger in the area. The English who loved these idyllic administrative enclaves in the remote hill posts built such relatively sophisticated abodes throughout the area. Karma had influence at the lodge. Before coming down to the plains to seek his fortune, he had briefly cooked for the lodge resident. With Karma's recommendation, the new caretaker treated me like royalty.

The lodge where I stayed near Karma's village (Illustration by Danny Uppal)

The next day, I invited Karma to come for dinner at the lodge and to bring his sister Aarti with him. I wanted to give her some souvenirs; things she could use when she went to the boarding house at her intended middle school. I reminded Karma to ask Aarti to bring her musical instrument

177

(veena) with her so she could sing a local Pahari song for us.

Around five PM, Karma came with Aarti. We sat down in the verandah overlooking the valley below. About two hours remained before the sunset. Without looking at me, Aarti nervously inched closer, lowered her eyes further, cupped her hands in a perfect lock, and in barely audible tones said, "Namaste Doctor Sahib." I reciprocated with folded hands but not with matching grace. I motioned for her to sit down next to me.

After the resident cook served spiced tea, I asked Aarti if she would play some local hill songs. She politely declined, but this was a temporary gesture. After some arm twisting by her brother, she agreed on the condition that she be allowed to sing a film song because she was more familiar with Bollywood film songs than with hill music. The Bollywood song she would sing would be very much like the folk songs of Chamba and she could play the veena. Before beginning, she retreated to the cottage to tune the instrument.

When we entered, we found Aarti squatted gracefully on the hard-carpeted floor. She straddled the veena between her knees and started singing while swaying gently.

"Mora gora rung lei le (**take away my fair complexion**)
Mohe shyam rung dei de (**give me the dark color of Shyama – Lord Krishna**)
Chhup jaoongi raat hee mein (**I will become one with the dark night**)

Mohe pii ka sung dei de (**Unite me with my beloved**)

The rendition was magical, although I thought a bit mature theme for a thirteen-year-old. In the high Himalayan hills, however, girls mature early, I had been told. Aarti was now deeply into the song. Her eyes were shut; she was swaying gently, and seemed oblivious of anyone around. She was in ecstasy. Even Karma was surprised at the intensity of her immersion.

Suddenly, I realized her words were not directed at any mortal soul. She was singing a devotional song dedicated to Lord Krishna. She was singing songs that for the uninitiated, might appear like earthly love songs but were actually devotional songs. To be in love and to be one with Krishna was the ultimate goal for millions of faithful. Such was complete devotion and unconditional surrender to the Lord. It occurred to me that the devotional theme was entirely fitting for the evening. After all, her own name Aarti meant evening prayer.

It was surreal. The sun was now a few minutes shy of disappearing behind the fir trees below. Unfortunately, no one had a camera to capture the scene that even the most accomplished Hollywood director would have difficulty visualizing. Soon the evening was over. Karma turned around and said, "Okay Aarti, bid Namaste to Doctor Sahib. Time to go home." He then asked me if I wanted to go for a walk in the woods the next day to watch the sunrise.

"Sounds wonderful," I answered as I patted Karma on the back.

The next day, Karma and I met for our morning walk. Everything was eerily quiet. There was no traffic, no sounds, only birds chirping. After a few minutes, Karma stopped. With a gentle tug on my elbow, he stopped me as well. Then he inched closer to me, took a deep breath and said, "Doctor Sahib, I have been meaning to ask you this. Do you like Aarti? Isn't she a sweet girl? I know she can talk some English. Last night I heard you saying a few things to her in English and she understood and enjoyed everything."

Without waiting for an answer he continued. He did not want to break his line of thought, fearing that if he did, he would lose the initiative. Then his opportunity might evaporate and he might not be able to summon enough courage to express what was to come.

"Doctor Sahib, Aarti will make a nice wife for a Ph.D. research scholar. She is on her way to leaning English. She will look," he said and hesitated, groping for a suitable word and then resumed, "she will look modern in the clothes that the girls at the university wear." He hesitated again and said, "She is a better cook than I am."

I was unprepared! There followed a long awkward moment when no

179

words were spoken. The silence was stunning. Even the noisy forest birds seemed to have decided to observe a moment of silence while waiting for the answer. I had to break the silence.

"Aarti is a beautiful girl. With your help, she is destined for college and when she graduates, she will marry a successful young man who may be a doctor or a lawyer. Just imagine Karma, what man would not want a wife with the looks and intellect of Aarti? You know that now she is just a child. Like me, the research scholars that I know off at the university are all twice her age. Let her grow up first. Maybe I can recommend someone in a few years, someone who is from a superior caste, maybe even a bright Brahmin boy."

Karma was disappointed but not ready to give up. He continued, "But Doctor, she will soon turn fourteen, a good age around these hills for a girl to be married, or at least get engaged so she can plan her future. Her fiancé can go to America, finish his studies and when he comes back, she would be waiting. Maybe this is written in her karma (fate)." Suddenly Karma realized what he had said. We both laughed. The laughter was short lived and I responded, "You are a good brother Karma. You will find a good match for your sister."

I looked at Karma. He had his face cupped between both his hands. He was sobbing, "I understand, but Doctor, I hope you can understand." I want Aarti to have good life. I do not want her to be cleaning dishes for rich people all her life, the way I have done. The way my mother did. She deserves better."

"She will not wash anyone's dishes except her own and maybe not even that. She will marry someone well-to-do and will hire her own mundu to do dishes," I assured him.

"I hope you are right," Karma said softly while still drying his eyes with the corner of his shirt. We were nearing his uncle's house where our paths diverged. I went to the lodge and Karma kept going straight on the path towards his uncle's house. Karma was going back to Chandigarh the next day. I was taking the bus to Baijnath to visit my sister.

CLOSURE OF THE THREE STAR EATERY

About three months after my visit to Karma's village, the "flat fraternity" started disintegrating. I received my acceptance at the University of Southern California and started preparing for my departure to America. Respected Surjeet Uncle had found a lectureship in Amritsar and would

180

move to his new location within two months. Maulvi married and decided to move into a house with his bride. Raji, the fourth roommate, found a residence closer to his secret girlfriend's home. This was a reckless move for him as the father of the secret girlfriend owned a gun. (A gun would be impossible for a typical person to acquire in India, but as the girlfriend's father was an ex-military officer, he had no problem.)

Karma was left with no alternative. He started looking at the university for other job opportunities. We encouraged him to bid for the canteen contract himself. This time he hit jackpot. He purchased the canteen contract and moved back to the university. Once there, the first thing he did was to hang a large nameplate in front of his shop saying: "*Mr. Karam Singh, Sole Proprietor.*"

The weekend before I was to leave for America, Karma invited my closest friends on the campus and threw a magnificent feast. He cooked his favorite dishes and invited two of his Kangra friends to help. This was a grand treat, the Three-Star dining all over again!

One day before my departure to the USA, I said good-bye to Karma and promised to stay in touch. I received occasional news of Karma while in the USA. Several years later, while visiting India, I went to the university to see how he was doing. He was away on that day, but I learned that Karma, the sole proprietor, was doing well. His business was booming. He had added food items that students wanted and he even established credit with his good customers who he could bill on a monthly basis. He had a student who helped him with bookkeeping. I was sorry to miss him.

YEARS LATER

My wife and I were touring India and decided to visit the university campus in Chandigarh. Karma was not there any longer. He had moved on. Very few people remembered him anymore.

At the chemistry department, we found a university employee who remembered Karma. He told us that Karma had sold his catering business several years before our visit. The business had grown steadily over the years and Karma made a little fortune from the sale. He also told us that Karma had put his sister Aarti through four years of college and she had married a well-educated man who was an accountant with a foreign company in Delhi, and by implication, was well-to-do. He also thought that Karma might be a grandfather and most likely living with his sister and the brother-in-law in Delhi.

Revisiting chemistry department to find Karma

Unfortunately, the employee did not have a forwarding address nor the married name of Karma's sister. I wanted to look him up in Delhi, but without a name or a mobile phone number, it was not possible. I wanted to see what Aarti looked like as a grown up woman and a mother. I wanted to congratulate Karma. I would have asked him to raise his right hand up in the air, do a high-five and yell, "We made it!"

(1) Rudi Brand's name arose from the method of brewing the libation. The word, "Rudi" or "Ruri" in the local dialect, meant a heap of cow or buffalo dung. The farmers had learned that burying a barrel of molasses a few feet below the cow dung mound yielded slow and steady fermentation. A measured amount of ammonium chloride (naushaader) would ensure controlled fermentation. Steady fermentation was assured by a constant thirty-five degree centigrade temperature under the well-insulated "Rudi." When the fermentation was complete, the mixture was distilled in a homemade still constructed from the lead pipes of abandoned truck radiators.

(2) Chandigarh was the first planned city in India and besides Le Corbusier masterpieces; it included projects that were designed by equally celebrated architects such as Pierre Jeanneret, Jan Drew, and Maxwell Fry. Chandigarh became an architectural jewel that could show the world the emerging face of India.

CHAPTER 14

SLOW TRAIN TO HER MAJESTY'S
SUMMER CAPITAL

It was the most exciting news I had heard in a long time. The women's field hockey team was going to Shimla for exhibition matches or for a tournament. The distinction was not important to me. What was important was that my friend Balraj (Raj) and I were invited to accompany the field hockey team in the "Women Only" reserved compartment. The invitation came from Cindi (1), the team captain and a local sports star. The idea of travelling to Shimla with my best friend Raj in the company of twenty young women for the seven-hour slow journey to Shimla was outrageously exciting and difficult to comprehend. Cindi told me not to tell to anyone that she had secured permission from the team manager to let her two "cousins" (Raj and me) travel in the same coach.

Cindi and I had become friends at the University in Chandigarh. She was a sophomore there while I was finishing my master's degree. I was also a part-time instructor and taught students who chose chemistry as their secondary (non-elective) subject. Cindi attended my chemistry class for one semester. Any socialization outside class, and especially away from the campus, between students and instructors was frowned upon, to put it mildly. This rule seemed silly to me. Cindi was only four years

183

younger than I was, and I was not her actual teacher. I did not score her papers (another more senior faculty member did). So I convinced myself that the "no fraternizing" rule did not apply to me. Moreover, my contact with Cindi was limited to fleeting hellos and brief chit-chats after classes.

Cindi was a terrific hockey player. I attended her matches whenever possible. She was small and thin, may be five-foot-three-inches tall, very agile, and aggressive. Although she was not beautiful in the supermodel sense, she was definitely attractive and sexy. Very sexy indeed.

Cindi played a midfield forward position and developed a scoring style that became her signature move. She would charge the goal, and then abruptly veer to the extreme left, and would toss the ball towards the net from a steep angle. Cindi learned this technique from a famous Indian field hockey player named Ramdas. Every time she scored from the unusually steep angle, spectators went wild and screamed: "Cindi, Cindi!" She always raised her stick in acknowledgement.

On one particular Sunday, she was in a critical game. The match had been scoreless; making the game dull. With three minutes left, Cindi broke through the midfielder then dodged the fullback near the striking circle (the "D" arc). She veered to the extreme left until she was almost at the penalty corner attacker's spot. The spectators sighed. They thought she had gone too far and missed her best chance. They were wrong. Cindi turned, lunged forward, and tossed the ball into the goal from a very steep angle. The crowd went wild and yelled, "Cindi! Cindi!" She waved at the crowed. She spotted me and waived again, this time at me. After the game ended, I waited while she finished the victory celebration with her team members.

She came up to me and said, "Thank you, sir, for cheering. I know you have been to other games before. I appreciate that and I admire your love of the sport." Her calling me sir was odd but not surprising. Although I was almost her age and not a real professor, I commanded respect. *Only in India!*

The five-minute conversation must have triggered something. Cindi and I started "accidently" bumping into each other at the large and busy campus. One time I finally asked her if she would like to have tea at the nearby canteen unless she was going to a class. She said she did not have a class at the time (that was a lie) and had tea with me. She told me about herself, her family, and that her goal was to get on the Punjab State women's field hockey team and ultimately the National Hockey Team, which had aspirations for Olympic competition. I wished her good luck. I also asked her if she would like to meet for tea again. She agreed and suggested we go to a different teashop farther from her classes where there was less academic traffic.

I did not see her for two weeks until we bumped into each other in the library. She came to me, lowered her voice and said, "Sir, I am mad at you. Why didn't you tell me that you have been accepted to a university in California and that you will be leaving us in a few months?" I was shocked by her emotional question and asked her how she knew this information. I had not told many people.

"It is all over campus," she said. "How many lucky souls from this campus get to go to a California university on a scholarship?" She had done her research.

I was in a hurry so I told her I would fill her in on the details of my plan the next time we met. We had promised to meet for tea every week on Wednesdays. On one Wednesday, she had an evening class, but she chose not to tell me. Instead, she proposed we go to dinner at the restaurant at the Mount View Hotel, the only decent hotel in Chandigarh at the time. I agreed. She said that she would have to be home before 8 PM.

"The restaurant probably doesn't even open by then," I reminded her.

"Then we will skip dinner," she said calmly.

The restaurant at the Mount View Hotel was not open when we got there but the small coffee and teashop was. While sipping the spiced tea, Cindi became serious. She said, "So sir, our tea rendezvous are short lived. I know you are going to paradise. New friends, new adventures, new scenery. Cindi will still be here and I know you will not come back because when people go to America they forget everyone back home. Maybe they want to purge all those memories."

The conversation was making me uncomfortable. I could not think of anything encouraging to say to her. My mind was savoring the news of my acceptance at the University of Southern California (USC) and I was anxious about my trip to America. I worried about such things as: what if I ran out of money before completing my studies, what if I failed at my studies, what if I did not fit in in America, who would I call for help if I ran into trouble? (I did not have a rich uncle back home to bail me out). My family was spending every bit of savings they had to buy my airfare to California. I was in no shape to have a girlfriend until I settled down after my education was completed.

Cindi noticed my silence and said, "I am sorry, I am not asking you for anything. Don't worry, relax."

"Cindi, you are also headed for big things," I assured her. "Just imagine being on the National Field Hockey Team." She found no comfort in my words but rather was in deep thought. The time was close to 8 PM. I reminded her of the curfew and we rose to walk to the bicycle stand. She gave me a quick hug and peddled away.

Two days later, she spotted me on campus. Another woman who was a member of the field hockey team accompanied her. She introduced me to her this way, "Sunila, this is my cousin Jas. He is a lecturer in chemistry and is headed to the USA in a couple of months for advanced studies."

"You lucky man," Sunila said with a touch of jealousy. Then she turned to Cindi and said, "You never told me you have a cousin on the faculty here. Why have I never run into your cousin before?" Cindi deftly changed the topic.

I had noticed Sunila before, as had every male student on campus. She was beautiful, almost as if someone transplanted her from a Bombay film studio to campus in preparation for shooting a college romance movie. She had poise, sophistication, and charm that was unique among the many beautiful women on the Chandigarh campus.

Sunila was an English major. She asked me if I know of a university in the USA that had a Ph.D. program in archeology. She specifically inquired about the University of Pennsylvania.

"Sunila, you know more about the educational opportunities in America than I do. Perhaps you should coach me before I go there."

Cindi was feeling left out. She turned to Sunila and said, "Sunila, let us break the exciting news to bhaji." (2) (Note: *I had persuaded Cindi not to call me sir since we had become friends. She decided to call me bhaji [brother] but sometimes she would call me veerji, which also means brother. She alternated between bhaji and veerji, both affectionate and comforting sounds. I preferred veerji, a nice term when you are concealing your true relationship*).

Cindi turned to me and said, "Our field hockey team has been invited to play matches in Shimla. Sunila and I are very excited. Maybe you can go with us to Shimla and you can bring your friend Raj with you. You should see Shimla before you go to America. Who knows, maybe you will never have a chance again or you may not even care."

"What a fantastic idea. How would this work? You girls will be in reserved compartments. When you arrive, you will be bussed to your hotel and Raj and I would be left hunting for a cheap, flea-infested room," I said.

"No you won't. You will be travelling with us in the same 'Women Only' compartment before you check into your fleabag hotel." She winked and smiled as she said that.

"That is a sick joke," I said. "You want us to get pulverized by the morality squads or by the railway police for travelling in the women's coach?"

Sunila came to the rescue. "Don't worry veerji, Cindi is right. You two are family. Cindi is the team captain. She has influence. I also have influence being the assistant captain. We have already talked to the head coach who will be travelling with the team but in another compartment with the rest of the coaching staff. According to Cindi, coach has agreed that you two, being family members, can travel with us. Coach probably feels that it would be a benefit to have two strong young men in the women's compartment on the slow night train with so many stops."

I was in awe. I did not know how to react. I wanted to convey the good news to Raj as soon as possible.

When I broke the news to Raj, he started jumping up and down like a monkey. At that time, a thought occurred to me. What if we were discovered? We would be ashamed and become the laughing stock of the campus. What worried me most was what if the news got to my professor in America. Could it kill my chances of going to the USA?

I expressed my concerns to Raj. He laughed and said, "Relax man. What if your professor finds out that you pretended to be a girl's cousin when you are not. Do you think he is going to cancel your fellowship? Come on! Americans do not care about such things, only Indians do. As for me, I think the scandal could make me more popular with the women here." His words were most reassuring. I thanked him. He resumed his monkey dance. I joined him.

A few days after that, I bumped into Cindi and Sunila who were walking together. I invited them to tea. As Cindi was late to her class, she suggested I take Sunila to tea because Sunila had some free time. At tea, Sunila told me about her family and her own aspirations. She was from Ambala, a fair-sized city not far from Chandigarh. Her family was well to do. Her father was a military officer and a substantial landowner. During our conversation, Sunila reiterated her desire to go to the USA to pursue an archeology degree and asked for my help. I said I would. Cindi soon joined us. She had no more classes for the day. We talked about the dream vacation to Shimla and agreed that it would be nice if we could spend a few extra days there after the games were over.

SLOW TRAIN TO PARADISE

Before we parted, Cindi discretely told me to meet them at the Kalka railway station near their train compartment just before the narrow gauge train was to depart. In view of the clandestine nature of our trip, she did not want Raj and me to join them before the train was ready to leave. That would allow too much time for probing questions from her teammates. We did as told. When the stationmaster blew the final whistle, we jumped aboard. Two of the girls started to block us by saying that the car was for women only. Sunila intervened. "Ladies these two young men are family. They are Cindi's cousins. They will ride with us. Mr. Ramesh Kumar, the head coach, has approved their stay in our compartment. They will be good to have with us on this all-night train with so many undesirable characters hovering around at the stations."

Raj interrupted her. "Ladies we will take care of any intruder who tries to misbehave. We are not carrying weapons, but we are moving weapons ourselves." With that, he did his best karate move and finished by shouting, "Hah!" Half of the girls clapped. The others were still trying to figure us out.

The train was moving by this time. We quickly grabbed two empty seats. Somehow, I ended up next to Cindi and Raj sat next to Sunila. I know he was dying to do a high-five but fortunately did not.

As the train ascended out of Kalka station, the compartment grew cold. Two hours into the journey, Cindi unrolled a small blanket and moved closer, allowing me to share the warm cover with her. This was the first time I had been closer to her than shaking hands. Sunila saw this and pulled out her own blanket. She motioned to Raj to share her blanket. She did not know Raj, so she kept a more respectable distance, but still allowed him to share the cover. Raj was not bothered by this. This was a small step for the man. He was in heaven. He could imagine the future.

Most of the team members were now asleep or dozing. Cindi and I were wide-awake. Cindi squeezed my hand under the blanket and we looked at each other. I motioned for her to be careful. Perhaps not everyone was asleep.

She turned her head to the other side, pretended to be asleep, but still clutched my hand. We must have eventually gone to sleep because when the train stopped, daybreak was near.

The stationmaster came into the compartment and shouted, "There will be a long stop here. There is a nice restaurant just a few yards uphill. It is serving early breakfast. Go ahead and enjoy, but come back to your compartment when you hear the whistle." The four of us dashed to the small restaurant and grabbed the best seats. Several other girls followed but most decided to sleep.

Train to Shimla

Our waiter was a delightful old man, fluent in English. After he served our food, he told us that he has been working there since the days of British rule and the place was better maintained at that time. "Before Independence, this restaurant was only open to Englishmen or other dignitaries travelling to Shimla. Ordinary Indians were not admitted. They could only eat at the fast food stalls on the platform. During those days, the train would stop for a long time on some days. The tradition was that the train could not leave as long as an Englishman was still having his meal. The station master would come in to check and give the green go flag only if no Englishman was still in the restaurant," he said speaking with regret that the good old days were gone. Then he said, "Ladies and gentlemen, now times are different. You must go back at the first warning whistle. No one is going to hold the train for you."

Soon the whistle blew. The waiter came back to our table. Raj gave him the exact cash he was already clutching with his right hand. The train started going uphill very slowly. You could feel the engine groan as the train attacked the incline. After a long time, the train halted at a big station. We had arrived in Shimla.

As soon as the train stopped, all hell broke loose. Passengers positioned to get out of the train in a hurry. Red-shirted coolies swarmed around the well-dressed passengers, trying to grab their bags. A local sports official welcomed the field hockey team to Shimla and prepared to escort them to their hotel. Raj and I said temporary good-bye to Sunila who was staying with the team.

View of the Himalayan Mountains from Shimla

Raj and I stayed with Cindi who was waiting for her cousin (a real one from her mother's side) and his wife. She would stay with her relatives who lived in Shimla. They spotted us and started waving. Cindi turned to her cousin's wife and introduced me saying, "bhabiji (sister-in-law) this is one of my professors and his friend Balraj who is starting his Ph.D. program in zoology. They are both field hockey addicts. I invited them to accompany our team and be our body guards during the long night journey."

The cousin acknowledged our contribution to the safety of his cousin by nodding his head the correct way and said, "I hope you were able to get some sleep, gentlemen. Those hockey women can be very rowdy. I know it from our Cindi." He pulled Cindi close to him and gave her a nice brotherly hug. Raj and I both felt a slight bit of jealousy.

The cousin then turned to us and said, "I am sorry gentlemen, we only have a small flat. I wish we could have accommodated you at our place, but you would not be happy there. I will drop you on the way at one of the inexpensive hotels where I know the owner."

"That will be very nice," we both said simultaneously. We happily hopped into his Ambassador car, driven by a young chauffeur. At the hotel, the cousin helped us secure a room and promised to see us later.

For the next two days, we did not see Cindi and Sunila nor did we go to their games. They were busy and we were busy with our own activities. On the third and the last day after their matches, Cindi invited us to go with them to the ice skating rink. Two of their other team members were also coming.

Shimla had many attractions and ice skating was one of the highlights. None of us had ever been to an ice skating rink before. We tried our skills at ice skating and fortunately succeeded in avoiding serious bodily harm. The onlookers were delighted with our clumsy moves.

After skating, we went for dinner, but we were in a pensive mood. Although we had one more day in Shimla, the thought of the end of the dream vacation had already started gnawing at us. Then Raj devised a new plan.

SCANDAL POINT

Our last day in Shimla was to be devoted to taking in as many sights and events as we could. We spent the whole day with Cindi and Sunila.

After breakfast, we headed to the Shimla Mall, a must see on every visitor's itinerary. It was early. At that time, there were very few people at the mall. Shops were just opening and we headed straight to the spot named Scandal Point.

Scandal Point, Shimla

Scandal Point is perhaps the most visited site on the Shimla Mall. It owes its popularity to a famous story from the British days. The story is that the Maharaja of Patiala State noticed a beautiful young English woman strolling near that location, introduced himself, and suggested she accompany him to his palace. Some accounts of the incident say that he abducted her, but that has never been authenticated. In any case, the young lady turned out to be the daughter of the Indian Viceroy. Horrified, the British banned the friendly Maharaja from all entrances to Shimla. Subsequently the Maharaja built a new palace on a hilltop only thirty miles from Shimla in a show of defiance (3).

Cindi and I headed straight to Scandal Point while Sunila stopped at a shop on the way. Raj accompanied her. Raj was still trying to win over Sunila but was not making much progress.

When Cindi and I arrived at Scandal Point, we were the only ones there. Cindi surveyed the landscape. Suddenly she emerged from behind me and planted a moist kiss on my lips. Two boys from a distance saw us and whistled. There were no policemen around, or this could have been a scandal of our own! In India, at that time, kissing any girl in public could get you in trouble. The consequences might include police harassment or roughing up by the omnipresent ruffians who sometimes assumed the role of morality police. If you escaped physical assault, you could count on a lecture from an elderly person.

Cindi and I immediately established a more appropriate risk-free distance between us when we saw Sunila and Raj coming towards us. I worried whether Sunila had witnessed the kiss and if my cover as Cindi's cousin was blown.

I could not see Sunila's expression from the distance. She joined us, smiled, and said, "Let us not hang around here long. We do not want to create our own scandals." I sighed with relief and convinced myself she had not seen anything. We had lunch at the mall.

After listening to the Scandal Point story, Raj came up with an idea. "Ladies and Gentlemen (he and I were the only men there), it would be a crime to end the trip so soon. I have been talking to the man at our hotel about what else we should see here in Shimla. When I told him that we were travelling with two young single women, he recommended going to Chail, the scandalous young Maharaja's secluded summer palace, the ultimate romantic place on earth. Need I say more?" He paused and waited for response.

"I like the idea," I said. "Let us go to Chail tomorrow."

Cindi raised her hand and said, "Count me in. I do not have to inform my parents. I will just inform my Shimla cousin and let him convey the change in plan. My parents are very liberal. They know I am in good company and I can take care of myself," she said with pride.

We looked at Sunila. She was thinking and finally said, "Yes, count me in, too, but I have to contact my parents in Ambala. I am sure they will not object knowing that I am in good company." Raj snickered a little but fortunately, Cindi and Sunila did not notice.

HIGHWAY TO HEAVEN

The next morning we took the bus to Chail. The ride to the palace exceeded our expectations. For the two-hour long bus trip, we had an unobstructed view of the snowcapped Himalayan Mountains, which towered thousands of feet above us. Raj sat next to Sunila in the bus and was trying to make small conversation. Sunila did not seem interested. Instead, she watched the beautiful scenery unfold. She knew Raj's stories could wait.

We found rooms at a small hilltop cottage. It was modest, clean, and had the best view of the mountains around. After we checked in, we went for a hike in the nearby woods. Situated at an altitude of 7,000 feet, the place was surrounded by forests of Chir pine and gigantic Deodar trees. It was a hiker's paradise!

Soon we ran into a charming young couple. They were more curious about us than we were about them. The man turned out to be the manager of the Maharaja's Chail palace. He introduced himself as Rahul and his wife as Komal. I introduced Raj and me as Cindi's cousins and Sunila as Cindi's field hockey teammate and her best friend. They wanted to know what brought us to Chail and how long we were in town. All this time, Komal was scanning our faces with extreme curiosity and delight. She seemed liberal-minded and very perceptive. She had figured out that we were not very legitimate, meaning that we were not on a parentally sanctioned trip. Perhaps she was thinking, "This is the face of modern India," although she and her husband were good representatives of that India.

Komal turned to her husband and said, "Darling, why don't we invite these young people to the palace tomorrow for afternoon tea?" Rahul agreed.

Tea with the palace couple was another clue that we were in heaven and not in Punjab. They gave us the grand tour. When we came to the Maharaja's dining room, we froze in astonishment. It was the most magnificent dining room that any of us had ever seen. Much of the furnishings, utensils, and the crockery was alien to us. Almost everything seemed imported. In one corner was a grand piano covered with a red cloth. We wanted to spend more time there. It was educational.

Komal sensed it and said, "We use this room only when Maharaja or his special guests are staying at the palace, but you are also special guests so we will have tea in this room." She pointed to the cook who was already standing nearby in anticipation of the Madam's commands.

Tea was served on a silver tray in ornate cups and was accompanied by fruits so fresh and sweet that I wondered their origin. They were not from the stalls Raj and I frequented. We were thanking our lucky stars. We must have done something extraordinary to merit this amazing experience.

All the next day, we explored the trails recommended by Rahul and Komal. We visited a small village in the hills and bought some local fruit. During the hike, I thought Cindi was trying to hold my hand. I quietly discouraged her, but both Raj and Sunila saw it. In the evening, we went to the Punjabi Dhaba (an informal diner where the food was cooked in an earthen oven) near us. The food was delicious and the Dhaba manager was a jolly bearded man.

The next morning, while I was waking up, Sunila tapped on my shoulder and motioned for me to come out of the cottage. She proposed that she and I go for a morning walk in the woods without disturbing Cindi and Raj who were still sleeping. Both liked to sleep late.

The morning walk was magical. Sunlight was streaking from behind the ridge. Sunila pointed to the sunrise. Then she asked, "Is Cindi really your cousin?"

I smelled trouble. "Why do you ask me this?" I tried to show utter surprise.

"Because I don't believe it. You never talk about family connections. And when I asked you a couple days ago from which side of the family she is your cousin, you changed the subject as if you did not hear my question."

"I can explain that now. She is my cousin from my father's side. She is the daughter of my aunt, my father's sister."

"Okay then why did she kiss you on the lips at Scandal Point? That is not very brotherly in our culture. We don't have many kissing cousins in Punjab. Cindi is your girlfriend, why can't you admit it Jay?" (Sunila had started calling me by my initial but she stretched the "J" and it sounded like "Jay" which I liked). "All this is deception. I do not blame you if you have a girlfriend, but Cindi is not the right one for you. She is a party girl, Jay. Do you know how many boys she is flirting with? Well I can tell you. Half of the men's field hockey team!"

My cover was blown. I could pretend no more. "I am sorry, Sunila. You are right. Cindi is not my cousin, but neither is she my girlfriend. She is nice to me and I have had tea with her on several occasions. The night train was the only time I had any physical contact with her other than just a hand shake."

"And what a nice contact that was in the train! While you may have fooled the others, I was watching. She couldn't have squeezed any closer to you and if she had tried both of you would have tumbled onto the floor!"

We both laughed even in the middle of the tense conversation. She repeated her advice. "Cindi is not your type, Jay. You can do better."

"I hear you," I assured Sunila. We turned around to go back. Cindi and Raj were waiting for us. I guess we were gone longer than intended.

"Hurry up you lovebirds. Your servants are waiting and the food is getting cold," Cindi said laughing as we were approaching. She could have fooled no one. The sarcasm in her voice revealed her feelings loud and clear.

I was well aware of her mastery of acid wit, irony, and sarcasm. The four of us sat down for breakfast. I could already feel the tension between the two women. Raj tried to diffuse the tension with his dumb jokes. It did

195

not work.

After eating, we went hiking as planned and were joined by two young men who were staying at a nearby cottage. Their company was welcome in view of the tension that had developed between Cindi and Sunila.

The hike was pleasant. The tension seemed to have evaporated for the moment. At dusk, it resurfaced. Sunila wanted to go for an evening walk. She invited Cindi to come along. Cindi declined saying she was too tired from the hike and why don't the rest of us go ahead. Raj, who was observing the developments with great concern, decided to stay back to keep Cindi company.

Sunila and I followed a slightly different route this time. Darkness approached. A fine drizzle started and we looked for shelter. We noticed a cottage with a small porch. The empty cottage was locked. We stood on the porch to wait out the drizzle. Suddenly Sunila started wiping away tears.

"What is the problem," I inquired. "Why are you crying? Are you hurt?"

"Yes, I am, but you cannot do anything about it. I cannot explain, but I am not happy even though I keep telling myself I am in paradise. I am not in a paradise, and I miss my family. I want to go home, and Jay, let me ask you, why is your phony cousin such a bitch? Why does she hate me? What did I do to her?"

At this point Sunila started trembling. I feared maybe she was getting sick. Maybe the drizzle made her too cold. I moved closer and she engulfed me in an embrace. She kept crying on my chest, drenching my shirt in the process.

We heard footsteps in the distance. The dark silhouette formed into a recognizable figure. It was Cindi.

"What is going on here?" she demanded.

"It was raining and Sunila and I found this shelter where we could wait for a while until the rain stopped."

"There is no rain here. I came through it. Am I wet? I think all the rain in the area probably fell on your chest." She pointed to my soaking shirt.

Cindi continued, "This was supposed to be a fun trip. Why are people crying? Did someone die?"

"No one died but Sunila is homesick. She misses her family. She has never been away for so many days," I said.

"Then tell Her Highness to quit crying and come to dinner. Tomorrow she can go back to her Palace in Ambala." Sarcasm was Cindi's forte and apparently, she had reserved her best jabs until now. Sunila and I broke the embrace and I took Cindi away from the porch. The drizzle had subsided. I asked her what was troubling her.

"I do not have a problem. The problem is you and the princess. There is nothing wrong with her. She is not missing her family. She is interested in you because she thinks you will bring her to America after you are settled there. She told me that Jay, bhaji, would help me get admission to a university in America. So now, she is clinging to her bhaji in the dark to secure that admission. Don't you realize she is not your type? She will not fit in America. She will be crying for her mommy as soon as she gets there!"

"Cindi you are making a mountain out of a mole hill. I made no such promises. She only discussed educational opportunities in America with me. I did not promise anything to her. How could I? I myself do not know how I am going to survive in a foreign land. Didn't I tell you the same?"

"Maybe, but I wasn't glued to your chest when you were telling me that. I was at a distance."

I decided not to argue with Cindi. I would not win. I do not know if anyone would. She was a competitor. She was the champion!

Sunila had already started walking towards the cottage. We caught up with her and returned with her. Cindi went straight to her room and closed the door.

Raj motioned for me to step outside. He had something on his mind.

"I feel sorry for you. I feel sorry for all of us. The dream trip has turned into a nightmare in two days. Both girls are mad at you, but maybe we can still salvage it," he said confidently.

"I am listening."

"May be we can swap girlfriends," he said.

"Swap what? Swap something we do not have. Are you crazy? We do not have girlfriends. What we have is two gutsy and smart women who trusted us to come along with them while they were taking risks. We screwed it up."

"Don't say we. You did it all on your own. Maybe it is not your fault either. Sometimes things just don't work out. My original idea was that I would couple up with Sunila while you entertained your friend Cindi. It was supposed to end up like those Bombay movies where everyone goes home happy despite all the challenges and misfortunes. I tried with Sunila, but we never bonded. She is more your type."

He hesitated and said, "The fact is that I get along well with Cindi. She likes me, but I never tried to get any closer to her in deference to our friendship and your relationship with her. We can give it a fresh try. With your permission, I can win over Cindi if that will not ruin our friendship."

"It will not ruin our friendship and you don't need my blessing. I am leaving India in three months. I have made no promises to Cindi and neither to Sunila. I will soon be out of the way but remember, Cindi has her own plans. Her goal is to be on the Indian National Field Hockey Team. Good luck to you, Raj, it is already too late, but go ahead." I sensed he was not ready to drop the idea.

We both said goodnight and went to bed. I woke up early as usual. Sunila and I were to make breakfast. I started towards the kitchen. Sunila was already there. Her suitcase was packed and was standing in the corner.

"Where are you going this early?" I inquired.

"Going home," she replied. "My vacation in paradise is over, the paradise is no more. Would you do me a favor? Walk me to the station so I can catch the first bus to Shimla to connect with the afternoon train to Kalka and then on to Ambala. I will send a message home for them to pick me up."

I did not know what to say except, "I am sorry, Sunila. It does not have to end like this, but if your folks are expecting you home tonight, you had better go. Let us have some breakfast first. Afterwards I will escort you to the bus."

I saw Sunila to the bus and gestured for a hug but she shrugged it off and hopped on the bus. I waved as the bus left. She waved back.

I walked back to the cottage and joined Cindi and Raj. No one said a word. Cindi wiped away tears and said, "I guess I am the bad one here, but I don't think I did anything wrong. I am hurt, too. I have feelings like everyone else."

"No, you did nothing wrong. No one did except it was all a dream, a dream we should have known would end badly." I tried to console her by giving her a hug. She pushed me back.

We decided it would be no fun to continue the trip. We had planned on two more days in Chail but decided to go home early. The next morning, we followed Sunila's footsteps and went back to Chandigarh, via bus to Shimla then the train to Kalka, and arrived in Chandigarh late at night. At the Chandigarh station, I offered to walk Cindi back to her home. She refused. I persuaded her to let Raj accompany her home in a rickshaw. As it was late at night, she reluctantly agreed.

I did not see Cindi or Sunila on campus for two weeks. One day, I cornered Cindi when she was coming out of her class. I suggested we have tea. She refused but softened up after I insisted and asked her to let me explain. At tea, she wished me good luck in America and asked me when was I leaving for the USA and from where? I told her that I would first go to my village, say goodbye to my family, then return to campus to say farewell to my Chandigarh friends. The next Friday, I would take the train to Delhi to catch my overseas flight. Raj would accompany me on the train and see me off at the airport. I asked Cindi if she would say good-bye to me at the railway station when I left. To my surprise, she said she would. She knew what time the express train to Delhi left. She had travelled that route more than once.

I did not succeed in making contact with Sunila. Raj told me that Sunila and Cindi were not talking to each other. Maybe they would patch up things one day, he hoped.

On Friday, Raj and I met at the train station. Cindi was nowhere to be seen. The stationmaster blew the warning whistle. It was a signal for passengers to occupy their seats. Three minutes from then there would be a second whistle that meant everyone should be on board, as the train would be leaving in a few seconds.

"Okay Raj, Cindi is not coming let us get inside," I said.

Raj scanned the surrounding area and shouted, "Wait, I think a woman is running to catch the train. It must be Cindi. Who else in Chandigarh has that kind of speed?"

It was Cindi. She was out of breath. "I am sorry I'm late. Have a safe journey. I don't know if I will ever see you again, but don't forget me and please send me a post card." The stationmaster motioned for us to hurry up. He also told Cindi to get on the train.

"I am not a passenger. I am here to say good bye to my cousin who is going to America." I gestured for a hug. This time she did not move away and let me hug her. The doors began closing. Raj and I jumped inside and started waving. She waved back. From a distance, I thought she was wiping away some tears but it could just have been my imagination.

During the train trip to Delhi, Raj and I reviewed the events in Chail a few weeks earlier. A famous verse from an Urdu poet crossed my mind so I recited it to Raj.

"Na hee Junnett milie Na visaale sanam
Na Idher ke rahe, Na udher ke rahe"
(I did not get to Heaven neither did I unite with my love)
(I am neither here nor there)

He became serious. He seemed to sympathize, but then he started laughing and said, "You deserve it. You screwed up!"

The train arrived at the Delhi station. We gathered all our belongings. I double-checked my passport, my visa, and the admission letter from USC. The next day I would be on a plane to Honolulu, Hawaii, my point of entry to another world.

From Los Angeles, I sent letters to Cindi. She wrote me back and apologized for her behavior in Chail, but she reminded me that I was equally at fault. She urged me to write back to her and promised that if I did, that she would send me a photo of her holding her latest trophy. She was sure I would like it.

She did as promised. The photo was impressive. She also wrote to me that her team had again been invited to play exhibition matches in Shimla. They would be travelling on the same night train but a month later and it will be colder then. She made no mention of Sunila.

A friend of mine at USC was going to Chandigarh to visit his family. I went shopping in an expensive part of town and bought a nice warm ladies coat and asked my friend if he would deliver it to Cindi for me. In one of the coat pockets, I put in a note, which said, "I hope you stay warm in the cold train." When he returned, he told me she was grateful and wished me good luck. She did not look as thrilled he thought she would.

Cindi did write back thanking me again and wishing me good luck. Our correspondence fizzled and ended soon afterward.

Six months passed. One day, coming back from the library at USC, I met a pleasant young lady. She said her name was Mary, she was from Savannah, Georgia, and she was in Los Angeles finishing her master's degree in social science. I invited her to tea at the campus canteen and we talked. Over the next seven months, we drank a lot of tea together. Two months before finishing my studies, I received an employment offer from Canada. I told Mary and asked if she would consider moving with me to Ottawa. She said she would consider it and let me know. Two months later, she joined me in Ottawa, Canada.

Update: Many years later, I told the Shimla story to Mary and told her I wanted to take her to Shimla with me. She said she would like that. Over the next twenty years, we visited India several times, but Shimla was not on our agenda. Then one evening last year, we were watching the season premiere of *Anthony Bourdain's, Parts Unknown. Tony explores Punjab -- one of the most beautiful and relatively unknown areas of India."* Bourdain's Punjab visit became one of his most popular shows on CNN. His travel to Shimla by the slow, narrow gauge train brought back many memories.

We have been together ever since.

We went to Shimla in January of 2015 along with my book editor, Greg Beckstrom, to research some of the stories. It was a tight schedule, but we decided to take the slow train to Shimla. My niece, Peggy Sidhu, booked us on a train similar to the one I had travelled on with the field hockey team despite the fact that a more spacious and comfortable train with reclining seats was now an option. The train ride brought back forty-year-old memories, and I decided to write this story.

I want to go back to Chail someday.

Endnotes:

1)   Cindi had a more authentic Punjabi name but she preferred to be called Cindi because it was an easy to pronounce adaption of her real name.

2)   Bhaji means brother.

3)   After the Scandal Point incident, the British banned the Maharaja from entering Shimla, the summer capital of India. This incensed the

powerful Maharaja who was a big supporter of the British Empire. The Maharaja vowed to build a new summer retreat for himself. He built the magnificent palace in Chail only thirty miles away from Shimla. After the independence and the absorption of Princely States into the Indian Union, the successor Maharaja donated most of his buildings to Chail Military School and Government of India.

CHAPTER 15

LAST STAND OF THE BLUE WARRIOR

Every year they arrived on time. Villagers were waiting. Especially excited were the young children. They expected a carnival, a sports extravaganza, and an endless party for the next three days discounting a possible skirmish among the visitors or the disciplining of an unruly spectator. They pitched their tents, constructed temporary earthen ovens, and helped themselves to the village water-well, playfields, or any other public utility without any permissions or permits because no such permissions or formalities would have been necessary.

The uninvited but welcome visitors were Nihang Singh's from the famous Budha Dal (the Old Warrior Band). They wore bright, navy-blue clothing adorned with saffron sashes and were heavily armed with traditional weapons. Most of them were middle-aged men, but occasionally there was a woman, a child, or a teenager. They rode horses and pulled wagons loaded with household essentials. The visitors were not gypsies. They were the ancient Sikh warriors who were sworn to keep the three hundred years of war traditions alive by reenacting the chivalry and struggles endured by Sikhs over two centuries of persecution by the Mughal Empire in Delhi.

They would gather in the village common area and put on a display of horsemanship, weaponry skills, and sports contests resembling Judo and Karate combats. Most of them had exceptional skills in these disciplines. Their favorite game was "Gatka" a traditional Sikh martial art for combat training. In Gatka, wooden sticks were used in place of swords. (Gatka is now offered as an organized sport in Punjab schools and colleges, along with fencing.)

Nihang sports were great entertainment in the villages where nothing else ever happened other than the daily grind of tilling the fields, milking water buffaloes, and other monotonous chores. The arrival of the Nihangs brought entertainment, which people could count on every year. Villagers rewarded the warriors with food, tea, milk, and sweets. The warriors brought their own cannabis. In the evening before dinner, the Nihangs would prepare a cool, tasty beverage of cannabis, crushed almonds, and unpasteurized milk. They garnished the drink with ground black pepper. The delicious peppery concoction was called "Sukha", a comforting elixir. Everyone was invited to share the meals, regardless of their religious beliefs or social status. Even their enemies were invited to share their meals (unless they posed an imminent threat to life and property) in accordance with the time honored Sikh tradition of "Guru Ka Langer" (Guru's Kitchen). Village adults were invited to drink the Sukha beverage. The more daring ones did. Before going to sleep, they engaged in an hour or two of high-quality gossip sessions. At the end of their day, they shouted their favorite slogans at the top of their lungs. That was their way of saying good night to each other and to the villagers who were generally half a mile away but who could easily hear the slogans. Their most popular slogans were:

Raj Karega Khalsa, Aaki Rahe Na Koi (The pure ones, meaning Guru's disciples, will rule. There will be no holdouts.)
Bolay So Nihaal, (Whosoever utters the following will be happy.)
Sat Sri Akal (God is immortal.)

Much of the conversation, especially with an outsider, was an exaggerated and upbeat version of the theme in question. Roots of this exaggerated account of things and events go back hundreds of years when this wartime vocabulary was developed to keep spirits up in the face of adversity. The slogans and the uplifting vocabulary resulted from 200 years of harassment of Sikhs by the Mughal emperors of India.

Like most children in rural areas of Punjab, I was fascinated with the Nihang paraphernalia, warlike culture, and their navy-blue attire; but most of all their sportsmanship and mastery of hand-to-hand combat weapons. As an adult, however, I became more fascinated by their vocabulary and the special Nihang "Lingua Franca" which they used somewhat successfully to deceive their enemy and to communicate with each other while on the run.

Nihang Bolay – A Language of Survival
Nihang Singhs evolved their own code language to satisfy their need to bolster their spirits. They called the coded war language "Bolay." Some examples are:

Sava Lakh: Meaning an army of 125,000 soldiers when in reality it referred to just one soldier. It is not certain how often, if ever, it fooled the enemy, but it was a morale booster. Nihang math was unique. To keep calculations simple, while one soldier was 125,000 (Sava lakh), two soldiers were an army of 200,000 (Do Lakh), not 250,000. The modified math made multiplications simpler in the days when the fighters on the run did not carry stationary or electronic calculators.

Slaying of a Sister F....ing Mughal; was the term for passing gas (farting). This was designed to convey that another despised Mughal enemy had been disposed of.

Donkey Tit Sucker (Gadhi Chunghna) was a euphemism for a tobacco-pipe smoker. In the Sikh tradition, consuming of tobacco was the ultimate sin. Consumption of other intoxicating agents could be forgiven but not tobacco smoking. Such intense dislike of tobacco was triggered by the Sikhs hatred of the Mughal enemy. Mughals were heavy smokers.

Chardhi Kala was a popular phrase. It essentially meant positive attitude, high spirits, and a mental state of optimism and joy.

Sukha was the name for a popular cannabis drink. The word meant comfort, relaxation, and peace giving.

THE BABY BLUE – MAKING OF A BLUE WARRIOR

My cousin Tej was fascinated with the Nihangs. The very first time his father took him to the Budha Dal rodeo in the next village, he was hooked. He had just started school. Like many kids in his neighborhood, he would miss school during the three day Budha Dal carnival but would easily make it up because both his mom and dad were educated and his mother was a part-time teacher. Tej was granted permission by his parents to enjoy, unrestricted, the greatest free show in town for three days. The only thing he was not allowed to experience was the cannabis beverage that flowed freely in the evenings.

Cousin Tej would dress in shiny blue fabric from head to toe, wear a pointed turban his father tied on his head, and adorn it with toy weapons. Among these would be a quoit (Chakra) that looked real. His fascination with the color blue earned him the nickname "Neela Parinda" ("Blue Bird" in Urdu language) from his mother who had learned Urdu in school. Sometimes his father would call him the Blue Warrior because of Tej's fascination with the Nihang warriors who wore navy-blue. His mother would often point out to others the blue tinge in his eyes although some imagination was required to see that. At school, he was an active and bright student; the pride of his parents. Life was good for Tej.

Tej grew up in the Nihang lore. When he was fifteen, he asked his parents to let him join a Nihang Dal (unit). His request was summarily rejected. His father and mother wanted him to go to college, acquire a western education, and become an engineer, doctor, or a military officer in the Indian Army. As a first step towards that goal, they enrolled him in a junior college.

Instead of continuing his studies, Tej dropped out of school and joined the "Nihang Fauj" (army). There were several bands of Nihangs. The granddaddy of all and the most prestigious was the legendry "Budha Dal" (the Old Warrior Band). Tej could not join this prestigious group right away. He was not yet accomplished in the martial arts necessary for entrance into the elite band. He opted instead to join one of the smaller groups. This afforded him a carefree nomadic life with no particular milestones to achieve. He had only to ride horses with a roving band of other Blue Warriors. They would go from one village to another, set up a tent village (they called it a cantonment) on the outskirts of the town, and entertain themselves and area residents.

A BRIEF NIHANG PRIMER

There is no consensus on the origin of the word Nihang, although some have traced it to the Persian word for a crocodile (نهنگ). Persians (Mughals) likened the ferocity of Nihang to fierce sea creatures. The colorful blue clothing of Nihangs probably comes from the concept of "Shiva Swaroop" meaning "Shiva's appearance" ascribed to the venerated Hindu God Shiva, the protector.

Their love of weaponry grew out of necessity. A fully outfitted Nihang Singh was armed to the teeth. On his arms, he would wear metal war bracelets (Kada). He would carry swords (preferably two – one curved and the other straight [Khanda]), a buckler (a shield made of buffalo hide [Dhala]), an iron chain, and a dagger in his waistband. Small weapons useful in close combat included a treshool mukh, or Trident (a small spear-like dagger that he could hide in his turban) and war shoes that had pointed blades at the toes (useful for kicking).

Nihangs mastery of weapons was legendry. Weapons and martial arts training were compulsory for a Nihang and they had a name for this training. It was called "Shaster Vidya" meaning weaponry science. The real weaponry science of the present day Nihangs, almost extinct, is being replaced largely by a safer and more sedate sport called "Gatka," which is played with wooden sticks instead of real swords.

ARTICLES OF FAITH – THE 5K REGIMEN

The hallmark of Nihang life, and in fact all ancient Sikh life, is the adherence to the five articles of faith, which are considered the five necessities of daily life. Each article started with the letter K. The 5K regimen most likely resulted from the harsh nomadic existence necessary for survival from the Mughal campaigns to exterminate Sikhs. Genocide of Sikhs started in earnest with Emperor Jahangir (father of Shah Jehan, the builder of Taj Mahal) and peaked during the beheading of the ninth Guru in the crowded Chandni Chowk in Delhi by Emperor Aurangzeb. (1)

For many modern Sikhs, the 5K regimen might appear strictly ritualistic and a morale booster, but it made practical sense when it came to survival under nomadic existence. Every Nihang Singh possessed the five Ks that included:

Kirpan – A small curved sword.

Kesh – Hair on the head and a facial beard. The beard was to match the ferocious Mughal looks. Long hair tied into a knot over the head cushioned the impact of a hard object like a club.

Kada – A heavy steel bracelet with sharp edges. This may have started as a wartime fashion or was a handy weapon in close combat.

Kangha – A wooden comb to keep long hair combed and contained.

Kaccha – A large oval underwear very tight at the mid-calf and which required some effort to put on and to take off. It has been compared to the chastity belt worn by some western women to protect against unwanted intrusion and rape. It was felt that a warrior constantly on the run should keep amorous thoughts under check to the extent possible. Probably the more important reason was that the large cotton garment covered significant parts of the skin against insects and rodents when sleeping on the ground in forested areas.

In addition to the 5Ks, another important component of Sikhism is Dastar. Dastar, Persian for turban, is a symbol of respect and pride for a Sikh. Nihang Singhs are famous for their turban headwear. The exquisitely tied tall turbans are pointed. At the top usually sits a trident, which can be used as a weapon for stabbing the enemy in close quarters. The sturdy tall turbans provided additional storage and support for other small weapons. Steel-reinforced turbans acted as helmets, affording effective head protection.

Note: In modern times, the US Government's primary safety regulator, the Occupational Safety and Health Administration (OSHA), exempts Sikhs from wearing mandatory helmets in recognition of their religious beliefs as long as a Sikh wears the traditional turban (1926.100; 1926.100 (2), Std. 1-6.5; hard hats – exemption for religious reasons.)

AN EVENING WITH THE BLUE WARRIOR

My mother passed away in India in 1992. Many friends and relatives came to her funeral. Cousin Tej was not among them but his elder brother was. I told his brother that I wanted to see Tej before my return to America. He promised to track him down for me. Two days later, Tej showed up all dressed in navy-blue with a saffron sash and supporting a nine-foot long spear in his right hand. He laid down his spear, leaned forward, and touched my knees as a sign of respect for the elder cousin. I motioned for him to sit down. We exchanged a few pleasantries before I asked my first question.

"Your family is not happy with your lifestyle, Tej. They feel you are wasting time. You are a smart man. They want you to go to college and get a degree. What happened? You were a high-scoring student in school. Maybe you are destined to go to England or to America for a higher education. Why have you adopted this nomadic life?" I challenged him.

"Bai (brother), I am not smart like you. I am not cut out for high academic achievement. I am happy the way it is, serving the Guru. Someone has to do it." At this, he launched into how rough the times were in Punjab and there was nothing he could do about such excesses. Sikhs were being harassed and punished for wanting an autonomous state. He felt that the Nihang Singhs were especially targeted because of their perceived threatening looks. In reality, they did not pose a threat to anyone. He continued, "Bai, you know we (Nihangs) don't bother anyone. We are just keeping alive the 'Mariyada' (tradition) of the Guru who gave his life fighting religious persecution. Someone must guard the faith. Would you know, Bai, that I have been stopped, questioned, and harassed by police without any reason? One time they wanted to search under my turban, an ultimate insult to a Nihang Singh. I refused. They roughed me up but let me go. You know, Bai; I would not let anyone remove my turban. I would die first."

Tej was getting emotional and agitated. I decided to change the subject. "I still think you should go back to school, get a degree, and find out what the rest of the world is like. Maybe get a college degree in America. You can still serve the Guru as a highly educated and devoted disciple. Many Sikhs are doing just that and earning a good name for the Sikhs and for India all over the world."

He perked up at my suggestion. "America must be paradise, Bai. Tell me more. I know it is not like here. I am sure in America, if you want to practice your faith, no one will bother you. Can you get stopped and searched just for practicing your faith?"

"Well, Tej, America has its problems, but no, you don't get stopped and harassed if there is no charge against you and you have not broken the law," I assured him.

"You are living in paradise, Bai," he reaffirmed his belief.

Tej offered to take me to the Nihang Singh academy in nearby Damdama Sahib, a sprawling complex and one of the five "Seats of Power" in the Sikh hegemony. There he would introduce me to the chief and let me experience the Nihang lifestyle. I was tempted but had to decline because of my tight schedule and my need to return to work.

"Thanks, Tej. Maybe next time, but I want to ask you questions about your fascination with the Nihang culture." (I wanted to know if this was just an excuse for him to avoid civilian life or if he really believed in his mission of protecting the faith.)

"Go ahead Bai, ask me anything," he assured me.

"You know Tej, your favorite slogan is: *Raj Karega Khalsa, AAKi Rahe Na Koi*", which means that the Khalsa (meaning pure but in reality, Sikhs) will rule while there will be no holdouts. "Do you really believe that Khalsa will rule the world someday and there will be no opposition? How do you suppose this will happen? Do you think America and Russia with all their might will just surrender to Khalsa when daggers and spears are all that Khalsa has?"

Tej had to think hard on this. He suddenly had a flash of lightning. "Bai, when the Guru uttered this, he was not thinking of Khalsa winning by force. Of course not. The Guru was convinced that even mighty powers would be persuaded with the depth and sincerity of the brotherly lifestyle of Khalsa and would join the Dal."

"That is a clever argument, Tej. It won't happen, but you are quick on your feet."

Tej seemed to have another flash of lightning and eagerly cut me off. "Actually, Bai, when Guru spoke those words, Guru was referencing the Indian subcontinent and immediate surroundings that were known then. America was not even discovered at that time, nor did anyone here know about Russia or the British Empire. Britain was not a factor until after Guru Gobind Singh." Tej looked skyward, folded his hands, and showed respect to the 10th Guru.

I was impressed with his referencing history to justify his hypothesis. "Your slogan makes more sense now when you put it that way, but I believe the Guru did not mean that the Khalsa (Sikhs) would rule the Indian subcontinent either. The Guru who uttered these words was very realistic. The 10th Guru was a man of the world, and don't you remember? Before he succumbed to his wounds inflicted by his trusted lieutenant, Pandha Khan, he so elegantly expressed the transitory nature of this world in his favorite language (Persian)."

"Dunya Muqam e Faani" (This world is transitory, mortal)

"Okay, Bai, then you tell me what you think the great Guru meant."

"I believe what Guru meant was that the truth will prevail. Who will oppose purity and truth? Have you forgotten what the word Khalsa means?

The Guru may have referred to only the truth and not a particular ethnic or religious group dominating the world," I tried to convince him.

I am not sure if Tej was convinced by my interpretation, but he complemented me on my explanation and said, "Bai, you are so smart, and that is why you are living in America and I am still here chasing water buffaloes." Then he laughed and said, "Well, I don't even chase buffaloes. I just loaf around." We both laughed and flashed the equivalent of a high-five hand slap (a gesture of celebration).

I next questioned Tej on the use of illicit drugs that Sukha passed at Nihang gatherings, saying this elevated the cannabis drink to the status of almost an offering sanctioned by the religion.

"What is wrong with Sukha?" he challenged me. "It is just another natural herb like many we enjoy in India. Sukha (ਸੁੱਖਾ) is a comfort-giver. It makes you feel relaxed, friendly, and peaceful. Cooked into Pakoras (ਪਕੌੜਾ), it is a delicious food. Bai, have you ever tried it?"

"Yes, Tej, I have tried the drink as well as the Sukha-laced Pakora fritters on numerous occasions when I was attending the Punjab University Campus in Chandigarh. I did not find it anything special, and I am not sure I would elevate it to the status of a Sikh ritual. Most Sikhs today do not condone the use of intoxicants, even the peace giving Sukha," I argued. I am not sure he agreed with my statement.

"Bai, the reason I say Sukha is peace giving is because there have been no cases of violence or aggression resulting from consumption of Sukha? We do hear, every day, cases of aggression and misbehavior committed by people under the influence of Sharaab (alcohol)." He paused and continued, "Bai, I never touch that stuff."

"I am happy for you because of that," I said, and dropped the topic.

BLUE RODEO

I asked him about his own weapons training and his horse-riding skills, all essential qualities of an accomplished Nihang. "Bai, I am a rookie, as you know, but I have become pretty good at horse riding. What I like most is riding on two horses running side by side during which I must stay on their backs until the finish line is reached. That is not easy. I will get better someday," he assured me.

"That is awesome!" I exclaimed. "Have you done that at a show?"

"I did but I will tell you about it if you promise not to laugh."

"Tell me, but I cannot promise I won't laugh."

He ignored that and said, "Bai, in my desire to impress the village folks, I chose the most difficult and daring act to perform. I tried to ride two horses in parallel while standing straight up on their backs."

Tej described his feat the following way. "The referee uttered the standard slogan (Bolay So Nihaal) and gave the go signal. The two horses ran parallel for a few seconds. I raised my arm and uttered the Jakaara slogan. The animals quickly sensed they were being commandeered by a novice. They felt no obligation to obey the rookie rider and started going their own merry ways. Just before the finish line, I came tumbling down and hit the ground hard. The crowd sighed. Several people started running towards me to render aid, fearing I was seriously hurt and could have damaged my spine. With the Guru's kirpa (grace), I was not seriously hurt. Before they reached me, I got up, raised my right arm and yelled,

Bolay So Nihaal (whosoever utters the following will be happy) and
Sat Sri Akal (God is Immortal)."

Tej told me that he was not the least bit embarrassed about his fall and he summarily rejected any offer of assistance. He started limping back to the start line. He was obviously in pain. Someone tried to offer a hand again, and again he would not accept help. The Charhdi Kala (positive energy) had taken over. The Guru was taking care of him and he needed no assistance from the mortals around him.

I was impressed with his positive outlook. I gave him a pat on the back and congratulated him for his courage. The exchange left me exhilarated and sad. I was impressed with his thinking prowess and the analytical nature of his reasoning. He must have had a high IQ, I thought, but sadly, no one will ever know. No one will ever care.

Time had come for me to leave. He gave me a hug and extracted a promise from me to look him up when I came back to India the next time. Then he would take me to the Blue Warrior academy in Damdama Sahib and introduce me to the chiefs.

DARK CLOUDS OVER PUNJAB

The nascent Indian democracy weathered several storms after gaining independence from the "British Raj" in 1947. The Punjab area generally bore the brunt of these events, including the bloodshed and communal genocide immediately following the 1947 partition.

The second blow to the Indian democracy was delivered in June, 1984 when the Indian Army, under the direction of Sikh General KS Brar, stormed the holiest of Sikh shrines in Amritsar in an attempt to flush out militants camped inside the complex. Several hundred people were shot to death within the confines of the temple. Some of them were militants, but a significant number were just innocent pilgrims. Among the occupants of the shrine was General Shabeg Singh, a Major General in the Indian Army. Major General Shabeg sympathized with the Sikh demands for an autonomous Sikh State. The Sikh State movement had also won many supporters in the USA, Canada, and the UK.

General Shabeg Singh was killed inside the temple at the hands of his own military. The precise number of militants and innocent people killed has never been established and probably never will be. Most Indian historians and impartial Indians agree that the attack on the Amritsar shrine was ill advised and badly executed. Even the name, "Operation Blue Star", was a cynical name because there was nothing blue or of star-quality about the operation. It was operation "Blood Red" from the start.

The results were predictable and tragic. The Sikh militancy and the secessionist movement turned increasingly violent as a result of the Golden Temple Massacre. The attack alienated even the moderate peaceful Sikhs resulting in an ever-escalating cycle of confrontation. It is a fact that majority of the Sikhs, including the official Akali Dal Party, did not advocate a separate Sikh country. Most well-educated and well-placed Sikhs were of the opinion that a separate Sikh state was not necessary or viable. Sikhs had always been a part of Indian society and culture and their future lay with India. It was hoped that the campaign would soon die down. It was not to be.

Six months after the Golden Temple attack, violence peaked on October 31, 1984, a day I will never forget. On October 31, I boarded the London Underground (tube) at the Paddington Station. I looked at the newspaper the man sitting next to me was holding. The headline exclaimed, *Indira Gandhi Assassinated by her Sikh Bodyguard*.

I went into a shock. I did not know what to think. I missed the station where I was to get off. I started visualizing what was to come. I did not have to ponder long. What I feared had already started. Sikhs were being dragged out of trains by their long hair and beaten to death or set on fire with lighted tires around their necks in Delhi, the Indian Capital. No one came to their rescue. Bands of police who usually hovered around Indian railway stations to ward off petty criminals were nowhere to be seen.

This was justice Indian-style. Instead of mourning the death of a popular leader inside places of worship and community halls, some Indians decided to punish every man who resembled the guard who shot Mrs. Indira Gandhi. The perpetrators of the violence, although known, have never been brought to justice because of their political ties.

Returning to my hotel in the Piccadilly area, I was greeted by the turbaned Sikh doorman. I told him I was a Sikh from Punjab and now a US citizen living in Michigan, USA. We shared the grief and wondered about the future. I asked him, "With your turban and obvious Sikh appearance, do you have any concern for your safety here in London? You never know where religious hot heads can surface?"

"Oh no, sir. A Sikh is never a target here in the UK just because of his appearance. This is the safest place for a Sikh. British people remember our service to the Crown," he said emphatically. I wished him good luck and went to my room.

In my room, I kept thinking about what he had said and his words made me sad and agitated. How ironic I thought. A Sikh in a foreign country thousands of miles away from home feels perfectly safe but not in his own country where his faith originated and where his soul resides.

The revenge killings subsided after a few days but the brutal police crackdown was just beginning. They were designed to punish anybody and everybody who ever uttered anything sympathetic about secession in a public gathering or even among neighbors. Young men in Punjab disappeared on even a tiny whispered rumor. Almost every village in Punjab had stories of kidnapping, rape, and torture of young men who ever mentioned the word Punjabi Sooba (Punjabi province), let alone "Khalistan," the proposed name of a separate Sikh country.

CULTURE OF INTIMIDATION AND ABUSE

In the annals of police brutality, the Punjab Police of 1980s and 1990s occupies a prominent position. In even earlier times when I was growing up, the sight of a policeman would send chills down my spine despite the fact that I never got into any trouble. (My mother made sure of that!) Still, I was terrified at the sight of a Punjab policeman. They seemed ready to thrash you at the smallest excuse, as if beating was the first lesson they mastered at the police academy. The second lesson was of an immense vocabulary of curses and humiliating phrases. (2)

Note: *By describing such fears, I do not imply that all police were brutal. There were, no doubt, some kind and caring souls who jeopardized their own safety to help others. Unfortunately, based on my experience, they were rare at that time. Perhaps most were just following orders from their superiors. This is evident from the recorded history that the top police officer in Punjab, under whose watch these atrocities and human rights violations occurred, was awarded one of highest honors by the Union Government in Delhi.*

VISITING PUNJAB IN TROUBLED TIMES

Several years passed before I returned to India. In the aftermath of Indira Gandhi's assassination, I postponed my trip to visit my family until times were better. Finally, I started making travel arrangements and contacting relatives about a visit. On my list of persons to see were Tej and his elder brother. Because I never had any contact information for Tej, I called up his elder brother who lived in Ludhiana, a large manufacturing city in Punjab. The brother was delighted that I was coming and assured me it was now okay to visit Punjab. I expressed my desire to see Tej during my visit and possibly to see his "Nihang Rodeo."

Suddenly the voice on the other end went silent. After a while, the brother apparently resumed his composure and said, "You will not be able to see Tej. He is very far away."

That was a strange answer. I did not comprehend it and blurted, "How far away? Where did he go? He was always around. Did he even have money to travel?" I challenged the brother.

"Bai, Tej is with the Guru. I am sure he is in peace. Six months ago, he was killed by the Punjab police. They claimed he was a suspect in the separatist movement and was a threat to public safety. All I know is that according to the police, he was at a public square in a grain market. They said he was brandishing his spear but not directing his attention to anyone in particular. He had his nine-foot long spear and the sword. When he would not drop his weapon, they beat him to death. We never were able to cremate the body because we did not receive it. We did not have any notification of

216

his death for many days. We were told that his body had already been cremated because they could not locate his family."

He continued, "You know, Bai, that cannot be true. They could have questioned some of the onlookers who witnessed Tej's death. Tej was a regular in the area. Someone could have led them to us, but the Government made no effort. This is not unusual around here," he said calmly.

I was stunned at the news and the casualness of it all. "Didn't you try to find out more? It sounds like a wrongful death to me!"

"Bai, it would have been futile. It would have invited only more trouble. Tej was not the only case. Hundreds of young men disappeared during the purge. Some were taken for questioning and never returned. Some died in fake encounters. Some were rounded up but released after the relatives paid bribes to the police. No one ever knew the charges."

We had a long awkward silence on the phone. I said goodbye to Tej's brother and promised to see him when I visited India.

During my next visit to India, I started piecing together the circumstances of Tej's death. I learned that Tej's life had been going downhill. He was often intoxicated. He had little contact with his family. Apparently, they were not happy with him. He was not the son or the brother about whom they could brag. He was a loser in their eyes. To make matters worse, he had secretly married a woman from a low caste and perhaps was just shacking up with her ("living in sin"). The family considered him a lost cause.

LAST STAND OF THE BLUE WARRIOR

On one fateful afternoon, Tej was standing in the busy intersection at a grain market. Farmers brought their wheat harvest to be auctioned at the open bidding of the market. This was a good place for Tej to show off his swordsmanship and his Gutka skills to the farmers who had just sold their crop and were flush with cash. They tipped him generously for showing off his weaponry skills.

On the fateful day, a crowd gathered near the grain market. Tej started his show by letting out his favorite cry of, "The Khalsa will rule one day and there will be no holdouts." Then he started twirling his three and a half foot-long curved sword to show his dexterity with the weapon.

Suddenly two jeeps pulled up and six policemen jumped out. Tej stopped his act, put the sword in its case, and watched. A hush fell over the crowd. One of the policemen pointed at him and shouted, "Is your name

Teja Singh Sidhu?"

"Who wants to know?" Tej replied.

"The Punjab police want to know. You are a suspect and must come with us," the man yelled.

"What is the charge? You need to show me the summons," Tej demanded.

"Our information shows you are a separatist, a threat to the peace. You can find out more at the police station, but for now, put that Barsha (spear) on the ground, take off your turban, remove your weapons, and put everything right here." The policeman pointed at the jeep.

"A Sikh warrior never takes his turban off on anyone's orders and neither does he surrender his spear, trident, and chakra to anyone except to the Guru if he so orders," Tej declared with confidence.

"The Guru is not here to give you that order. Do what we tell you on a count of five otherwise there will be consequences."

There was a stir in the crowd. A few people fled the scene.

Tej would not budge. Instead, he raised his left arm and let out his favorite slogan, "Raj Karega Khalsa ..." Before he finished his slogan, three policemen, who had already positioned themselves behind him, knocked Tej to the ground and started kicking him. His spear fell to his side and his beautifully tied turban rolled off his head along with the trident. His right hand was bleeding because he had fallen on one of the weapons dislodged from his turban.

Tej was still shouting his slogan and not completing it because of the blows he was receiving. A fourth policeman had joined in the beating, using his rifle butt. Tej was now shouting obscenities and reminding the policemen that the Guru would punish them some day. His warnings had no effect. The police kept pounding until he stopped complaining. He had no willpower left to resist. He just lay there. More onlookers left.

One of the policemen bent over to listen to his heart and gave a signal to others. Apparently, Tej was not dead. The signal was to finish him off. The beating resumed. Someone in the crowd yelled, "Stop beating the dead man. You can't make him anymore dead."

Policemen looked at the crowd. What idiot would dare say that? The man had already disappeared. He knew better.

The beating continued until the officer in charge gave the signal to stop. Tej was lifeless. Several women in the front row covered their faces with their headgear. Several uttered "Wahiguru" (Guru is great) and "Hare Ram" (Oh Lord!) to express their horror. Two policemen covered Tej's motionless body with a white sheet and loaded it into one of the jeeps. The police sped away.

YEARS LATER

After piecing together the story from several sources, I lost my appetite to visit Tej's brother and again delayed my trip to India. I tried to expel the circumstances of his death from my memory. Perhaps I succeeded. Later, I went to India on several occasions but did not pursue information about Tej's death. Tej was forgotten. No one celebrated his birthday or mourned the anniversary of his death. He did not exist.

In 2015, when I was writing this book, Tej's memory kept popping up in my mind. I decided to visit his brother. Previously, this brother had not been willing to discuss the issue. Perhaps he had been afraid of possible Punjab government incriminations.

After a sumptuous lunch at my cousin's modern house, I reiterated my concern over Tej's violent death. Apparently, my cousin, Tej's brother, was expecting this and decided to discuss the matter. He was confident that the political environment had changed. Reopening the issue of his brother's death would not land anyone in jail. Punjab was now at peace.

He went into a storage room and brought out some rumpled brown papers. He told me that he did file a claim of wrongful death almost twenty years ago. Among the papers he showed me was a handwritten postmortem (autopsy) sketches and notes. The autopsy listed the deceased as Tej Singh, son of Sarban Singh, and was signed off on 9/7/95, which in India would be July 9th, 1995.

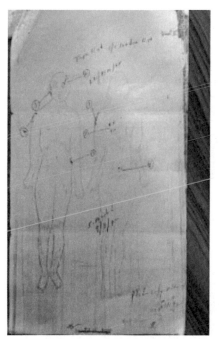

Multiple wounds covered Tej's body. My book editor, Greg Beckstrom, and I poured over the autopsy report and debated as to which one was the fatal blow, although neither of us had any forensic training. Then it dawned on us. Why fuss? What does it matter?

219

1) Aurangzeb (1618 – 1707) was the 6th Mughal emperor. He was the son of Shah Jehan, the builder of the Taj Mahal. His relentless pursuit of power and religious persecution brought him into conflicts with many Indian religious and ruling groups including Marathas, Rajputs, and Sikhs. In 1670, the 9th Sikh Guru Tegh Bahadur decided to challenge Aurangzeb on his persecution of Hindus and Sikhs and anyone who questioned his authority. Aurangzeb ordered the Guru beheaded in a public display in the Chandni Chowk intersection in Delhi. (A memorial in the form of a temple called "Gurdwara Shish Ganj Sahib" now stands at the spot of the Guru's execution.)

Guru Tegh Bahadudur's young son, Gobind Singh, took over the cause after his father's execution and fought with the Mughals all his life. In 1705, just before his death, Guru Gobind Singh wrote a long poignant letter called *Zafarnāma* (Punjabi: ਜ਼ਫਰਨਾਮਾ, Persian: ظفرنامہ) to Aurangzeb in which he rebuked the emperor for his weaknesses as a human being and for his excesses. At one point, the Guru reminded Aurangzeb that he and his henchmen had broken their oaths sworn upon the Qur'an. Guru also stated that in spite of his several sufferings, he had won a moral victory over the Emperor who had broken his vows. In one of the most quoted verses of the Zafarnama, Guru Gobind Singh justified his taking up of arms against the Emperor.

Chu kar az hama heelt e dar guzshat,
Halal ast burdan ba shamsheer dast.
"All modes of redressing the wrong having failed, raising of sword is pious and just."

2) Punjab police had a vast arsenal of insults and curses to suit the occasion. In ascending order were: *Son of an owl* (Ulu da Patha), *Son of a pig* (Sur da bachha), "mother f---er, and "sister f---er." The last slur was considered so vile that the recipient would suddenly lose all restraint and lash out. In Punjab, a slur to your sister's honor often resulted in a violent reprisal.

CHAPTER 16

ADDICTED TO HEAT

Rajesh and I looked forward to our visit. Both of us had been to Tokyo before but had never visited anywhere else in Japan. Our assignment in Sendai, about 200 miles north of Tokyo, was to conduct a health and safety risk assessment for a multinational US-based company. The trip required travel on the high-speed Tohoku Shinkansen train from Tokyo to Sendai, one of the largest cities in Japan. The train ride itself was an adventure, but more exciting were the culinary experiences that awaited us in Sendai. Rajesh's culinary excitement was, however, somewhat tempered by the prospect of having to endure Japanese food, more known for savory "Umami" flavor profiles than hot spices, for a week.

SEEKING HEAT IN THE LAND OF THE RISING SUN

Rajesh is a third generation Malaysian whose forefathers migrated to Malaya from South India. He never lived in India, but an addiction to spicy food was embedded in his DNA. For him, the spicier the pepper, the more he liked it.

I also consider myself somewhat of a capsicum addict. Compared to Rajesh, however, I am a pepper wimp! My "heat threshold" peaks at slightly above the jalapeno pepper on the Scoville scale and definitely under the cayenne pepper rating. Unlike Rajesh, I do not suffer withdrawal if I do not get my capsicum fix.

We were met at the train station by two company safety representatives. They introduced themselves as Hitomi (the one with beautiful eyes) and Akira (the bright one). They were very pleasant and spoke excellent English. They proposed that we go directly to dinner at a nearby and well-known restaurant before it closed as the dinner hour was passing.

221

Afterwards, we proceeded to the hotel after a quick stop at a karaoke bar.

The restaurant they selected served authentic Sendai delicacies which included Gyutan (beef tongue), Sendai oysters (served raw or fried), and Sasa Kamaboko (a fish loaf made from pureed flounder). Jisake, the local sake brew, accompanied all this.

At Hitomi's request, the waiter explained the preparation of each dish including the historical context. As the waiter explained, Hitomi translated it all for us.

Rajesh decided to have Sasa Kamaboko, the white fish. I also decided on the white fish. I selected the same dish as Rajesh so we could share the unique experience and talk about it later with each other and our friends.

Our food arrived accompanied by the customary o-jigi, a precisely executed thirty degree bow. The Sasa Kamaboko we ordered had a distinct and heavenly aroma. Hitomi explained the proper way to eat the unique dish. That was interesting, but I was ready to dig into the food as soon as it arrived. Not Rajesh. He was scanning the table in search of something. Hitomi and Akira noticed this too and asked Rajesh what was needed? Before he could respond, I intervened, "He is looking for hot pepper sauce. Rajesh likes his food spicy!"

"Not a problem," Hitomi said. She pointed to the nearby black pepper (actually powdered white pepper). Rajesh politely declined the offer. He had already seen it at the next table. He seemed reluctant to tell our hosts what exactly he was looking for.

"I think he is looking for something hotter, I mean spicier than white pepper. He is used to eating really spicy food," I reiterated.

Our hosts were anxious to comply but were at a loss to come up with the right ingredient. Akira had a thought. He talked with one of the waiters and in hushed tones explained what the foreign guest wanted. The waiter left and soon returned with kai choi, a Chinese mustard called takana (タカナ) in Japanese.

Rajesh and I looked at each other. Chinese mustard was not what Rajesh had in mind!

Hitomi had another idea. She decided that the missing ingredient was tōgarashi, a Japanese version of hot pepper. She told us that togarashi was a type of a capsicum and to foreigners, it is introduced as the Japanese chili pepper. One variety called *Shichimi Tōgarashi*, is a mixture of several ingredients that vary by maker. She asked our waiter to check if the restaurant stocked Shichimi. It did not.

All hopes for a fiery elixir seemed dead, but Hitomi was not ready to give up. She motioned to our waiter who had continued to hover near our table. She whispered something in his ear. The patient waiter performed a fifteen degree o-jigi, retreated and whispered to the two nearby waiters. Both of these men dispersed immediately to fulfil the request.

The situation was getting awkward. "I am sorry to hold up dinner," Rajesh said with grace. "Hot pepper is not so important. The food looks delicious just as it is. Perhaps it does not need any additional ingredients. Let us eat." He then raised his glass of sake and said, "Gan bei!" (Cheers!), not remembering that we were in Japan, not in China. He recovered quickly and corrected himself. "Kanpai!" he said in well-rehearsed Japanese that he had mastered on his previous trip to Japan.

As soon as we put down the sake glasses, the two waiters reappeared, each carrying a small bottle with some kind of sauce. Both of them had dashed to nearby fast food restaurants in search of the pepper sauces.

Rajesh examined the bottles. A broad smile appeared on his face. He lifted one bottle and then raised it in the manner of proposing a toast with a fine wine, gave the thumbs up sign, and thanked the waiters. The bottle he picked with great delight had the coveted Tabasco Brand® Pepper Sauce label.

We started to eat. The three waiters were in no hurry to move away from our table. They were anxious to see the results of their efforts. They hung around, pretending to straighten out the adjoining tables but their attention was fixed on what was to happen next.

Rajesh poured a generous portion of the Louisiana hot pepper concoction on the exquisite fish preparation, took a bite, looked at the waiters, and once again gave a thumbs up sign. The waiters clapped.

When we were leaving the restaurant, our waiters made sure to shake hands with us and especially with Rajesh. They motioned to another staff member to take a group photograph that included them standing as close to Rajesh as possible. We agreed that our dining experience eclipsed the bullet train ride in excitement.

CULINARY GIFT FROM THE GODS

Capsicums, known as peppers, have been cultivated in the Americas for thousands of years. They are now grown worldwide and have become the key ingredient in many regional cuisines.

Capsicums have various names, which depend on the area where they are grown and the variety of pepper. The spicy varieties are commonly called chili peppers. The large, mild forms are called red peppers, green peppers, or bell peppers in North America; Shimla Mirch in India; and just capsicum in some other countries. The term "chili" comes from the Nahuatl (a Mexican language) word *chilli,* the variety cultivated in Mexico since 3000 BC.

Capsicums contain a chemical called capsaicin (methyl vanillyl nonenamide) which is responsible for producing a burning sensation in the mouth. While most animals find it unpleasant, some humans love it. The amount of capsaicin in the pepper fruit is highly variable. Consequently, each type of Capsicum has different amounts of perceived heat.

MEASURING HEAT – THE SCOVILLE SCALE

Pungency/hotness of chili peppers and spicy foods is measured in Scoville Heat Units (SHU), dependent upon the capsaicin concentration. The scale was invented by Wilber Scoville, a pharmacist in Texas in 1912, and has become a standard worldwide rating system despite its imprecise and subjective basis.

The Scoville scale is not a method for measuring capsaicin concentration, the component responsible for the "heat content." It is, rather, a subjective logarithmic scale based on sensitivity of human testers to capsaicin. It is used by businesses to rate the pungency of thousands of food products around the world.

The range of the "heat" present in varieties of hot peppers is reflected in the vastness of the Scoville Heat Units that range from almost zero for common Bell peppers to over a million SHUs for the Indian Bhut Jolokia pepper, two million SHUs for the Trinidad Scorpion pepper, and over two million SHUs for the Carolina Reaper pepper, the recently crowned world champion.

Pepper types	Scoville heat units
Carolina Reaper	1,400 000 - 2,200 000
Trinidad Scorpion	1,200 000 - 2,000 000
Ghost Pepper	855 000 - 1,041 427
Chocolate Habanero	425 000 - 577 000
Red Savina Habanero	350 000 - 577 000
Fatali	125 000 - 325 000
Habanero	100 000 - 350 000
Scotch Bonnet	100 000 - 350 000
Thai Pepper	50 000 - 100 000
Cayenne Pepper	30 000 - 50 000
Tabasco Pepper	30 000 - 50 000
Serrano Pepper	10 000 - 23 000
Hungarian	5 000 - 10 000
Jalapeno	2 500 - 8 000
Poblano	1 000 - 1 500
Anaheim	500 - 2 500
Pepperoncini	100 - 500
Bell Pepper	0

Above: Scoville ratings of common varieties of Peppers

Capsicum heat-seekers continuously seek out the hottest varieties. As a result, the champion title has changed hands several times over the past five years. The Guinness World Records in 2007 certified that Bhut Jolokia, the Ghost pepper grown in India, was the world's hottest chili pepper. The Indian Ghost pepper is rated at more than one million SHUs and is one thousand times hotter than the Tabasco pepper.

A Bhut Jolokia (Ghost Chili) vender in Australia

The reign of the Indian Ghost queen was short lived. It was replaced in 2012 by the Trinidad Moruga Scorpion pepper. Moruga's reign was even shorter. In December 2013, the *Guinness World Records* rated the Carolina Reaper pepper, a crossbred of the Indian Naga (Ghost Chili) and the Mexican Habanero, as the world's hottest pepper. Carolina Reaper topped the Scoville scale at two million SHUs.

Trinidad Scorpion –The Kama Sutra secret?

Bhut Jolokia, the Ghost Naga Chili

PEPPERS, PEPPERS, EVERYWHERE

Although a food item, chili peppers have found many other uses. The main ingredient, capsaicin, is used in Native American medicine as well as in modern medicine as a circulatory stimulant and an analgesic. Claims have even been made promoting its cancer-fighting properties, but no legitimate scientific information exists to authenticate this claim. Police Departments use an aerosol extract of capsaicin, called pepper spray, to incapacitate an aggressive person and for riot control.

THE KAMA SUTRA EDGE?

Claims have also been made declaring capsaicin as an aphrodisiac with powers rivalling those of some well-known pharmaceutical products. These claims refer to the varieties with a high Scoville score, particularly the Trinidad Scorpion pepper. One vendor promoting scorpion products at a town fair had the following warning posted in his shop: "Not recommended for individuals taking nitrates for chest pain."

Such claims of its erotic powers have never been proven. Perhaps modern pharmaceutical products in the market today using the same warning are more reliable.

Spanish conquistadores became aware of the culinary prowess of chili peppers and took them back to Europe (from the Americas). They also brought them to their Philippines colonies from where they spread throughout Asia. The Portuguese brought chili peppers to India. Indians took the pungent European gift to new heights with most unusual, innovative, and sometimes unlikely uses of the hot commodity.

From India, chili peppers made their way back to Europe through the British troops and civil servants who after years of service in India had become addicted to the pungent fruit. Many of them craved hot, spicy foods upon returning to the UK. Even a few of the Viceroys themselves fell victim to the pepper rush. Thus started a culinary revolution in Britain culminating in the opening of a large number of Indian restaurants throughout the UK. This phenomenon has resulted in London becoming one of the best locations to find authentic Indian food outside India. In a recent national poll, "Chicken Tikka" was voted as the National Dish of England to the delight of many food enthusiasts and perhaps to the dismay of traditionalists.

In today's context, can you imagine what Indian food would be without chili peppers? I cannot. Given that chili peppers arrived in 1600 with the Portuguese, it is hard to imagine what Indian cuisine was like for the thousands of years of the country's history prior to the introduction of ubiquitous peppers.

Indians often carry their love for hot peppers to extremes.

Zubin Mehta, the renowned classical music conductor who has led some of the most prestigious orchestras in the world, is known worldwide for his love of hot peppers, specifically "Bird Chilies" known as Cili (Chili) Padi in several South East Asian countries and a popular ingredient in the Malayalam (Kerala) cuisine in India.

Stories abound that when Mr. Mehta arrives at well-known restaurants, the head chef soon appears with a small plate, which he places next to Mr. Mehta. The celebrated conductor takes the hot chili peppers from a silver dish, which he brings to restaurants. The chilies are to be delivered to the chef who prepares customized fiery dishes laced with the music director's favorite chilies. Knowing this, Alan King, the great comedian once remarked. *"He (Mehta) is the only person I know who puts chilies on Mexican food and Indian food."*

LEMONADE WITH A SCOVILLE TOUCH

During one of our trips to India, my wife Mary and I were invited to an evening of music, food, and fun in Patiala, an erstwhile princely city in northwestern India. The function was the annual gala of the local Rotary Club. As soon as guests were seated, out came white uniformed turbaned waiters carrying lemonade in tall glasses with crushed ice sprinkled with rose water.

Mary took a sip, looked at me, and asked, "Did you try the lemonade?"

"No, I have not but I will. What is different about it?"

"Taste it," she replied.

I took a sip. It tasted different because it had generous amount of salt, black pepper, and, I believe, a pinch of Cayenne pepper. I could not guess the Scoville score of the rose-flavored lemonade. Although we both like lemonade, we now avoid lemonade when travelling in India, but order fresh lime juice, which is also delicious and comes with Scoville score of zero.

CHINESE CUISINE INDIAN STYLE

Growing up in India in the 1950s and 1960s, I never tried Chinese food. I do not think many people in India at that time knew what Chinese food looked or tasted like. Exceptions were those who lived in or near Chinatown in Calcutta. There is nothing in common between Indian and Chinese cuisines. The spices used are different, the cooking styles and preparation techniques are different, and the vegetables are different. Moreover, bread, which is the main food item in North India, is not a part of Chinese food.

During my second and third return trips to India, I started noticing the popularity of Chinese restaurants. They were everywhere. "Let us get Chinese tonight," was often heard. Eating Chinese food was a fashionable thing to do. When wealthy Indians in Delhi or Mumbai grew tired of everyday Indian food, they would head for a "Manchurian Chicken" restaurant.

My relatives in Patiala invited me to a restaurant in town specializing in Chinese food and asked, "Would you like to have something different from the Indian food you have been happily devouring for a week?" Despite my reservations, I agreed after learning that the restaurant served both Indian and Chinese dishes.

Manchurian Chicken was everyone's favorite along with traditional Indian dishes. Out of curiosity, I tasted the Manchurian Chicken. It was a strange experience. The taste was familiar but alien at the same time. It tasted neither Chinese nor Indian because I am familiar with both cuisines. I am also familiar with American-style Chinese food including all-time American favorites Chop Suey and Mu Shu Pork. Because of my frequent travels to China, I have developed an appreciation for authentic Hu cuisine from Shanghai, Cantonese Dim Sum, and fiery dishes from Szechuan and Hunan provinces. India's Manchurian Chicken had no similarity to any Chinese cuisine that I knew.

I asked the waiter about the recipe. He probably did not want to reveal the chef's secret formula but did reply, "Sir, I am not the cook, but I know the special dish has some of the best ingredients which include onions, garlic, turmeric, green chili peppers, red Naga chili peppers, chicken stock, and also spring onions, and soy sauce sautéed in ghee (clarified butter).

It sounded exactly like Indian cooking except the soy sauce seemed to be the secret ingredient. The Manchurian Chicken recipe was supposed to contain fiery Szechuan peppers, which have a special flavor and the heat every Indian seeks. Szechuan peppers would have been hard to find in Patiala. The chef had no problem substituting with hotter Naga peppers.

I wanted a native Chinese person to tell me how authentic Indian Chinese (also called Indo-Chinese) food was and the opportunity soon arrived. A well-travelled Chinese lady I knew from Shanghai happened to be in Baroda, India on the day I was also there on a business trip. We decided to have dinner at her hotel. She was anxious to learn about Indian food and asked me to recommend some well-known Indian dishes.

I drew her attention to the Chinese dishes the restaurant also offered. She was surprised and pleased. I urged her to try the all-time favorite Manchurian Chicken. She took a bite. Her eyes opened wide and she responded, "Interesting! Very interesting!" (This is usually what people say when they are not sure whether they like something, but they want to be polite.)

I prompted her, "What do you think? How does it compare to Chinese food in Shanghai?"

"This food is not really Chinese, but I like it," she replied and helped herself to a generous portion.

I am still baffled by Indian people's fascination with Chinese food, but I know the reason. It is the pepper pursuit and Indians have raised the ante. Chinese dishes in India are more generously peppered with high Scoville rated chilies. The secret for the popularity is not in the spices or method of cooking. The secret is the Ghost Naga pepper, which packs one million SHUs.

BEER TADKA

You may not be familiar with the term "tadka" but you are probably familiar with beer. Perhaps you have heard of "dal tadka" if you have ever been to an Indian restaurant because tadka is the basis for many popular Indian dishes. The sautéed mixture of onions, garlic, ginger, and other spices is generally prepared at the beginning of cooking and before adding the main food items such as lentils, vegetables, or meat. Other spices used in tadka can include cumin, mustard seed, fennel seed, red and green chilies, and sometimes a few additional secrete ingredients, all sautéed in ghee.

However, have you ever heard of "beer tadka"?

The Indian pepper pursuit finally caught up with the current beer craze in India. My friend Mihir told me of a concoction called "beer tadka" one night at a dinner in Delhi. I thought he was joking. He was not. He told me about a brewery in Bangalore, India that brews this bizarre concoction.

Anticipating a trip to India, I wrote to my friend, Chitra, to inquire about buying a six pack of beer tadka. Chitra located a microbrewery in Bangalore that makes the product. Apparently, it is not readily available outside Bangalore. I suppose I have to wait to savor this unique brew until I have the opportunity to visit Bangalore.

Peppered alcoholic drinks have been around for years. Most people know about Bloody Mary cocktails and spiced ales. Pepper vodkas are also around, as I learned from my travels in Russia, but beer with curried flavored tadka sounds very exotic.

Recognizing the ingenuity of Indians, more applications will no doubt be found for capsicum. The possibilities seem endless: Tea tadka (actually, I have heard of it), lemonade tadka (I have tasted something close), and ice cream tadka? Why not? Fried ice cream is a popular dessert at Mexican restaurants all over the world. All that is needed is a dash of Naga pepper or the Trinidad Scorpion pepper.

CHAPTER 17

PREETI GILL GOT MARRIED – ALMOST

Preeti Gill was not shy but neither was she extraordinarily outgoing. She was sophisticated, wickedly smart, and deliberate in all her actions. Her large smoky eyes gave her a friendly, approachable appearance. Overall, she presented herself very well as a tall, attractive, confident, and modern Punjabi woman. Her real name was Parneet but everybody called her Preeti.

Preeti went to a prestigious woman's college and became a medical doctor, a common goal for bright Indian students and especially for women. Preeti did well in college, graduated with honors, and specialized in pediatrics. She had initially wanted to be a dentist but relatively early on in her studies decided to be a pediatrician. She loved children and looked forward to having her own someday. Not long after she had graduated from college, she faced a critical decision – should she seek a job or get married? Neither of these choices promised smooth sailing. She wanted to stay close to home but also wanted a husband who was interested in international opportunities.

The jobs available for pediatric doctors in her vicinity of India were not what she had hoped for as the pay was low and there were few opportunities for advancement. Her parents had paid a lot of money for her to reach this stage in her education and profession so she wanted to be able to manage the high cost of living by herself in expensive Chandigarh.

Instead of settling for a job with few prospects, she began focusing on her other option. Why not get married and postpone her career plans? Once she married, she would know where she would live. Only then, she would hunt for a job and explore the opportunities in the area where the newly married couple would settle. The plan was discussed with her mother and father. They agreed wholeheatedly.

Preparing to embark on this plan, she soon realized that going through medical college was a breeze compared to the task ahead. In all the years she had attended her prestigious medical school, Preeti had not met any man she fancied enough to the point of wanting to marry him. It was evident that she was going to need help finding a husband.

In old India, finding a husband was easy. When her father and mother married thirty years earlier, their parents handled everything. Preeti's parents had little to do with the marriage except for making the invitation lists for the wedding ceremony. Preeti's grandparents had the resources, savvy, and wisdom needed for the critical decisions regarding selecting suitable mates for their children (Preeti's parents). Moreover, they had the experience of living in an arranged marriage. Most of all, the grandparents believed that they knew what was best for their son and daughter, especially the daughter (1).

Preeti faced different challenges. Her parents were ready to help with the hunt for a husband, but they knew times had changed from when they were married. They understood that in these times they could suggest, but not dictate, whom Preeti would marry. They were also aware that well-educated girls in North India had few choices; not that there were fewer boys than girls, but college-educated girls in Punjab were choosy. When they graduated, they emerged more sophisticated and articulate when compared to the boys who had gone through the same curriculum and upbringing.

"Women work harder. They do not indulge in wasteful and silly pursuits, and women are better behaved." I have heard this from several women including my own niece, Navjot Sidhu. There are no profound reasons for this phenomenon. Nevertheless, I am convinced that in Punjab, on average, women are more polished and articulate than the men of similar ages. It is possible that the same holds true in other parts of India.

Preeti's parents were open to all groom search options including placing matrimonial advertisements in the *Times of India* and the *Chandigarh Tribune*. The matrimonial advertisements read:

"Wanted: Handsome Jat Sikh boy, under 30 years of age, from a respectable family, for a fair-complexioned girl, 28 years of age, 1.7 meters tall and graduate of Lady Hardinge Medical College (LHMC). Only a doctor, an IAS (Indian Administrative Service), a PCS (Punjab Civil Service) officer or an engineer need apply. Preference will be given to a NRI (Non-Resident Indian) (2) medical doctor practicing in the USA. Reply in confidence with full particulars, including photos."

Preeti's advertisements ran in both the Delhi and Chandigarh newspapers for three weeks. Many applications were received. Three applicants qualified for follow up meetings. Priority was established among the three. Two of the men lived within a fifty-mile radius of Preeti's home. The third one lived 250 miles away in a New Delhi suburb. Distance negatively affected his priority rating. The third candidate must wait until the two who were close by were screened.

Preeti's mother and father readily approved the next steps. Preeti was told that she could invite her first pick for lunch at the Shangri-La restaurant or another place of her choice and she could decide if a second meeting was warranted.

The first suitor, a PCS (Punjab Civil Service) officer, flunked the Shangri-La luncheon test. He was smart and witty, but had ugly teeth and was bit overweight. Apparently, Preeti prized good teeth in men. The second in line was a mechanical engineer who was invited to the restaurant. He was good company and easily passed the Shangri-La test of good companionship as well as the dental inspection. The two agreed that they would meet again at the Ritz, the local cinema, to watch a movie. This was common practice.

The cinema had reserved seats, which eased the seating dilemma. The next challenge was to find a romantic moment for holding hands. Unfortunately, the violent, action-packed movie that was playing at the cinema that afternoon did not inspire a tender moment.

The mechanical engineer passed the movie-screening test so he was placed in the "possible" category. Before a decision would be made Preeti wanted to meet the man from Delhi whose performance at a restaurant lunch meeting would be crucial to determining if he merited a movie invitation.

The Delhi man was a medical practitioner. This time Preeti and her mother would go to Delhi. If there were no Shangri-La restaurant in Delhi, another suitable venue would be found. Preeti's mother would not go to the restaurant with the couple but would have her meal at some nearby place to give the couple privacy. The mother had to shadow Preeti because she felt safety was not assured in an unfamiliar big city.

Preeti's family sent a message to Delhi regarding the details of the meeting but received no response. A week passed, nothing happened. Then came the devastating news. Too much time had lapsed and in the meantime, the man had become engaged. Apparently, he was a hot commodity.

Back to drawing boards went the planners. They decided upon a second trip to the Ritz Theater for one more movie rendezvous with the mechanical engineer who had been placed on the possible list. This time the movie would be more carefully chosen and would be preceded by dinner.

Unfortunately, things did not go well during the second movie visit. Apparently, the man became too aggressive. He started groping Preeti like an automotive mechanic anxious to learn all about the workings of an exotic Italian Ferrari. Preeti stopped him but was disgusted and wanted to leave the theater. She discretely stayed in her seat until the end of the film so as not to make a scene. After the movie ended, she said a hasty good-bye to "Mr. Hands," saying, "It was interesting." She then darted to a waiting rickshaw and yelled, "35 L Model Town please."

TECHNOLOGY ENABLED

Her thoughts next turned to technology. After all this was 2016. People were moving away from newspaper advertisements. Indians had discovered the Internet, smart phones, iPads, and websites for such purposes.

Preeti had never looked at the matrimonial websites. She was not even sure if there were such sites in India. She talked to a lady doctor intern at the medical college. The intern was a Christian girl from India's Northwest province, home to a tribal area that was heavily populated by Christians, many of whom were quite westernized. Her name was Francis. Preeti asked Francis about internet dating sites. Francis recommended "Christian Mingles.com." Out of curiously, Preeti explored the site and quickly decided it was not for her. She was not a Christian. There was no point wasting time. No devout Christian man would want to mingle with a five-foot seven attractive Sikh lady doctor.

Preeti also looked at "eHarmony.com." She found nothing of interest there. It was not for people like her. She wondered if anyone had thought of "Indian Mingles" or, better yet, "Sikh Mingles.com," but no such websites existed.

After considerable searching, good news came. She heard about a flashy new website exclusively for Indians who wanted to mingle (correction! to marry – mingling with opposite sex is not very Indian.) The site was called, "Shaadi.com," literally meaning "marriage.com."

Preeti registered and waited for something to happen. In the very first week, she hit the jackpot. She connected with a NRI (Non-Resident Indian) (2) Punjabi doctor, well-settled, and practicing medicine on the United States east coast.

Email messages were soon flying across the oceans at the speed of light. Text messages followed, the first content was brief and boring but this soon

236

turned romantic. Many were adorned with smooching emojis, signaling ultimate approval. Skype chats followed. Group photos and "selfies" were exchanged. Ultimately, family photos were sent and family introductions were made. To all involved, this seemed to be a match made in heaven. All agreed that the time had come to make commitments in the form of a small "deposit or a "reservation."

RESERVE, CONFIRM, AND FLY

Preeti was now only three steps away from matrimonial bliss. She knew that modern Indian marriages had become more formal, festive, and costly than in the past. More money was available, a choice of marriage palaces/party houses had sprung up even in small cities, and Punjabis were always looking for an excuse to dance the Bhangra, the harvest dance. Preeti started planning for the three events to come. The first would be "Roka" which literally means STOP! Functionally it means, "Grab" the opportunity. In commercial aviation jargon, Roka would be equivalent to making a reservation for the flight you wanted to take and it buys you some time to make the payment (commitment). Roka is, therefore, simply a "reservation" to buy some time before an official engagement. If things deteriorated in the meantime, Roka could be smashed in a moment like a cheap Chinese toy. That is not to say that no money is spent or no fuss made during Roka. In fact, plenty of fuss is made as sugar-laden sweets flow, dinners are organized, and photo albums are prepared.

Preeti's Roka festivities went as planned followed by a period of calm until the engagement was set. Preeti invited a larger circle of friends and family for the engagement festivities, which were similar to the Roka but on a grander scale. Gallons of Solan Whiskey, a local whiskey popular from the days of the British, were downed and the harvest dance was performed even though the harvest had long been completed and the bounty sent off to markets.

For Preeti and her fiancé, the elaborate engagement ceremony was remotely controlled. Through the use of technology, the 9,000 mile span between them was effectively bridged. The immaculately dressed groom-to-be was beamed into Preeti's living room in full color. He was wearing a mauve Gucci Marseille silk suit with a hunter green necktie. The image was so clear that the bride and groom could almost kiss each other. They did not try. Kisses were not appropriate in public. All enjoyed the lavish engagement ceremony. Guests wondered – with an engagement like that, what would the "Shaadi" (marriage) be like?

Preeti's NRI American Fiancé

They did not have to wait long for the Shaadi announcement. The wedding would be three months from the engagement. All that was needed was for the groom to line up another doctor to tend to his patients while he was away, to make travel arrangements, and to decide on the honeymoon details.

A large wedding palace was booked, a catering contract was signed, and a well-known Sikh priest was secured by Preeti's parents to perform the "Anand Karj" ceremony. A sufficient stock of Solan Whiskey was procured along with dozens of cases of Kingfisher beer.

An estimated 200 guests from the groom's side and 150 guests from Preeti's side would be attending.

THE DOWRY CALCULUS

The night before the wedding, the groom's father proposed a small informal get-together at his house for the parents, the groom, and groom's grandmother. Preeti was not invited. This would not have been odd as the bride usually did not make herself accessible until just before the ceremony when she would enter the room ceremonially, escorted by her bridesmaids.

Preeti before the wedding ceremony

239

After dinner concluded, the groom's father leaned towards Preeti's father, lowered his voice and said, "Mr. Gill, your daughter has bagged the most eligible Jat bachelor around. Yes, there are other Punjabis in America, but not many of them bring home a quarter million American dollars every year. Your daughter will be living like a princess in America and will be the envy of every Punjabi girl back home."

"Yes, no doubt, Preeti is the luckiest girl and we couldn't be happier. We always wanted our Preeti to have the best because she deserves it. She is special, very special!" Preeti's father choked up as he said those words. Preeti's mother wiped her tears with her silk scarf.

At this point, the groom excused himself for few minutes as if previously rehearsed and his father then inched even closer to Preeti's dad, lowered his voice until barely audible and said, "To show that we recognize my son's value and hard work, an appropriate dowry is required."

Mr. Gill's jaw dropped. He steadied himself a bit and said, "Yes, we do appreciate the boy's worth, and how much do you think would be appropriate?" Mr. Gill was trying to recall the bank statement he had received only a few days before.

"It is hard to put numbers on such things but I think you will agree that fifty percent the boy's annual income (3) should not be out of line."

Mr. Gill sank further into his cushioned chair. He was good at mental calculations having been a math teacher. Without any calculator, he figured that the $125,000 US dollars (purportedly half of the groom's yearly income) would be roughly seven million Indian rupees, a royal sum.

"Sir, we do not have that kind of money. Let us give seven lakh (seven hundred thousand Indian rupees) now and let the ceremony roll. Then we can see what we can do."

That was not a satisfactory answer. "That would be an insult to my son. Please try to arrange the appropriate amount before Sunday afternoon, the day of the wedding," the groom's father firmly declared.

Mr. Gill and his wife rose without saying anything and left wondering how in the world they were going to meet this ransom. They must have thought of saying, "To hell with you," but those words were not in their vocabulary.

"Just what the doctor ordered!"

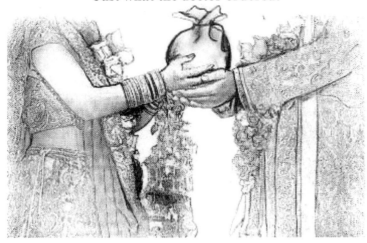

They thought of ways to solve the problem. They wanted Preeti to be married. They had waited for this for a long time. She was their life. Yet they did not have 0.7 million rupees to spare. Just seven hundred thousand rupees would pretty much wipe out their savings.

"With the Guru's grace, something will work out. It always does. There will be a way. I think they will understand," Preeti's mom tried to console her husband. "Now get some rest. Tomorrow is your dear daughter's wedding, a very big day."

The next morning, preparations were in full swing. Mr. Gill went to the bank and withdrew seven hundred thousand rupees (a little more than $10,000 US dollars) thinking this would save the day and the wedding would go as planned.

The guests arrived. Pleasantries were exchanged and congratulations flew. Minutes before the ceremony, the groom's father pulled Mr. Gill aside and asked, "Do you have the money?"

"Yes, I went to the bank as soon as it opened and withdrew seven lakh (seven hundred thousand) rupees. That is all there was," Mr. Gill pleaded.

"Seven lakh? Seven lakh?" The groom's father shrieked in anger trying to control the decibels. "That will be insult to my son."

Mr. Gill turned away, muttering inaudible sounds. He went straight to his wife, whispered something in her ear which she relayed to Preeti's uncle. Preeti's mother ran to the adjoining room where Preeti, surrounded by her bridal maids, was being made up. Her mother broke the news about the ransom demand.

241

Even before her mother finished, Preeti dropped her wedding gown and darted out, stopping near the holy book around which the wedding ceremony was to take place. She looked at the crowd, which was now visibly alarmed. Preeti yelled, "Ladies and Gentlemen, this wedding is off. Please go home. We apologize for the inconvenience. Please leave." Then she turned towards the groom and his family and said, "Please go away immediately. We do not want to see your faces. Vacate this place before something terrible happens." Then she cupped her face with both hands and started crying.

Preeti's uncle stepped up. Preeti was like a daughter to him. He lost his cool. He started yelling obscenities at the top of his lungs at the groom and his father.

The groom's guests made a hasty dash for the exit.

Her uncle was yelling, "You bastards, you robbers, you can go to hell where you belong." Then he looked straight at the father and yelled, "Your NRI son is a f-ing idiot. He does not deserve Preeti!" (The uncle had served in the military and had an enviable vocabulary of American curse words).

Suddenly he leapt upon the groom, who was only a few feet away, and started pummeling him. Other people from Preeti's side joined in the bashing. Some slapped the father who was the architect of the dowry scheme. Shortly thereafter, the NRI doctor was bleeding. His face was swollen. The doctor needed medical assistance.

Someone called the police who arrived promptly and escorted the groom and his father to the police station. The groom was given first aid. Afterwards, both he and his father were criminally charged for violating India's Anti-Dowry Act.

The story of the marriage fiasco with photos of the injured groom hit the front pages of regional newspapers and was covered nationally. Preeti received dozens of requests for interviews and TV appearances, all of which she declined. She stayed in the house, gave no interviews, and accepted no phone calls. She had had enough!

Once again, she had to start her search afresh. This time her marital ads would read, "No Greedy NRIs wanted. Only educated, civilized men with love in their heart need apply!"

BONUS STORY

Not all dowry stories have such a bad ending. In doing my research for this book, I came across another story that I thought would be nice to share with readers. The short story below was published in early 2015 in a newspaper in Northern India.

Urea Fertilizer Dowry Saves Dying Wheat Crop!

Rama Mandi: Wedding dowry is supposed to include cash, furniture motor vehicle, gold, clothes, or electrical machinery. At the nearby Bagha village, the dowry truck delivered 18 bags of Urea fertilizer.

Knowledgeable sources reported the unusual story wherein Mr. Amandeep Singh, a farmer from Bagha village, was the recipient of the unique dowry payment at his January 31, 2015 wedding.

Looking at the pale wheat crop greatly worried farmer Amandeep. Through the matrimonial intermediaries he expressed his worry to his potential father-in-law. Feeling the pain of his would be son-in-law, Amandeep's father-in-law, Gursewak Singh, procured 18 large bags of precious Urea to give to the groom as a dowry for his daughter's wedding.

The deeply gratified groom (Amandeep) was heard saying;

"Although I feel a bit embarrassed about the fertilizer gift, the fact is that receiving the Urea is a happier event than my marriage."

Translated from Punjabi by Jas Singh

Endnotes:

(1) Indian weddings have undergone gradual change over the decades since Preeti's parents were married. The system has evolved from a "shot in the dark" where the bride and groom first met on their wedding day into various scenarios providing some degree of choice in the matter. My friend Rajan (not his real name) who hails from Tamil Nadu, in South India, told me his own story.

Rajan's parents and friends launched a vigorous campaign to find him a bride. They succeeded in arranging an interview with the prospective bride who seemed like a good match. Accompanied by his mother, father, and his sister, he went to bride's house in a nearby village to meet the family. They all sat down around a table loaded with food. Two of the food items on the table were not to be eaten until initiated by Rajan. One of the items was "Laddu" – a sweet, round pastry made of chickpea flower, sugar, and ghee (clarified butter). The other was "Omapodi" – salty, crisply fried chickpea flour noodles sprinkled with carom seeds. After a few minutes, the bride entered the room, said Namaste (greetings), and introduced herself. Small talk followed. As minutes passed, tension built up. Finally, decision time arrived. If Rajan picked the sweet Laddu, it would signal "yes" but if he picked the salty Omapodi, it meant the deal was off, and everybody could go home. Rajan hesitated a bit, made his move, and picked the salty noodle snack. A hush fell over the room. It was pin drop silence. The visibly upset bride got up, said "thank you," and left the room.

(2) In Indian jargon, NRI means "Non-Resident Indian," a term applied to Indians living oversees who presumably have permanent visas or are eligible for citizenship, or are citizens. They are a hot commodity in the Indian dowry market because of their incomes or earning potential. United States and Canadian NRIs have the greatest opportunity to demand big dowries. Some take full advantage.

(3) The fifty perecent of man's first year income is a convenient dowry calculation formula but has limitations. It is best suited where the man has a regular job and verifiable income. One can think of situations where the groom has income from sources other than salary. The dowry math gets more difficult in those cases. Even more complicated is calculating the "dowry worth" of a swindler, a thief, or a hired hit man. This requires greater mathematical ability, but the fifty percent of average yearly income formula still could be applied with only minor modifications.

More difficult would be calculations where the wealth is from the livestock owned. For example, how many goats would be required to please an NRI doctor earning $250,000 US dollars who lives in a Chicago suburb? I also wonder how the dowry would be decided if a groom wanted to be paid in manure. Chemical fertilizer in agricultural zones in India is in serious shortage. Farmers are desperate to get the fertilizer at any cost. Some politicians are using their influence to divert the granular white gold (Urea) to their districts through clandestine means. The problem was brought to light in early 2015 when a farmer groom demanded several tons of urea from the bride's family as a dowry. The story was a hit in the local papers.

CHAPTER 18

BRIDESMAIDS GONE WILD

Paul and Bonnie decided the time had come to get married. They had followed each other through college, and when Paul secured a good job with a high tech computer company in Silicon Valley, he asked Bonnie to marry him. She happily accepted. Soon their thoughts turned to what kind of wedding they should have. Both opted for an unusual, non-traditional wedding – wild and exotic.

Paul's father had a suggestion. He would take Bonnie and Paul to his village in India and organize an old-fashioned Punjabi wedding, which would incorporate customs old enough to be unfamiliar to many Punjabis today. Modern Punjabi weddings, unlike traditional ones that last several days, are much shorter affairs. In addition, modern Punjabi weddings now usually take place in "Wedding Palaces" or in hotels.

Paul's father saw no point in taking his son and Bonnie all the way to India to wed them in a hotel or at a wedding palace. He thought that the wedding should be in a family home. To accommodate hundreds of guests for the ceremonies and the meals, he arranged for a large shamiana (tent) adjacent to his nephew Sher Singh's house.

The proposal met Paul and Bonnie's objectives. Bonnie's parents also liked the idea although it was clear that Bonnie's father would not be able to attend the wedding. Bonnie's mother, Carol, however, would make up for the dad's absence with her enthusiasm. Paul's father contacted his nephew in Patiala and asked if he would arrange a traditional Punjabi wedding replete with singing of the Sythniyan (Punjabi satirical wedding songs) and the nonstop Bhangra dance. Above all, he was to arrange some almost extinct wedding rituals including the groom teasing session with the girls from bride's side of the family.

The details of the rituals required were provided to the Patiala nephew as follows: for the ceremony, the groom was to be dressed up in a golden

245

sehra (a flower-decked veil like headdress), and he must arrive at the bride's house on a horse to the accompaniment of an Indian brass band. A fully decorated elephant would have been even better if one was available for rent.

"No problem," Sher Singh, the resourceful nephew, assured Paul's father.

News of the upcoming wedding spread like wildfire among the families and friends. Carol, Bonnie's mother, became the most sought after woman in her suburban Michigan neighborhood. Ladies demanded details. What would Carol be wearing at her daughter's wedding? Would she be able to communicate, not knowing a word of Hindi or Punjabi? Could she eat Indian food and, most importantly, would she, a woman, be able to drink alcoholic beverages? Several friends of the couple in the USA expressed their desire to attend the wedding. This would afford them the opportunity to visit rural India in the knowledgeable and secure company of an Indian group. They also wanted to join the couple on their honeymoon at the legendry Lake Palace Hotel in Rajasthan. (1). The Lake Palace Hotel had been one of the favorite palaces of the Maharaja of Udaipur during the British days.

Soon all the planning was completed and the air tickets were purchased. Many of the guests and wedding party flew to India together. The wedding party arrived in Delhi three days before the ceremony to give everyone a chance to rest, overcome the jetlag, do some shopping, and visit a few local attractions. All the ladies had their wedding garments tailored, Punjabi style.

Once the group arrived in Patiala, the bridesmaids briefed Bonnie about the rituals that would take place and the beauty parlor treatment that would transform the Michigan woman into a bejeweled Punjabi woman suitable for any Maharaja's harem. The first big event on the agenda was the mehndi ceremony for the ladies. Everyone adorned their hands and arms with mehndi paste while they sang songs about young women contemplating married life. As neither the groom nor the bride maintained a home in Patiala, the bride adopted the home of Sher Singh, the resourceful nephew, as a base for the ceremony. The groom stationed himself at the home of cousin Surinder, another resourceful nephew.

A decorated horse was brought to the groom's residence. Here the groom and his best man, a young cousin, mounted the horse and led the brass band to the bride's adopted home. Upon arrival, the groom found that he could not gain access to his bride until he had correctly answered questions posed by those on her side. This was easily accomplished. Gifts were exchanged.

The wedding was to take place under a huge tent, designed to hold the estimated 300 guests. Many old rituals were included: Jago, Batna/Haldi, Sythniyan recitals, and more. No one, however, explained to Paul, the verbal hazing ceremony that was to come on the eve of the wedding. The surprise would speak for itself.

Bride and groom in front of the bride's temporary home

RITUALS FORGOTTEN

Paul looked forward to his wedding. He wanted it to be an authentic, traditional ceremony in every detail as it had been in the days when his father had grown up in the village. He had read about Punjabi wedding rituals. He learned about Jago (wake!), the dance performed the night before the wedding to welcome the bride. During the ceremony, a family member, usually an aunt, led the procession carrying on her head the Jago, a big brass vessel studded with clay lamps (divas) lighted with mustard oil. Bonnie learned about Batna/Haldi, a ritual where a paste made from turmeric and mustard oil was applied all over her body by the bridesmaids in an effort to

247

bring out the best of her natural baby skin. The bright yellow spicy bath sounded exotic, but she wondered if it would make her skin itch.

Paul searched other Asian wedding rituals. These included the South Korean custom where after the wedding ceremony; friends of the groom took off the groom's socks, tied a rope around his ankles, and beat the soles of his feet with a dried yellow fish. This was done to toughen the groom to face the even more difficult challenges that would come on his wedding night. Paul also learned about the Eastern Malaysian tribal (Tidong community in Sabah) ritual of not allowing newlyweds to go to the bathroom for a long time. That sounded painful to him.

Such concerns were soon allayed. He was assured that Punjabi weddings did not involve physical torture, just clean fun and perhaps some verbal abuse that held no malice. These rituals sounded harmless to him. He believed he could sail through the process without too much embarrassment and without physical discomfort. His internet search of Indian wedding rituals, however, did not prepare Paul for the "groom teasing" ritual that was to take place in Patiala. In its purest form, this ritual has become almost extinct and even if some folks remembered it, they did not want to enact some of the crude aspects of it. His Indian cousins decided that Paul should experience the real thing because it was his heritage and just clean fun.

For the verbal hazing session, Paul needed an asset he did not have. It was the all-important Sarbala, the sidekick. Sarbala shields the groom and responds to acidic taunts and puns, and mildly vulgar inquiries from bridesmaids and other young women. The women, in complete freedom and absence of usually pervasive censorship, enjoyed a "free-for-all" female session with the groom and the sidekick. For Paul, a bilingual Sarbala was a necessity.

At the beginning of the teasing ceremony, a session of friendly insults and frank discourse would take place in Punjabi language. Paul was born and brought up in upstate New York by his Indian-American father and his American mother. He never learned Punjabi at home except for a few curse words he picked up from his cousins on previous visits to India. He needed a Sarbala who was fluently bilingual, about his age, and ideally, someone familiar with American slang and lifestyle.

Paul would have preferred to have one of his University of Michigan buddies, maybe Mike or Kody, with him at the wild session with the women, but that was not possible. Neither would it have been practical because none of his Michigan friends could have helped him fielding the insults and innuendos hurled in Punjabi. Paul had heard about some tricks that would be played on him, like the women stealing his shoes and demanding ransom for their return, but not the raunchy verbal battles.

As luck would have it, a Sarbala meeting these specifications was found. It was a distant relative of Paul's who had been educated at the Dehradun Academy, an elite English school high in the Himalayan Hills. His name was Virender, but everyone called him Vimto (2) which he liked. The name Vimto conjured up visions of someone westernized and fun loving. Which he was. Vimto grew up and was educated in India, but to most Indians he looked as American as Paul. He sported a hipster windswept hairstyle with slicked backsides and a shiny luster. Vimto knew about American customs as he had been to San Francisco for a month visiting relatives. Paul and Vimto bonded immediately.

On the wedding eve, the groom's hazing ceremony took place under the large ornate shamiana tent in a corner reserved for the groom, sidekick Vimto, and the women. No other men were permitted in or allowed even close enough to hear the discourse of the ladies, Paul, and the sidekick. The bride was not permitted in this session because she was not supposed to mingle outside her ladies' entourage until the wedding ceremony had taken place.

It was a "free-for-all, no holds barred" session. Nothing verbal was off limits to the approximately one hundred ladies, almost all of whom were young except for a few brave middle-aged souls. No physical contact was allowed or possible because the ladies sat at a safe distance from the groom and the Sarbala, who were both positioned in the middle of a semicircular arc. The giggly and rowdy ladies surrounded them. Older ladies were permitted but chose not to attend, a wise decision as the session was for the young ones. They had earned it. Surprisingly, the hard-core religious puritans who would otherwise have been horrified and ashamed of girls taking verbal liberties only common to boys withdrew from the ceremony and let it go uncensored. It was the custom. It was a refreshing and delightful ninety minutes of unfettered freedom in an otherwise conservative and restricted environment.

The verbal barrage started as soon as Paul and his sidekick entered the tent. This had begun under the direction of a modern-looking young female. Her name was Armani.

It is a beautiful name; a name, which translated as "wish" or "desire." Armani was five-feet-six-inches tall, had jet-black hair, smoky eyes, and slim features. Her blown out, slightly curly hair made her look flirty, inviting, and seductive. She had an intense piercing gaze, which transmitted a message in a universal script, "Talk to me. Do not look sideways, engage me, say something to me, and if you do not like to talk, say it with your eyes. I understand more than one language."

Armani introducing Paul

Heads always turned when Armani walked by. Based on her demeanor, use of American slang, and mastery of a few profane English words, she must have attended college. She became the self-appointed master of ceremonies. This was not co-incidental as she had previously played such roles. She was a popular figure in the neighborhood. Every bride wanted Armani to enliven her party, sing pointed "sithniyans" (wedding puns), and to intimidate even the most jaded groom.

Armani fired the first shot and challenged Paul on his suitability to marry their "sister" (the bride). She asked Paul what made him confident that he was good enough for her sister. The sister theme prevailed throughout the discourse even though it was apparent that Bonnie had no "sisters" in India. That did not matter. It was a female sisterhood. The women had adopted Bonnie. The friendly fire and the puns hurled in Punjabi were translated into English by Vimto and Paul's answers, translated into Punjabi, were conveyed back to the giggly crowd resulting in a thunderous response each time. The questions came in rapid fire and were difficult for Vimto to translate quickly, but he did a job that could be the envy of a seasoned diplomatic interpreter.

The G-rated dialogue heated up to the PG-13 (3) level and headed towards R-rated (4) dialogue. Children were there but were naturally sheltered. The adult material was subtle and consisted mostly of innuendos and suggestions. The youngsters did not understand anything. They just giggled when the adults went wild.

Armani raised her hand and lobbed a verbal grenade, "Okay, Mr. Smart, are you strong enough? I mean have you been exercising regularly for the tough task ahead of you?" Paul understood the gist of her remark from the two English words, smart and strong, even before Vimto translated. The girls giggled. Vimto straightened up, consulted with Paul, and gave the answer in Punjabi. The giggling intensified and some girls whistled.

Armani was on a roll. She pointed at Paul and said, "Amreekan (American) boy, do you know the task ahead of you? Are you enough of a man to make our sister happy, I mean happy, happy!" she winked.

Vimto jumped up. Without translating to Paul and without waiting for his instruction, he blurted out loud in English, "You bet your sweet a.., he is. Don't believe me? Check him out. Come on, tigress!" Vimto was excited. He had not yet exhausted his American vocabulary.

Paul cupped his eyes with both hands and said, "Oh, no." He realized Vimto had stepped over the invisible threshold. He motioned for Vimto to shut up. A dozen women in the crowed giggled. The ones who understood English covered their mouths with their hands. Paul thought for a second, turned to Vimto and said, "Okay, man, you have done it. You can't go back. Now you have to tell what you have said to the rest of them in Punjabi. You owe them."

Vimto repeated his prose in perfect Punjabi, and this time, added a few other syllables of his own. Before he completed his translation, all hell broke loose. A thunderous applause erupted. Many of the ladies were delirious and rolled uncontrollably on the floor. Armani was not about to give up. She looked at Vimto and said, "Okay, we accept your challenge. We will test him to see how clever your friend is. Give us a minute."

Paul and Vimto looked at each other in bewilderment, wondering what kind of a test was in store. They did not need to wait long. Two young girls emerged from behind the pack. They carried a large glistening brass pan with handles on each side. In the middle was an upside down, seven-inch diameter, greased bronze bowl. They walked up to Paul, put the pan containing the upside down bowl in front of him, giggled, and retreated. Armani looked straight at Paul and said, "Now Amreekan boy, let us see how clever you really are. Show us if you can upright the inverted bowl with one hand." Paul eagerly put his right hand around the greasy bowl ready to pick it up, confident that the task was a piece of cake. The slippery pot wiggled out of his hand like a scared rabbit and spun around the greasy brass pan making several circles. Paul wiped his greasy hand with his wedding gown, steadied himself, and tried to reach below the slippery vessel. Every time he touched it, the bowl sped away from him. He tried several times but with the same result. Each time the object wiggled away from him, raucous laughter ensued.

He was getting frustrated but confident that he could do it. He had heard stories about grooms who had been given simple math skill tests which some had failed with humiliating results (5). Being a University of Michigan business school graduate, Paul was not worried about failing any math test from a bunch of schoolgirls, but up-righting the greased bowl proved to be a challenge. He did not want to fail this test. He was a systems engineer. He hated to lose. He knew he could solve problems if he concentrated.

When wiping his greasy right hand, he noticed that the nail on his index finger had grown too long. Insight, like a flash of lightning, struck his brain. He pushed the bowl firmly against the lip of the pan, inserted his overgrown nail under the rim of the bowl, and lifted it enough to allow the tip of his index finger to fit securely underneath. He then put his left hand under his right wrist to give the hand added support, and in one swift jerk lifted the heavy bowl, causing it to fly out of the brass pan onto the floor. The bowl landed on its side and started rolling towards the raucous crowd. An oily trail was left on the carpet of the tent floor. Chants of "Aja, Aja" (keep coming, keep coming) filled the tent. The bowl headed straight towards Armani where it finally died only inches from her feet. A standing ovation ensued!

"He did it. The Amreekan boy passed the test!" The onlookers were shrieking in joy. Paul stood up and raised both hands in victory like a victorious wrestler and questioned, "Anything else?"

"Yes, there is one more test," said Armani. Then she motioned and two of her friends fetched a small table and two chairs and placed them in front of her. She was planning to be the referee for an arm-wrestling match to come. A five-foot-seven-inch tall, muscular girl occupied one of the chairs.

She was introduced as Gagandeep ("light of the universe"). The girls called her just Gagan. Gagan was a sophomore at the Patiala Medical College. She excelled in sports. She was a shot putter and a disc thrower with several trophies to her credit. For an accomplished athlete, she was not big or heavy but was taller than an average Patiala co-ed.

"Okay Amreekan boy, there is one more test. Let us see how strong you are and if you can arm wrestle Gagan without losing a limb," Armani challenged Paul.

Paul started to get up, but Vimto interrupted. "My brother, Paul, will have no problem wrestling Gagan. He is strong with very long arms and has the grip of a Gecko (lizard)," Vimto said and continued, "He does not want to hurt your champion, but more importantly it does not behoove the groom, the hero of the occasion to be wrestling with a little girl. Wrestling is my job because I am here as the groom's bodyguard. I can arm-wrestle with Gagan and beat her, but let me tell you, Paul is stronger than I am."

Vimto's proposal was accepted. Armani showed interest in Vimto, a very eligible bachelor. She motioned for Vimto to occupy the chair facing Gagan and she stood in between Gagan and Vimto as a referee.

Both Gagan and Vimto placed one arm on the table with their elbows bent and touching the surface. They gripped each other's hand. The goal was to pin the other's arm onto the table surface with the winner's arm over the loser's arm. The match started with a slight edge for Gagan. The struggle continued for several minutes. Gagan appeared to be winning. Suddenly, Vimto started to gain on Gagan, perhaps because of his longer arm. Whatever the reason, he appeared to be winning. Four girls leapt out of the pack and wrestled Vimto down to the ground before he could claim victory. Pandemonium broke out. The "no physical contact" rule was shattered. Shouts of "stop it, stop it," went unheeded. It looked like Vimto and the girls were enjoying the contact. Two others joined the action. Finally, Armani yelled, "Cut it out ladies before it gets out of hand." They stopped. Vimto rose and raised his hands in a sign of victory that mimicked Paul's action when he had flipped the greased bowl.

With calm restored, attention turned to singing and dancing. Armani started reciting a couplet called, "Boli". At the conclusion of the song, the entire contingent broke out into a clapping symphony called "Giddha." Armani began dancing. Several girls pointed at Paul, motioning for him to dance. Reluctantly, he rose and started dancing Bhangra, American style. Vimto followed him, accompanied by more applause. The unrehearsed Giddha went on for twenty minutes. Whenever it appeared to be ebbing, it would erupt in another corner like the "wave" at a Detroit Lions football game.

The adults nearby could hear the singing and the applause but would not dare to enter into the fun. It was verboten, off limits to them. Most of them would never know what was said and done. The bride could not hear anything. She was far away and surrounded by her maids. Custom dictated that she would not show her face until the time was right. The one hundred lips would remain sealed.

Sidekick Vimto and Gagan, the Patiala sports star, in an arm-wrestling match

WHAT HAPPENS IN A PUNJABI TENT ON THE WEDDING EVE, STAYS IN THE WEDDING TENT

PS: Vimto and Armani are now married living happily somewhere in Queensland, Australia. Paul and Bonnie are proud parents of two young girls, Jennifer and Stephanie. They live in Portland, Oregon.

(1) **Lake Palace:** Realizing that this was an American contingent on a special wedding tour in India, the Lake Palace management gave the newlyweds the "honeymoon suite" that was once the favorite of the Maharaja. The hotel manager gave all wedding guests a tour of the suite. The suite was glamorous and sumptuous. In the middle of the living room, an ornate swing hung from the ceiling. The swinging bed had enough room for a couple in a tight embrace. When one of the male guests asked what

254

the purpose of this was, the manager winked and said, "Sir, I am not sure, but the Maharajas were very eccentric and sporty." He then proceeded to show the guests the marble bathrooms with gold fixtures studded with precious turquoise stones.

(2) **Vimto** was a popular English soft drink in India at the time. It was a cocktail of grape and raspberry juices with black currants, herbs, and spices.

(3) **PG-13** Mature material. Parental guidance recommended for readers under thirteen years of age.

(4) **R-Restricted**. Suitable only for readers above 18 years of age.

(5) **"Indian bridegroom dumped over a failed math test", BBC News, 13 March 2015:** An Indian bride walked out of her wedding after her bridegroom-to-be failed to solve a simple math problem, according to police in Uttar Pradesh. The bride asked the groom to add fifteen and six. When he replied seventeen, she called off the marriage. Reports say the groom's family tried to convince the bride to return, but she refused, saying the man was illiterate. Local police said they mediated between the families and both sides returned all the gifts given before the wedding.

CHAPTER 19

BUREAUCRACY PAR EXCELLENCE

Growing up in India, I never thought about bureaucracy even though it pervaded every aspect of our lives; mine, my family's, and that of everyone else important to me. I had heard the term and knew what it meant, but assumed that things were this way by the intention of authorities. Protesting or complaining about it was unthinkable, useless, and wasteful. I just tolerated it. My tolerance limit was exceeded when I went back to India for the first time, eight years after I had immigrated to the USA.

THE PLAYBOY CENTERFOLD

My routing from New York to Bombay (now Mumbai) was through Beirut, Lebanon. Beirut was still the "Paris of the East" and had not been destroyed by the fighting between rival political and religious factions. As luck would have it, my airplane would be the first one to touch down in Beirut in the New Year. The airport authorities organized a grand New Year's Eve celebration right inside the airport terminal. Every passenger on an airline landing within an hour of the New Year was greeted with champagne and hors d 'oeuvres when they arrived and upon re-boarding their flight, each man received a bottle of Lebanese vodka and each woman a bottle of perfume. The gesture was most generous and appreciated by all.

I tucked the free vodka bottle into my carrying case along with my two bottles of Scotch whisky, which were to be presents to my relatives, and re-boarded the flight to Bombay. The vodka bottle was exquisite! "It looked like real Waterford Crystal," I said to the man sitting next to me who had also received a bottle.

He smiled, introduced himself as Latif from Lebanon and said, "Yes, the bottle is great but the stuff inside probably tastes like kerosene. The Johnny Walker Scotch you are carrying makes a nicer gift," he said while laughing.

Hearing the phrase "tastes like kerosene," lowered my enthusiasm about my free gift. I was familiar with the kerosene, having done most of my studies before the sixth grade under the light of kerosene lanterns.

My flight arrived in Bombay after midnight. A long line formed at the customs and immigration desks. The area had the appearance of a trader's caravan due to all the luggage being carried. Much of the luggage was comprised of electronic gadgets not easily available in India at the time. When my turn came to declare my goods, I voluntarily took out the two bottles of Scotch whisky and the fancy bottle of Lebanese vodka and pushed them in front of the customs inspector.

"You must pay a hefty duty on two of the three alcohol bottles, sir," he said while calculating the duty. "You are allowed only half a liter of whisky duty free." I did not want to pay the duty he calculated and neither did I want to part with my bottles of Johnny Walker, but I had a backup plan. I would give the man the Lebanese vodka that tasted like kerosene as a gesture of goodwill, and he should let me through, I figured. Fortunately, something else which he might enjoy even more caught his eye. He was peeking at the front page of one of the magazines I was carrying in an envelope. It was a recent issue of Playboy magazine, a relatively new and very popular adult publication. He pointed at the stack of magazines and asked, "What kind of magazines are those? I have never seen this kind in India."

"They are sports magazines," I replied. "They are popular in America but may not be suitable for Indian youths," I said trying to keep straight face.

"I need to see if they can be permitted in the country," he said and pulled one of the dozen out to examine. The centerfold photograph opened effortlessly. He pulled the magazine closer so that other people in the line behind us could not see and to permit himself a closer look. With one glance at the featured model, he froze. The more he concentrated on the woman in the centerfold, the more intrigued he became.

The already long line was getting longer. I smelled an opportunity. "If you are not sure, why don't you keep that one and examine it later when you have time," I said. "If the magazines need to be confiscated, please let me know and I will take them to the police station in Patiala to be destroyed promptly." To show that I was serious, I gave him my phone number where he could reach me in Patiala. The magazine was exactly what he wanted.

"Good idea," he said and carefully put the precious magazine from

America in his satchel. He then yelled, "Next!" Simultaneously he turned to me and said, "You are free to go, sir, and enjoy the scotch." He winked as he said that. I winked back.

I told the story to each one of my relatives and friends lucky enough to receive their issue of Playboy with centerfolds. They also treasured their gift.

EXCHANGING MONEY IS A TIME CONSUMING TASK

My second return trip to India was an important one. I was excited because I would stay at the fabled Ashoka Hotel, which I could not have afforded when I lived at home in India. Now, as I had a pocket full of greenbacks (US dollars), it would be possible. I would be welcomed as a special foreign guest, I imagined. I would go to the Connaught Place, hunt for souvenirs, gorge on authentic Indian food at some of the best eateries in Delhi, and look up my old college friends who had settled in Delhi.

The first order of business was to get some US dollars exchanged into Indian rupees. I entered a bank in the Connaught Place area to get some Indian rupees before I proceeded to my hometown in Punjab. When I walked up to the man at the desk, he motioned for me to sit down without looking at me. He adjusted his black rimmed glasses and asked, "What currency are you carrying?"

"US dollars," I replied while pulling a wad of money from my coat pocket.

"How much exchange do you need?" He inquired.

"Two thousand US dollars," I replied.

The clerk almost fell from his chair. He did not say if the amount was over any limit. Instead, he stared at me and asked, "Where did you get that kind of American money?"

"I am paid in American dollars," I replied.

"How is that?" he said incredulously as he adjusted his glasses again and challenged me. "Young men around here don't earn that kind of cash and certainly not in American dollars?" He examined my Indian passport again (I did not become a US citizen until 1972, the following year.)

"I am a permanent US resident, employed, and well paid by my company because I am skilled and qualified," I replied calmly.

He adjusted his glasses again and yelled at the nearby orderly, "Babu, bring some chai (tea) for the Sahib. Bring the kind garnished with cardamom, cloves, and cinnamon."

I sipped on the herbal tea while he counted the money and examined it to make sure it was not fake. He told me that a lot of counterfeit money had been circulating. Real American dollars were hard to get because of the stringent currency trading limits at the time. I already knew this. No one outside India would exchange Indian rupees into US dollars, although the reverse was easily possible. Thus, a black market had been created. Every Indian living in the US was aware of this. If exchange had been available, I would have exchanged my US dollars before leaving Syracuse, New York. Another way to get currency exchanged would have been for me to give a newly arrived Indian (usually a student) in the US, the needed American dollars which he could not obtain in India before he left for the USA. I would then receive the equivalent amount in rupees from his relatives when I arrived in India. It would have been a fair deal. Unfortunately, I had not explored such an exchange before leaving the USA.

The man counted the wad of money three times until he was satisfied that the amount was right and that the new crisp bills were not counterfeit. That was, however, not the end of his cross-examination. It was just the beginning. He had many doubts.

He challenged my qualifications. He wanted to know all about my employer. Why had he not heard of that company before? What kind of job title did I hold? None of the questions had anything to do with him giving me the money. Then he told me to come back after lunch because he had to clear this transaction with his boss to make sure I was eligible for the exchange. At that moment, his boss was at lunch.

I left to get my lunch at Narula's, a landmark restaurant in Connaught Place. Narula's was a pleasant place. No questions were asked. The establishment was eager to feed me. I experienced no bureaucratic delays. I had a nice lunch for about $1 US dollar (about seven rupees) and I was out of there in less than an hour. I returned to the bank and waited for the clerk. I approached him again and he said, "Sir, the amount of exchange you want is above my boss's authorized limit. Only his boss can approve it and he is at a different branch across town. We will send the Chowkidar (watchman) to take the papers to him and you can come back just before closing." Then he added, "It would expedite things if you give some money, a tip, to the man going to the other branch in this awful heat." As a hint, he picked up one of the twenty dollar bills to help me with the math.

I was not shocked. I gave him three one-dollar bills (about twenty-one rupees) and told him to enjoy lunch tomorrow at Narula's restaurant for his efforts and the services he had rendered which were beyond the call of duty. I encouraged him to buy the Chowkidar lunch as well. Three US dollars would be more than enough to have a decent lunch for two at Narula's. He took the money, did not say anything, but looked like he was satisfied with my offer.

I decided to wait until the Chowkidar returned from the other branch. The clerk looked at me a few times as I waited, then went into his boss's office. He emerged after five minutes and said, "Good news! In deference to your time and need, the boss decided to authorize the amount even if he must go above his authority. Just bear with me for a minute." He then completed a long form and handed me a thick brass token with an engraved number and told me that I could present the brass token at any of the five windows with iron bars. Within a few minutes, I would be on my way with the local currency.

It was not to be. The first window I went to was not authorized to dispense $2,000 dollars' worth of rupees. Window number five was, however, that window had a line. When my turn came, I presented the brass token. The man behind the bars shook his head and said, "Sir, it could take a while. Why don't you have a seat? I need to count the money three times to be sure and verify with my supervisor to get his approval to dispense the cash. In the meantime, if a line forms again at the window, I will call you before the others in line. Please stay in sight."

Fifteen minutes passed before the man reappeared behind the window.

There was no one else in line. He gave me the cash, thanked me, but did not retract the hand that had just dispensed fifteen thousand rupees in my stretched palm. I pulled out a five-rupee note from the wad he had just given me and handed it over to him. It was a bit shy of a dollar, but generous, I suppose, because the man gave me a big smile. I left without a smile. I was one hour late for my next appointment. Happily, I finally had some local cash.

On the way, I kept thinking, did I just bribe two people? No, I did not, I convinced myself. I had just paid the bureaucracy tax.

GETTING A TRAVEL PERMIT IS A RISKY TASK

A few years later, the health of my sixty-year-old mother suddenly took a downturn. According to her Indian physician, she might not have long to live. My wife Mary and I wanted to visit her before her condition deteriorated, but 1986 was not a good year to go to India. Punjab, India had just endured its worst communal riots since the 1947 partition. Wounds opened in the aftermath of Indira Gandhi's assassination were still raw and Punjab was experiencing communal rivalry and revenge killings. Entry to Punjab was restricted even with a valid Indian visa. Punjab entry visas for foreign passport holders were issued in Delhi on a strict "need only" basis. Knowing of the difficulties, my wife and I still decided to go. Upon our arrival in Delhi, we found things normal; at least on the surface. The narrow streets around the Chandi Chowk were crowded, but there were no foreigners to be seen there or at the famous monuments around Delhi.

The next morning, my wife and I went to the Punjab permits office early to stand in line to get permission to go to Punjab. Already fifteen to twenty people were ahead of us. The permits officer handed us two separate forms to complete and asked us why we wanted to go to Punjab. We explained the reason. He checked our passports, reviewed the forms, stamped the forms in several places, and said, "Tomorrow is Saturday. We are open half-days on Saturdays, but the fact is that on issues of importance like this, nothing can be done until Monday or Tuesday. Actually, even if I expedite your request, it will take at least three days for the CID (Criminal Investigation Department) to give you a clearance certificate."

The words "criminal investigation" hit me like a rock when used in reference to a travel document, but I did not show it. "If that is what it takes, we have to live with it. We will enjoy the sights of Delhi and come back first thing on Wednesday morning. Hopefully there will still be plenty of time to get to Punjab," I told the officer.

"Good idea," he concurred without looking at us.

On Wednesday morning, we arrived at the office early. We were the first in the line. "Sorry to disappoint you, but there is no news from the CID. They are very busy these days. There are too many bad characters around," he said. "Frankly, to save you too many trips, I advise you to check in two days." That meant Friday. We looked at each other in disbelief. We had no recourse.

On Friday morning, we were again the first in line and entered his office. When the man started to say "sorry," I interrupted him, "Officer, why do you need a Criminal Investigation Department report on a couple of people who are here just to visit an old, ailing relative? You have our documents, you can question us as long as you wish to make sure we are not bad people, so why the CID check?"

"To be honest with you sir, it is your US passport. The Government is very leery of people of Indian origin with surnames like yours arriving from the US and Canada because they cause trouble, but I don't mean you personally."

I was getting frustrated and felt insulted. My voice was rising, causing concern to my wife. "Look officer, isn't it obvious that I am not here to cause any trouble? If I were, would I drag this woman with blonde hair and blue eyes with me? If I had bad intentions, I would have come alone, changed into the clothes of a farmer, wrapped a decent dhoti around myself, gotten lost in a sea of Indians, and hopped on the train to Patiala."

The man took off his glasses, looked at the ceiling, and smiled. He had a nice smile. With a smile on his face, he looked human instead of like a bureaucrat. The transformation was miraculous. For one moment, he had shed his tough armadillo-skin and had bared the natural baby skin of his birth. Without his bureaucratic skin, he looked just like a typical Indian; curious, humble, and accommodating.

"I guess you have a point," he said with a smile. "Give me your passports." With a chop chop, he stamped the permit on both passports. "Be careful while in Punjab," he said and shook our hands.

We darted out of the office to catch the express train leaving Delhi in just three hours. While on the train, we discussed the events of the last six days and concurred that the man had the authority to grant us the permits all along and probably on the very first day. Why didn't he exercise that authority?

"Then he wouldn't be performing his duty. He wouldn't be a bureaucrat!" my wife replied. We enjoyed our stay in Patiala and extended

262

it for a week to happily watch my mother recover from a near-death experience.

A TRAVEL STOP THAT SHOULDN'T HAVE BEEN

Returning home from Kuwait in November of 2013, I was looking for an easy route to travel back to Hawaii. This was not an easy task. Something caught my eye. An Indian airline offered passage through Delhi that could connect me to my international flight back to Honolulu. It was not the shortest route and it would require a long layover in India, which would deter many travelers. For me, it was an opportunity, I thought. It was a cheaper flight than other options and I could have breakfast with my favorite niece Peggy, a student at the Lady Hardinge Medical College in New Delhi. This would give me a chance to catch up on some gossip related to my extended Indian family and to savor authentic North Indian cuisine.

This was not to be! Problems surfaced immediately when I checked at the airline (Indian) counter at the Kuwait airport. My transit in India would not be the regular transit where passengers do not need to go through customs and immigration, just to change flights without leaving the airport.

"You need an Indian visa to go through India," the agent casually informed me.

"I am not visiting India, I am just changing planes in India," I said. The travel agent had told me that this was a regular everyday routing that many passengers travelling from Kuwait to Western destinations preferred." I continued, "What happens if I don't have an Indian visa but hold a confirmed airline ticket that your agent sold me without any hint that I would need an Indian visa. An Indian visa is not something you can get in a hurry!"

"Then you stay one more day in beautiful Kuwait and arrange alternative routing," the young agent said with a smile.

I did not find the situation funny and got into an intense argument with the agent that the airline or their agent had an obligation to alert the passengers about the need to have an Indian visa to travel on this routing. He said it was my responsibility to check. We had come to an impasse. At that point, I told the agent that, in fact, I did have an Indian visa, a five-year business visa that permitted me to have unlimited entries. "Sir had you told me that in the beginning, you would have saved my time and yours."

"I am sorry, but I wanted to make a point!"

"You made it," he said gingerly, proceeded to give me the boarding pass, and wished me a good time in Mumbai. The mention of Mumbai produced another shock. I thought I was spending all my layover in Delhi, at breakfast with Peggy, my niece.

"Your point of entry in India is Mumbai," the airline agent said casually. "That is where you will clear immigration and customs, and after a long wait, you will take the domestic flight to Delhi where your international flight to the USA will originate. Your transit in Delhi is very short. Please do not make any plans to go out of the airport," he cautioned me. That was the worst news I had heard until now. I thought of ways to tell Peggy that our breakfast of paranthas and pooris accompanied by spiced perfumed chai was off.

I cleared the dreaded customs desk in Mumbai without a hitch and sat on an airport bench for hours before boarding the plane to Delhi. I was able to send email and text messages to Peggy and her dad in Patiala expressing regrets for missing my breakfast with Peggy.

Upon my arrival in New Delhi, a well-dressed young man was waiting for me as I exited the airplane. He had perfect English and pleasant manners. "Welcome to Delhi, Mr. Singh. I am here to assist you and to take you to the international gate. We have to clear Indian immigration for your exit from the country. The airport is crowded as always, but with my badge, we can skip the lines. You have a tight connection because the plane coming from Mumbai was twenty minutes late." He offered to help me with my brief case. I declined his gesture.

I was surprised and delighted with the encounter with my young escort. India is changing, I thought. I should spend more time in the changing India because I like so many things here, I told myself. We breezed through the checkpoints and reached the immigration desk. We skipped the long line but headed towards a special immigration check. The young man escorted me into a small cluttered room, wished me safe journey, and left.

A man about fifty-five years old and somewhat overweight was waiting for me. He motioned for me to sit on the green sofa beside him and asked for my passport. He flipped through all 120 pages of my well-travelled passport, looked at each stamp as well as records of my earlier Indian visits, and inquired, "What is the purpose of your travel through India?"

"To return home," I replied.

He took off his glasses, stared at me like a deer frightened in the bright headlights, pointed at my US passport and said, "I thought your home was in the US."

"Yes, it is and that is where I am going by the cheapest means possible," I said.

He had no counter to this, but he was not satisfied. He had not yet earned his pay. He looked at my passport again, looked at my birthdate and said in Hindi,

"Abhi Kaam kyon Kerte ho?" (Why do you still work?)

This was the strangest and most offensive inquiry so far. I did not want to show anger. My flight was about to leave. It was time to go but I had to answer.

"Kaam (work) is good," I tried to assure him in "Hinglish," a language composed of fifty percent Hindi and fifty percent English and spoken by almost every educated Indian. I quickly switched to English because of my lack of Hinglish proficiency.

"Many people past their sixties are very productive," I assured him "Moreover, work keeps me young and healthy," I reminded him. I could not avoid looking at the advancing bulge in his stomach as I said this.

He stared some more and said nothing. He had run out of inquiries. He handed me my passport and the boarding pass. "You are free to go. Your flight may be waiting for you at the gate," he said.

The time was two minutes past the departure time. He did not offer to lead me to the gate. That would be beneath his rank. I made the dash to the gate five minutes away.

They were waiting for me at the gate. "Just go in Mr. Singh," the anxiously waiting airline agent said to me without even looking at my boarding pass. "We have been waiting for you, sir." I looked at my watch. It was six minutes past departure time. Holding the plane for me would have been a major favor, but there was a more important reason for holding the plane. It was important to get the troublemaker out of the country!

I have much more travel to do, including many more trips to India.

I have one wish. When I am ninety-nine years old, in good health but toothless, I will go to India with all my documents in order. The immigration officer will look at my toothless grin, observe my jet-black hair (better living through chemistry), verify my birthdate, smile back at me, and say, "Welcome back, Dr. Singh".

(1) Hong Kong-based Political and Economic Risk Consultancy Limited ranks bureaucracies across Asia on a scale from one to 10, with 10 being the worst. On this scale, India scored 9.21 and fared worse than Vietnam, Indonesia, the Philippines, and China. The report said that Indian bureaucrats were rarely held accountable for wrong decisions.

Press Trust of India news agency: "This gives them [bureaucrats] terrific powers and could be one of the main reasons why average Indians, as well as existing and would-be foreign investors, perceive India's bureaucrats as negatively as they do."